PARTY GOLD

PARTY GOLD

A Cyrus Grant novel of suspense

VICTOR SHEYMOV

CYBER BOOKS PUBLISHING

LCCN: 2012950675

ISBN-13: 978-0985893071

Cyber Books Publishing

http://www.cyberbookspublishing.com

In loving memory of Alexandra Jejero

ALSO BY VICTOR SHEYMOV

TOWER OF SECRETS
A Real Life Spy Thriller

CYBERSPACE and SECURITY
A Fundamentally New Approach

Communism is not dead; it is just
morphing into a sovereign criminal system.

CONTENTS

x

Chapter 1

He heard the heavy office door open quietly behind him. Cyrus Grant stood near his office window, overlooking Pershing Park and Pennsylvania Avenue. Not a single cloud marred the perfect midday sky. The beginning of October is definitely the most beautiful time in Washington. Investment banker Cyrus Grant was handsome in a muscular way, but not like any male model. His perfectly tailored gray suit neither accentuated nor concealed the features of his fit six-foot body. He would look at home on any sports team, that is if he was a bit younger. His blue eyes had begun showing a little more ice and a few light wrinkles subtly signaled the change. If one looked very carefully, one would notice a few gray strands in his brown hair. A perfectly straight nose, well-defined chin and small ears would have made his face look patrician if not for his too athletic neck which more suggested all-American. The open expression of his face enhanced that impression.

Cyrus did not turn. He knew his secretary would just leave the papers on his desk and leave as quietly as she came.

Instead, a soft and casual fatherly voice said, "Glorious day. Best view in town, isn't it?"

Cyrus turned to see a slightly overweight man with a large, balding head and small brown eyes moving toward him. The head of the company, in his threadbare tweed jacket and ill-fitting trousers, was a jolly man.

Cyrus received his slap on the back. "John, I thought you were in New York."

"I was. Had dinner last night with a couple of local hot shots and stayed overnight. Canceled lunch with the other two and got back ten minutes ago."

"Anything wrong?"

"No, just got bored. I guess I'm getting too old for these fishing expeditions called 'we have a good general idea, let's see if we can do some business.' If you have an idea, develop it, send me your proposal and then I'll see what it's worth."

"I see."

"Are you free for lunch?"

"Sure. Occidental?"

"Fine."

They went to the elevator.

Jones & Bleach was a boutique investment-banking firm, well known in the small circle of blue ribbon international merchant bankers. But beyond the rolodex of major players in the game its name generally appeared in many of the Wall Street announcements of new securities issues. In the long list of the underwriters it was invariably in the bottom quarter, read only by the pros. Jones & Bleach has never participated in a controversial deal. After more than half a century in the business, the firm rarely looked for deals; the deals came to the firm. It had developed a reputation for checking out its clients thoroughly as well as anyone the firm dealt with. For many in the business, Jones & Bleach's presence in a deal was one of the telltale clues that the deal was "clean" and that no major controversy would be waiting in the wings. John Porter was the pillar of that conservative image. He was the Chairman, CEO and a main shareholder of Jones and Bleach. He had bought the company twenty-five years ago mainly with borrowed money that had long been paid off.

Few people knew that right after the acquisition he had transferred the ownership to a trust, a common arrangement for those who have to deal with estate taxes. Nobody ever bothered to look for the trust document itself, and if anybody had, they would not have found it. Not only was the document itself missing, but also the old lawyer who set up the trust was long dead. And nobody paid any attention to the fact that the key employees of the firm did not receive actual shares of the company as their profit-sharing incentive, but only their "equivalents," redeemable for cash upon the termination of their employment, a common arrangement in closely held corporations. So the sole owner of Jones & Bleach was the JMP Trust, and the sole trustee of that trust was John Porter. But no one would care about such details of a sixty-odd-year-old company. Since everything prior to 1929 was prehistory, as far as Wall Street was concerned the firm had been in business forever.

A dozen investment bankers worked at Jones & Bleach. Half of them were principal players, like Cyrus Grant, and the other half were up-and-coming on a long, long probation. The top half was all Senior Vice-Presidents and the lower half was Vice-Presidents. About thirty research and support personnel completed the operation. This rather dull firm saw insignificant personnel turnover, which most people attributed to relatively high pay, consistently twenty percent above the industry average.

The Occidental Grill was in one of the most prestigious locations in town. The Willard Office Building was in the middle of the Washington Universe: a block from the White House, across the street from the Treasury and next to the Willard Hotel with its restaurants.

"Good afternoon, Mr. Porter." The maître'd winked at his assistant to take care of the customers in front and, spotting the men entering the door, took a few steps forward. "Good afternoon, Mr. Grant. Your table is ready, gentlemen."

"Hello, Mark. How are things?"

"Picking up. Beginning of the season, you know."

They followed Mark and exchanged a few "hellos" with other diners, who were eating and talking but never missing anyone coming in.

Once settled in their booth, John perused the specials, and asked, "So, did you have a good sail?"

"Fabulous, as always in Maine." Cyrus intercepted John's look across the hall at a Washington Post reporter trying to bribe his way to a booth next to where Steve Grant, a Managing Director of Solomon's Washington office, and a Chief of Staff of a famous Senator were settling down, and added, "What a place."

John smiled, "Matches the town. Everyone's playing the game." e middle of lunch Cyrus began to feel uneasy. This small talk, focused on vacation places, sounded all too familiar. John had not given him any special assignments for more than a year. John knew Cyrus better than anybody in the world, even better than his own mother. He was his *de facto* adopted father. Cyrus had not wasted his time around this remarkable man; he had learned a great deal from him. If by the end of lunch John had not discussed any subject of substance, something very important must be about to follow.

Why worry? I'm not in the business anymore. No more assignments, no more stunts.

But his uneasiness refused to go away. When they were leaving the restaurant, John, in as casual voice as they come, suggested, "Gorgeous weather. How about a little stroll? I've been sitting too much lately, you know."

What's going on? I've retired, damn it. Cool down, play along, let's see what it is all about. Matching his tone, Cyrus replied, "Sure. How about the Mall?"

"Great idea."

They crossed E street, passing half a dozen stretch limousines, perpetually waiting for their VIP Willard Hotel guests, and walked through Pershing Park in silence. They crossed Pennsylvania Avenue and were walking by the left side of 15th street, along the Commerce Department building, when John chuckled and broke the silence.

"Wondering what this is all about?"

Cyrus did not answer, just looked at John, perhaps revealing a slight irritation that John read his thoughts so easily, and John continued.

"Of course I remember that you've retired. I'm retired as well, but the only difference is that I just don't know it yet." Cyrus slightly nodded and John went on, "But this has nothing to do with intelligence or this country's top national interests. Just business. Cold-blooded business."

Sure. That's why we are having this chat here, instead of sitting in your office.

"However, this business can draw on your past expertise." At the word 'past' Cyrus sharply glanced at his mentor, but no apparent offense was meant. *Well, no one likes their expertise to be "past." But that's the way it is. That's the reality. Accept it.*

John was looking at Cyrus and his reaction did not escape the old fox. Something flickered in his eyes. As if nothing happened, he continued, "I have a business idea. Have you heard of the 'Party Gold'?"

"Just some hints a couple of years ago. Wasn't that something to do with Gorbatov's last few months in power when it was rumored they got some money out of the country?"

"Yes. To be a little more specific, that 'some money' was between 70 and 200 billion dollars."

Cyrus stopped and looked at John incredulously. "That's a lot of loose change." He knew John too well to question the reliability of his information. *That's what it's all about! But I can't imagine that John has ever contemplated dealing with shady figures by helping them invest that money. You tricky old man, you never let anyone know your hand. What are you up to now?*

In the dullest of his voices, John concluded, "So, nobody knows where that money has gone. The Russian government would love to find it and would pay a commission. Five percent would be in order, I guess. So, how would you like to find it and earn the commission for the firm?"

Cyrus stopped again, this time standing stock-still. He couldn't believe his own ears. *No. He's pulling my leg.* He just laughed.

"You know, John, I've got a better idea. Why don't we lease a good yacht and go treasure hunting in the Caribbean? Plenty of sunken ships out there. With the gorgeous weather starting in a month or so, it'll be a diver's paradise, and much more fun. Besides, the odds for success are immeasurably higher. Want me to make arrangements?"

"I'm serious."

"So am I."

"Cyrus, I really am serious."

"What? Are you trying to tell me that you want to jump into highly questionable activities, on par with some junky private investigators, jeopardize the firm's reputation, come up with nothing, and end up being the laughing stock of Wall Street? After that, all the calls we'll get will be from the *National Enquirer* at best.

"Did you notice that in last year's ITT deal we were not on the list of the underwriters, nor the Bank of America deal last month?"

"So?"

"Well, those were just some of the early warning signs. Contrary to popular and uninformed belief, the business in general is not doing too well. Our firm is doing even worse than the norm. We have to do something, and rather quickly, to survive."

"How come? I thought we were doing quite well."

Having crossed Constitution Avenue, they were walking on the

Mall passing the Museum of Natural History. An endless line of tour buses was parked along Madison Drive, waiting for their tourists. Small-time vendors of t-shirts and all sorts of useless souvenirs were waiting for their victims, not trying too hard and knowing all too well that they had their captive market.

"You know, of course, the history and the real purpose of our firm."

Cyrus began to feel bored. "I know. Top priority national security issues."

John's tone changed to that of a history professor, good enough and arrogant enough to disregard the indifference of his youthful audience. "Nevertheless, let me give you a few minor details that may shed some favorable light on my business idea. Besides, you might need to know this in the future."

"Why is that?"

John Porter gave Cyrus the long, sad look of a very tired man. He did not answer, sighed, and continued, "Back at the time when I," he chuckled, "bought Jones & Bleach, it was recognized that all the existing organizations were unsuitable for certain types of highly sensitive intelligence operations. You cannot operate really quietly in an organization with thousands of people. On top of that, if the organization is part of the government, there are no secrets. Sooner or later everything comes to light. However few, there are some things that must never come to light. So, some 'companies' were created. Pretty transparent. Boilerplate, nothing that stood out. But they were just kidding themselves. Do you know where all the clandestine efforts of this sort fall apart?" he asked suddenly.

"Lack of real expertise in the cover field?"

"That's one of the reasons, but not the main one. The main reason is only one, money."

"You mean funding for the operations?"

"Precisely. The money has to come from somewhere. And that somewhere has only one final address, the Treasury. And money always, always leaves a trail. For an interested party it's just a question of persistence, and unfortunately, that interested party does not have to be a foreign power. Some of our beloved politicians sometimes forget what they were elected to do, which is to uphold the national interests of this country. And they can proudly sacrifice the most critical and sensitive interests of the country to settle their squalid scores in their personal power game. Of course, some of them have quite legitimate concerns about the abuse of power. But occasionally they also do real harm, albeit with the best intentions. Remember, the road to hell is paved with good intentions. So, whatever the reason, there's always a danger, especially for a really clandestine operation."

"So, that's why you've always been so concerned with our profits."

"Of course. We've never gotten a penny from the Treasury, even as a loan, even indirectly. None." They looked at each other. Cyrus sensed John's revealed deeply held pride.

John took a breath and went on. "As you well know, intelligence operations, particularly quality ones, cost a fortune. And then some. So, it was not humanly possible, considering the things we've done, to do it without some sort of help. And we were getting that sort of help. Sometimes we got into a deal we initially had little to do with. Nobody knows how, and nothing was in writing, of course. Nothing was ever said, really. Just a hint at the highest level, and the recipient of the hint had a choice whether to understand it or not. Most people on that level do. That's all."

"So, that's why from time to time, out of the blue, you get an invitation from a big shot in New York to participate in a practically done deal and get a piece of the action?"

"That's right. Some of them probably think that something underhanded is going on deep down below, like we are managing somebody's 'blind trust' or something along those lines, but that's OK. If they've gotten to the level they are on, they're smart enough not to even think about it. Usually they've perfected the art of selective memory."

"I didn't realize that's how it worked."

"You did not need to."

Why do I need to now? Cyrus did not ask. He also knew John Porter better than most people. They walked by both buildings of the National Gallery of Art, turned onto Pennsylvania Avenue and started heading back toward the office.

John continued, "So, to complete this security picture, during every change of administration, the incoming President is given the combination to the Personal Safe of the President of the United States, which has very few items in it. One of them is a sealed envelope containing only one sheet of paper detailing the ways to communicate with me at any moment."

"What's written on that envelope?"

"I don't know."

"Who else knows about this setup?"

Cyrus caught John's look and immediately regretted the question. They didn't say a word for quite a while.

They passed the square-looking FBI building, whose architecture seemed to loudly declare the bureau's respectability and legitimacy, and were approaching the Freedom Plaza. Cyrus came back to reality.

"This is all very interesting, but what does it have to do with anything?"

John stopped near the memorial in the small park and slowly said, "I am getting signals that the current President is not very fond of this setup. He is so concerned, particularly after that Iran-Contra thing that was bungled so badly, that he has refused any further support and is even considering squashing the firm altogether."

The word "current," and the way it was said, struck Cyrus.

"You sound as if you are speaking from a position of eternity."

"In a way, I am. I think this firm is a national asset and I intend to save it. All I need for that is money." He sighed and concluded in a weary voice, "Think about it, Cyrus. Everything I have told you. Give me your answer in a couple of days. Meanwhile, to help you make an informed decision, I have a file for you to read. Stop by my office."

Cyrus suddenly felt a heavy weight on his shoulders.

They took an elevator and walked to John's office. Following John, Cyrus passed the reception room with his secretary's desk and all the attributes of executive secretarial power occupying about a third of the room, and proceeded into John's office. Cyrus winked in response to the secretary's smile, put his hands forward as if he were water skiing and humbly mumbled, "Here I am, in tow again." He then made a couple steps mimicking the Pink Panther. She laughed, "Cyrus, the rumor was that you've grown up. Now I see it's all wrong."

Although it was large, the office did not feel at all spacious. It created a sense of containment despite plenty of light from its three windows overlooking the same park. Heavy, floor-to-ceiling mahogany panels were filled with personal mementos, not books. A large and massive desk stood in the middle of the right wall, facing the entrance. Two side tables encircled the occupant's position, as if he were about to withstand an infantry assault. A huge antique Persian rug covered most of the floor from the desk to the opposing wall. Two comfortable leather armchairs and a couch surrounded a square table at the other end of the room. Two Victorian oil landscapes and an English hunting scene, all beautifully framed and lighted, were the only objects on the walls. A couple of French bronzes on stands between the windows completed the furnishings of the chamber.

Cyrus closed the massive door behind him and sat in an armchair. John walked to one of the panels and opened it. Inside was a bookshelf. In fact, only the panels along the outer wall and the ones with the paintings were decorative. The other panels disguised the accessories of a very active high-level executive: bookcases, file cabinets, closets, a bar and, of course, safes.

John squeezed his right hand between the left-most book and the back wall of the case and pushed. When he released the pressure, the whole bookcase popped out about an inch. He pulled it and, when the bookcase softly had slid forward a foot, he swung it out, like opening a door. This revealed a safe. He dialed the combination, opened the heavy door and took out a three-ring binder. He closed the safe door, swung the shelf back and pushed it forward. It clicked softly into place. John closed the panel and put the binder on the table in front of Cyrus, then sat down in another armchair.

"I've been watching this deal for a few years. Here you'll find the last couple of years' glimpses." He gave Cyrus a poignant look heavy with wisdom and weariness, but he concluded in an incongruously routine voice, "I must go back to work now. Let me know what you think." Even under the most elaborate audio surveillance nobody would think of the encounter as anything more than a routine business assignment. That was the rule of this office, which had never been broken.

Cyrus took the folder and stood up. "All right John, let me do some digging. I'll let you know if any of my clients are interested." He opened the door and turned, "Oh, and thanks for lunch; it was delightful." One had to know him very well to hear a slight note of sarcasm. John did.

He stopped at John's secretary's desk. She was impressively attractive despite her sixty years. She was tall and her trademark dark business suit fit her still slim figure well. Her face had acquired a few wrinkles, but presented a calm and confident beauty. Noticeable gray in her still abundant dark hair reinforced that image. Her brown eyes expressed that kind of friendly but distant intelligence that made men uncomfortable to even think of flirting with her. She had always been considered unapproachable, particularly after her husband's death.

"Joan, why is it that every time I pass your desk, you get younger and younger, and I feel older and older?"

"Stop it, Cyrus. Your charm doesn't work here. For me you're still that young clumsy boy who could never hand me the rose he'd taken the trouble to get every time he came to visit."

That was not true. His charm always worked with her. They shared a fondness for each other since John first brought the fifteen-year-old for a tour of the office many years ago. She viewed him as a younger brother and took him under her wing when he started working in the firm.

Cyrus nodded at the rose on her side table. "And still, you always have a fresh rose on your desk, and still, it's red," he kept teasing her.

"You know perfectly well, young man, that every morning I place it here myself." She changed her tone: "You'd better tell me how you, the shining star of modern capitalism, are doing."

The hidden hint at his "retirement" was not a pleasant reminder. Perhaps he was just getting too sensitive. Cyrus chose to avoid the topic. He looked her straight in the eye and lowered his voice, slightly nodding toward John's door, "How is the old man?" He immediately noticed a trace of sadness, if not pain, in her eyes.

She paused. "He's all right." She paused. "I guess, he's struggling, perhaps with himself. Through all these years and all the troubles, I haven't sensed anything like this." After a brief moment she blurted, "Cyrus, for God's sake, what's up? I used to know everything. Now I'm not so sure."

Suddenly, Cyrus felt uncomfortable. He felt like a young boy afraid to tell his mother about trouble among his friends. "How would

I know?"

Her stern voice was persistent, "Cyrus, don't try to lie to me. You can't."

"I've got to go." He moved out of the room, but suddenly he stopped at the door and turned. He just couldn't deal with Joan like that. "We'll talk some other time." His voice was still noncommittal.

"All right, I'm very patient, as you know."

Cyrus carried the binder to his office. He nodded to his secretary as he passed through his reception room, and she followed him into his office. He put the binder on his desk, unlocked the rings, and took all the pages out. "Mary, please take care of this."

"Sure." She handed him two large manila envelopes. He put the pages in the envelopes, opened his attaché case and put them in.

She knew what to do. A simple security precaution. Some staff saw him with the binder, so his secretary would fill the binder with materials on some other deal and leave it on his desk. Just in case.

"I think I'd better go home now. You can go too, if you want."

"Thanks, I will, as soon as I finish this stuff. I have a few errands to do."

Being Cyrus' secretary was not an easy job. Sometimes it meant doing nothing for a few days, but then it could mean working thirty-six hours nonstop at a maddening pace. So, take your rest when you can.

"Mary, do I have any appointments tomorrow?"

"No, just five o'clock drinks with Gates from the Prudential at the Old Ebbit."

He thought for a second. "All right, keep it on. I'll be here tomorrow afternoon." He put his coat on, took his attaché and headed out. "See you tomorrow." He was gone before she answered.

There was not much traffic yet. Cyrus took Fifteenth Street to Constitution, crossed the Roosevelt Bridge, and turned onto the George Washington Memorial parkway. He liked the drive between his house and the office. He got off the Parkway and took Chain Bridge Road, heading south. In less than a mile, having just passed the main CIA entrance, he turned right onto Georgetown Pike. At Langley High he turned right into Langley Oaks, the large neighborhood favored by foreigners, mostly diplomats, and some relatively young professionals. His friends often asked him why he'd chosen it and he could never answer precisely why. But as far as he was concerned it was a perfect location.

Cyrus drove into the garage and walked to the mailbox, then went back into the garage and closed the garage door behind him. He often wondered why people had main entrances. He could not even recall the last time he had used his. He unlocked and opened the door from the garage into the house and entered his kitchen. The security system started beeping and he dialed the code. He closed the door, thought for a second and turned the security system on again. He took his coat off and went to the basement to turn on the sauna, one of the best features of the house. It would take an hour to heat up properly. Then he went back and took the two packages out of his attaché. He went upstairs. One of the three bedrooms served as his study, another one was a guest bedroom, which made little sense since he rarely, if ever, had guests in his house that did not sleep in his bed, and the third was his master bedroom. He opened his bedroom door completely so it swung into the room slightly beyond ninety degrees. He then reached to the top edge of the door and pushed down a small wood button, flush with the surface. If someone looked at the door from above, it looked like an ordinary shaft, part of the conventional structure of the door.

Now the whole doorjamb popped out, except for the hinges. He pulled the jamb out a foot and a half. A flat container rolled smoothly out. It was divided into eight slim inch-deep cells, each the size of a regular sheet of paper, and each with a four-inch high stop, so that a stack of papers inserted there would not fall out accidentally. Most of them were empty. He put the packages in the two top cells and slid the container back in. It fit back into place perfectly with a quiet click. Nobody would notice this safe, even if they inspected the door closely. Even a metal detector would be thrown off, since all the parts were made of ironwood. The brass-covered hinges were really made of hardened steel. However, as with many high security arrangements, the main concern was not the loss of the contents. Someone getting close enough to try was bad enough itself. The main concern was to detect the attempt and to know as early as possible that it had been compromised. So when Cyrus slid the container out, his first move was to look at a small plastic counter set into its innermost lower corner. Every time the safe was opened, this counter added "1" to the previous four-digit number and Cyrus always remembered the last one he had seen.

Putting the documents into the safe was a routine precaution, automatic. He would only take the documents out when he was actually working with them. He did not want to read them now. He needed time to consider the conversation with John. And to relax.

He went down to the living room and sat in his favorite chair in front of the patio overlooking his quarter-acre backyard. One of the beauties of this house was that it was adjacent to Langley Oaks Park, so the view was much better than a small backyard would normally allow. He sat contemplating the three old, large and beautiful oaks in front of him and the undergrowth that flourished in the neighboring ravine. Just beyond lay the park that extended as far as the beautiful rapids of the Potomac River.

Cyrus already knew some of the things that John told him today, and he realized that John had endeavored to create a grander context for Cyrus' own association with the firm's mission and, no doubt, to remind him of his old sense of priorities. Cyrus had to admit that John had achieved that. Sitting alone in his living room, he became lost in memories.

Chapter 2

Cyrus remembered John as far back as he could remember anything. John's early contact had been sporadic and somewhat fleeting, John was had always been a great influence in Cyrus's life. John would disappear as suddenly as he appeared, but he always spent time with Cyrus during his visits. He always brought presents for him, and those presents were as unexpected as John himself. John had been his father's best friend, and John and his wife Margaret were close to Cyrus' mother as well.

Cyrus remembered well that day in 1968 when he returned home from school and found two officers in Navy uniforms in their living room. "Father's friends," thought Cyrus. His mother's eyes were red, and her face was pale, as if carved in marble. One of the officers tried to usher Cyrus into the garden in their back yard, but Cyrus sensed something and refused. He went to his mother, and the same strong feeling that made him refuse to go outside made him stop. He would never forget her voice, chillingly calm, but with an unbearable underlying tension. "Cyrus, your father is not coming back." Cyrus was very disappointed. His father's tour was supposed to be coming to an end in two weeks, and the preparations were well underway to welcome him home. Cyrus wanted to ask why his father's tour had been extended, but the same feeling blocked his question. He just looked at his mother. The silence became intolerable, at least for the adults. With the same dull voice his mother said, "Cyrus, darling, your father is not coming back to us at all. He is dead."

Cyrus did not remember any particularly deep feelings at the time, except huge disappointment. His long planned trip to Disneyland was going to be postponed again. All the feelings came much later.

John and Margaret came to the house that same evening. Then after a few days they all flew to Washington. Cyrus remembered the funeral at Arlington cemetery. The casket was never opened, despite Cyrus' requests, and his suspicion that his father was not in it fueled his hopes for several years. After an admiral gave the flag to his mother, he turned to Cyrus, took a large insignia out of his pocket and gave it to Cyrus.

"This is your father's insignia. He was a proud SEAL. Keep it with the same honor with which he wore it."

Cyrus took the insignia. "Do I have to become a SEAL to have one of my own, so I can wear it?"

"Yes."

"Then, how can I become a SEAL?"

"For now, you have to study hard. When you grow up, we'll talk about it."

After the funeral his mother went to visit her aunt, and John and Margaret took Cyrus to Disneyland. He was marginally happy. During the trip he asked a lot about the SEALs. He didn't quite get it; he only understood that they could swim well under water, but, somehow, his determination to become one of them intensified. He figured that the sooner he finished school, the sooner he could become a SEAL. Cyrus also had another reason to hurry. He'd heard a lot about the Vietcong, and he wanted to kill a lot of them to pay them back for his father, and he'd have to do that before the war was over. So, back from the trip, he was determined to graduate from high school ahead of his class.

And he did. Thanks to his mother's insistence, he had already started a year ahead of his age group when he entered the school. After his father's death he was determined to graduate from high school as soon as possible. During these years, Cyrus saw John and Margaret on a fairly regular basis. Initially, John did not involve himself closely in Cyrus' education; however, in time he began supervising Cyrus more vigilantly. Cyrus had earned all the necessary credits to graduate by the time he had just turned 16.

Cyrus' perception of the world changed following his father's funeral, but his dream of becoming a SEAL remained unchanged. He knew that the SEALs were physically outstanding, and he was determined to be likewise. This stood him in good stead, because, as the youngest kid in the class, he was frequently subject to bullying. So, thanks to his drive, and his natural ability in sports, he could hold his own in any company.

With great effort, John convinced Cyrus not to join the Navy immediately after graduation. He convinced him that he was simply too young for that kind of discipline and training. Strangely, Cyrus was not disappointed that his efforts to graduate early did not lead to joining the SEALs right away. Although he did not feel any push from John to go to MIT, that push was there, undetectable, but definitive and firm. Cyrus would come to appreciate much later that this was John's style. So, Cyrus applied to MIT and was given early admission.

Somehow, Cyrus did not go to the Navy when he became eligible. Again, he did not feel any push from John, just an argument that he might be better off in the Navy with the MIT diploma under his belt. He did well at MIT. Moving faster than his class became a habit, and by Christmas of 1978 he had one semester left before his graduation.

Suddenly, things changed. Cyrus was stunned when John suggested he quit MIT and join the Navy.

"John, you spent three years convincing me to graduate from MIT first. Why should I quit now, a few months from my graduation? It defies logic."

John casually said, "Not really. In the Navy, and in the SEALs in particular, you need knowledge, not a diploma. You already have the knowledge. A diploma is just a piece of paper."

They were close enough for Cyrus to realize that John had something up his sleeve.

"John, what's this all about?"

John grew serious. "Cyrus, you've grown now. Do you trust me?"

"Completely. You are like a father to me, you know that."

"Then do what I say. You've wanted a career in the Navy; you've wanted to become a SEAL. I guided you to the best of my abilities. Now you can have what you want," John paused, "and, maybe, more."

Cyrus was about to respond when John added, "And don't worry about the MIT diploma. You can get it later."

Cyrus shook his head. "John, you've never been vague with me. Please, don't start now. What does all this mean? And, what the hell does 'more' mean?"

John responded in a very quiet voice, "Cyrus, either you trust me, or not. If you do, do what I say for now and I'll explain everything to you later. If you don't, well, you are a big boy now, and you're capable of making your own decisions."

A long pause followed. Cyrus thought of his life to that point and the role John had played in it. Finally, he agreed. "All right, John. I've grown to trust you implicitly. I'll do what you want. But I expect an explanation soon."

"I'm honored by your trust, Cyrus. I'll give you the explanation as soon as I can, in a year, maybe."

"What's the big secret?"

"There are national security secrets. For now, just take a semester off at school and tell them you need to think about your life, what you're going to do with it." John chuckled. "I guess it's a fashionable thing to do these days with you youngsters."

In the months that followed Cyrus puzzled over this peculiar Christmas conversation.

Enlistment in the Navy went very smoothly. With his MIT background Cyrus became a machinist mate in only six months, instead of the usual year. Now the door to the SEALs was opened.

Cyrus applied and was accepted as a candidate. Cyrus passed the battery of tests, leaving no doubt in anyone's mind as to his qualifications and abilities, an accomplishment shared by no more than ten percent of the accepted one percent of applicants.

At first, he thought that the tests were mostly physical. Later he realized that, while being certainly highly physical, they mostly tested the mental toughness of the candidates. The "hell week" of almost non-stop physical activities made him wonder if he really wanted all this. But Cyrus realized that the point of it was to demonstrate that humans can endure much more than most people can imagine. Mental toughness was more important than physical toughness. It was almost unreal to see that big guys with perfect muscles were breaking down and quitting, but seemingly weaker guys could keep going. The relentless tests gave way to a merciless week of training that pushed each candidate to his limit or beyond. Cyrus passed. It was not easy, but his memories of his father helped him persevere.

Cyrus hardened during the subsequent twenty-six-week

training. He was no longer a schoolboy; he'd become a warrior. He went through rigorous training in many types of combat. He became an accomplished diver, and a competent skydiver. He was proficient with almost any weapon from any country he could lay his hands on. He was trained in unconventional warfare. If he did not have a weapon, he could make a one from almost anything. He understood that his mind was the most formidable weapon of all.

He passed the final exams with excellent grades, and was assigned to the SEAL Team One. By SEAL rules, every candidate had to complete six months of probation in a SEAL unit before he achieved his 'Budweiser', the SEAL insignia, and officially became a SEAL. Needless to say, Cyrus was proud.

In the middle of August 1980, a week before his official inauguration as a SEAL, Cyrus was summoned by the Unit CO.

"You have one week's leave to visit you mother."

Cyrus was very surprised. Not only had he not been scheduled for this leave, he had not asked for it. He became worried and quickly asked, "Anything wrong with my mother?"

"Not that I'm aware of."

"Why, then?"

"SEALs do not question orders."

"Aye-aye, Sir."

He found his mother in good heath and spirits, and she knew nothing of the origin of the unusual order. Cyrus was left wondering. Then, on the third day of his visit, it all dawned on him. The phone rang, and Cyrus answered.

"Hello, Cyrus. John."

That was it. "Hello, John."

"I heard you're home. I'm in town. See you in half an hour."

John came for the evening and suggested that they leave the next morning to go sailing for a couple of days. All three of them went to John's place in Boothbay Harbor, in Maine. During the day Cyrus' mother and Margaret spent time together and John and Cyrus went sailing, and they all spent the evenings together.

They sailed out of the inner harbor, not as far as the open ocean, but staying in the outer harbor, just across from the yacht club. John steered into the wind and dropped the anchor.

"Cyrus, now it's time for me to level with you."

Cyrus nodded.

"As you know, I've been trying to help you since your father died."

Cyrus nodded again, but did not respond. John continued, "Your progress meant more to me than anything else, with only one exception: national security."

Cyrus' eyes showed genuine surprise. As far as he knew, John was a businessman and, his patriotism notwithstanding, had nothing to do with national security.

John smiled. "For your information, my primary business is national security. My investment banking business is a cover. A good one but, still, just a cover."

"So, are you telling me you work for the CIA?"

"God, no. I wouldn't touch that outfit with a ten-foot pole."

"Are they so bad?"

"Yes. First, they're totally incompetent. Second, and even more important, they have no idea what intelligence is about. They think that it's about who out-crooked who. When in fact intelligence officers must be squeaky clean. A lot of extremely important things are done on trust. One's word must be kept. If you lose credibility, you lose everything. You can dupe someone once, and that's it."

"Why are they successful then?"

"They're not. They just manage to keep most of their failures secret and take credit for other people's work. They don't operate the aerial and satellite intelligence; that's NRO, National Reconnaissance Office. They just take credit for it. Signal intelligence is the NSA, the National Security Agency. Sometimes CIA manages to take credit even for that. Their analysts are utterly incompetent. They either take their "analysis" out of the media, or they are dead wrong. And, they've bungled their own business, human intelligence."

"How come they recruit a lot of spies?"

"Cyrus, they haven't recruited anybody for a long time; they just take credit for it. They're so obvious anywhere in the world that those who want to be recruited come to them, and those who don't, just stay clear of them. In fact, they thrive on the image of this great country, take advantage of it, deplete that image, and then take credit for mysterious successes, too secret to tell." John paused. "But enough about the CIA. You will have many opportunities in the future to figure it all out for yourself."

Cyrus was surprised by this outburst by the usually very reserved John. It could only have been caused by a lot of real frustration, and his anger seemed grounded in good reason. "So, whom do you work for?"

John took a while to respond. "Cyrus, what I'm about to tell you is one of the most guarded secrets in national security. All the secrets you've dealt with so far in the SEALs are a bit pale in comparison. If it ever comes out, I will have to deny it altogether, including this conversation with you."

Cyrus felt slightly offended. He did not say a word, and John continued, "I work for the President, and only for the President. Once in a while, a crisis pops up. A crisis that cannot be solved by any government intelligence body, something too sensitive to risk exposing government involvement. That's where I come in. I provide the highest professional-level operational solution to the crisis. And total deniability for the government if something goes wrong. I am totally disposable. There is no link between me and the government."

"Does it mean that you're taking orders directly from the President?"

"Better than that. The President describes the problem to me. He never suggests a solution. He can't. He must be totally clean. The President can raise his right hand and swear truthfully that he never ordered any action, nor did he know of anyone who did. I'm the one who finds and implements the solution. I'm the only one who's responsible for everything."

"That's a pretty tough position to be in, a ready-made scapegoat."

John smiled. "Good motivation not to fail."

They were silent for a while. Then, Cyrus asked, "You didn't just tell me all that to widen my intellectual horizons?"

"That's right." John smiled, and then became very serious, almost formal. "I'm offering you a job."

Cyrus laughed. "And my 'Budweiser' fits well into the picture."

"Of course, but not only that. I've guided you very carefully right from your childhood, hoping you'd come through."

"And that's why you encouraged me to learn flying?"

"Sure, and I sent you to an old friend of mine for that so you'd learn from the best."

Cyrus started thinking the offer over when John intervened. "Don't say anything now. It's too serious to decide on the spot. Take your time. But no one, no one can know what I've just told you, not even your mother." John sighed, "Just one more sin on my soul."

The next day, Cyrus, attracted by the mystery and utmost importance of the mission, was leaning toward accepting the offer. One thing bothered him, though. SEAL. He had a hard time giving that up after pursuing it as his primary goal for so many years.

In the boat again, he said, "John, everything you've told me about your outfit sounds interesting, but I really wanted to become a SEAL."

John detected in the tone of Cyrus' answer a need for a discussion, rather than a refusal.

"Well, it's entirely up to you, Cyrus. But there is something I want to make clear to you. It may look like SEAL is a place for heroes. And it is, don't misunderstand me. However, that's not the only place for heroes. Our organization requires no less heroism, believe me. If you join us, you'll operate mostly in a hostile environment, and you'll be alone. Alone is the key. Very few heroes can do that. It is one thing to face danger with a group of your buddies, and it is entirely something else when your nearest buddy, and support, is a thousand miles away. Psychologically, it's much more difficult. But you're one of those men who are psychologically fit to do that. On balance, I'm offering you a more dangerous job than the SEALs do, but all the skills that you've learned there may someday save your skin. We never know what we're going to face. Any other service can occasionally decide that something is not their job, but we don't have that luxury."

"I appreciate your honesty, John. Truthfully, it's very tempting, but I still don't know. I need your help, your advice."

"I can't give you advice. First, I'm not impartial. Second, I can't be responsible for getting you into something, which can easily cost you your life. I can answer some of your questions, but you're still on your own."

"Is what you do really that important?"

"Absolutely. If something can be solved by any other means, we're not involved. You can't find a place where your personal contribution to the national security, in its purest form, is greater, if that's what you're asking."

"Then, I'm interested, John. What should I do to join?"

"That's the hard part, Cyrus. You'll have to do a lot of things first. I also have to ask you for a great personal sacrifice."

"What's that?" asked Cyrus cheerfully.

"I know it means a lot for you, but you'll have to give up your 'Budweiser.'"

"Why? I passed all the training and tests. The official ceremony is just days away, and you're asking me to do that?"

John answered in a very calm voice, "Precisely. One of the reasons that we are very effective is that we have a perfect cover. Each of us is untraceable to any intelligence organization."

"What does that have to do with it?"

"Simple. You needed SEAL training, and you've got it. However, if you're officially enrolled, you're on the national register, and on a lot of other lists as well. We can't afford that. SEAL training is a red flag for any counterintelligence check, and you'll have plenty of those later, believe me."

"But all the lists are secret. What are you afraid of?"

"They are secret only to the general public. Any intelligence organization worth a damn has them. That's a reality."

"But I've already been involved in the program."

"True, but only in 'working papers.' The attrition rate is very high, and it's all very tentative until you're officially in. These working papers aren't kept very well either, nor for very long. Your name will disappear in a while."

"And how am I going to get a discharge?"

"Very simple. Medical discharge. Either injury or an illness. Your personnel file will remain 'machinist mate'."

Cyrus was shaken by the prospect of the demise of his childhood dream, but he was also impressed by the thoroughness of the security consideration in John's outfit. "Is that why you got me out of MIT in the middle of the show?"

"Absolutely. You have to account for all the time in your life, leaving no 'white spots' to indicate any intelligence training. See, you'll go back to MIT and graduate. The total time spent would be just slightly above nominal, but well within the average. If somebody digs deeper they'll see you made a try for the Navy, didn't like it, and reverted back."

"Is it that important?"

"Of course, if you do it right."

Cyrus was too impressed to pass up the opportunity. "All right, John, you've got me. But how am I going to get a medical discharge?" He chuckled, "I bet, you have a friend in the right place."

"Of course. I have a lot of friends in a lot of right places."

"I'd like to go back to the Unit to say good-bye to the guys."

"No. You've got to learn to leave without saying good-bye. You'll need it a lot."

They were silent for a while, but Cyrus grew intrigued and asked, "Are there any other sacrifices that I should know about?"

"Certainly, a lot of them. But you have to be fair to me, Cyrus. All the skills you've acquired with my guidance will be useful to you if something goes wrong, and you want to live a normal life span."

"I know, John. I never doubted you."

"Thank you."

"When can I start working for you?"

"In a few years."

"What?"

John smiled. "What you're going to do requires a lot of skills and knowledge. You've just started your training."

"You mean training for a few years?"

"Yes. Training and studying." John chuckled. "But it will be fun, don't worry. Just get your MIT diploma first."

And Cyrus did. In December of 1980 he passed all the required exams for his graduation.

Christmas 1980 brought exciting news to Cyrus. After the New Year he left for Oxford, England. He made sure he was seen hanging around there, making an early 'get acquainted' trip, preparing to enter the University in September. In fact, he spent most of the time in the Fort, the MI-6 training facility. John considered it "the best training in the world," and by some mysterious means, John got him there. The training groups were extremely small, and the Fort was famous for its facilities, location and scheduling. The several groups of trainees in the Fort never encountered each other. Each trainee was exposed only to the instructors and to his peers in his own group, and everyone used an alias. At John's insistence, Cyrus also let his hair grow long before going to England.

The training itself was fascinating. Cyrus was impressed by its emphasis on details, meticulous planning and preparation. By the end of August his initial intelligence indoctrination was over. After a week home with his mother, he returned to Oxford to continue his study. He stayed at Oxford for two years, spending his summers at the Sorbonne in Paris 'to get used to the cosmopolitan environment, and to develop his network,' as John put it. All in all, it was a lot of fun. In fact, Cyrus sometimes caught himself forgetting his main mission.

His next assignment came in the fall of 1983 when he enrolled in Harvard Business School with John's peculiar admonition that it was no longer the "unparalleled school it used to be, but you've got to go through it." Cyrus found this characterization accurate. The atmosphere was a bit stuffy. Indeed, its 'Who's Who society, early cynicism and elitist pretentiousness among the students somewhat poisoned his stint there, but the study was interesting and the approach was drastically different from Oxford.

After the first semester, Cyrus took a leave of absence and returned to England to continue his advanced intelligence training at the Fort and in the field. By the end of 1984, Cyrus had had the best possible all-round training for intelligence.

Having missed a year, Cyrus returned to Harvard in January of 1985 to continue with his MBA study. Overall, he found it most useful for developing a network for his future as a banker in John's firm. He graduated in June of 1986, and although he enjoyed his studies, he had grown restless and decided to confront John.

"John, I'm getting tired of studying. Being a perpetual student is not exactly what I had in mind as my life's endeavor."

John laughed. "I've been waiting for this for some time. You've got a little more patience than I thought. Good. Pretty soon it'll be over, but believe me, you'll have moments when you'll wish you were still a student."

"John, I'm serious."

"So am I. You've accomplished a lot, Cyrus. At twenty-six you have managed to get the best intelligence training available on this planet, SEAL training, plus you have MIT, Oxford and Harvard under your belt. That's about as good as it gets on our side, you know. No less important, you've also become good at your regular job. That's hard to do, but it's absolutely essential for intelligence work." John paused and continued, "Yes, in order to be convincingly genuine, you need to be very successful in your cover career. On top of that you have your intelligence work. With us, that's where you can't afford a failure. So you have to be able to work hard at both jobs simultaneously. But working hard is not the real point--you have to deliver at both jobs.

"All that is well and good, but when can I start working?" Cyrus persisted.

"Soon. You need just a month of our company's initial training, but before that I want you to spend a couple of months at the CIA 'Farm'."

"What? Why would I need that? I've heard enough about them to stay as far away as I can."

"You'll need it. Not that you're going to learn anything useful there, but you have to have an idea of how they're trained. This will give you good insight into how they behave and perform. You'll know what to expect from them."

"Why would I need that?"

"There are so many of them out there, and you'll be bumping into them once in a while. Besides, it's not inconceivable that some day you may have to use their technical support services. 'In the blind' of course, when they'd have no idea of what is going on."

Cyrus shook his head. John added. "One more advantage of that is that you'll have to master one of the most difficult tasks: getting by their instructors as someone with no intelligence knowledge of any kind. They are not the most impressive, but nevertheless they are trained intelligence officers." After a pause, John concluded, "You check in on Monday for the short course training. You will drop out in two months. Alias, of course. And take care of your appearance; I don't trust them at all. I've made all the arrangements."

Cyrus shaved his head, put on a Brooklyn accent, and plunged in.

In two months he was all too happy to vanish from the dreadful place. His eyes were sore for the next two weeks from wearing the contact lenses that made his eyes brown. His jaws were sore from wearing dental inserts that made his speech different and also further changed face. With his altered eye color and the drastic transformation of his physiognomy emphasized by his bald head, Cyrus felt confident that no one from school would ever recognize him. He had many enthusiastic chats outside of class with his instructors, and listened attentively to their war stories.

By the time he was pulled off the course he had a pretty good feel for the people the "Farm" was churning out. John's objective was achieved.

Following John's regimen, Cyrus honed his MI-6 training. Now, by Christmas of 1986, he was finally ready to work.

Chapter 3

"Cyrus!" called an unfamiliar, cheerful female voice. Having made his way through a small team of uniformed and white-gloved doormen at the entrance, Cyrus Grant walked briskly up the stairs of the Waldorf-Astoria lobby. With a light, unhurried motion he stopped and turned around.

A blond knockout of about twenty-eight, dressed in a black business suit that showed the lines of her perfect body better than any evening gown, moved up the steps toward him. Her dark blue eyes sparkled as if she were genuinely glad to see him.

Cyrus quickly placed the face at Bear Sterns, but he couldn't quite recall the name. His upbringing kicked in, and he automatically took a few steps down towards her. Behind the woman he saw two figures entering the main door of the lobby. One was slim and short, and the other looked like a bear. *Better to be lucky than good. Having worked for being good all my life, I'll gladly take luck any time. Let's start negotiating.* He smiled cheerfully, shook her extended hand and immediately turned his way upstairs beside the blonde.

She saved him some embarrassment by quickly saying, "Hi Cyrus, I'm Sherrill Maxwell. Remember me?"

Pretty loud voice. They should hear it. The pair now was not more than twenty feet behind, and they slowed down to maintain the distance. "Hello, Sherrill. Of course I do. Bear Stearns, isn't it?"

That was a welcome reassurance for her. She hadn't been that sure that he would remember. "And we also met at your uncle's birthday party last fall in Greenwich."

That was the sixty-fifth birthday gala in Connecticut in October. "Oh, yes, Old James' birthday-retirement hoopla. Actually he's my aunt's husband."

"All the same, he's a nice man."

Cyrus chuckled, "As far as bankers go."

She laughed. "Don't be so cynical. There are no saints within a hundred miles of this city." Seeing that they were not too far from the main ballroom, she quickened the pace. "Actually, the last time I saw you I wanted to buy you a drink. How about that?" She looked him straight in the eye with a slightly challenging look, provoking his competitive instincts.

That's a pretty fast pace. On the other hand, New York is New York. She's certainly very attractive. And obviously competitive. All right. He met the challenge with his eyes. "Splendid. But we'll negotiate who's buying the drink for whom. Frankly, that was my," he paused briefly and looked at her, "idea as well." They were entering the ballroom, which was hosting the World Bank cocktail reception. "Great. We'll serve our obligatory time in this zoo, and then we'll think of something."

"Great. Forty minutes or so?"

He nodded.

The World Bank President and a Vice-President were greeting the arrivals. The VP knew Cyrus.

"Hello Cyrus!" he called and offered his hand to welcome him. "What a lovely lady you have with you! Let me introduce you to our President."

What friendly energy. You can't last long, greeting everyone with this enthusiasm. Slow down to one out of five. "Hello, Jack. Great to be here."

"George, let me introduce my dear friend Cyrus Grant of Jones & Bleach. He is also a nephew of Mr. Coldwell, who just retired Vice Chairman of Chemical Bank."

"Glad to meet you, Mr. Grant. We made a few deals with your uncle. Great man. Is he still in the business?"

Cyrus sensed that the pair behind them had caught up and were standing close behind. "Honored to meet you, Sir. My uncle is still on the Board of Directors. Let me introduce Ms. Sherrill Maxwell of Bear Stearns."

"Happy to meet you, Ms. Maxwell. Any business that attracts such beautiful ladies must be a good business." Everyone laughed, and the President smiled at Cyrus, "I take it the two companies are joining forces?"

"We've just started negotiating." Cyrus and Sherrill looked at each other.

"Well, good luck. And welcome to our small party." There must have been five hundred people in the room and more to come.

Cyrus and Sherrill became separated right after passing the welcome party. Somebody grabbed Cyrus by the arm. "Hi, Cyrus. Glad you're here."

"Hi, Jimmy. What's up?"

"Look, we're working on a deal in biotech. There's some room there. Care to join?"

"Another start-up?"

"No, no. Expansion. Doing quite well already. A joint venture in South Africa."

"Are you mad, Jimmy? Biotech in South Africa? Give me a break."

"Listen, its really good. Mandela is bending over backwards to create a good business environment. A lot of things that are impossible here are a no-brainer there. And with North Africa a mess, guess who's going to supply the whole continent."

"Well, kind of radical, but makes sense. How much?"

"About twenty million. Total of eighty."

"Tell you what, talk to Peter Sames, he's handling most of the biotech, certainly in that range."

"Don't know him. How about an introduction?"

"OK." Cyrus took a small notebook out of his pocket and made a note.

"Thanks, Cyrus. See you around."

Before another encounter Cyrus stopped a waiter. He took a twenty-dollar bill out of his pocket. "Get me a quiet corner table in the Oak Room for two for dinner. Seven o'clock. My name is Cyrus Grant."

"Yes, Sir. Right away, Mr. Grant."

Cyrus roamed around for another thirty minutes. *What's taking them so long? Any mistakes? No, doesn't look like it.* He felt relief when a slim man with an outrageous tie emerged about fifteen feet in front of him. The man suddenly recognized him, waved, and started working his way toward Cyrus with the bear-like figure in a dark blue suit in tow.

"Cyrus, my friend, how nice to see you again!"

"Hello, Jeffrey. How've you been?"

"Good, good. How's business? I heard that you are looking to do something in Russia."

Cyrus opened his mouth to say that the rumor was not true, but he didn't get the chance. "By the way, I want you to meet someone. Let me introduce Mr. Dronov. Yuri, this is my dear friend, Cyrus Grant, an investment banker. One of the best." The style didn't surprise Cyrus. He'd known Jeffrey for a number of years, and generally tried to stay away from him, but it was virtually impossible since Jeffrey was everywhere.

The men shook hands, and Dronov replied in a heavy, unmistakably Russian accent, "How do you do, Mr. Grant." The Russian's face was rough hewn, with a heavy nose that dominated rather formless lips, and small piercing eyes under heavy lids and bushy, half-gray eyebrows. A mass of thick gray hair had obviously not been touched by a barber in a month.

"Pleasure to meet you, Mr. Dronov."

Jeffrey gently stepped in, "Mr. Dronov is visiting. Incidentally, he is a former general, believe it or not, with the KGB." He laughed loudly on his own. "Everything's changed now hasn't it? We're all friends now and, maybe, business partners."

Cyrus raised an eyebrow. "Oh, that's interesting. So, is it Mr. Dronov, Comrade Dronov, or General Dronov?"

"Do you speak Russian?" Dronov suddenly half-asked, half-suggested in Russian.

Jeffrey's jaw fell, and Cyrus' face clearly expressed puzzlement.

Elaborate? Lay it out? Holding back may look suspicious. No, play it cool. "Just a little bit." Answered Cyrus, also in Russian.

"More than a little, Mr. Grant, I didn't know that investment bankers were so modest. But the main point is, please don't be touchy. Given your background, some hostility would be understandable, but try to realize that communism is gone. Besides, in any system, there are people who just do their job, whatever profession they happened to be in. Old wounds are better off not disturbed."

"Background?" Cyrus was not quite ready for such a turn.

"Obviously, you speak good Russian, but your slight accent suggests that you come from the "first wave" of Russian immigration here. In those circles the word 'comrade' is used exclusively as a slap in the face."

"General, don't tell me that you derived all that from my few words of Russian."

"Yes, I did. The way you pronounced my last name suggested that you speak Russian. And the way you said 'Just a little bit' completed the picture."

"You amaze me, General. Are all the guys in the KGB that good?"

Dronov smiled, "Just the generals."

The waiter quietly came from behind and said in Cyrus' ear, "Your table will be ready in fifteen minutes, Mr. Grant."

Cyrus responded, without turning, in a half tone, "Thank you very much," and continued in a normal voice without any pause.

"You're right. My mother was Russian, my nanny was Russian, and I had a chance to practice in the émigré community," Cyrus responded to clarify things. He paused, trying to find a way to make up for the small embarrassment. "So, have you been in the States before?" He smiled, "Your English certainly suggests that."

"Yes, I've been here as a 'Resident' or a Station Chief, as you call it."

"So, you know this country inside and out, I guess."

Dronov laughed, "I wish. It's still a puzzle to me in many respects."

"Oh, don't be so modest. But what business brought you here this time?"

"Plain and simple. You call it job hunting. I got together whatever money I had saved, jumped on an Aeroflot, it's cheaper, and now I am staying with an old friend, testing his hospitality."

Jeffrey, silent for a long time, jumped in, "That's what occurred to me, Cyrus, when I spotted you. I thought that your company might need the talent and expertise of a man like Mr. Dronov."

"Well, Jeffrey, the rumor you've heard, if there was any, is not true. We're not doing any business with Russia. As a matter of fact, as far as I know, all the companies that jumped into that are trying to get out and salvage whatever money they can."

He paused slightly, watching Jeffrey's face express clear disappointment, and the stone-faced General nod gracefully, and continued, "So, I guess, the employment prospects in this area, certainly with our company, are pretty bleak, I'm afraid." Then he added with a slight hesitation, "However, there is something I'm working on right now. It relates to a company connected with Russia, but based in the West."

Where the hell is Sherrill? She is the best way to bail out, and I need it soon. "What are your capabilities right now, Mr. Dronov?"

"I know organizations, I know people. Quite a few, actually. Russian, mainly. In Russia and abroad. I know a lot about them; as we say in Russia, I know 'who is breathing with what.' If I don't, I can find out, quickly and reliably."

"How reliably?"

Dronov smiled, "Very reliably."

Finally Cyrus spotted Sherrill ten feet behind and slightly to the side of the general. He gave her a long, inviting look. She started moving toward them. "The thing is that one of our clients is considering forming a joint venture with the company in question and we are to help them to put the deal together. So, I need to know a little more about that company than I do in order to be comfortable with that deal."

He turned to Sherrill, "Sherrill, let me introduce Mr. Dronov. I guess you know Jeffrey."

"Hello, Mr. Dronov. Hi, Jeffrey." The men responded.

Jeffrey tried to seize the moment, and obviously remembering the remark about the table, he jumped in again, "That's great. Let's chat about it over dinner."

Cyrus' voice iced, "I'm afraid I'm already committed. Besides, I don't want to overextend your time, gentlemen. So, if you have any interest in a temporary thing, Mr. Dronov, we can talk tomorrow, but I have to be honest with you, I can't promise you much."

"In my current circumstance I'd be grateful." Dronov's answer was simple and humble.

Cyrus put his hand around Sherrill's waist, she did not move. The feeling was pleasant. "How about joining me for breakfast tomorrow morning?"

"With pleasure."

"Splendid. Eight forty five, hotel The Crowne Plaza. Do you know where it is?"

"Must be a new one. But I'll find out."

"Just off Times Square. Good night."

Cyrus and Sherrill started making their way through the room. He had to lean to her ear to be heard in the increasingly noisy room. "I hope we don't have to stay in this zoo much longer."

"I'm ready to leave any moment. Any ideas?"

"One to start with. I've booked a table in the Oak Room for dinner."

She looked at him. He noticed a momentary sparkle in her eyes. "Well, you're living up to your reputation so far. I'm starving."

They skipped out of the room and went downstairs.

As they finished dinner there was no doubt in their minds what would be the next move. Cyrus was a little surprised that Sherrill excited him that quickly. He definitely felt younger. "I guess I'm supposed to escort you home, but I'd rather take you to my hotel, however shocking that may sound to you." He leaned to her ear, "I want you."

He noticed the same instant sparkle in her eyes. She was definitely in a mood to tease. "Well, if that excites older men more, why not?"

He gently squeezed her arm just above the elbow. "We'll see who is 'older' very soon."

Walking through the lobby, he stopped at the concierge and ordered champagne and a fruit basket sent to his room at the The Crowne Plaza right away.

When the taxi slowed as it approached the entrance of the hotel, Cyrus noticed a station wagon with a ZY license plate parked in the street just near the corner of the hotel. *Gee, the Russians are really serious about the whole thing. Leave no stone unturned. It's right where the telephone cable should go into the hotel trunk. What an honor!* He knew they must eavesdropping on all the hotel telephone lines, most likely just to listen to his phone.

An hour and a half later, exhausted, they were lazily grazing the fruit. Sherrill was slowly sipping champagne.

"Cyrus, the good news is that you're a terrific lover, the bad news is that you know it."

Cyrus looked at her with a quiet smile. "Tell me, what made you pick me up tonight?"

She laughed happily. "You were a target of opportunity."

"No, seriously, why?"

"Darling, you have quite a reputation among girls. When Gail, your cousin, brought me in for your uncle's birthday, we gossiped about you, and I got turned on. We made a bet, but you failed to pay any attention to me, so I lost. Tonight was my revenge. Satisfied?"

"What kind of reputation?"

"The most eligible bachelor, straight, charming, terrific in bed, wealthy, very well connected, and a little strange."

Cyrus chuckled, "That's all overblown. But why strange?"

"You seem to be available and not available at the same time. Though rumor has it that you have no trouble engaging women, I also hear that you are totally cold and unresponsive to the flirtations of even the most beautiful women. You, Cyrus, are always in control. When you consider all these things together, it's a bit strange."

Cyrus noticed that she had taken on a slightly more serious tone, and he tried to turn it back. He put his hand on her naked back and said with a smile, "Well, a short while ago, at times you were in control."

Her brown eyes turned serious. "That's only because you let me."

He quickly changed the subject. After another half an hour Sherrill decided to go home. She did not want Cyrus to escort her, but he insisted.

When they arrived at her apartment building, he kissed her goodbye, then once more, then again. After that, without saying a word, he let the taxi go and went with her upstairs.

At two in the morning, as he was getting into a taxi, he saw the car that had followed them from The Crowne Plaza, still waiting seventy yards up the street. He was tailed back to his hotel. The station wagon was still there.

Cyrus went up the elevator to the twenty sixth floor. Exiting the elevator, he came to a marble table with a lamp and flowers in the corridor. He put his hand underneath the table and searched. The envelope was taped to the table top from underneath. He carefully took it off, put it in his pocket and went to his room.

Once in his room, he glanced around to ensure that there were no gaps in the curtains before taking the envelope from his pocket and opening it. Two sheets of familiar thin water-soluble paper contained a typed letter. He sat in an armchair and started reading.

"Audio surveillance of Bear and Mule. 01.24.95"

18.37 Outside the Waldorf-Astoria hotel.

Bear: Why are you so sure that he doesn't work for the CIA?

Mule: My dear general, real investment bankers, and he is a real investment banker, do not work for that shit pot. First of all, there cannot be any incentive. These guys make at least half a million dollars in a very bad year. What would they make with the CIA? Secondly, if such collaboration becomes known, even just rumors, their reputation is tarred and they're untouchable. Forever. It's a strong deterrent, you know."

18.42 Entrance of the Waldorf-Astoria hotel.

Mule: Unintelligible.

Bear: Nodded, no sound.

19.15 Reception room for the World Bank. Sound quality poor.

Bear: We can't lose him, let's move.

Mule: Don't worry; he's going to be here for another thirty minutes.

Bear: I said, let's move.

Mule: OK, OK.

Mule: Cyrus, my friend, how nice to see you again!"

Cyrus skipped his part in the transcript.

19.26 Outside the reception room.

Bear: Sonofabitch! He just dumped everything for a skirt he met five minutes ago. What an arrogant bastard!

Mule: I've told you, he's kind of a playboy, wealthy, you know. He doesn't give a damn if he misses a deal. He likes to say that there's always another deal.

Bear: It's hard to believe that he can be good in his business when he doesn't seem to care.

Mule: Don't worry, it's just his style. He's a top-notch investment banker, one of the best. If he starts working, he goes all the way. By the way, why do you need a good investment banker, General? To manage your pension plan?

Bear: Oh, shut up, Jeffrey. None of your business.

Bear: Jeffrey, are you sure that you can afford that much time with me?

Mule: Absolutely, don't worry. Everyone's dealing with the

Russians these days. We're friends now, remember?"

That was the end of the first page. Cyrus smiled as he read the last passages. *Well, the station wagon is still there. I shouldn't disappoint them.* He took his notebook out of his pocket, dialed his office, and the code for his voice mail. He listened through all five messages and then dialed the number for his secretary. "Mary, please ask Peter Sames to call Jimmy Peters at Solomon in New York. He's got a biotech deal in South Africa. Sounds a bit crazy, but it may be worth looking into. It's right up Peter's alley." He went through the few notes he'd made at the reception and responded to a couple of his own messages. "That's all. I'm not sure yet when I'll be back. So, have a good time without your favorite boss. Bye." He paused just a second, and then recalled something. "Wait, one more thing. Tell John Porter that I am about to hire a strange guy here. Well, temporarily, of course, as an independent contractor. Believe it or not, he's a former KGB general. He seems to know his way around in some quarters. Trycorp is keen on fiddling around with that Seebercorp, and I'm supposed to check it out, but I don't even know where to start, so he can be useful. Now, that's all, bye."

He hung up, went back to his envelope and started reading the second page.

"Intercept of Bear's telephone call to Carno. 01.24.95 19.34 from a pay phone in the main hall of Grand Central.

Bear: Hello, Vitali, this is Pavel.

Carno: Hello, Pavel, how are you?

Bear: Sorry to disturb you at home, but I just started talking about the deal we discussed with you earlier with that small company. I need to be sure that the company is reputable. You know how many crooks there are in New York. You promised to help through your friends in the Commerce Department. We may not have too much time or too many opportunities, so, I'd like to make sure that there are no slip-ups."

Carno: Pavel, don't worry. We're checking them out now. There will be no slip-ups. We'll let you know, as agreed.

Bear: I certainly hope so. Thank you, Vitali. Good night."

At the bottom of the second page there was a note, "We're sure you know about the station wagon by the hotel's trunk of the hotel and the tail. There may be more, but nothing was detected. Obviously, they are playing it very seriously. Good luck."

At the bottom there was a happy face and a handwritten note, "Adequate sleep makes men strong!"

Cyrus smiled broadly. *Bastards.* He went to the bathroom, put the two pages in the sink and opened the faucet. Almost instantly the rice-based water-soluble paper turned into jelly and disappeared down the drain. The envelope went into the other part of the facility as the water drained. It was time to get some sleep.

The phone rang at 8:10. Cyrus answered. A sweetly nasty female voice said, "Good morning, Mr. Grant. I hope you had a good night's sleep. This is your wake up call."

"Joan? What's up?"

"Mr. Porter wants to talk to you," and she added in an even sterner voice, "Now."

The phone clicked softly, and John's voice came on the line.

"Good morning, Cyrus. I take it you had enough to drink last night."

"Hello, John. What do you mean?"

"I mean that I've got word that you started hiring KGB generals for us. Are you sure you're all right?"

"John, it's not that bad, you know." His voice was still slightly sleepy. "We need someone to navigate in that crowd of communists-turned-capitalists. How am I supposed to verify the eligibility of Seebercorp for the deal with Trycorpr when I'm totally at a loss? I don't even know where to start. This guy apparently knows that whole crowd. He seems to have all the connections." Cyrus took a breath after the monologue.

"Cyrus, you should know better than that. Politically, it's explosive. Can you imagine the uproar if somebody were to find out that Jones & Bleach employs KGB generals? You can do all the tap dancing in the world explaining that, but nobody would deal with you," he made a short pause, "or me, simply by implication."

"Well, we don't have to hire him. Suppose I just use him for a one-shot deal. And pay cash. But John, one way or the other, we need somebody like that. Could be worse, you know. This may well be a case where the devil you know is better than the devil you don't." He paused. "The alternative is to bail out of the deal, offending our good client, and people would talk about that, too."

There was silence on the line for a while. Then John's voice came to life, but it sounded less certain than before. "You've got a point, but I still don't like it, Cyrus."

"All right, let me talk to him. Frankly, I don't have a feel for him yet. If I have any doubts, I'll dump him. If not, it'll be a cash-for-services one-shot-deal with a clear outsider. Me personally. OK?"

After a longer silence, John said, "Very well. I know nothing about it; it's your play. But Cyrus, please be careful. I don't want you to get in a mess." Then he added, "By the way, what's your protégé's name?"

"Hmm, General... General..." he paused, "General Drobonov, or something like that." John met Cyrus' response with a disapproving silence.

"Don't worry, John, I'll handle it." He switched subjects. "By the way, the other deal, the Cresco."

"What about it?"

"I'm afraid we'll need to raise about fifteen million more, and quickly. I asked them to take another look at the assumptions in the business plan. If it comes back the way I think, I'll need to see you on that one."

"When?"

"In two days, Friday afternoon."

"No way. On Friday I have a family function."

"Sorry John, I've got to be in London Monday."

"OK, OK. I see you love to make the old man work. If worst comes to the worst, why don't you drop by on Saturday? Say, for lunch."

"Thanks, John."

They hung up. I wish, General, you could have heard this now, before we meet. And I hope you play it right, even without that luxury. Cyrus quickly put himself together, and went downstairs to the restaurant.

General Dronov was sitting in an armchair in the lobby near the restaurant. He rose when Cyrus approached. His smile was brighter than Cyrus'.

"Good morning, good morning, Cyrus!"

"Good morning, General. Sorry, I'm a little late."

They moved toward the restaurant. "Not to worry, you're still young. Young people are always late. You don't mind that I call you Cyrus, do you?"

"Not at all."

"Call me Yuri. My friends call me Yuri."

The restaurant was not crowded. Most of the guests had had their breakfasts and had left to make money. They took the corner table, away from the window. After they ordered, Cyrus started the negotiation.

"I was quite impressed with your improvisation last night, Yuri. But let me be blunt. There is very little chance of employment in our company at the moment. On the other hand, I, personally, need some assistance. What can you do for me?"

The assault, but neither his face, nor even his eyes showed it must have surprised Dronov. "Well, that's a very broad question. Do you have a couple of days for the list?"

Cyrus laughed. "OK. Let me be more specific. One of our good clients is considering a joint venture with a company headed by a former Soviet, with most of the employees former Soviets, and extensive connections in Russia and around it." He paused, and saw the general was listening carefully. "Well, since we're handling the transaction for our client, we need to know how legitimate the company in question is."

"Can you be a little more specific as to your criteria for legitimacy?"

"Actually, there's plenty to consider. Is the company sound financially, is the source of its money legal, is it involved in any sort of questionable activities, is there any suggestion of drug dealing or money laundering, where is it based in Russia, and are they reasonably honest or not. Those kinds of things."

"That's quite a lot." The General smiled. "But not really difficult. What I can't do is check out their activity in Western banks. But I can get the same information from the inside."

Cyrus' face showed surprise. "That would be quite a lot of goodies, you know."

"I know. But it's not a problem."

"Then I'm impressed. Provided, of course, that you deliver."

The General took this as a put-down. Dronov said quietly, "Cyrus, I didn't become a general in the KGB because my uncle was in the Politburo. I never had an uncle."

"Sorry, I didn't mean to offend you. Some people I deal with don't deliver. It happens, you know." The general did not answer, and Cyrus asked, "What is a fee that would make you comfortable?" His eyes were quizzical. He was wondering how the general would handle this sensitive matter.

"Oh, a thousand a day, plus fifty percent bonus for success, plus expenses, of course."

"OK."

Dronov laughed, "I shot from the hip. Should I have asked for more?"

Careful. Don't become too friendly, but don't overplay it either. Cyrus smiled and just said, "No."

"You're a good businessman."

"Your guess is very accurate. That is, if you were guessing."

Chatting about the cost of living in New York, they finished breakfast and moved to a small restaurant lobby doubling as a bar area in the evening. The restaurant was generally deserted at that time of the day; they saw only one man there reading a newspaper, apparently waiting for his appointment to come down from the room. They sat in the armchairs in the opposite corner.

"So, when do we start, Cyrus?"

"Right now."

"Oh, I see you really mean business. Well, I'm ready," the General chuckled, "Do all investment bankers move this quickly?"

"All the good ones. We don't have time to waste." *Let's see how good your cover is.* Cyrus paused, and when the General did not respond, he went on, "You are leaving for Toronto on the two o'clock flight. Let's start there. Later we probably will have to go to London. You have a couple of hours to pack your bags. If you give me your details, I'll take care of the tickets, and I'll join you in Toronto on Monday."

"Well, I've got a bit of a problem here, Cyrus. I'm a Russian citizen, remember? I need a visa to enter Canada."

Cyrus sighed in exasperation.

Dronov rushed to correct the impression. "It's not that bad. I have friends here, in the Russian UN mission. They can fix it quickly. I can go tomorrow."

"All right. You'll find me at the Intercontinental. It's better if you stay there too."

"Agreed. Can you brief me now, so I can give it some thought?"

"Sure. One of our clients is looking for opportunities for exports and perhaps some investments in Russia and is not familiar with the territory. They came across a company called Seebercorp and are thinking of a joint venture, and our firm is to handle the transaction. We know nothing about Seebercorp except that it got a little bad press a couple of years ago, which in itself may or may not mean anything, and the fact that the company is headed by some Boris Birnshtein, an émigré with allegedly high-level connections in Russia. So, we want to know if this Seebercorp is a reasonable bet for our client. Or, the way you put it, 'what it is breathing with.' That's about it."

"That doesn't look too difficult. But there still is that aspect I mentioned to you; I cannot verify their transactions in the Western banks. That should be your job."

"Don't worry about it. That's the easy part. Just find out everything you can on Seebercorp and Bernshtein."

"OK. So, I'll go inside."

"Inside?"

'Of course. Otherwise, the information is not very reliable."

"Well, in that case an additional bonus can be in order."

Something flickered in Dronov's eyes. "Very good, then we're all set." And, after a pause, he added, "Oh, by the way, Cyrus, I'm a bit ashamed to admit this, but I have no money now and would appreciate it if you could advance me some."

Well, you certainly play it cool. You have no visa, you have no money, you're flat on your ass, General. Sure. If you are so meticulous, it must be a very important game for you. You just confirmed it to me. "Of course, Yuri. Let's walk to a bank right now and settle that. Is a couple thousand sufficient? And I'll be paying for your ticket and hotel."

"Yes, of course."

Cyrus went upstairs to get his coat.

Chapter 4

Cyrus took the Dulles Toll as a shortcut out of the Virginia suburbs. In no time he reached Dulles Airport and jumped south to Route 50 via Route 28. He turned west and, as expected, hung in slow weekend traffic to Middleburg where the steady stream of cars slowed to a snail's pace. Past Middleburg it became more bearable. The beautiful Blue Ridge Mountains were close and looked inviting. About four miles after Middleburg he turned right onto the small road, leaving the weekend tourist crowd behind. He crossed another local road, and after about a mile, he turned left onto a private gravel driveway. He passed through about two hundred feet of thick underbrush and obviously unkempt forest, and entered a beautifully landscaped English garden that looked as if it had been this way since the day of creation, but in fact, was carefully designed and maintained. After gently weaving through the slightly hilly landscape for another two hundred yards, the driveway circled in front of a large Tudor mansion. A small house, apparently for the help, was partially visible behind the farther end of the main house. Cyrus parked the car, took his attaché and walked up the stairs to the main entrance. The door opened and John Porter made a few steps forward to meet his guest.

When they entered the house, Margaret Porter walked to the foyer.

"Cyrus, dear boy, you certainly abandoned this old woman. I haven't seen you for ages." She kissed him and led him to the living room.

"Hello, Margaret. I have no excuse, but I've missed you."

"I know, I know. Tell me how you've been."

The large living room was paneled with black walnut wainscoting, and the paneling extended all the way to the ceiling around a marble-mantled fireplace. The decorative horses and ducks customary in the homes of this part of Virginia countryside were noticeably absent. Instead, several eighteenth- and nineteenth-century oils adorned the walls. They chatted for a few minutes, and Margaret, always tactful, left to make sure that "lunch would be served properly." John and Cyrus settled comfortably into two deep armchairs in the library.

John's face lost the social expression. "Well, what do you think?"

"I think, it went pretty well, I..."

John interrupted him. "Wait. First things first. Are you going to take this assignment?"

"Come on, John, I'm in it up to my ears. What do you want, a signed contract?"

John chuckled, ignoring the obvious irritation. "At least that's settled. As always, I want things to be clear. Go on."

"By the way, it's hard for me to believe that their interest in me is entirely coincidental. How did you manage to steer them?"

John smiled. "Let's just say that it took me a year to set up. But it was far from settled. I just got you on their short list. And let's leave it at that."

"You're an old fox, John. What really amazes me is your ability to see a few moves ahead."

"That's the key to success in intelligence. The very core of it. Without that you'd be just reacting, and you would end up being tricked and manipulated at every turn." John hesitated. "Well, *revenons a nos moutons.* Where are we now?"

"I guess we're in the game. I don't see that I've made any detectable mistakes so far. They swallowed everything we gave them. What bothers me is that they're so pushy."

"You know as well as I do, in high level intelligence, and they obviously are in that league, there is only one reason to be pushy. A serious deadline is leaving them no alternative but to push. So, they must be in a hurry."

"OK, but why are they in a hurry?"

"That's what we don't know. It's for you to find out, among other things. As a matter of fact, we don't even know who 'they' are, do we?"

"No, but we can guess. It clearly looks like the KGB, namely its current foreign intelligence arm successor, the SVR."

"Well, that's an assumption. All we know is that Dronov retired a couple of years ago, had an out-of-the-blue, one-on-one meeting with the SVR head Sviridov, allegedly got carte-blanche and took off to recruit a topnotch investment banker. He seems to be taking the bait with you. That's all."

"No. We also know that with Gaidar's help Yeltsin got hyper about money hidden abroad by Gorbatov and his cronies from 1986 through 1991, totaling between seventy and two hundred billion dollars. We do know that in 1993 they started asking everybody, including Kroll and the FBI, to help find the money; they even cooperated to some extent with Kroll. And on the top of that, we know that a year later, in the fall of 1994, they stopped cooperating and started blocking all attempts at investigation.

Why, we don't know. One explanation is that they found the money, but it doesn't look like it."

"Precisely. If they found it, we would've gotten a hunch. And, Dronov, after a meeting with Sviridov, wouldn't be looking for an investment banker."

"To manage the fund?"

"No way, they wouldn't let anyone do that."

"Then, we can be reasonably sure that, one, they haven't found the money, two, they are in a hurry, three, they have no hope of finding it on their own, and four, Dronov has been assigned to do that, using a Western investment banker."

"And five, they will kill that investment banker as soon as the money is found or even as soon as they have enough clues to finish the job on their own. You're on the spot, Cyrus, and I want you to clearly understand that. I want you to have no illusions." John looked Cyrus straight in the eye.

Cyrus chuckled. "I do, and let's get on with it. You want me to do the job or what?"

John nodded. Both knew that that was what each one had to say. After a pause he said as if thinking out loud, "All right, but we still aren't sure who they are."

"True, but isn't that slightly academic?"

John was still thinking out loud. "No."

"Why? Same goal, same players."

John looked at him, and for a moment was slightly at a loss. Then he said quickly, "The set of rules they'll play by and their final goal will depend on who they are."

Cyrus was not convinced, but said nothing.

At that moment a phone rang. John answered, listened for a few seconds and hung up. "Cyrus, something came in downstairs. Let's go take a look."

They stood up and walked to a door at the back of the hall. They went through that door and downstairs to the basement.

Just next to a poolroom there was a vault door with a combination lock and a security system keypad on the wall next to it. Cyrus knew it was a decoy. The combination lock would click detectably and for a pro wasn't too difficult to pick. Regardless of what combinations were attempted, the security system would unlock on the seventh one tried. The trick was that the door would close ten seconds after the last entrant went into the vault and couldn't be opened from the inside. And the moment the door opened, an alarm would go off in some nasty quarters owned by the Pentagon. The heavy safe in the vault itself was, of course, empty.

John and Cyrus passed the vault door and entered an inconspicuous storage room. John pushed a bolt in one of the shelves and a small wall panel above it moved aside, revealing a small keypad. John dialed a combination. One of the storage racks in the opposite wall silently moved with part of the basement's concrete wall, revealing a doorway. They entered a brightly lit room with racks of various pieces of electronic communications equipment and computer terminals. The door shut silently behind them. There was a desk with an armchair, two tables and a few rolling office chairs in the middle of the room. One more door led to yet another room.

"What's up, Jim?" John asked a man on duty. Cyrus and Jim nodded to each other.

Jim put two pages of computer printout on the table. Like every other piece of paper in the room, it was water-soluble.

At the upper, right corner it was marked:

"Source: FBI".

"Method: Visual surveillance"

"Time & date: 1028 101095."

The note was short: "Subject party patrolling an entrance marked "Salisbury Farm" off Rt. 719 in VA. 2 cars, shuttling between Rt. 743 and Rt. 619. Same situation at the "Salisbury Farm. Service entrance." off Rt. 619 on the West side."

Cyrus chuckled, "They know your back door, John."

John nodded. "Leaving nothing to chance. Check and double-check. As always, when they're serious." He turned to Jim. "Jim, has anybody arrived in the last hour through the back entrance?"

"No, sir."

"Make sure nobody leaves here before 2300."

"Yes, sir."

John looked at the second page. It had just arrived and was marked: "Peter to John."

John read the message. "NSA Operations confirmed that: 1. Russian New York Station requested a visual on Cyrus Grant on possible contacts with any known or suspected US intelligence officers, marked "no further consequence for your station." 2. A satellite overhead of 77-49W, 39-02N marked "urgent" was transmitted to the Russian Embassy at 0212 101095." Those were the coordinates of John's mansion.

"No wonder they know about the back door. Let's go upstairs."

They returned to the library and Cyrus was puzzled. "John, why are they making such a big deal of it? They're just risking attracting unwanted attention. It would be much safer to play it low."

"I can see only one reason for that. They want to make damn sure that you are not connected to the government. It's clear they are making sure that you haven't arranged a meeting with anyone from the CIA. As far as attention goes, they think they can't lose. They can only attract attention if you do work for the government. And what that means is that they plan to give you access to some sensitive stuff."

"I guess you're right. But there's another question: "Aren't 'they' the Russian government?"

"Not necessarily. First of all, there's a mess over there. All sorts of private enterprises in Russia are conducted through government facilities these days. They haven't developed the concept of conflict of interest yet. So, all we know is that some government people are involved. Secondly, why would they use a retired general instead of a government official, like they did with Kroll? Something is escaping me here."

"All in all, John, we know that I'm reasonably clean and will probably be cleaner when I meet Dronov again. By the way, don't forget to mention a couple times "Cyrus told" and "Cyrus thinks" in regard to the Cresco deal." He chuckled, "After all, that's my only reason for being here today. Here is the file and the memo."

Cyrus took a folder from his attaché and put it on the side table. "Sure."

Margaret walked in and declared in a tone that would not tolerate any insubordination, "Whatever your business is, I'm starving. And I hate cold food. Let's go. You'll never finish your business anyway."

After lunch John and Cyrus returned to the library.

"So, how was Canada?"

"I talked to a couple friends there who are well wired into everything in the country. Nothing, except a few companies like Seebercorp. By the way, that outfit is a sewer. We should not touch it with a ten-foot pole. So, we'll have to kill the deal with Trycorp. But don't do it now. Wait till I send you the stuff that Dronov gives me."

"Is it that bad?"

"Yeah. Seebercorp is a corruption broker for the whole former Soviet Union. They deal openly and bluntly. Trycorp could find itself in the middle of a few scandals a while from now."

"I see. But nothing at all on the missing funds? There should be some traces in Canada. Their laws are just too convenient for the purpose."

"Nothing, John. I was surprised myself. Every sizeable movement of funds with any question mark on it belongs to the current wave of corruption in Russia. Nothing on those earlier transferred funds."

John sighed. "All right. What's your game plan, Cyrus?"

"Well, I have to make certain assumptions here. One, that Dronov will move to recruit me; two, that he'll present it as his private little enterprise. Perhaps, he'll hint that some powerful friend of his could be involved, also on a private basis; three, he'll give me a relatively free hand; and four, he'll limit my involvement to outside of Russia."

"I agree, those are pretty reasonable assumptions."

"I'll go to London. Hopefully, some of my contacts can help. See, given the sheer amount of money involved, at least a large chunk would have to go through London. After that, hopefully with some clues, I guess my next stop would be Switzerland. Then I have no idea where anything I'd find there will lead me. Cyprus, Liechtenstein, the Caribbean, who knows?"

"So, you think that after sifting through the records, combined with fishing for rumors of large, hushed-up deals, you'll get wind of what happened?" John's tone was skeptical.

"Yes. Hopefully." Cyrus paused, "Any other suggestions?"

"While I'm not impressed by how solid this plan is, the answer to your question is, no. Besides, we've got to start somewhere."

He paused. "One point I would like to emphasize, though. You've got to find out what Dronov and Co. already know. And the sooner, the better."

"Oh, don't worry about that. They'll definitely want to shorten my search. So, as soon as I start digging they'll start correcting and directing me. By doing that, they'll show me what they know."

"Be careful here. Dronov is an old poker player, so don't count too much on reading him."

"But in this case he doesn't have much choice, does he?"

"I wish I shared your optimism," John sighed. "Well, what kind of support are you going to need?"

"Don't worry about that. As always, I'd rather have none and just use my own connections." He paused, "I'll send you the bill later."

John laughed, "I know your bills. Most employers would go broke with you. I'm the only one who can tolerate such bills. By the way, I still don't remember you giving me a business reason for chartering that Lear to go from Paris to Fiji for three days, nor did you ever mention who exactly was on that plane."

Cyrus gave a sheepish smile. "Well, John, we'll talk about it when I'm back."

"Hell we will. Your memory will start failing. As usual."

They were silent for a while, returning their thoughts to the task at hand.

"All right. Do you remember all the emergency procedures?"
Cyrus nodded.

John looked Cyrus straight in the eye. "One more thing, Cyrus. Under no circumstances do you go to Russia. Is that clear?"

"I'm not crazy."

"I guess that's all. At least for now. It's about time for you to go."

"Right. See you, John. I'll drop by to say bye to Margaret."

He waved his hand and walked away without turning.

John opened his mouth to say, "Be careful," but after a moment's hesitation, he just turned to the window and stood there, thinking. He was not comfortable with the smooth beginning of this operation. He couldn't put his finger on why, but he didn't like it.

Chapter 5

An hour after the Concorde landed, Cyrus was in his Mayfair hotel. The first man Cyrus saw in the lobby was Dronov. Cyrus waved and went to check in. Given his frequent stays there and his name on file, he only needed to sign the prepared card. Cyrus sent his luggage to his room and went to greet the patiently waiting Dronov.

"How's everything?"

"Just perfect. How have you been?"

"Good. Dropped by to see my boss, spent two nights home for a change, and here I am."

They moved to the bar. "Any luck on your side, Yuri?"

"I wouldn't call it luck, but I've got what you wanted." Dronov took out a folded manila envelope, straightened it, and put it on the table in front of Cyrus.

Cyrus opened the envelope and looked through the papers inside.

"My God, this is quite an outfit." He paused, reading some parts. "General, I'm impressed. I won't ask how you got this, but not only does it come from inside, it could only have come from three or four people in the company."

Dronov smiled.

"This is incredible. They have a seedy relationship with every crook in the Russian hierarchy."

"Not really. There are many dealing with other companies of that kind. But you are right, they've got top of the line clientele."

"So, I take it, you don't even need to dig any further here, or anywhere else?"

"That's right. No need to."

"Well, then, I thank you. Your fee is well earned. Along with an additional bonus of ten thousand." Cyrus paused, and added, "I'd like to have your card, Yuri. In case of future eventualities." That was a nice but clear 'good bye.'

Dronov was not ready for this abrupt end. Stumbling slightly, he said, "Cyrus, I need to talk to you."

Cyrus did not understand. "Yuri, I appreciate the quality and speed of your work, but as I told you from the start, we don't have any opening for you at the moment. If something comes along, I'll let you know right away. I promise."

Dronov knew he had no options. Either play it now, or drop it. "It's not that, Cyrus. You probably think that I was about to ask you for a job again?"

"Yes. Isn't that logical?"

"It is. But it's not the subject. Something much more important." He paused, and added, "And very, very profitable."

Cyrus was still skeptical. "Come on, Yuri. Please, don't tell me that you have friends running a business in Russia and there's an opportunity to invest a few million at an unbelievably high return with virtually no risk. These days that's as rare as a Mexican in California. The problem is, every one of those deals I know of has gone sour as soon as the money is transferred to Russia. I have a lot of friends here, and a lot of social calls to make, so time is hard to come by for me."

"No, Cyrus. Nothing like that. It's highly confidential, too. So, I would suggest a walk, for that matter."

Cyrus laughed. "General, are you implying that somebody is spying on us here?"

"You see, Cyrus, over the years my former line of work has made me pretty well known in intelligence circles, including here in London. So, when I show up, they get curious to see if I'm up to something. A regular precaution, you know. As a matter of fact, they browsed through the papers I just gave you."

"Yuri, the last thing I want is to be involved in some kind of spooky story. It looks to me that any association with you has a price."

"Not to worry about it. As I told you, they looked through these papers. Incidentally, because I knew that and I let them do it, I did not leave the other papers in my room. So, they have a pretty good idea that I'm working for you. Nothing wrong with that, considering the subject." He chuckled. "They probably just feel a little sorry for you, that's all."

"By the way, how do you know that they looked through these

papers?"

"Oh, some very old tricks of the trade. Nothing fancy."

Cyrus did not respond, still trying to get over the revelation.

Dronov pressed. "Cyrus, you have nothing to lose here. Half an hour of your time with a chance that you might like something."

"All right. I owe you that much. You've impressed me more than once, let's see what's up your sleeve this time." Cyrus noticed a cold flicker in Dronov's eyes. Facing Cyrus' patronizing attitude and arrogance, he had all along played humble. *That's precisely what I want. The more emotions you show, the better off I am. So far, so good.*

Once out of the hotel, they walked toward Hyde Park. Dronov did not waste any time.

"Cyrus, are you aware that the communists of the Soviet Union, just before its demise, transferred large amounts of money abroad?"

"I heard some rumors to that effect a few years back."

"Have you ever given it any thought?"

"Not really. That kind of thing is inevitable. Almost every ruler moves his plunder abroad, hiding a few million here and there for a rainy day. Everyone is disgusted, but in practice there's nothing that can be done about it. It would probably cost more to catch them than the amount recovered. Why?"

"What if I tell you that the amount is in the billions, perhaps as much as two hundred billion dollars?"

"Two hundred billion?"

"Yes."

Cyrus stopped. "Yuri, give me a break. Do you realize what two hundred billion is? Do you know how difficult it is to move one billion without red flags going up everywhere?"

"Nevertheless, this is the fact, confirmed."

"Are you saying that that much money was moved abroad, and nobody noticed?"

"Exactly."

"Yuri, it can't be done. I know that much."

"Cyrus, I'm not crazy, and treasure hunting is not my type of recreation. I can tell you only that it has happened. Here is the confirmation." He gave Cyrus another envelope. "The White House is aware of the situation, as well as your Treasury, the FBI and the CIA.

None of them could help the Russian government find it. Neither could one of the American private security companies. The fact was confirmed, but everyone failed to find the money. Now it's up for grabs."

"So, what do you expect me to do? Find it when everyone else failed?" Cyrus paused. "If what you're saying is true."

"Yes. After you study these papers, you will see there is no question of whether it's true or not. Then, you make your decision. I believe that together we can find it. I wouldn't suggest taking it for ourselves, but if we return it to the Russian government, a healthy commission of several percent should keep us comfortable for a while. I believe that, even with your earning habits, it should be attractive enough to get involved."

Cyrus noticed that Dronov's tone had slowly turned from humble affect to almost terse, commanding. He was about to start paying Cyrus back. *Good. The more emotions you have, the less analyzing you'll do. The better off I am.*

"Well, Yuri. Needless to say, I'm in shock. My gut reaction is to forget the whole thing. However, I've learned to take you seriously. I'll read these papers overnight and we'll talk tomorrow."

"Good. I was sure you were a sensible businessman."

"And meanwhile, let's have supper. I know a nice Portuguese restaurant not far from here, Corabella. I usually drop by there when I'm in London."

"Sounds great. I love Portuguese food."

In the morning they met over breakfast.

"Have an interesting read last night, Cyrus?"

"Fascinating. I would never have imagined something like that could actually happen in real life. Seems more like fiction."

"No matter how it looks, it's real. Very real."

"So, you're trying to recruit me for the task?"

"If you will. I'd rather put it in a different way, though. I propose a partnership."

"Fifty-fifty?"

"I'm afraid, not. I have two partners already. So, it looks more like a quarter."

"I'd like to know who the other partners are."

"I can tell you about one, but not now." He looked at Cyrus in an expressive way.

Cyrus smiled. "Oh, yes, I forgot. We're being watched."

"Cyrus, please. This is serious business. I understand that you also take precautions when you handle confidential business matters. Just consider that this one is no different. It is a confidential business matter."

"All right, all right. It's just that I've always been fascinated by the way spooks conduct their business." *Careful. Don't overplay it.*

"Cyrus, get serious."

They finished their breakfast and went for a stroll.

Cyrus started without a warm-up. "Yuri, I must say that I was really fascinated by what I read in your papers. This is a very interesting proposition. For one, the potential fee is impressive, by anyone's standards. As a matter of fact, it would be the highest fee I've ever heard of being paid. Professionally, I must say, I almost want to do it. See, what happened goes against my training and experience. To find it becomes almost a matter of professional pride. I just refuse to believe that anyone can hide a sum like the money in question."

"That is precisely what I was counting on. Your professional curiosity. So, I take it, it's all settled."

"Not exactly. As I said, I almost want it." Cyrus paused. "There are some hard questions in my mind. One, it sounds too good to be true, and I know better than to jump into this kind of thing. Two, I have to question who I am dealing with. The last thing I want is to get involved with a bunch of spies. Please, forgive me for being blunt."

"Quite to the contrary. Knowing where you come from, I perfectly understand your hesitance with intelligence. I know that Americans are not too fond of it. However, as far as you are concerned, it would be just your professional involvement. Nothing else. No intelligence, no clandestine stuff. None. Just be a good banker."

Cyrus still had some doubts. "Are you saying that I would have a free hand? I mean completely, without any poking into what I'm doing and who I'm dealing with, without a carload of heavies following me everywhere?"

"Of course. By the way, it would be counterproductive. Cyrus, you've read too many spy novels." Dronov smiled.

"Who is your partner?"

"Primakov." Something like triumph shone in Dronov's eyes.

"Who is he?"

"Oh, brother. Do you read any newspapers, Cyrus?"

"The business sections, mainly."

"He is the head of the SVR, Russian intelligence service." Seeing Cyrus' reaction, Dronov interrupted him with a gesture, and hurriedly added, "This is a purely private endeavor, as I told you. And his presence would enhance all. On the other hand, you don't even have to know that, if this makes you happy."

"As a matter of fact, I'd prefer not to know."

"All right. So, we agreed?"

"And you guarantee that it is a purely private endeavor, and that I wouldn't be working for a foreign government?"

"Absolutely."

Cyrus smiled. "Then, yes. I just can't resist the temptation, I don't know why."

"Splendid." Dronov shook Cyrus' hand. "Welcome aboard."

"But Yuri, I want to warn you. If I ever see your spooks spying on me, the deal is off."

Dronov laughed. "Don't worry, Cyrus. I know you Americans. You're obsessed with your privacy. No surveillance. I promise."

Sure.

After a short silence Dronov asked, "Any ideas how you're going to approach the matter?"

"Of course. I don't think it should be terribly difficult. That kind of money is impossible to move without a trace. Luckily, we happen to be in London, through which most of the world's money passes one way or another. I'll call on some of my well-wired friends. Something should crop up there."

"Is it that easy?"

"No. That's just a beginning. The trail will probably lead us to Switzerland, Cyprus, the Caribbean or something like that."

"How long will it take?"

Oh, you are in a hurry. "I have no idea. Let's just start digging, and we'll see what we're dealing with.

Chapter 6

Cyrus rang the doorbell. In a few seconds he heard the lock click and, to his total surprise, a cartoon-like computerized voice cracked, "Please, come in. Feel at home, but don't forget that you are not. Ha-ha."

Cyrus opened the door and stepped in. A tiny foyer led to a landing, which opened into a large living room with four couches, several chairs and a few small tables, all placed without any noticeable system. The ample floor space was largely covered with rugs and numerous pillows, indicating that many guests preferred sitting on the floor. A closed door off the landing apparently led to a basement, and a dark wood staircase along the wall led upstairs. A rather large kitchen, visible from the landing, opened to the living room without a door.

Cyrus was deciding what to do when he heard footsteps coming down the stairway and a tall skinny figure in a brightly colored jogging suit appeared at the landing between the first and second floors.

"Cyrus, I thought that you'd have changed more. I would've easily recognized you in the street. At least, no surprises on this front. Glad to see you, anyhow." He said all this in one continuous stream without even a breath. A few seconds later Cyrus was shaking Nicholas' hand.

"Hello, Nicholas. It's been a while. I reckon, you're a big boy these days."

"That's for sure. Don't even think of bullying me now the way you chaps treated me back then," laughed Nicholas, obviously referring to his older brother and his friend Cyrus pushing him around during their days at Oxford. "A drink?"

They walked into the living room and Cyrus landed in a chair. "No, thanks." Nicholas sat down too.

"OK, I'd like to ask you how you have been but you're in a

hurry, I take it." Nicholas quipped, "I'm yet to meet an American who is not. By the way, why is it that you're the only American whose accent doesn't irritate me too much?"

"That's because years back you knew all too well that I'd punch you in the nose if it did."

"You bully," Nicholas squeezed a mean smile, "but I shall pay you back when you're ninety and I'm still just eighty one."

Cyrus laughed, and Nicholas changed the subject. "Well, how can I help you? Alistair was rather vague on what brought you here."

Cyrus took a deep breath and thought about how to tackle this touchy situation. He understood that he could not afford to give Nicholas a bunch of crap if he wanted to have any hope of his help. Nor did he want to do it. On the other hand, telling the truth was absolutely out of the question. "Well, in a couple of words, I'm looking for gold."

"Wrong place, Cyrus. None here, I'm pretty sure. Talk to my brother, he's the rich one." Nicholas was smiling, waiting for the story to develop.

"To make a long story short, my company was asked to find some funds allegedly stolen from Russia between four and ten years ago. So, they assigned me to do just that, and I am having a hard time figuring out where to start. Alistair thought that you might be able to help with your computer wizardry."

Showing any surprise would be beneath Nicholas' dignity. "How much money is in question?"

"Billions. Many billions."

"You mean rubles, of course?"

"No, dollars. Or pounds, if you wish."

Only a pause indicated Nicholas' surprise. Finally he managed to respond, "Well, the more, the better. Easier to find. But I would've thought that Russia was very poor these days."

"Not for everybody. Let me brief you. Allegedly, Gorbatov and company started squirreling money away outside of Russia, shortly after Gorbatov came to power, in eighty-five, eighty-six. That was going on until he lost power in ninety-one. They used communist party channels, the KGB and God knows what else. Yeltsin's government could not find it. The question is, where's the money and who's keeping it."

"I presume you've tried banking channels."

"Of course. No luck there. So, can you help, somehow?"

"Cyrus, all I can do is use my computers along with my brain. The information you're looking for should be in a computer or computers, somewhere. That's where I have a shot at getting it. The problem is finding out where it is. If you told me what computer has it, I'd try to get it. Without knowing the address, I can't help you. I reckon, neither you, nor my brother know that, or even have a suspect company." He paused, "Or do you?"

"No. We had a few suspect companies, checked them out. Nothing. I have a couple more to go, and I'll check them out too, but I'm certain I'll get the same result. They're just too small for this kind of money. That's the problem. If either Alistair or I knew where it was, we'd find out the rest by analyzing their outside transactions."

"Well, I can send a few messages out to my friends, I can post a few on some bulletin boards of the Internet. Let's see what people know. You'd be surprised how friendly the chaps on the Internet are. With some luck we may get a few leads."

"Nicholas, that's absolutely out of the question. It's too sensitive. Even the fact that I am snooping around. Besides, if somebody knew anything about it, the KGB would have gotten wind of it before now. As far as I know, they haven't."

"You mean that the KGB is looking for that money too?"

"Sure."

"Well, that makes it fun." Nicholas's eyes gave sparkled. He loved a challenge. He paused. "Let me think a bit. Meanwhile, I would like to show you my lair."

On the way to the staircase Cyrus glanced at the kitchen and saw a few large signs like "FOOD" on the refrigerator, "DIRTY DISHES" at the sink, "DRINKS" at one of the cabinets. Those were clear indications of Nicholas' lifestyle. Apparently, friends came and went practically at will, sometimes in numbers. The environment was obviously self-service.

The second floor was basically a large room lined with bookshelves and four computers, each with its own workstation. In the middle there was a long table littered with magazines and computer printouts. There was a huge desk near the window with yet more magazines and a few books on it. Cyrus could see another smaller room in the back, with three electronic workbenches and a couple of computer skeletons, shelves with books and computer parts, and a window. .

"This is where I live, Cyrus." Nicholas sounded almost apologetic. "My bedroom is on the third floor," he added, looking around. It was obviously a rare occasion to have someone from another planet walk into this room and force Nicholas to look at his home through another world's eyes. His long reddish blond hair and his clothes, however, fit the environment and completed the overall picture.

"What a place!" Cyrus was looking around with genuine interest. "You really love this stuff, don't you?"

"Of course, and frankly, I have a hard time understanding how somebody can not."

"Well, Nicholas, the fact that all of us are different makes this world fun, doesn't it? Can you imagine what a boring place it would be if all of us were the same, even perfect? To me, that's a horrifying thought."

"You're absolutely right. The problem we often have, though, is accepting the right of others to be what appears to us to be wrong."

"Sure. But I enjoy going to places different from mine. Gives me a better perspective."

They sat in comfortable chairs in the middle of the room next to the long table.

"All right Cyrus, *revenons a nos moutons.* You're saying that at the moment there are no identifiable deposits that fit your description."

"Correct. And you are saying that you cannot identify one either, other than going around to your friends or posting an ad on the Internet."

"Precisely. And you're saying that one, it's unacceptable to do that, and two, it wouldn't work anyway."

"True."

"A pretty picture. It means that either we have to come up with a compromise of some sort, or with a radical idea. For lack of a radical idea, at least on my part, let's see if we can compromise, maybe lower our goals a bit."

Cyrus went through his choices and options in his mind.

Suddenly, he felt that something was hatching. "Look, Nicholas, I started running through our options and something just occurred to me. I just started this search, but some other people have been trying it for some time. Obviously, they didn't find the money, but maybe, just maybe they found out something. Something that could be helpful to me. After all, it's always much better to start any search midway than at square one."

"That sounds reasonable. Who else was searching?"

"Kroll," he paused, "and the KGB, of course."

"Who is Kroll?"

"They are an American private investigations company, which was hired by the Russian government to help locate the money. Later they dropped out of the deal. But the KGB surely knows everything Kroll found."

"In other words, the KGB has the most complete file on the subject?"

"Yes. You aren't seriously considering hacking into the KGB computer, are you, Nicholas?"

The flicker in Nicholas' eyes announced that he had taken the bait. "At least it's worth thinking about."

"Come on, come back down to Earth."

"Cyrus, the Russians are one hell of an adversary. They have programmers as good as anyone, maybe better. Since they weren't spoiled with good computers they were forced to use their brains more to achieve the same results. Besides, their math education is probably the best in the world. On the other hand, nothing is impossible as far as computers go."

"Do you seriously think you can beat them?"

"I can try. Can we somehow figure out their computer phone number?"

"I don't know. But even if we do, are you hoping to hack it?"

"Relax, Cyrus. That's my field. There is plenty of password-cracking software out there. If anyone is stupid enough to have a password from a dictionary, it's easy to crack. Besides, I've done some software of that sort on my own, just for fun," a sheepish smile briefly crossed his face, "At least it wouldn't hurt us to try, would it?"

"Not unless you're playing with the KGB. Then all the bets are off."

Nicholas opened his mouth to say something, but then suddenly jumped up, went to the window, stood there for a few seconds, and started pacing the room. Cyrus was wise enough to sit tight and quietly watch the tall, skinny figure in a jogging suit as he walked and muttered feverishly to himself.

Five minutes later Nicholas suddenly stopped in front of Cyrus. His eyes were shining. All his usual awkwardness that made him recognizable a mile away had vanished. He prowled like a graceful tiger.

He gave Cyrus a triumphant look and said, slowly enunciating each word, "A new positive control Trojan worm introduced through a bait message with a preliminary server hack. That's all."

"A what?" Cyrus realized that he hadn't a clue as to what Nicholas meant.

It took Nicholas a while to focus on where he was and who he was dealing with. His face expressed clear disappointment that the dude in front of him was genuinely incapable of understanding not only the details, but even the sheer magnitude of his great discovery. Slowly, his face regained his regular soft, kind and slightly uncertain expression.

"Sorry, Cyrus. I got carried away. I think I've found a rather elegant solution to our problem. We don't even need to know where the KGB computer is to hack it. Let me explain. Are you familiar with the term Trojan?"

Cyrus chuckled. "Sure, but that was a while ago, I can barely remember."

Nicholas laughed. "I mean in the computer jargon."

"I heard it, but I don't really know what it is."

"Well, this a malicious program that is delivered through an innocent looking content. The same concept. "

"I see."

"So,

"Sounds a bit pretentious, don't you think?'

"Not when you consider it. Listen to me. Do you know what a so called 'computer virus' is?"

"Sure. It's when somebody sends you an email with some program that messes up your computer, deletes its memory and does other nasty things, isn't it?"

"Yes. Often people call it a 'virus.' Technically, if a malicious program delivered through the e-mail, it is considered "virus", if it enters the target computer through some other way, it is a "worm". Generally, it's called malware, short for malicious software. Actually, it's not just a malware; it's a destructive malware. But who told us that the malware has to be destructive? Nobody. It's just an assumption. In fact, a virus can be anything. Aside from other options, in can be just a program that controls a target computer and commands it to do what the virus' master wants. Anything, within that computer's capabilities. For instance, it can command the target computer to call my computer here and to give me full access to all its files." Nicholas stopped and finally took a deep breath.

Cyrus was struck by the simplicity and potential of such an approach. "Wait. Are you saying that once the virus is introduced in what you call a target computer, that computer, perhaps unbeknownst to its master, can serve whoever the virus commands?"

"Precisely. And there are practically no limitations."

"Nicholas, are you saying that nobody has thought of this possibility, and that there is no defense against it?"

"Not quite. There is a technique called 'firewall' that is supposed to stop any malicious software that tries to enter a computer."

"Sounds like an aircraft firewall."

"Yes, except that the firewall works to some extent in an airplane, but not in a computer." Nicholas chuckled. "They should've called it "fig leaf" instead of 'firewall'."

"How come?"

"See, security of computer access over a network consists of a combination of computer networking and cryptography. The problem is that networking guys usually don't understand cryptography, and cryptographers don't understand networking. By the way, a few folks in your NSA understand that, but most people don't."

"So, what the bottom line – I'm a little confused here."

"The bottom line is that this "firewall" can only detect a known malicious code, and even then very poorly. If I write a new piece of software, it will go unnoticed and act as designed. I can also make sure that it self-destructs after its mission is complete."

"Nicholas, are you saying that there is no solution to this?"

"Not at this time, and it's a fundamental problem. The only thing you can do is to separate a computer that contains sensitive information, and never allow it to go to the Internet and communicate with unknown computers."

"What if they do?"

"Then we are out of luck. But all this is very new stuff known to very few on a scientific level, and most operators are not even aware of it. So, we have a shot here."

The Party Gold somehow moved to the back burner. Slowly, still not able to comprehend all the consequences for any computer user, Cyrus said, "Nicholas, do you understand what that means for computer security as we know it?"

"Yes. It goes straight to hell."

Cyrus didn't even listen to the answer. He was almost talking to himself, "And for world banking?"

"A very expensive mess."

Cyrus was compelled to give Nicholas a good lecture about the potency of the weapon he just invented, when he suddenly realized that somebody else could come to the same realization. Or, perhaps, already had. He made a conscious effort to return to the business at hand, and just said quietly, "Well, no matter how much we know, we still have no idea how vulnerable we all are."

"True." Nicholas was a scientist, not much invested in the quotidian world.

Intellectually, Cyrus felt dizzy. "Have you got any scotch?"

"In the kitchen cabinet." Nicholas answered automatically without even noticing that he'd said it.

A trip to the kitchen brought Cyrus closer to reality. Boy, he needed that drink. Cyrus was surprised to find a bottle of Dalwhinnie in the "DRINKS" drawer. He'd rather have it with soda, but there was none. On the other hand, he'd take a good scotch with water over a mediocre one with soda any day.

In a short while Cyrus found himself thinking more or less straight again. "Nicholas, we still have a problem here. In order to introduce the control virus into the KGB computer we need to hack it. So, no matter how ingenious the virus solution is, it doesn't seem to be something we can use."

"Incorrect. When the Greeks made their Trojan horse, they couldn't just bring it into Troy, could they?"

"So?"

"Well, they left it outside the city wall and left. Then Trojans brought it in themselves didn't they?"

"True, so what?"

"We'll do the same thing. We'll post a message for them on one of the Internet boards, and they'll take it in themselves," he chuckled, "complete with the worm."

Cyrus looked at Nicholas. Now he saw not a boy, the younger brother of his friend, but a man possessing frightening power. "You know, Nicholas, I think I've unleashed something that could frighten a lot of people. I'm glad we're working together, not against each other."

"I can't work against old friends," Nicholas said simply.

"All right, what message are you going to post for them?"

"That's your job, Cyrus. You should know what they'd grab. As far as I am concerned, it should be at least three pages long."

"Why do you need that much? It's not easy to concoct something convincing that long."

"There are two possibilities. Either they are using an automated sweep of the Internet boards of their interest, meaning a computer looks for key words in all the messages and, if it finds any, downloads the whole message for future reading by their analysts. Or they do the same thing using an operator. If they use a computer, we're all right even with a short message. An operator, on the other hand, would read the message, essentially doing the same screening job as a computer would do. But he would certainly see the whole first page and, if curious, would look at the second. The point is not to let him see the end of the message where the commands are. He'd immediately figure out that something was fishy. So, we have to make sure that the second page is boring, so he won't go to the third page."

"Psychologically, this is very good."

"Maybe, but there still is a possibility that an operator would catch it. For that we need a pre-hack." He took a short breath. I can hack a server that the message is going to be on, and make sure that the message the operator is seeing on his screen is not the message that he downloads. It's a bit tricky, but it can be done. It is much easier if we put it on a server that I know well."

"You are playing them, looking three moves ahead."

"I just know the routine. Everyone follows it. So, you need to do an essay. Exciting first page, boring second page, and stop after two or three lines on the third page. I'll do the rest."

"Forgive me, but just out of curiosity, how do you know what kind of computer the KGB is using?"

"I don't. Chances are good that it's one of four types. So, I'll write a program in all four systems with the instructions to disregard the ones that the computer doesn't understand." Nicholas paused, and concluded, "Let's get working. Which system are you used to?"

"Microsoft Word."

"Splendid, take that one," he nodded to a computer in the corner, "Let me pull it up for you." He walked to the computer and, without taking a seat, pulled Word onto the screen. "And I will do my cooking." He stepped to another computer, sat down and ceased noticing Cyrus. Or anything in this world, for that matter.

Two hours later, after a few rewrites, Cyrus was reasonably satisfied with his creation. He moved to a comfortable armchair. He carefully reviewed their approach, trying to find pitfalls. So far, he saw none. After all, he concluded, it wouldn't hurt to try. Provided, of course, that the poking around was cleanly anonymous.

There were no sounds except the slightly audible traffic in the street and the quiet clatter of Nicholas' keyboard, occasionally interrupted by an intermittent sigh or chuckle. A fancy, modern world map clock on the wall showed the dark wave of night approaching Moscow, which corresponded with the increasing noise of the afternoon London rush hour from the street. *Amazing. I never thought that those things actually worked.*

Nicholas' voice brought him back to the task at hand.

"OK. I guess we're in a reasonably good shape. Have you finished, Cyrus?"

"Yes. It should do."

"Let me see." Nicholas rose, walked over and looked at the screen with Cyrus' message.

Cyrus felt offended. *I understand that you're a computer genius, but this is too much. You'll never know half of what I knew about* these things ten years ago.

"Oh, Cyrus, I'm not questioning you. I just need to figure out which board to post this thing on, and that depends on what you wrote." Nicholas' tone was clearly apologetic.

Not bad. You have a high level of sensitivity too. I didn't think I was that easy to read. "Sure. I don't mind at all. Two minds are always better than one. Check it out, too."

Cyrus' note read:

"Anybody know anything about several years' worth of strange movements of huge sums of money through the world banking system?

I've been working lately on specialized financial software for a major bank in New York. To test it, I used it on historical data going back up to ten years. To my great surprise I found some major abnormalities in the flow of funds starting in about 1986, and involving many of the major financial institutions in the world. It seems to have stopped about 1992. To be more precise, the abnormalities peaked around 1991 and gradually disappeared by the end of 1992.

Some of the funds appear to have originated in Russia. Could it be related to the Party Gold funds secreted by the communists while still in power? At this time when the people of Russia are trying to finally build a democracy in their country and are in desperate need of money, I thought that the people of the Internet could help them to find the money that rightfully belongs to them...."

The note further described some of the transfers, but in very general terms, without mentioning any specific transfer or institution. It went on, raising the possibility of an international conspiracy involving major financial institutions helping the communists hide their plunder. And, of course, it briefly mentioned several companies in a separate, clearly speculative, attempt to identify the circle of conspirators.

At the end the note invited the Board participants to contribute to the subject, exposing the thieves along with the ever-suspect conspirators, major financial institutions.

Nicholas finished reading. "That's good. I'd have bought it if I bumped into it on a board. Where did you learn how to do that?"

"I'm an investment banker, remember? You have to learn all

sorts of skills there."

"Well, I think we should put it on several boards, that would be more reliable, but hacking them would take some time."

Cyrus thought for a second. "I don't think so. It could look suspicious, like we wanted to make sure somebody wouldn't miss it."

"All right, that's your department. But I know one board where it would fit well."

Cyrus was not sure about some security aspects. "Nicholas, I want you to understand that this is not a game, and if it is, it's a serious one. We need to do it very cleanly. Not only to make sure that the KGB takes the bait, but also to make sure that we're safe, particularly you."

"Come on, Cyrus. Who am I supposed to be afraid of? KGB spies? First of all, they don't give a damn about me. Secondly, they have enough problems of their own in Russia now, and thirdly, I'm in England and they just wouldn't dare."

I wish you knew better. God, how often people refuse to be careful of what they don't know.

"Nicholas, since I got you involved in this thing, it's my responsibility to make sure that, at least, you don't suffer. Leave that aspect to me, OK?" He paused, and then continued, "So, I presume that you can post the message truly anonymously, so there will be no way to trace it to you later. Besides, for my own reasons I don't want the KGB to know that their information has been siphoned, and more specifically, that I have it. I'm not the suicidal type, see."

"Personally, I'd rather get in their face, but if you wish, it's easy for me to put in several layers of insulation, each one of them being sufficient in itself."

"Splendid. But one other thing bothers me more. No matter what you do, you're instructing the KGB computer to call you. That defeats everything else. Can you make it call somewhere else and talk to you indirectly?"

"Yes, but that wouldn't be too reliable. I'd rather not do it that way."

Cyrus wanted to respond, but he saw the wheels in Nicholas' mind turning again and said nothing, patiently waiting. Nicholas jumped up, paced the room for a few minutes and sat down again.

"I think we can find a way to do it without a trace. Is that what you want?"

"Absolutely."

"Then listen. I can include some self-destruction controls. When the target computer receives the message, it will save it in its memory, on the hard disk. Depending on the procedure they use, the virus would be activated either immediately, or when pulled up for processing and reading, or when transferred to a different file. I can modify the virus so it not only instructs the computer to do what we want, but also to erase itself from its memory afterwards, leaving only the message text there. Would that satisfy your ever increasing requirements?"

"Perfect. How long would the message be on the board?"

"On a busy board, oh, maybe three days. But I can send a request to that host to erase it as an error any time." He paused a little. "Wait. I can simply break into the board host and erase it myself at any time. As a matter of fact, I don't even have to break in. The host's manager is a friend of mine, and I have the password."

"Now we can go ahead and test your newly designed weapon."

Nicholas smiled, "It's not a test. It's the first use."

You're arrogant too. Well, at least that's deserved.

Suddenly, Nicholas added, "Hopefully." Cyrus did not even want to think of the possibility that somebody was already using such a control virus.

In half an hour Nicholas finished his last touches to the virus and composed the whole package.

"Well, Cyrus, let Operation Trojan Horse begin."

"You look a great deal like Napoleon," needled Cyrus.

Nicholas laughed, "Let me put a patch on my eye. I'd prefer to look like Nelson."

Nicholas played something on the keyboard, and declared, "See. Now I'm in the Boston University computer, entering the Net from there." After some more key strokes he continued, "And now, ladies and gentlemen, welcome to the friendly Stanford computer."

The next announcement was, "Now, welcome to the Internet again, this time from Stanford. Then we go to New York University and from there, into the Net again."

A couple of minutes later he pronounced, "Finally, we are putting the message on the board."

In a while he logged off in the reversed sequence. "That's it. The virus is out. Let it do its dirty job and self-destruct. Like a classic spy."

At the last remark Cyrus felt an uneasy chill between his shoulder blades.

Nicholas sighed and added, "All we can do now is wait."

"How long do you think we have to wait?"

"Could be an hour, could be a day. At very least, we definitely have the time to go out and have dinner. I think we deserve one."

Cyrus did not want to take chances. He did not want to expose Nicholas' connection to him by accidentally bumping into an undesirable somebody.

"I'd rather have something here and not take chances of missing the call."

"Oh, don't worry. I built in a command that the communications have to wait twenty-three minutes after a human stops touching the keyboard. This reduces the chance of any supervision. But if you want to eat here, that's no problem."

"Good idea, but why twenty-three?" Cyrus was puzzled.

"Oh, I don't know. Just twenty-three."

They ordered dinner from a nearby Italian restaurant where Nicholas was a regular. When Cyrus remarked that it was a much better alternative to American pizza, Nicholas just quipped, "It all depends on where you have friends. These guys have known me for years, and if I asked, dinner would be complete with music and a good singer.

"So you are a professor at the London School of Economics. Have you developed any taste for business yet?"

"No, and I'm not likely to. First of all, I'm not a professor; I'm an adjunct professor. Second, I teach computer science only and fully intend to keep it that way. Third, I do some consulting and software development on the side. It takes time and effort. But generally, I enjoy dealing with computers more than with people. My family thinks that it's antisocial. Perhaps. I still prefer it that way.

Cyrus clearly felt a defensive undercurrent in his voice, probably exacerbated by a long family dispute about traditions, culture and social life.

He touched Nicholas' arm. "Nicholas, it doesn't matter what

you do. It's how you feel about it that counts. So, don't worry about it. With some patience the situation will take care of itself. Maybe your family will see that though they don't understand it, you love what you do and that you're damn good at it."

Perhaps not so much his words but the tone of his voice comforted Nicholas. He looked at Cyrus. "I'm glad you understand."

Well after dinner the buzzer on one of the computers went off. They rushed upstairs.

Nicholas watched intently as the monitor filled up, and he suddenly cracked up with laughter. Cyrus was looking at him with obvious puzzlement.

Through his laughter Nicholas squeezed, "The FBI, Washington D.C. computer is offering full access to its files and what you're watching is its main menu. Do you want it?"

Cyrus' mind rushed. "Are you mad? I'm an American citizen, and if we go any further there, it's a serious crime. Sign off, right away."

Nicholas' eyes flashed a mischievous sparkle. "Want a password, just in case? The computer will give us one on request right now."

"Damn it, Nicholas, sign off. I don't care for this brand of humor."

Nicholas chuckled and signed off. Cyrus took a deep breath.

Nicholas was smiling broadly. It's working. Then he started laughing again.

"Now what?" Cyrus' voice betrayed some irritation.

"Nothing. I just realized that we made our appeal too broad. Now we have to brace ourselves for a lot of friendly calls. See, it will happen to any computer that retrieves our message, and the FBI was just the early bird. I hope there won't be too many takers. But luckily, I have a system here, not just four computers. So, if one is busy, the call will be transferred to another."

"My God, we really released the jinn. Now the whole damn world will be after us. The last thing I need at the moment."

"Don't worry. It's fully anonymous and the virus will self-destruct in every one of them." He paused and added, "At your wise request, I must admit."

Cyrus was speechless. The magnitude of what they'd done just now dawned on him.

In a few minutes the University of Minnesota was on line with another friendly offering. Within two hours Nicholas got rid of a dozen of calls, including Kroll, the CIA, several universities and three obscure private companies nobody ever heard of. The MI-5, MI-6 and the MOSSAD, were dismissed by Nicholas.

Just after midnight their prey finally showed up. The caller introduced itself as the Russian Ministry of Fisheries computer. Having done that, it displayed a menu in Cyrillic.

"Damn. That's a surprise I was stupid enough not to foresee."

"Not to worry, Nicholas. I speak Russian. My mother was Russian, remember?"

"Oh, yes. Thank God. I totally forgot. So we have to work together. And quickly enough, I hope. There is always a chance that somebody will see it in Moscow."

Cyrus glanced at the map-clock. Unlikely. All the duty officers in the world are taking a nap, if they can, at this hour. The before-shift change rush will start there in two hours, maybe one and a half.

Nicholas flipped a switch, disconnecting the other computers so they wouldn't be distracted by other calls. They started working. Cyrus was reading the menu and Nicholas was at the keyboard. Most of the directories and files were coded, so Cyrus had to poke into the actual files here and there to see the subject. He felt like the proverbial kid in a candy store. His professional heart was bleeding. Such a wealth of information at his fingertips and he was tempted most of the time. But he was a professional, and he knew better than to let himself be distracted. Finally they found the tree. The golden tree. Project "IGLA," "NEEDLE" in translation. *Somebody has a sense of humor over there. It's one hell of a needle, but still, they are looking for a needle in a haystack.*

"Nicholas, download the whole damn thing, can you?"

"Certainly. I have enough memory for that." He gave the command.

A second later a message popped up. Cyrus cursed and translated, "Security regulations strictly prohibit manipulating a whole project directory!"

"Let's go a level down." Nicholas' fingers were flying over the keyboard.

On that level they struck lucky again. The first branch of the tree started downloading.

We've gotten lucky again. With these fifteen directories we have a chance. With over two hundred on the next level, we wouldn't. How long will this luck last?

Nicholas was thinking in parallel. "The guys have a 28 kilobaud modem. That's pretty good. So do we. If not for that, it would take forever."

The procedure was running in a pretty routine manner: a series of commands and then just over fifteen minutes of downloading.

Half an hour later, during the next downloading, Cyrus realized their omission.

"You know, Nicholas, we were dumb enough to forget to ask the password. Just in case."

"You're right." Then Nicholas smiled, "I thought you didn't want anybody's password." A joke under pressure is usually appreciated. This one certainly was.

"No, just the FBI. Many don't matter. But I certainly want this one." Than he added, "And Playboy, if they call. Would you?"

Nicholas laughed. "OK. The first chance we have is at the next change of directories, but that would delay the whole thing for about two or three minutes. Or, we can wait until the end and take our chance there."

"Do it at the next change."

An hour later, just over an hour and a half from the call of the "Fisheries" computer, the transfer was complete. The final sign off was surprisingly anticlimactic; both Nicholas and Cyrus were exhausted, and Operation Trojan Horse was over.

Nicholas became irritated with the continuing flow of calls, so he sat down, quickly concocted a program instructing his computer to get rid of other callers appropriately, and poured himself a drink.

Chapter 7

Cyrus had to call John. He knew that John would leave the country only under the most extreme circumstances. In Cyrus' mind this was an extreme circumstance. John was surprised, but he agreed. He chose the estate of an old friend in Oxfordshire, England.

It took John ten hours to arrange things in Washington during his absence and to get to England. By that time Cyrus had more or less sorted things out in the product of Trojan Horse, the files of the KGB computer.

"Cyrus, shame on you. You can't abstain from making the old man travel, can you?"

"Sorry, John. I didn't really have any choice. Look at what we've got here."

John briefly looked at Cyrus' outline of the contents of the files. "What the hell is that?"

Cyrus had a chance to have some fun. As casually as he could manage he said, " Oh, some KGB files on the subject of concern."

John looked at Cyrus. He was stunned and did not bother to cover it. "Say, what?"

"Oh, you know, some Moscow files on that Party Gold. Fresh from the KGB."

"How did you manage? Even if you'd recruited the general, it wasn't enough time to go to Moscow, fetch them, and get back."

"There was no need to. And, I didn't recruit the general. So far, he's 'recruited' me." Cyrus chuckled, "We've done it from London."

He told John about Nicholas and the Trojan Horse.

John was silent for a minute and then slowly said, "I trust you understand, Cyrus, the implications of this," he stumbled, "trick. I mean the whole computer security issue. The NSA would be walking on their ears."

Cyrus got serious. "I do. That's one of the reasons I asked you to come here. However, I must insist that nobody, NSA included, uses it before my little business is finished."

"Hard, but I'll do it. But how about that friend of yours? He could start talking or playing with this toy."

"No. He's a good guy. By the way, I promised him one million pounds for forgetting about this trick forever, and another one in case this endeavor succeeds. In other words, I bought it from him."

"That's a good deal. If he keeps his end, though."

"He will."

"By the way, you said 'one of the reasons.' That makes me a little nervous."

"Well, John." Cyrus was looking for words. "The whole thing doesn't look good. There are two types of Russian money in the West now." Cyrus smiled. "The old money and the new money."

John did not pay any attention to the joke and kept listening.

The old money is the Party Gold we're looking for. The new money is a mixture of the recent plunder smuggled out of Russia by those in power, with some part of it representing legitimate profits of some legitimate business people kept abroad. All I've seen so far is the new money. Through all my contacts in Canada, here and in Switzerland that was all I could trace."

"Are you trying to tell me that those billions disappeared without a trace?"

"Precisely. Every lead I had ended up in that category."

"How about the KGB files?"

"They've found some, about ten billion. They've kept quiet about it and are working on the recovery. I don't think they'll get much more, though."

"Why?"

"What they've found are mainly gold deposits that were obviously similar to the funds we are looking for. They were transported out of Russia, hurriedly and pretty sloppily, in the last month of Gorbatov's tenure. They were flown by military transport planes, which is how the KGB found the trail. I'd say that venue has limited potential."

"I see." John paused. "Any suggestions?"

"I have a hunch that the key to the Party Gold is in Russia."

"I don't like it, Cyrus. One, it scares the hell out of me. Two, why are you so sure?"

"Mentality. Those who hid the money felt very confident in Russia, and they were rather uncomfortable outside of it. It is very important to realize, that their goal was to hide the money abroad, not the key to it. Where would you hide something which is small, easy to transport, and very valuable? On your turf, or on somebody else's?"

"Come to think of it, you're probably right."

Cyrus continued pressing. "So far we've been looking for the movement of capital, not the key. True, such sums are very hard to conceal, particularly in large chunks; however, we've found nothing. Why? Because they used a mechanism that the Western banking system is not equipped to detect."

"Come on, Cyrus. We know this system inside out. They don't. Are you trying to tell me they've found something in our system that we are not aware of?"

"Yes. Don't underestimate them. We use this banking system for a wide variety of purposes, and moving money around in a clandestine way is not very high on our list. If someone looks at the system with a really focused, limited objective, they should be able to exploit it for their own purposes. Thirty years ago that would have been impossible, but now, the way the international financial system has evolved even in just the past ten years, we don't really understand it ourselves."

John sighed. "You're right there. We really don't know the monster. We have no idea what kind of tricks it can play with us, never mind the Party Gold venture."

The conversation died for a while. Then, John broke the silence.

"All right, are you trying to tell me that you want to give up?" Cyrus was about to respond, but John suddenly continued, "But the answer to your upcoming bright idea of going to Russia is no."

Cyrus laughed. "John, I just want to stop a pointless chase. I ran out of options here. The bottom line is that we have to look for the key, not the treasure." He paused. "But in regard to going to Russia, I still think that it's not that bad. I'm sure that the General will invite me, since he doesn't have a choice. He'll probably ask me to browse through their banking records with the hope that in my Western banker's mind something will trigger an association that will lead to the key."

John sighed heavily, and did not say a word.

Cyrus went on. "John, I really don't see much danger in it. The danger comes only if I find the funds, and they figure that out. Needless to say, I'm not going to let them know if that happens. I'd be careful, John. I promise."

John laughed. "You know, Cyrus, over the years I've gotten a pretty good sense of your definition of being careful. It scares the hell out of me." He shook his head. "Cyrus, do you think I want to watch you on that high-wire again?"

Cyrus felt sympathy and tried to discharge the tension. "Oh, don't worry, John. We can't possibly have any communications. So, no watching."

John laughed. "Can you ever be serious in a serious situation?"

John's face grew concerned again. "OK, Cyrus, I have no choice but to agree. Do you know why?"

"Because it was my idea, not yours."

"No. Because of my gut feeling. And my gut feeling is that it's not just money, it's something bigger."

"Why?"

"I've dealt with communists a lot. And every time it looked like just money, it later turned out to be something bigger. That's what makes me nervous. And the fact that until now we haven't found a damn thing makes me even more nervous."

"Are you keeping something from me, John?"

"No, I've told you, it's just a gut feeling." After a pause, he added, "But a strong one."

Cyrus hesitated. Then, he went ahead. "Speaking of gut feeling. I sensed that back in Washington, but I couldn't quite nail it. So, it may be more than just getting some money for the firm. If that feeling of yours is that strong, John, I've got a conceptual question."

John smiled. "Well, I have the feeling it's a nasty one. Shoot."

"If you feel like explaining, why are *we* doing it? Why not the CIA or why not the State Department which can talk to foreign banks through their governments?"

John sighed. "Here we go again. Why? Because the CIA does not function as an intelligence agency, that's why. They are going downhill, no stops in sight. They have come to the point of total incompetence. Their main job is Humint, human intelligence, right?"

"Yes"

"Have you heard of the "tooth-to-tail ratio?"?

"Yes. It's a ratio of the tooth, their fighting capability, to the tail, the ballast or the 'support' and 'miscellaneous,' in their organization. "

"Right. It's very low now. They've become a common, stinking bureaucracy. Bureaucracy is bad anywhere, but it is totally incompatible with intelligence. With the amount of people involved in approval of whatever they have to do, you have two things happen. One, you have a leak before an operation is even approved. Two, by the time it gets approved, it becomes counterproductive. Most of the stuff never gets approved. If you're a bureaucrat, your instinct is to play it safe. Nobody is going to punish you for doing nothing, but if something goes wrong, you're thrown to the sharks."

"Why not cut the fat over there?"

"No known bureaucracy has shrunk; they can be destroyed, but not shrunk. But that is only half of their problem."

"What's the second half?"

"Their personnel. They missed the point in the very core of the business: intelligence is an extremely honest profession, which is universally recognized among all the older intelligence services around the world. You have no other way to go. The CIA for some reason thinks that intelligence is about who is a bigger crook. You can get away with it once, but not twice. In real intelligence the result is removed from the action in time. Sometimes, for years. It's a long-term business. Destroying it takes only a quick action."

"If they have a good head they can understand that."

"Hell, no. Not with their long standing personnel policy. In intelligence you've got to take bright and very honest young people and teach them dirty tricks, while still preserving their integrity. They do just the opposite. They take stupid jerks and try to keep them reasonably honest. That's a losing proposition."

Cyrus smiled. "Why stupid?"

"Because no smart college guy would ever consider a career there. Even if the CIA wanted to, it couldn't compete in the university graduates' market. Sure, I know a few good, honest, and intelligent guys there. They went in because they wanted to serve their country, but they got accepted by mistake; they are an aberration."

"That's a pretty grim picture, John."

"Sure. And there's no reason in sight for it to brighten. The bottom line is that if we opened a cash-for-information kiosk in every capital's flea market, we'd have a hell of a lot better intelligence, and we'd have saved a lot of money."

John did not stay for dinner. "I'd rather have a bite and a nap on the plane." He picked up all the Trojan Horse materials and left.

The next day Dronov did not fail to meet Cyrus' expectations. After Cyrus gave him a detailed report on the status of the search, the general grew quiet and serious.

Cyrus had nothing to add, and the silence continued until Dronov spoke.

"Well, Cyrus. Of course, this is not good news. But I must admit, this is not entirely unexpected." He looked at Cyrus, and rushed to put in a disclaimer. "Don't get me wrong, though. I respect your expertise, no question about that. Besides, the report you've just made shows that your reputation is well deserved."

"Thank you."

"It's not you. We'd already done some good searching, as I'm sure you guessed. And, we also came up empty-handed. This simply means that those who hid the funds used such unconventional methods that all of us drew blanks."

"Clearly. I must say I'm surprised. Not only am I personally not capable of cracking this nut, but I don't know anyone else who can either. At least at the moment." He made a pause. "I'd like to encourage you a little bit, Yuri. Nothing can be hidden forever, particularly anything that size. I'm sure that sooner or later something will surface. Somehow."

Dronov sighed, and his face turned grim. "Time, I'm afraid, is what we don't have."

"I don't understand."

Dronov shook off his deep thoughts. "Never mind. I tell you what, Cyrus. How would you like to have a trip to Moscow?"

"What? You must be kidding, Yuri. What am I going to do there? Talk to all the spooks you'd supply?"

"Don't rush, Cyrus. Just stop and think. Spooks are none of your concern. That's what I'm here for. On the other hand, if you go through the old banking records, with your vast knowledge of the Western financial system something may trigger an association. That something can give us a missing clue."

"Come on, Yuri. I have no idea even how your banking system used to be set up. I heard it was weird, but that's all. It's not enough, you know."

"Don't worry about that. I'll find people who will brief you on that, and quickly. But none of the people over there has your expertise. That's the point. That's why you have a chance to find that clue. You don't even know what you know, Cyrus."

Cyrus just shook his head, unconvinced. Dronov pressed on.

"You have to understand, Cyrus. The people who hid the money covered their tracks in Moscow, and they did it well. But they covered them against Russian experts. They could not possibly cover them against a person like you, since they did not have enough knowledge of your knowledge. Does that make sense to you?"

"Well, it does. Some."

"I'll make a great deal for you. You'd stay in a first class hotel, have first class food and service, and I can get it for you at less than half the price. Besides, I would have thought that it should be of interest to you to visit the country of your grandparents."

Cyrus laughed. "You know, Yuri, you have great persuasive powers. You'd make a in the States."

"I'm glad you're open-minded enough to agree. To tell you the truth, I never doubted it."

Chapter 8

Cyrus knew the reputation of the Russian Customs and the Border Guards.. To his surprise, he and Dronov moved through the passport control functions unharassed. *Well, this is the first sign that I will be watched very closely around here. Let's see how you are going to play it.* He turned to the General.

"Yuri, I've heard that it's usually very unpleasant to deal with the Customs and *Pogranichniki* here."

"True. I just pulled a few strings. No big deal, it's easy for me. I also arranged the transportation from the airport."

A black Mercedes was waiting for them. Inside, Dronov said, "Cyrus, since you prefer to stay in a hotel, I made a choice for you. Of course, if you don't like it, you can choose another at any time. I can get you into any of them. For the time being, I put you in the Savoy. It's old, comfortable, not too big, and located in the middle of everything. Personally, I much prefer it to Metropol, never mind the Mezhdunarodnaya."

"Thank you. I've heard the name."

"Yes. It was renamed Berlin, But now, it's renamed back to Savoy. You'll find a lot of familiar names of places and streets. A few years back many old names were restored."

"So I've heard."

"By the way, the palace you see on the left is Peter the Great's Palace. Beautiful, isn't it?"

Cyrus looked at the magnificent complex surrounded by walls. He had seen pictures of it before. "What's there now?"

"The Air Force Academy."

"I see."

Twenty minutes later the car pulled up to the distinct facade of the Savoy. Dronov helped Cyrus check in. Ever since its construction the hotel housed one of the best and, probably, the most pompous restaurants in Moscow. Cyrus looked inside the main dining room as they passed.

"My God, it looks like this room was cut out of Versailles and brought here. Nothing short of a tailcoat would look right in this room. I didn't know anything like this still existed in Russia."

"Well, the old places were filled with filth for eighty years. Those that survived are now coming back."

Cyrus was pleased with his suite. Tall ceilings lent the rooms an airy feeling, and the windows overlooked a relatively quiet Rozhdestvenka Street.

"Cyrus, you'll find virtually everything you may need here, provided, of course, that you give decent tips."

Dronov left and promised to come back for dinner.

Cyrus went downstairs to a souvenir shop and bought a good Moscow map and a couple of tour guides. He went to his room and sat down to study them.

At seven Cyrus heard a knock on the door.

Dronov looked refreshed and happy. "Well, I hope you find everything satisfactory here, Cyrus."

"Yes, of course. Frankly, I'm a little surprised to find this kind of facility in Moscow."

"Many people are. The point is that this place is going capitalist much faster than anybody could have imagined. Ready for dinner?"

"Yes. Downstairs?"

"No. You'll have plenty of chances to dine here. I'd rather show you some more exotic places. I've made the reservation, and your car is waiting for us."

"My car?"

"Yes. You have a Mercedes with a driver around the clock. I arranged it at a reasonable price. See, getting around could be a bit of a problem here. Public transportation is a nuisance, taxis are a mess, and ordering a car every time you need to would be annoying and, frankly, not much cheaper. Of course, you can rent a car, but I wouldn't recommend it."

Well, I understand that you want to keep me under your watchful eye, General, but this is quite crude, really. On the other hand, it could be to my advantage. When I really want to slip away, your guys will be too comfortable to be vigilant. Yes, this is a better way. For me. "I see. All right, amen."

After a half-hour drive they arrived in the countryside, which Cyrus estimated to be due west of Moscow. By his study of the map, combined with some previous knowledge, Cyrus figured that they were roughly in the area where former Party bosses had their dachas.

Suddenly, Cyrus found himself in a mid-nineteenth century Russian country inn. The architecture, waiters' uniforms and the menu looked very genuine. A small Gypsy band was playing old Russian music.

"Surprised, Cyrus?"

"Yes. This is just like in the stories I've heard and in the books I read as a child."

"Surprising as it may be, a lot of Russians cherish their heritage." Dronov smirked. "When they can afford it."

Studying the menu, Cyrus found what he thought was extinct, *kulebyaka*, an old Russian dish featuring three sorts of delicatessen fish layered and baked in dough. A couple of dozen kinds of vodka fit well in this enclave of the Old World.

After they ordered, Dronov came to the point. "Cyrus, your search here will be limited to the Central Bank. As I told you before, you may detect something that others missed."

"The location for the search is logical, but I don't like the sound of your 'limited.' It sounds like a threat."

Dronov smiled. "Just a friendly warning. If anything you find leads you anywhere else in this city, leave it to me to deal with it. First, you're not equipped for that. Second, there are a lot of unfriendly folks around here, and some of them could become nervous if you snoop around. Remember that those very people who stole the money are still here. I just don't want you to get hurt."

"Is it that serious?"

"Of course it is. Look, it's easy here to find somebody to kill a man for ten bucks. For a hundred bucks you can find a pro."

No, General. You're lying. The main danger comes from you and your organization. And you want me under your control. "Well, how come snooping in the bank is not dangerous?"

"Simple. I have connections there. Call them partners, if you will."

Hell, no. This is government control, the current government. Easy, now. You've heard enough; don't make him suspicious. "I see.

So, if I get a lead to some other organization, I should give it to you and we'll see what we can do together."

"Precisely."

After a delightful dinner Dronov said, "It's a good time to show you a different spot. And, to introduce you to your assistant."

"Oh?" Here comes the girl.

"Yes. Let's go to the Metropol. You may find it a little irritating, but it's the place to show up once in a while. Several restaurants, bars, night clubs, you name it. We'll have after dinner drinks with the guy who works in the bank and can get anything you want over there. He's my good friend and can be trusted.

Sure.

At a posh bar in the Metropol, just a block away from the Red Square, they met a man of about thirty, medium height, weight, build, as well as medium brown hair; the man's facial features were medium too. Nothing remarkable. Even his dusty-blue eyes were too medium to describe.

A perfect specimen for an intelligence operative. Nothing to hang onto. Half an hour later you wouldn't recognize him in a crowd.

"Nikolay," he introduced himself, "Call me Nick."

"Cyrus, Nick will get whatever you need at the Central Bank."

"All right. This sounds very reassuring."

Dronov smiled. "Well, it's not easy to get anything in this bureaucracy. So, you'll appreciate Nick's value in the time to come." He paused. "Actually, you're not going to work in the bank. You're going to be in the archives."

"Oh? I didn't realize that."

"Yes. All the records of the transactions over three years old are transferred to the archive." Dronov paused again. "Cyrus, I'd also like to ask one thing of you. Please, keep as low a profile as possible on the premises. Remember, I arranged it on a strictly personal basis. It's hard for you to appreciate this, but, believe me, there are plenty of nosy people everywhere. And some of them are mean."

Cyrus laughed. "Well, this sounds like some sort of spy business."

"You may look at it that way. Everything is messed up and mixed up: the government, private business, criminals, politicians, everything. It's impossible for me to describe to you what is going on in Russia now. Just hold your judgment for a later day, OK?"

"All right. But it all sounds very intriguing."

Dronov turned to Nick. "Nick, how is Cyrus' Russian? I've been with him too much lately to hear it objectively."

"It stands out a bit. Not that there is any accent, but just the usage and the phrase composition make it very clear that he learned it eighty years ago. I think it will be unnoticeable in a couple of weeks."

"Well, then we have to have some kind of a story for the bank. Nick, you start a rumor in the bank that Cyrus has been raised by his grandmother in Latvia. But generally, Cyrus, let Nick do the talking. Try to stick to short phrases, and listen to the way they all talk."

"Yuri, I'm an American citizen. If I lie about who I am, I'm afraid I will become easy prey for the KGB. They'd have something to hang on me. That's a chance I can't take."

Dronov must have been a little irritated, but he did not show it at all. "All right, let Nick do the lying. If you're pressed, make a joke. Make sure that you say it as a joke. Say you're an Eskimo or an Ethiopian, and you forgot which one."

You old rascal, you know all the tricks of the trade. Cyrus laughed. "That I can do, sounds like fun."

"Speaking of which, I'm going to leave you and go home. I need rest. Cyrus, here is my cellular phone number; the phone is always with me." He handed Cyrus a business card.

"Well, that's pretty westernized, isn't it?"

"Do we have a choice?" Dronov shrugged and added, "But I like it anyway. Bye, boys. Have fun." He left.

Cyrus and Nick were sipping their drinks. After a while Nick came to life. "I'm glad to meet you, Cyrus. It's an honor for me to meet a famous American banker."

Cyrus lowered his head.

Nick modestly continued, "I can get you anything in this town. Just say what you want."

This is yet another message: 'Don't try anything on your own, you're well caged.' Why are they so pushy with it? What are they afraid of? Well, this is for you to find out.

Cyrus did not answer, and Nick, as a well programmed and oiled machine, continued, "Girls, boys, gambling? By the way, all of that is available right here."

Cyrus looked at him and said sternly, "Look, I have no interest in boys whatsoever. If I want to gamble, I'll go to a casino. If a want a whore, I'll choose the one I like."

It was not clear whether Nick got the message that he was being too pushy or was just responding to the next piece of input. "I'm just trying to help you, Cyrus. Moscow is a pretty unusual place. There is much more to it than meets the eye. If you gamble, you better know where, or, you can get duped, robbed, beaten, killed, or all of the above. If you pick up a whore, you better know which one, or you can get duped, robbed, infected, beaten, killed or all of the above."

"Even in a place like this?"

"Absolutely."

Let's see how great a hurry they are in. It's an indication of their timetable. "Then I'd like to just relax here for the time being."

"Very well."

Nick started asking a lot of questions about America. Cyrus realized that it was just personal curiosity.

Half an hour later Nick suggested a tour of the Metropol facilities. They walked to see a night club, a restaurant. When they entered another bar, Nick suddenly said, "Oh, see that corner on the right?"

"Yes." There were several small tables grouped together, and a company of about a dozen men and women in their twenties and thirties were apparently having a party.

"I see a few friends there. Would you like to join them for a short while?"

This looks like a pressing schedule. "Sure. Why not?"

Cyrus followed Nick to the corner. Nick shook a couple of hands and kissed a couple of cheeks in this already warmed-up crowd. Then he declared, "Guys, let me introduce my guest, my friend Mr. Cyrus Grant. He is an American visiting Moscow to study the business environment here. Incidentally, he is of Russian descent and speaks Russian.

The ceremony required Cyrus to shake exactly half of the hands present and say a few words to every one's master. Somebody fetched two more chairs for Cyrus and Nick, and the mandatory toasts followed.

As was customary in Russia, particularly when a foreigner is present, every toast was bottoms up. In half an hour Cyrus felt quite warmed up himself.

To his left was an extremely attractive brunette. "Laura," she said when they were introduced. By this time the whole crowd was in a self-perpetuating mode of loud conversations. Everyone spoke loudly, and no one seemed to be listening. Nobody seemed to notice that disparity, either.

Laura's voice suddenly changed from fashionable exhibitionist-cheerful to a calm, almost confidential. "I love your Russian, Cyrus. It makes me almost envious."

Cyrus chuckled, "Laura, please don't make fun of my accent and my poor Russian."

"Not at all. Truly, I meant what I just said. By the way, you do not have any accent. But your choice of expressions is a little," she hesitated slightly, "old-fashioned, too proper. It's like your language is coming straight out of Turgenev or Tolstoy."

"That's pretty much how I learned my Russian. It must sound very funny to you."

Laura smiled. "At first. And then it's apparent that your Russian is very correct, pure." She paused. "You see, our language is so corrupt, full of slang. It's losing its original beauty. That's why I almost envy yours."

"Well, your assessment is very flattering. However, I fully intend to upgrade my Russian while I'm here. I don't want to speak strangely."

"I understand. Besides, it's inevitable that you'll change, whether you want to or not. But I hope you don't."

"You seem to be very sensitive to language, Laura."

"Perhaps. My father is a professor of literature. I always wanted to be an author, but for now I have to settle for writing. I'm a journalist."

Well, I take it this is my seducer-designate. Textbook case, accelerated to the extreme. Should I mix up their cards or just play along? I am not deep enough in the game yet to try to draw a mistake from them by scrambling. Why don't I play along for now? So, let them have my full cooperation.

"Oh, how interesting." Cyrus paused. "By the way, it's a great party, but it's a bit too loud here for my taste. How about continuing this conversation somewhere quieter?"

Laura smiled and looked him in the eye. "With pleasure. But, by this I do not imply any promise."

"Neither do I."

Laura just laughed. Cyrus turned to Nick.

"Nick, I'd like to take off. See you tomorrow at my hotel."

"Of course. Your car is at the entrance. Black Mercedes with number 53 on the windshield. How about ten o'clock?" Nick smiled and winked. "She is a beauty, isn't she?"

Cyrus smiled. "Make it ten thirty."

Following Laura through the bar to the hall, Cyrus had a chance to appreciate her impeccable figure. More than that, there was something magnetic for him in the way she walked. The rarest combination of grand grace and girlish joyfulness with which she maneuvered between the people and objects in the crowded bar, making her way outside without ever touching anybody or stopping. She was more comfortable on her high heels than most women were in tennis shoes. As is common in Russia, she had left her boots in the cloakroom. In the hall with its bright lights Cyrus saw a beautiful face with good cheekbones and a high and open forehead framed with a thick dark brown coiffure. Her straight nose had the thin and graceful nostrils of a thoroughbred. Her face would have looked sculpture-cold if not for the wide open brown eyes, so soft that they more than compensated for the classic features. She stopped and, waiting for Cyrus, turned. The soft light coming in rays from her brown eyes complemented the grace of her pose.

This is the most beautiful creature I've ever seen.. I probably look like a sixteen-year-old boy at his first adult ball. Cyrus resisted the temptation to touch his jaw to make sure it had not fallen.

When Cyrus caught up with her, she smiled. She was obviously used to stunning men. Most women in this situation display either open triumph or extreme boredom, perhaps to reinforce the impression. She simply ignored the obvious, which for Cyrus was a display of tact he rarely found in beautiful women.

Cyrus finally regained his composure. "Well, I'm at a disadvantage. I'm afraid you'll have to choose our next destination."

She laughed. "As a foreigner, you are forgiven. By the way, it also gives me an opportunity to choose and not seem either capricious or presumptuous. So in a way I'm glad. I know a wonderful quiet piano bar in a restaurant not too far from here. Let's get our coats and catch a taxi."

"That won't be necessary. I have a car and driver here."

"Oh. Then, you must be really important. How come you hang around without a dozen aids and guards?" Her tone was needling, but playful, not hostile.

"I've got one chaperone, and I just dumped him where he belongs, at the bar."

Cyrus couldn't help it. Out of the corner of his eye he was watching the effortless grace with which Laura changed her high heels to the boots. She did it while standing up near the wall. *It looks like she's not too spoiled. She didn't even bother to try to find a seat to do that.*

"Laura, please forgive me. Why do Russian women change their shoes? In the States women wouldn't bother to do that."

She looked at him with surprise. "Never thought of that. Maybe, it's just a desire to look feminine. We always wear high heels. And economics, perhaps. We don't have too many good shoes, so we don't want to ruin them. Very often the weather here is so terrible." There was no pretense at all in that very straight answer.

Twenty minutes later they entered a bar in another posh restaurant. Cyrus' first reaction was surprise. The room, which was actually split in two by the bar and a piano, looked more like a boudoir. Heavy dark red drapes half covered several niches along the walls. The maitre'd measured Cyrus with a very testy look, decided favorably, and escorted them to one of the niches in the farther half of the room. The ambiance reminded Cyrus of a turn of the last century men's club with highly questionable activities. When Cyrus realized that it was just a very legitimate, high-class piano bar, he had a hard time keeping a straight face. Laura noticed that.

"Anything wrong, Cyrus?"

He burst into laughter. "Well, by Western standards, this place looks like a posh and pretentious cat house. I realize that it's not, but just the look of it throws me."

She also had a good laugh. "I would have never imagined that. Here it's just an attempt to look respectable."

Half an hour later Cyrus knew that Laura was a graduate of the

Moscow State University, and was now a reporter for the
Komsomolskaya Pravda, specializing mainly in investigative
reporting. She had studied ballet for nine years, and piano for ten. She
inherited her father's affection for Russian literature, and her thesis
was a study in late Nineteenth-century authors. When she realized the
conversation was becoming an interview, she bristled.

"Well, we're talking about me all the time. How about you? Are
you a rich American banker trying to make a good deal in Russia?"

Banker. It's a mistake, my dear. Nick never mentioned this
word. He said "an American, studying business."

"First of all, I'm not a banker. I'm an investment banker."

"Is there a difference?"

"Oh, yes, a world of difference. Crudely speaking, a banker
counts your money and gives you a loan. Any idiot can do that. An
investment banker designs the financial structure of a deal. He brings
people and money together, he makes things happen. That's the core
of any substantive transaction."

"Too vague for me. Perhaps, later you'll educate me on that
one. But what are you doing here? Trying to make one of those cozy
politicians-criminals-entrepreneurs-foreign bankers deals?" Her tone
was brash, if not slightly sarcastic.

Cyrus was surprised by the transformation of a beautiful woman
into a sarcastic, seen-it-all reporter. "Not really. Just studying the
Russian banking system."

She laughed. "Studying what? In a case you've been
misinformed, there is no banking system in Russia. There are a bunch
of money enterprises, jointly owned by former Party and government
officials, currently democratic politicians, and criminals of all grades.
Their main, if not only, goal is to handle the money the above
individuals gained in illegal transactions, launder that money and
channel it abroad. That's all. So, is this what you are going to study?"

Good Lord, what is this? "Precisely. How come you know all
that?"

"I'm a reporter. One of the things I'm currently working on is
exactly that, the corruption of the Russian banking system. Another
one is researching the money stolen from the state by Gorbatov and
his cronies before he was thrown out of power."

Why do they treat me like this? It's so crude, so rushed. Why?

Wait, they just confirmed you as a nonprofessional. If you show that you're dismayed, you've blown your cover. Additional check? Maybe.

"That's very interesting, Laura. I'd be delighted to talk about all that later."

"All right. But we can as well discuss it now."

Russian culture. Very intense. Often, very direct. There is no "not-until-after-desert" rule like the British. Business can be discussed before they serve you a first drink.

Cyrus made an effort to return the flow of conversation to a social mode, and he was surprised that Laura switched as easily away from the topic as she had moved into it. She was once again a beautiful, charming and disarmingly direct woman.

"Laura, at the expense of sounding banal, and I'm sure that you've heard it so many times, I still would like to tell you that you're an astonishingly beautiful and charming girl."

Laura laughed, "It's a matter of taste." Then she tried to relieve the situation. "But I'm glad that your taste favors me. You too must be very popular among the girls."

Cyrus ignored the second remark. "It must be very hard to be in such a position. Or, very amusing. I'm sure every man you meet tells you that."

Laura laughed again. She was clearly teasing him. "Much less than you think."

"Not true."

She surprised him again. "It is. The beautiful girl syndrome. Everyone assumes that she already has a lot of invitations, and so does not invite her. So, she often ends up without an invitation to the ball. To make things worse, she has to support the reputation and behave discouragingly, leading to even deeper isolation. And, very often, in the end she marries the ugliest man around."

Cyrus did not know how to react. All his experience and social skills somehow were of no use now. Laura apparently felt his uneasiness and came to his rescue. She looked at him directly, dazzling him with the warm light of her eyes, and said, "Cyrus, I want to know more about you, about your family. Do you have any brothers or sisters?"

Cyrus told her his story, carefully avoiding ideology.

In the middle of the night they rode to her apartment. The car stopped at the entrance of her building, and Cyrus found himself being indecisive, being afraid to spoil the enchantment. Subconsciously, he was also afraid that she might proposition him. As they got out of the car, he took her hands in his, but the moment he opened his mouth to say something, she quickly interrupted him, "Cyrus, please, don't."

They stood awkwardly near the door like high school kids. Then, Laura hurriedly took a business card from her purse, wrote down another number, and gave it to Cyrus. Apologetically, she said, "Forgive me. I just don't want to spoil it all. Good night." She kissed him on the cheek, quickly turned around and ran through the door.

For a few moments Cyrus stood motionless outside her building. His brief reverie interrupted by the sound of an engine running in a car parked slightly to his right. Then he slowly turned, got into his car and said as if he were speaking to himself, "Hotel, please."

Glancing over his shoulder, he noticed the parked car enter the travel lane without turning on its lights. Cyrus did not look around again but concentrated his focus on the driver's eyes and reactions in the rearview mirror. He too had detected surveillance. What should have been a ten-minute ride took almost thirty because of the driver's circuitous route, confirming the tail.

Trouble in River City already. Someone is onto Dronov, and it's not the locals. With all of their static posts, they would have no need for this clumsy mobile surveillance.

The general was upbeat at the late morning breakfast with Cyrus and Nick. The cluster of wrinkles around his eyes, despite an otherwise still expression, suggested a hearty smile.

"Well, Cyrus, I hope you had a good starting glimpse at Moscow last night."

"Yes, it was enchanting." Cyrus kept a straight face to preclude any further discussion of the matter.

Nick kept silent.

The conversation turned to business.

"Cyrus, Nick is going to brief you on the banking system at the time in question. He's pretty well familiar with it. If he cannot answer your questions, he'll find somebody who can."

Nick nodded, "No problem."

Dronov looked at Nick as if asking for something, and Nick gave him a three-by-five card. The general glanced at it, took out a pen, and wrote something. He gave the card to Cyrus. "Here are a few phone numbers you might need."

Cyrus took the card. There were public emergency numbers, the numbers for the hotel, Nick's home and cell, and the car driver's cell numbers, all written in perfect and meticulous, almost feminine handwriting. Dronov's cell number was written in by him with firm, clear, but slightly casual large letters.

It's about time to make some fuss. Cyrus studied the card, slowly put it in his pocket and coldly smiled. "I hope I'm wrong, but it seems to me that the message I'm being served now is to stick to you, gentlemen, and to those supplied by you. I wonder if a warning not to violate this cozy setup is to follow."

Nick moved slightly in his chair, clearly uncomfortable with the directness with which Cyrus expressed his observation.

Dronov smiled. "Cyrus, please, try not to see what isn't there. Nobody is trying to put you in a cage. I've already told you that, keeping in mind where you're coming from, it would be counterproductive. Your reaction is very natural for an American. You are all obsessed with freedom. However, there are some considerations I would like to submit to you. Mainly, it's your own security. Unfortunately, Moscow is not a very safe place. In a way, you are my guest here, and I am concerned about your safety, as you would be for mine in New York."

"But I wasn't," snapped Cyrus.

"I wasn't your guest there."

Cyrus was unconvinced and grumbled, "I'm a grownup and up to now, somehow, I've managed to survive."

"There is another point here. As you can imagine, there are some people here who will be very unhappy if we succeed. Unfortunately, we don't know who those people are, but I can assure you that they can be malevolent characters. Besides the possibility that you might get hurt, the fewer waves you make around here, the better chance you have of finding what we're looking for."

Cyrus suddenly smiled, "General, I'd like to tell you an old story. A woman complained to a doctor that her husband didn't pay any attention to her sex-wise. The doctor invited the husband for a chat and asked a few very direct questions. He was astonished when the man admitted that he had a few mistresses, some incidental affairs, and used prostitutes on occasion. "Why then don't you have any sexual interest in your wife?"

"Well," the guy answered, "I do not reproduce in captivity."

Dronov laughed and Nick faithfully followed. Cyrus continued, "In other words, like it or not, I'm not going to be in your pocket here. Or, anybody else's for that matter. I go where I want, with whom I want, and when I want. And hiding, whether it is in the office, or in the street, is not my modus operandi." *I hope I didn't overplay it.*

"Forgive me, Cyrus, but this is clearly a misunderstanding. You probably read too many spy novels about the KGB. Of course you're free to do whatever you want. I'm just talking about basic safety. My business is to warn you, the rest is up to you." He sighed slightly and looked at Nick as if saying, "See, this is a typical American, and there is nothing we can do about it."

Nick returned an understanding look, and Dronov added, "As you wish. Just give me a call when you're in trouble."

"I will."

Cyrus decided it was a good time to insist they wait until Monday to begin combing the archives of the Central Bank, because he wanted to determine their urgency and because he simply needed some time to get himself acclimated to the situation.

"Incidentally, General, I'd like to take this first weekend here in Moscow to get acquainted with the area. You know, get my bearings and do a bit of exploring. Can the archives wait until Monday?"

"Well, Cyrus, I understand that this is all quite a bit to take in at once, but we really don't have much time for entertainment and sightseeing. Don't misunderstand me, we hope that you will enjoy yourself while you are here; indeed, we've made it clear that we can arrange anything you wish. However, sacrificing the entire weekend when we have so much to do does not seem wise or in anyone's best interest. Trust me, you will have plenty of time for leisure and culture."

"Forgive me, General, but things have been moving very quickly for me since our meeting in New York. Honestly, I don't think I will be any great asset to you until I've had the opportunity to get established and I can calmly and carefully assess the situation."

Dronov sighed in frustration and replied, "Cyrus, I think it is a waste of valuable time, but if you insist, I must allow it. Nick and I will meet you at your hotel at 8:00 am on Monday; I trust you will be ready." Then he quickly added in a somewhat more pleasant tone, "Please call us if you need anything."

Chapter 9

The weekend slipped rapidly past and Monday's wake-up call came all too soon. Cyrus awoke still feeling as though he'd somehow been swept along in some breakneck current, but he also found himself eager to begin his search in Moscow.

He showered and dressed quickly and went to the lobby to meet Dronov and Nick. However, when he left the elevator he found only Nick waiting for him.

"Good morning, Nick. Where is the General?"

"Morning, Cyrus, I hope you are well rested and ready to begin after your weekend. Unfortunately, the General will not be joining us after all; something rather pressing has come up. Well, let's head over to the archives."

Nick brought Cyrus to an old drab four story building of indeterminable age. A small sign "Ministry of Finance" at the entrance was equally unimpressive. Nick waved to the guard behind the glass on the left, who was lazily reading a book and obviously not interested in anyone's coming and going. The guard nodded without any sign of interrupting his reading. They took an elevator to the fourth floor and stepped into a long corridor with a worn-out parquet floor and light blue walls. A single dirty window at the end offered little light and the few dim light bulbs hanging from the ceiling provided barely enough light to see the signs on the brown wooden doors lining both sides of the corridor.

They came to the second to last door on the right. There was no sign on it, just the number 427. Nick took a key out of his pocket and unlocked the door, and they entered a room only slightly more impressive than the corridor. The room was fairly large, about four hundred square feet, with ten-foot ceilings, ornate moldings in the corners and an equally ornate plaster circle in the middle, surrounding the hook of a crystal chandelier. The ceiling and the top four feet of the walls were reasonably white. The rest of the walls were painted in a light bluish-grey. Two large windows with oak frames and windowsills matched the oak of the door. One large desk was in the corner near the further window, the other, a small one, was humbly stuck to the wall. At the left wall there was a leather couch with a large coffee table and two chairs. A large Uzbek rug covered most of the parquet floor. The walls were free of pictures, or any other distractions. The only thing hanging on one of the walls was a blackboard. A mid-size safe and a small table with a coffee maker completed the furnishings of the room.

Nick said, "Well, this is your office. I'll be using the small desk, if you don't mind."

"Of course not. It's not bad at all, certainly better than I expected."

"I'll bring you a laptop computer later. What do you prefer?"

Cyrus chuckled, "Well, that sounds like full service. I'd prefer a Mac with Microsoft Office, if you have it."

"I'm sure we do."

"Perfect. Why don't we get cracking?" Cyrus sat at his desk in a comfortable leather chair. The desk was empty, with only a lamp, a telephone and a notepad on it.

"All right. Let me call the man who is going to help you here. He retired from the Central Bank and is a deputy head of this archive now. If anybody knows the operations of the bank, he does." Nick dialed a number.

Five minutes later a bald, plump man in his sixties came in.

"Cyrus, this is the deputy head of the archive, Valery Stogov. Valery, this is Mr. Cyrus Grant who we've talked about. He is working for the World Bank and is studying our banking system, starting from the eighties."

"Pleasure to meet you, Mr. Grant. I'd be delighted to help if I can."

After five minutes of small talk Cyrus said, "Mr. Stogov, I am ashamed to admit my total ignorance in regard to your banking system, past or present. So, I would appreciate if we start with you explaining the structure of it in the mid-eighties."

"Of course. It was very simple, actually." Stogov rose, went to the blackboard and started drawing.

An hour later Stogov suggested going into the archive itself.

They went to the third floor.

The huge hall was filled with racks of carefully stored large books and file boxes. Stogov took one of the books, put it on a nearby table, and started explaining the procedures for the transactions in the bank.

After just a few sentences Cyrus was shocked. He could not help it and said only half-jokingly, "Please, forgive me, Mr. Stogov. Are you sure we're in the nineteen-eighties room, not the eighteen-eighties?"

Stogov and Nick were not offended and cracked up.

"No, seriously. I would have thought that by that time you had computers."

Stogov, still laughing, answered, "Sure, we had them. Two. And both were of capabilities below a modern laptop. So, they were used to compute the balances and so on, but all the transactions were recorded in the ledger, and the accounts manually."

Cyrus felt like he was in a museum. He just shook his head.

"We did not have good computers at the time, Mr. Grant, we did not trust those that we had, and we could not accept the computer responsibility."

"What?"

"Well, you see, when you sign a ledger, your signature is on record. It's tangible, it's obvious. You always know for sure who's responsible. The way we saw it, the computer seemed an easy way to an uncontrollable system."

"All right. We've got what we've got."

Stogov began explaining the entries and the accounting system.

Six o'clock came before they knew it. On the way to the hotel Nick asked, "Any plans for tonight?"

Cyrus looked at him but did not notice any sign of needling. "I haven't thought about it yet. At any rate, don't worry about me. I may decide to do some explorating."

"Of course." Again, no sign of a smile.

Back In his hotel room, Cyrus took a long shower.

Deep inside he knew that that very evening he'd call Laura, but he did not want to admit it. Well, nothing wrong with playing along. They obviously want you to get involved with her. So, why not, to see what they really want?

But his training and experience were not for nothing. Cut the bullshit. You know that it's an option if, and only if, there is no chance of becoming emotionally involved. And, if there is such a chance, then it's wrong. Dead wrong. And you also know that you're about to become involved. And, the fact that you cannot explain that is irrelevant.

He was sitting in his bathrobe near the telephone with Laura's card in front of him. For the first time in his operational experience Cyrus was conflicted. Professionally, he knew all too well that any emotional involvement could be deadly. Personally, he desperately wanted to see her. There was only a small, almost imperceptible threshold to cross. And he crossed it.

Well, in the first place, she's probably not at home. He dialed the number.

"Hello." She was home.

Cyrus felt a rush of adrenaline, something he had not felt for some time. "Good evening, Laura, this is Cyrus Grant. How are you?"

"Oh, good evening, Cyrus. I was hoping you'd call."

"How could I not? I was wondering if you have any plans for tonight."

"Not really, unless you suggest something." That was Laura. Direct as only a beautiful woman could be.

"Well, then, I'd like to suggest we spend this evening together."

"I'd be delighted."

Cyrus caught himself feeling like a sixteen-year-old boy unexpectedly receiving a "yes." He was embarrassed by his own pause and said, "How about dinner at my hotel restaurant."

How original. Idiot.

He quickly added in an apologetic voice, "I don't know any better. This is virtually my first day here."

"It's a very good restaurant but awfully expensive."

Cyrus chuckled. "Don't worry. I'm a rich American banker, remember?"

"Oh, yes. And riding in a Mercedes limousine."

"Speaking of which, I would like to send it for you. What time?"

"I need half an hour."

"Thank you." She paused. "Cyrus, I'm really happy that you called."

"So am I. See you soon."

Cyrus called the driver and then the concierge to make a reservation. He dressed, poured himself a scotch, and sat down in a chair, trying to reconcile his predicament. His thoughts were far from clear. Every professional warning automatically met a rationalization.

Cyrus looked at his watch and rose to go to the lobby to meet Laura. At that moment he heard a gentle knock. He opened the door and there she was. Her smile was inexplicably shy and sly at the same time. Automatically, Cyrus stepped aside to let her in.

"Oh, I'm sorry I'm late, but it's great that you decided to drop by." He felt his words sounded lame. They were.

Still acting automatically, he helped Laura with her coat. He managed to take it off her shoulders just before moving around her. At that moment he felt the warmth of her body. He slowed his motion and looked into her face. She moved slightly closer to him, and her slim body trembled. That was more than Cyrus' manners and training could withstand. He let the coat drop.

Cyrus took her in his arms and carried her to the bedroom. Laura looked up at his face and whispered, "I couldn't help it." He kissed her again.

Two hours later, emotionally and physically exhausted, they were lying silently in bed. They were afraid to speak, afraid to scare off the wonder of the illusion and return to cold and unforgiving reality.

Finally, Laura whispered, "It was crazy, wasn't it?"

"Yes. Wonderfully crazy."

In the morning they had a huge breakfast in the room. On the way to the archive, Cyrus dropped Laura off at her apartment.

"Do I have to invite you again tonight?"

Laura laughed, "No. Six-thirty?"

"Sure. I wonder if I can wait that long."

She stepped out of the car, told the driver "Go," and shut the door. She knew that if she just looked back every one of the day's obligations would go to hell, so she didn't.

Chapter 10

In his office Cyrus found Nick browsing through *Penthouse*. Cyrus was glad to find freshly brewed coffee. He poured a cup and dropped into the armchair.

"Any bright ideas on where to start, Nick?"

"Cyrus, we exhausted all the bright and all the otherwise ideas about a month before your arrival. Now it's your play."

Cyrus thought for a while. "I presume there was a master list of all the foreign bank accounts. Can we get it?"

"There was no full master list. Many accounts were secret and were maintained by the KGB or the Central Committee, not by the bank. Those are off limits. The rest, pretty much regular accounts, were on the master list of the Central Bank. Now, many of those records are missing."

"Can we get whatever is left?"

Of course. I'm not sure how much help that would be, though. We already looked through those. And not just once."

"I see. Let's take a look at that anyway."

"As you wish. Anything else?"

"Yes. Let's take another tack. We're looking for a sizable chunk of loose change. So, why don't we pull all the accounts for those years involving balances exceeding, say, one billion dollars, at any point in time. And we do that not from the account master list, but from the routine records."

"You want to see if they missed something while covering their tracks?"

"Yes. People make mistakes, you know."

"All right, but it will take a while. Let me place an order." Nick disappeared, and returned ten minutes later.

"We'll have the results year by year, to speed up the process."

"Good. Meanwhile, tell me how the bank handled money abroad during the communist years."

"Disbursements?"

"No, deposits."

"Very simple. You can easily disregard the projects. Those were done for 'friends,' who either paid for them in barter, or did not pay at all. The rest was our sales of raw materials. Say, enterprise A sells a chunk of oil. A contract stipulated a deposit of the proceeds into account X at one of our handful of banks dealing abroad. That was the end of the deal for the enterprise. The bank reported the deposit to the Central Bank and waited for orders as to what to do with the money. Usually, the order was to pay for something bought in the West."

"Wait a minute. How did that enterprise treat the income?"

"It didn't. Often, it didn't even know for how much the material was sold for. All it was told was to ship a certain amount of material to a certain address."

Cyrus felt he had entered an alien planet. "Who did deal with the income, then?"

"The ministry that enterprise belonged to. Every enterprise belonged to a certain ministry. The ministry did all the negotiating."

"I see. So, the ministry kept the budget, right?"

"Right, but nobody really knew what that budget was."

"Come on, I'm trying to get serious here."

"So am I. Have you heard about the different types of rubles in the Soviet Union?"

"Yes. Internal and external."

"Not exactly." Nick stepped to the blackboard and started drawing a diagram. "There was a 'paper ruble,' used for the payroll and for shopping by mere mortals. There was an 'accounting ruble,' used for transactions between the enterprises and the ministries. There was a 'Comecon ruble' used for transactions between the Comecon countries, the so called 'Socialist Camp.' There was also the so called 'golden ruble,' tied to the dollar for accounting with the West."

"I didn't know all that."

"I reckon nobody did outside of the Soviet Union. But that's not all. The kick was that all those types of rubles were not convertible into each other, there was not even a ratio for accounting purposes."

"Good God! How did you do the budgeting then?"

"Simple. We added them all up. Many enterprises used all four types of rubles in their business. Some equipment came from the West, some from the Comecon, some materials from other enterprises. And the payroll was paid too. So, in the budget it was all added together and labeled as rubles."

"I hope you're not pulling my leg, Nick. But how did you do business like that?"

"We didn't. There was no business here as you know it in the West. It was very simple, actually. You get your plan from the ministry, negotiate it down, if you can, and fulfill it, if you can. Ship your product where you were told to, get your load of paper rubles to meet the payroll, and that's the end of it."

"Nick, swear it's true. I still can't believe it."

"I swear it. You better believe it. You need to know the real story," he chuckled, "not the analysis of your experts."

My God! And we listened to all our "experts" from the fucking CIA and others. With a straight face they went on about something like a "one tenth of one percent change" in a particular line of the Soviets' budget and drew conclusions that our major policy decisions were based on.

"So, you're telling me that you didn't really know your budget and didn't really have one?"

"Precisely. And we didn't need to. We had objectives to achieve; we had plans to fulfill. We had resources, manpower and money to play with. That's all."

Cyrus was stunned. He thought for a while, trying to digest what he just learned. He shook his head, forcing himself to return to the task at hand.

"All right. I guess, at least we're lucky here that we only have to deal with transactions with the West."

"That's for sure."

"Tell me then, what was the relationship of the ministries with the 'foreign' banks?"

"Indirect. It wasn't like every ministry had its own bank. Those few banks each served several ministries."

"So, the balances were kept by the ministries?"

"Sometimes, but not necessarily. The ministries fulfilled the plan, they stated their needs, and that's it. It wasn't their business to control the revenues."

"But who was running the show, then?"

"The Gosplan did. The State Planning Commission. In a routine way. They tried to balance the act. But the real master was the Central Committee of the Communist Party. They gave the orders, they stated objectives. They could intervene at any moment, at any moment take any money, or anything else for that matter."

"So, they could order any transfer, and nobody would ask them why?"

"Not only that, they could order that done with no records left. So, at best, you can have a record 'CC order.' Sometimes, nothing at all. They could order the previous record erased, or even conceal that the money had been received in the first place."

"How could they cook the books?"

"Very simple. We have a lot of pages missing from the books."

At least this is something. If we have a missing page, we can get a close fix on the date. Obviously, they had their favorite Western banks. Going to those banks and looking up those dates might provide a clue. Thank God, those banks must have their side of the transaction records.

"All right. The next thing we have to do is take a look at those books with missing records, whether it's a torn page, or anything else."

Nick marked his notebook.

Step by step, they started mapping their strategy.

A week later Cyrus was totally frustrated. There were no results. Clues showed up, just to disappear in the quagmire of the communist past. Cyrus had a small list of suspect banks, but he knew how difficult it would be to get the records from those banks, and how long it would take.

One day Nick took Cyrus to a "friend's country house" to meet Dronov. Cyrus quickly recognized all the attributes of a KGB safe house.

The General was upbeat and friendly.

"Hello, Cyrus. It seems like eternity since we met last. I just did not want to bother you. It wasn't a lack of interest."

"Hello, Yuri. I appreciate the free hand you gave me. Unfortunately, I have nothing encouraging to report so far. Whatever leads we got quickly vanished with the missing records."

"Well, no surprise to me, you know. But I take it you are leaving no stone unturned."

"Trying not to. We seem to need a fresh approach. I'd like to take this opportunity to ask you a few questions."

"Shoot."

"You knew that system inside-out. Can you name all the possible ways that the funds could be transferred abroad? Regardless of whether it is relevant or not."

Dronov chuckled. "That could be close to committing an act of treason, under certain circumstances. Let's say, I can provide you with the theoretically possible ways."

"Deal."

"One is a simple transfer from an account in a foreign bank to another foreign bank. Another one would be to sell a commodity to a Western company and deposit the proceeds straight into a secret account. The third would be to physically transfer gold, platinum, or diamonds to a depository at a bank abroad. The fourth one would be to transport foreign currency in the same manner. The fifth one would be to transport objects of art from national depositories abroad and sell them. The sixth would be to do the same with nuclear material or chemical weapons to certain parties, eager for this kind of stuff and able to pay. That's about all I can think of at the moment."

"How about making a deal with a large drug cartel, South American or Asian, to provide delivery and laundering capabilities in return for money deposited abroad?"

Dronov laughed. "Is it a guess, or do you know something, Cyrus?"

"Just heard some rumors a while back."

"Possible, but I personally think it's unlikely."

"Why?"

"In this case you don't solve your problem. The problem is laundering large chunks of money. They didn't need the money; they needed to transfer it quietly. Drug dealers have exactly the same problem themselves. How could they help each other?"

"Well, it's logical. So, you're saying that this kind of activity did not take place?"

Dronov was clearly uncomfortable. "I'd rather stop going any further into this. I can just tell you that in intelligence you try to keep all the doors open. You never know what you'll need tomorrow. But on the scale we're talking about, it does not make sense."

"All right. Let's look into the possibilities you've just mentioned. Transferring funds from one foreign bank to another is what we're looking into already. The second one is a commodity sale. Can we trace that through the ministries?"

"We already did. The amounts shipped are known. The amounts paid are not. They're in the bank's records that you are studying."

"I see. What about shipments of gold and diamonds? On the one hand, it takes a good planeload of gold for just half a billion dollars. So, we're talking a total of two four hundred plane loads. A lot of people involved to transport it, and a lot of rumors. On the other hand, half a billion dollars is still a lot of money." Cyrus remembered some references in the KGB computer files about such sums and wanted to check the level of Dronov's candor.

"We traced several flights like that to Switzerland and to the Far East. Then, we lost their tracks."

"All right. How about diamonds?"

" Diamonds are easier to transport, but they are more difficult to sell. The market would be saturated."

"True. I remember, though, that Mr. Oppenheimer of DeBeers was called out of retirement as an extraordinary measure, and came to Moscow for no known reason, spent a few days here, and went back happily into his retirement."

Dronov was surprised. "You're really well informed, Cyrus."

"That's part of my job."

"Well, there is something there. I suspect a collateralized loan. We cannot prove anything so far, and we're looking into it. I doubt you can help us there. At any rate, it could only be a portion of the whole thing."

"So, you want me to stay away from it?"

Dronov looked Cyrus in the eye. "Please."

"All right. How about a shipment of currency?"

"Practically impossible to find. Again, it could only be a fraction of the total. Once again, you cannot possibly help here."

"And, finally, nuclear materials."

Dronov's face turned grim. "We could not find any of that business. If it's true, we all have much bigger problems than chasing money. None of those folks know how to maintain it, forget about a possible use. I don't even want to think about it."

"As a banker, I don't care. As a human being, I must say that somebody had better."

There was quiet for a while. Then Cyrus broke the silence. "So, we're back at square one."

"Looks like it." Dronov paused. "Do you have anything at all, Cyrus, any tiny clues?"

"I have a list of suspect banks in the West, the traditional bankers so to speak. And suspicious dates around the times the records disappeared."

"That's something."

"Not really. Believe me, it will take a long, long time to get into those banks and to compare the two lists against each other. If it can be done at all."

"All right. Any suggestions?"

"I'd like to ask you a few more questions. Who was responsible for those transfers?"

"The General Secretary, of course. Gorbatov."

"He wouldn't do it himself, would he?"

How about those two suicides?

"Cyrus, it's a dead end. And, once again, it's outside of your field of expertise."

"Well, then I have to keep digging until I hit a brick wall, I guess."

"Cyrus, I respect your persistence. I also respect your professionalism. I also happen to believe that if you don't give up, something will come your way. I don't know what, how and when, but it will."

I hope so.

"I wish I was as optimistic as you are."

The rest of the meeting was dull. They agreed to meet in a week and left as they came, separately.

On the way to the hotel Cyrus' mood brightened when he thought of Laura, and then sank again. *Yes, Laura.*

He knew that what he had done was subject to an unconditional anathema in his profession. Having an affair with a suspected opposition intelligence agent could be condoned only under extreme circumstances, and strictly under the condition of no emotional involvement. By now he knew all too well that this was not the case.

He was emotionally involved. Deeply involved. He loved her, he adored her to the point that he was performing his tasks on autopilot. He was certain that it was mutual, but that was not much solace.

During the past week their mutual affection and relations had accelerated with the speed and inexorability of a hurricane. They both thought of nothing else, felt nothing else when together. And while they were separate each was constantly present in the other's subconscious. The situation was becoming unbearable, but Cyrus had passed the point of trying to find a solution. He just swam with the current, and the current was as hot as flowing lava.

When Cyrus was not working they spent all their time tiogether. Laura showed him Moscow, the way only a true Muscovite can show it to a dear friend. They never discussed business. Many times Cyrus caught a fleeting shadow on Laura's face, which passed quickly without a trace. He knew exactly what it was: a mirror reflection of his own dilemma.

When he returned to the hotel, Laura was in the room. She was dressed in a warm sweater and black slacks. She kissed him, leaning in with her whole body, but this time he felt more of a gentle sadness than passion.

"Hello, darling. I just came in." She paused. Then her voice turned unnaturally joyful. "How about a short walk. The weather is so unusually good for this time of year that it's hard to pass up."

Suddenly, for the first time alone with Laura, Cyrus felt his autopilot kick in. "Great idea. I don't even want to change."

They went outside and walked to Kuznetski Most, turned right, then left and came to Theatrical Square. Laura did not say a word during the fifteen minutes that they made their way slowly along the crowded streets. Laura went to an empty bench near a dry fountain in front of the Bolshoi Theater. They sat down. For a minute nothing was said. Then Laura finally spoke.

"Cyrus, darling, it's unbearably hard for me, but I must tell you something which can…," she stumbled, took a deep breath, and went on, "Oh, God, I don't know what it can do, but I cannot go on like this any longer."

Cyrus squeezed a smile. "Oh, the devil is not as frightening as it's painted." An old Russian proverb.

"It is." She took another deep breath, and plunged headlong in.

"Do you remember you asked me before if I was the most beautiful KGB agent? A semi-joke every foreigner makes here? Remember that I just laughed it off?"

"Yes."

"Well, it's true."

She saw Cyrus open his mouth and quickly went on. "Don't say anything now. Please. Let me finish, while I still have the strength."

Cyrus just nodded.

"It's not the KGB. The KGB split a while ago. I am an officer of the SVR, the Foreign Intelligence Service. All the other things I told you are true. I do have a degree in literature, I am a reporter, I do work for the *Komsomolskaya Pravda*, I do write articles, and so on. But I also went through two years of special training, I know a little English, and I am a lieutenant, senior grade."

She made a gesture to stop him again, as if he was going to interrupt her, inhaled deeply, and continued. "It's not like you in America see it. It's not about persecutions, it's just intelligence gathering. It may be a disgraceful profession in America, but here it is a very respectable one. Nobody forced me to join; I did it voluntarily, out of a sense of patriotism, if you will. It's not that I'm a 'sparrow' sent to seduce you. I am investigating the same matter as you, and I was tasked to watch you to see if you find something and try to hide it from us. In that case I'm to find out what it is and pass it on to my superiors. What I just told you amounts to treason, but at this particular moment that is my least concern. I've just told you all this because my conscience made me, despite my professional responsibilities. You can despise me for what I am, you can hate me for it, but it's true. I will love you no matter what, and nobody can take that away from me. But the last thing I want is to enjoy your love under false premises. If you decide to dump me, I will understand, and I will not blame you."

Laura cast her eyes down. Then, with visible effort, she looked at Cyrus with great intensity. Cyrus smiled. The warmth of that smile answered Laura's unspoken question.

"I don't remember revealing that I love you. And you forgot to mention it too."

The tension made Laura react slowly. First, she kept staring at him, then she burst into almost hysterical laughter, inspired by both fear and relief. At that moment, she knew she had not lost Cyrus. And that was what mattered most. When the outburst ended, she had tears in her eyes.

Unable to hide her happiness, she said through the tears, "I don't consider it to be a revelation that true love does not require words. And if you deny my assertion, I'll call you a liar."

Cyrus put his arm around Laura's shoulders, pulled her close, and whispered into her ear, "This was the most unusual admission of love I have ever heard of."

They sat in silence for several minutes. Then Cyrus asked, "How come you never discussed business with me? You totally neglected your duty."

Laura detected Cyrus' joking tone. "That's because you're a sex maniac. Every time we're alone, we end up in bed."

"First of all, that's entirely your fault. You're too wonderful. Secondly, you never complained. Does that tell you something?"

"That was not a complaint, it was a compliment."

They looked at each other and walked briskly back to the hotel.

After dinner in the hotel restaurant they went for a walk, this time toward Red Square. Suddenly, Laura asked, "Cyrus, why are you doing this? For the money?"

"I don't really know. Money is part of it, but, frankly, there are many ways to make money, and this is certainly not the most efficient. Dronov talked me into it. Adventure, perhaps. Why?"

"I was wondering about it all along. You never looked like a treasure hunter."

"Let me explain. I've hated communism all my life. I still hate it -- for what it did to Russia, to many countries round the world, for the many millions of people it killed, many more than any other political system. In my view, the even bigger evil is that it corrupted the souls of many whom it did not kill. Somehow, a lot of people think that that's all over now. That's not true by any stretch of imagination. Communism is not just an ideology. It's a mentality. It is still alive. In Russia, for instance, it is still the prevailing mentality, and it pervades all aspects of life. It will take a couple of generations, at best, to get rid of it."

"I know it. It's horrible beyond description. That was one of the reasons I went to work for intelligence. I was hoping to change that, to accelerate the process."

Cyrus nodded, and continued. "So, somehow, I feel that these stolen billions are a continuation of communism, an attempt to reincarnate it. I can't prove it, I can't explain it, but I strongly suspect it. This is one of the reasons I'm in this game."

"I understand. You know, the more I work for the SVR, the more I feel that what you've just said is true, true to the extent that sometimes I feel despair and helplessness. That mentality is still with us, the country is being looted wholesale and piecemeal. I don't know what to do. I want to fight, but who? The windmills?"

Cyrus had never suspected the depth of Laura's ideological despair.

"Since you asked me about this treasure hunt, I can tell you that the most important thing about it is not just to find it, but to return it to the country openly, so that people know about it and the politicians have less of a chance to misuse it. In other words, it corresponds perfectly with what you just said about the current system."

Laura became almost agitated. "That's exactly what bothers me. Do you know that the whole setup for you is to prevent exactly that. To get the money quietly. And only the devil knows how these billions are going to be used."

"That's what I'm determined to prevent. I'll be damned if I let it happen the way they want."

"Cyrus, darling, you don't know these people. You don't know how ruthless they can be. You cannot even imagine the danger for you."

Cyrus smiled. He was touched by Laura's desire to warn him, to protect him.

Laura was offended. "Why are you smiling? You think I'm a weak woman? I've been trained, well trained."

"No, my dear. I'm just smiling at the irony of the whole situation. It looks like we have no choice but to work together for the same goal."

Laura thought for a moment and nodded. "Yes. But regardless, even if I did have a choice, I'd make the same decision anyway."

I'd choose for you to be far away, in a safe place. I'd rather have no guardian angel than have you in danger in that role.

He gently squeezed her shoulder. "So, we're partners?"

"Partners."

Chapter 11

The partnership worked. He was amazed by Laura's transformation when they discussed business issues. More precisely, he was amazed by Laura. One moment she was an irresistible beauty, a witty socialite with the slightly arrogant confidence of a society lioness, the next moment she was a sexless, sarcastic, seen-it-all reporter, and then she could turn into an insecure girl, vulnerable and even desperate for love and home.

From Laura he got a good handle on the inner workings of the Central Committee in its final years in power, who had been involved in handling its money for confidential matters, and the mechanics of its interaction with the bank. Yet knowing all that still did not enable them to zero in on anything concrete. None of those channels could handle money of such magnitude.

But within a week Cyrus felt that at last he was heading in the right direction. Laura's knowledge, complemented by Cyrus' own experience at the bank, provided a solid platform for a final assault. Cyrus did not know where and when that assault would take place, but he had an instinct that told him he was close.

During one of their frequent walks through the central Moscow streets, Cyrus summarized the situation.

"So, speaking of our little endeavor, we still don't have a concrete target."

"True."

"Two people we are interested in are dead: Georgy Pavlov, who was in charge of the Party finances for twenty years until 1983, and Nikolay Kruchina, his successor until the communists' departure from power."

"Yes, but the fact that both of them 'committed suicide' by jumping out of windows within a few days of each other tells us something. It tells us that they mark the real trail."

"By the way, what's the significance of jumping out of a window? Is it some kind of a communist ritual? I mean, if somebody wanted to get rid of them, why so primitively? I always heard that the KGB was pretty resourceful in this regard."

Laura laughed. "No, there is no such ritual. I guess, somebody wanted to post a message, not just to kill them."

"What message might that be?"

"If you know something, don't even think of trying to be cute. We're serious, and this is what will happen to you."

"I see. Then we have to find whoever who worked for them."

"But this is precisely the point, Cyrus. That's why I had so much trouble finding anyone who knows anything even remotely connected to handling money in the Central Committee. Besides, that money, I'm sure, was handled through some unconventional channels, not through Kruchina's subordinates."

"Laura, I think I'm on to something. Look, why would they kill Pavlov, who left the job two years before Gorbatov even came to power? He certainly didn't handle the transfer and, most likely, didn't know about it."

"That's a good question."

"Because he knew where the money had been parked abroad and how much."

"You're right. There is no other reason. But it doesn't cover all the money. Some of it was transferred hastily at the very end, in 1991."

"Well then, we have something. The money consisted of three parts. One, was stashed away abroad over a long period of time, and it's either still there, or it's been moved and hidden again."

Laura interrupted him. "It was hidden again. I know their style. No way would they leave it in an old place."

"All right. The second part was transferred from within Russia over four years, during a relatively quiet time. Probably very carefully. And the third part was transferred in last few months, hastily." Cyrus recalled those reports of some planeloads of poorly packed gold shipped to Switzerland.

"I think you're right. This means that our best chance at unearthing the money is with the latest, less strategic transactions.

"The point is, Kruchina seems to be the bottleneck. We have to find people who were around him."

Laura sighed. "I know. But I've exhausted…," she suddenly

stopped, and after a short pause went on, "You know, I've got an idea. One of my friends' sisters is married to Kruchina's nephew. That's a lead I never thought of."

Cyrus looked at Laura. She explained, "I have a dacha, a country house. For many years the same gang of kids went there every summer. We grew up together."

"I see. You never mentioned that."

"Well, actually, it's my uncle's house. I was very close to him and spent many summers at his dacha. My parents did not have one."

She told him a few stories about her childhood times at the dacha.

Cyrus heard her, but was preoccupied with the task at hand. "Laura, I'd like to ask you a question. Very general. Don't analyze anything, just give me your reflex reaction. In this country, if you're head of state and can't really trust anyone, who would you choose to trust if you had to trust someone? I mean what category of people."

Laura thought for a few seconds. "The KGB cipher clerks."

"Why?"

"Traditionally, they are a caste, a special caste. Keepers of the state secrets. They had two masters, the KGB on the one hand, but in some respects only the Central Committee on the other. They never talk. They've always been considered the most reliable, most loyal group. They undergo the strictest selection process of all, the strictest training of all. Nobody knows what they do, even in generalities."

"All right. Then what is the most secure place in their domain?"

Laura laughed. "You know, this is a really funny coincidence. My uncle is the boss of that place."

" The same uncle you've just mentioned?"

"Yes. The place is in Yoshkar-Ola."

"Yosh what?"

"Yoshkar-Ola, the capital of Mariy Autonomous Republic."

"Where is that?"

"Cyrus, you should brush up on your geography. North of Kazan."

"Good God! What's your uncle doing there?"

"They have a top-secret installation for the government to move to there, in case of a nuclear war. It has a long-term depository for ciphers."

Laura told Cyrus what she knew about the installation, located just outside of Yoshkar-Ola, and about the compound where her uncle lived.

"What's his name?"

"Portnov. Nikolay Portnov, KGB major. Want to visit? I can make an introduction, but there is no way they'd let you go there. But if you do, my uncle is going to be in big trouble." Laura smiled at the ridiculousness of the idea.

Cyrus was uncommitted. "Let's think about it. Nothing is impossible as far as I am concerned."

"Sure." Laura did not take the idea seriously.

They changed the subject and turned toward the hotel.

Two days later Laura could barely wait till the end of dinner. They let the car go and strolled through small streets of old Moscow toward the hotel. Laura was excited as never before. Somehow, through someone, she had discovered an old lady who had been Kruchina's personal secretary for many years. She had retired shortly after his death. Laura went to see her and found out that Kruchina had gone to his dacha the morning of the day Gorbatov left for his Crimea vacation, just before the August 1991 coup. Kruchina mentioned to her that Gorbatov was going to drop by Kruchina's dacha on his way to the airport.

Laura talked the lady into meeting "a good personal friend," that is Cyrus, the next day for further discussions and some serious money. The lady agreed, given her affection for Laura and severe financial difficulties. That meeting was to take place tonight.

Cyrus was trying to figure out a way of getting rid of the surveillance without arousing too much suspicion. He had often noted surveillance in the street and was genuinely puzzled. If they had Nick, Laura, and the drivers with him all the time, why would they need the surveillance? That surveillance was very professional, very good indeed. They always stayed far behind, changed people and cars all the time. Cyrus knew he could not afford any rude break. That would reveal too much, and his status would be immediately reevaluated, and the consequences would be severe.

The telephone on his desk rang. Cyrus answered.

He was surprised to hear English. "Hello. Do not say any names. Do you recognize my voice?"

That was Laura. That was the first time that Cyrus had heard her speaking English. Her accent was not too heavy, but distinct. Given the different language her voice sounded different. But it was unmistakably Laura. She obviously knew that since Cyrus had always spoken Russian, they didn't have an English speaker listening now. It would take them a while to translate.

"Da." In Russian. With the corner of his eye Cyrus noticed Nick at his desk, reading.

"Listen to me carefully. You are in grave danger. Your only chance is now. Go to the basement of the building. In the boiler room there is a service door to the outside, in the back. You just need to break a small lock. The security system is off now. Do not take your car. Do you remember the place where we formed our partnership?"

"Da."

"Go there and wait for me. Do you remember my car?"

"Da."

"Be at the walkway when I turn off the bridge."

"Spacebo."

"I love you. Don't answer."

"Poka." 'Bye in Russia. Cyrus hung up.

Cyrus' brain was working full speed. He took a diskette, put it in the computer, and entered the command. The hard disk started clicking, copying the files to the diskette. He turned to Nick.

"Nick, that girl on the second floor, Tanya, just called."

"Oh?"

"She's all excited about something. Did you ask her to search for something?"

"Yeah, but that was a while ago."

Cyrus glanced at the computer. The copying was complete.

"Can you go find out what it's all about? Probably nothing, as usual. Meanwhile, I'll finish something on my computer that I want to show you."

"No problem."

The second Nick left, Cyrus took the diskette out of the computer and put it in his pocket. He grabbed his coat from the hanger and rushed out. In the corridor, he went to the fire exit leading to the basement. Cyrus did not see anyone. He found a small piece of pipe near the door, and in no time Cyrus was in the back yard of the building. He walked to the corner of the building. Luckily, the trolley was coming to a stop. Cyrus ran, and jumped in. A look outside assured him that no one was following, everything was quiet. The trolley rolled passed Cyrus' waiting car. He did not sit down. Two stops later he left the trolley and slid into a vacant taxi.

What could possibly have gone wrong? The only thing plausible is tonight's meeting. Well, when you've got to go, you've got to go. Now, what about Laura? She's burned, no question about it. She has to go with me. All right. Laura will find a place to hide for a while. The only trip I have to make is to the cache.

Cyrus changed taxis, and thirty minutes later he was near the Rossia hotel. Its main entrance was actually a large deck overlooking the Moscow river and the Moscvoretsky bridge. The steps in front of the entrance to the hotel led down to the embankment where he had had that key conversation with Laura, after walking from Theatrical Square.

Cyrus went to the railing. The pick-up place was just fifty feet below and right in front of him. This way he'd see Laura approaching and see if she was being followed. Not finding him there, she'd go around the block and he'd get in on the second pass.

Cyrus wasn't surprised to realize that he liked the idea that Laura had to go with him. At that moment, he saw Laura's car. A small, mustard-colored Lada, the Russian variation of a Fiat-124. Laura used it almost all the time she wasn't with Cyrus. She had given him a ride a couple of times. Cyrus was amused at how proud she was to be a good driver. He hadn't appreciated that women drivers were still not too common in Russia.

Laura stopped in the right lane at the traffic light on the other end of the bridge. The left window half opened, as always. "To keep the windows clear." A light military truck stopped behind her. In the second lane Cyrus saw a heavy Chaika, the favorite limousine of the second tier of the former Soviet elite. The traffic light turned green, and Laura accelerated. She knew that she was going to make a sharp right turn at the end of the bridge, so she did not drive too fast. The next thing Cyrus saw made him freeze.

The Chaika drove in the next lane, just behind Laura. Then, it began overtaking her. But the military truck behind Laura kept accelerating hard and was closing fast. At that moment Cyrus understood everything. *Go! Go! Gas to the floor!* He did not shout, and she could not hear.

The Chaika overtook Laura at the end of the bridge and made a sharp threatening move to the right. To avoid a collision, Laura instinctively turned the wheel to the right. She probably did not even have time to hit the brakes. The military truck, moving slightly to the left, hit the left side of the Lada's rear bumper with the right side of its heavy front bumper.

The tiny Lada effortlessly became airborne on the curb, went over the walkway, narrowly missing two pedestrians, and through the rails. The Chaika went on without slowing down. The military truck quickly made a U-turn and sped in the opposite direction.

His blood running cold, Cyrus saw Laura's Lada making its rainbow flight. It plunged into the murky, icy water of the Moscow river, the roof hitting the water first. A surprisingly big splash and a dull thump were all the Lada's impact with the water produced.

As he ran down the stairs, Cyrus saw large bubbles surfacing in the middle of the river. When he stopped at the rails of the embankment, all he saw was the steady current of the freezing Moscow river. He felt nauseous.

.A crowd was gathering quickly.

"Poor guy, they'll never find his body before spring. Drunk, I suppose. Oh, they speed like crazy, these young people, all the time," muttered the old woman standing beside Cyrus.

Cyrus turned.

Something clicked in Cyrus' brain. His training took over. *Get away from this area. Fast.*

He sped up the stairs to the main entrance. It took a tremendous effort not to turn. On the other hand, he did not need to. The graceful rainbow arc of the Lada was now burned into his brain for the rest of his life. He hadn't suffered nightmares before, but now he knew what his nightmare would be.

Cyrus took a taxi. "Kalanchevka." That was a square, housing three rail stations. His brain was working at full speed again. Clothing. The first thing to do. Then what? An exfiltration would require a few days' wait. Where would they not expect me to hide? Slums. Hide in the slums. OK. The second thing is the cache and a message to John, Cyrus sighed, to advise him of a full-blown failure.

He got out of the taxi and went to the Yaroslavsky train station. Without wasting any time he proceeded to the restroom. Large, stinky and dirty, it was full of men shaving or otherwise taking care of their personal hygiene. Cyrus looked at the crowd.

One man, about his size, attracted Cyrus' attention. He was obviously just off the train. He wouldn't have a half-empty bag if he was leaving Moscow. His bag would be full, and, most likely, he'd have several. So, he should have some money. And, he wasn't too drunk, just a little bit. Worn and dirty as it was, his attire was what Cyrus needed. He rubbed his eyes hard. Now they were red. He made a little disarray with his clothing too. Now Cyrus was well dressed, but drunk.

The man was washing his hands. Cyrus moved next to him. He splashed his face, and moaned. "Oh God, what a hangover."

Etiquette required sympathy. "Yeah, in America they have pills for that. Here, no way. Just another drink."

"No money, see. I spent it all."

"Hmm." That was an unwelcome pitch. Against etiquette. Now the man had the right to become rude to Cyrus.

Suddenly, Cyrus looked at him. "Look, I see your wardrobe could use an upgrade." And he glanced at his own coat.

The man obviously didn't know what cashmere was and how much it was worth, but he knew enough to see an opportunity. "Well, I don't suppose it's worth a bottle, but I can give you one."

"No way. Two."

"No."

Cyrus was pushy. He needed two bottles, for currency. "How about if I add the suit and the shoes?"

The man was wondering how far he could push his luck.

"And the hat too."

"Deal."

They went to adjoining stalls and made the exchange. Cyrus kept his underwear. Buying an old bag on the sidewalk just outside the station was no problem, and five minutes later Cyrus was on his way, making sure nobody was on his tail.

Making his way through the station, he looked at the train schedule. The first line told him the Kazan express was leaving in ten minutes. Cyrus stopped. Laura's uncle in Yoshkar-Ola suddenly came to mind.

They'll fish me out in Moscow. Chances I can stay undetected are too slim..

The temptation was there. Suddenly, he saw the tiny Lada on its deadly rainbow arc.

Oh, what the hell. I'd rather fight to the end.

Also, although he didn't want to admit it, Cyrus didn't want to return to John empty-handed. He didn't even want to think about that.

Cyrus turned sharply, and went to the cashier. Amazingly, tickets were still available, and ten minutes later he had the cheapest ticket on the train and was lying in his berth, heading to Kazan.

Chapter 12

Ten minutes passed before there was no one in the observable vicinity. Cyrus hesitated for a few more seconds. What if he's hostile? Not much to fall back on. Well, that's been my modus operandi lately. At least I'm sure he's alone. What the hell. Go.

Cyrus left his cover and moved to a small house. He walked along the edge of the concrete walkway without leaving any footprints in the slush either on the walkway or on the grass. Then he made two jumps, first touching down on the edge of the top step of the front porch stairs, then bouncing off onto the small front door mat. He glanced back. No footprints. Still no one around. He carefully knocked on the door. No answer. He knocked again, just a little louder. Footsteps moving toward the door were a welcome relief. Hopefully.

"Who's there?"

"I'm a friend of Laura's, here just by chance."

The door opened. A short man in a rather ordinary wool warm-up suit and slippers looked surprised. Thinning gray hair made him look older than he actually was. "My God, have you walked from town, or what?"

He ushered Cyrus in, closed the door and quickly helped him out of his soaked raincoat. Cyrus took off his hat and bent down to fiddle with his shoe laces, thinking of how to start a conversation.

"What weather you have down here. There must be something to compensate for it."

"I wish. Come in." The man gestured toward a room down a short hallway. They passed the kitchen entrance on the left and stopped at the entrance of the small living room. Thick curtains covered a window facing the street. A couple of chairs, a sofa and a shelf along the right wall with books and memorabilia were complemented by a low table in between and a Sony TV set in the corner. Cyrus also noticed quite a few objects of foreign origin, but none of them looked very new. He turned to the host and extended his hand.

"I'm Kirill Turov. Just came from Moscow." That was true. Almost. Turov was his mother's maiden name.

"Glad to meet you. Vladimir Portnov, as you know, I guess. Have a seat."

Cyrus glanced at the chairs and chose the least worn one. Besides, an open book rested on the lamp table near the other one. If you don't want to subconsciously irritate your host, avoid taking his favorite chair.

"So, how was your trip?"

"Not too bad, I think. I've had better ones, though."

Cyrus noticed Laura's photo in an elaborate wood carved frame. She was laughing with that laugh he wouldn't forget for the rest of his life. He clenched his teeth. The next question was what he was waiting for and what he was afraid of.

"Well, how's Laura? Still the same tomboy? It's about time she settled down, you know."

"Not good." Cyrus lowered his head. It took him more effort than he'd anticipated to raise his face again and look Vladimir straight in the eye. The silence was so tense at that moment that the words he was barely able to squeeze out were almost redundant.

"She is dead."

Vladimir's face turned pale, and his lips and eyes narrowed. He slowly leaned his back against the chair. Very slowly and calmly he asked, "What happened?"

Cyrus did not answer. Vladimir caught his glance toward Laura's picture. He knew that Cyrus' silence meant something extraordinary, something bad. After a long, long half a minute, Vladimir sighed heavily. "She was like a daughter to me."

"I know." They sat there, each sunk in his own memories.

Finally, Vladimir rose and, stepping heavily, walked to the kitchen. The refrigerator door clicked, and he came back with a bottle of vodka and two glasses. Without a word, he poured both full, gave one to Cyrus and they drank, bottoms up.

"Vladimir, she was murdered."

Vladimir's face hardened. Slowly, he turned to Cyrus.

"Who?" Just one word, but it contained everything: sorrow, fury, and a frightening promise of revenge.

Cyrus paused, and said firmly looking in his eye, "KGB." He deliberately avoided the new names of the old outfit. This way Vladimir's response was more telling. It was almost ideological. He saw Vladimir's fists clench.

Vladimir was visibly struggling to control himself. His movements and speech became slow. Deliberately slow. Cyrus felt the enormous emotional struggle in him.

Almost casually, Vladimir said, "I want to know everything." That calmness bordering on casualness was usually the result of being slightly too successful at controlling oneself.

At that moment Cyrus knew that Vladimir would be a very patient listener, for whom time did not matter much, so he wanted to make sure he didn't miss any detail that might conceivably increase the certainty of Vladimir's revenge.

"You have to know something before that. First, you might want to know who I am."

"If it matters." He was a gentleman. That meant "If you want to tell me, fine, but I understand that you might have your own reasons and your own problems. It is not important to me."

"I prefer to deal with our guards down. So we can see each other's faces. I know who you are, so let's get even."

"Go ahead." He looked at Cyrus with interest.

"First of all, I'm an American."

This time Vladimir's face showed emotions. Mixed emotions. "Shit. You sound like an old boy from Peter."

Cyrus was glad to notice that Vladimir used an old nickname for St. Petersburg, not its communist name of Leningrad. He smiled. "Well, you're partially right. My mother's family is from Peter. Emigrated during the Revolution.

Vladimir did not respond. Stonefaced again, waiting for explanations, now surely in order.

Cyrus wanted to claim some psychological territory right now, no matter how small it might be. "Well, does it make sense for me to continue, or would you rather kick me out right now?"

"Do you know where I work?"

"Yes."

Vladimir nodded. He made another trip to the kitchen and returned with a plate of pickles. They had another drink, this time followed by a pickle.

"I reckon this business will take a while." He paused, "You must be hungry, Kirill."

"Not much." In Russian culture that meant "I'm starving." Cyrus wanted to give a sigh of relief, but he knew he couldn't afford one.

Vladimir was the one who sighed. "Let's fix something. I'm hungry too." They went to the kitchen. Cyrus sat and watched Vladimir warming up a roast. His motions were very mechanical. He was deep in his own thoughts, somewhere far away.

"Mind eating in the kitchen?"

"Of course not."

They consumed the meat, accompanied by potatoes, and had another drink, all virtually in silence. Cyrus knew all too well that he couldn't refuse to drink and, surely, he was glad that he had had some practice time in Moscow. Otherwise, at this rate he'd soon be under the table.

During tea, Vladimir turned to Cyrus. "You were close to her." The sound of this half-question intimated that in his thoughts Vladimir was somewhere else.

"Yes, very."

Vladimir's voice suddenly turned firm, even terse. He was back. "Now tell me what happened. Exactly."

For an hour and a half he told Vladimir about the General's approach in New York and what happened in Moscow. He gave a truthful account, with the exception of anything related to John Porter and the operation "Trojan Horse." As far as Vladimir was concerned, he was just an investment banker who had gotten more excitement than he'd bargained for.

Several times during the story Vladimir shook his head. The end of the story came as a painful reminder that they both would never see Laura again. Vladimir's face showed intense interest during the story, and at the Moscow part it turned grim again. Cyrus was almost sorry that he was putting the man through this. For a while they were silent again. *Silence seems to be the theme of the day. Well, sometimes it's more eloquent than any speech.*

Finally, Vladimir spoke. "So, did she start helping you when she fell in love?"

That's a pretty cheap trap. You can do better than that.

"No, earlier. She told me that she felt that I was doing something good for Russia." That was true.

And she also felt that I was defenseless. Back then it was all right, but now I feel really guilty about that.

Cyrus did not anticipate the next turn of conversation. Vladimir interrupted his thoughts. "How did you, in an emigre community in America, perceive communism and communists?"

Cyrus shrugged, "We hated both."

"But you didn't seem to do much about it, did you?" A slight sarcasm in Vladimir's voice was obvious, but Cyrus felt something else there too.

"Well, there were a couple of reasons for that. Russian émigrés were so entangled in little squabbles among themselves, that there was no way even to think about any sort of unity or a united front. Russians possess a very interesting trait. Have you ever noticed that Russians fight best against each other? Look at all of Russian history. There was no 'external' war where Russians displayed such courage, selflessness and determination, and such little mercy, as in a fight with other Russians. They couldn't even agree on their first Tsar and opted for inviting a Swede." He took a breath, "That was one reason. The only exception being if Russia is attacked. That was partly why the communists won the Revolution and the Civil War in the first place. They were the only truly united force in 1917."

Vladimir smiled. "Interesting. I've never thought about it, but you've definitely got a point here."

"And there's a second reason: there were too many people in the West who benefited from communism in Russia, directly or indirectly. Liberal demagoguery, which by the way was perfected by the communists, took its toll. When most people in the West finally understood what was going on, they realized that they were in danger too, and by then it was too late. The country that had been kidnapped by the criminals had become too strong, and could not undo the evil without the famous 'mutually assured destruction'."

"That is hard to believe."

"It's true. I can give you a perfect example. Have you ever heard of Ambassador Davis?"

"No."

"That idiot was American Ambassador to Moscow, and he returned to America in 1938. He held a press conference right on board the ship in New York harbor. You know what he said about the situation in the Soviet Union at the time? 'They are engaged in a very interesting experiment!' And he said this right at the height of Stalin's purges, at the time when the American people were trying to make up their minds about communism. Many were fascinated with the idea. You think he didn't know what was going on? Bullshit. He just had his own agenda. As did many others."

"Still, for me that's hard to understand. I can understand it if somebody is brought up in a communist society, bombarded with propaganda from the age of three, but I can't understand it from somebody who was raised in a country where he could read whatever he chooses."

"It's not that simple. In the seventies Lenin was voted by the United Nations as one of the great humanitarians of all times. Who did it? The Soviet Union with a dozen allies? No way! But the people who did it would now rather forget the whole thing. They are certainly not interested in taking responsibility for who knew what and when, and who did what and when."

Cyrus noticed that he was getting emotional. He paused. "Vladimir, why are you interested in all this stuff? It's too late anyway."

"Well, I'm just trying to sort things out for myself. Who is who and where I stand, that sort of thing."

Cyrus was about to try to turn the conversation closer to his point of view, but suddenly, Vladimir said, "Do you want to hear my story?"

"Of course."

"First of all, if anybody finds out that I have an American guest, I'll probably get shot."

"Come on, now? With the Cold War over?"

"Precisely. Do you know what I do?"

"Vaguely. I know that you are a KGB major and you have something to do with ciphers."

"Let me clarify. I was working in a cipher department. My career was going pretty well. Before being promoted I took an assignment abroad as a cipher clerk, to get some hard currency, you know. Posted in New York. There I committed the most horrible sin for a cipher clerk. So called double-enciphering."

"What's that?" interrupted Cyrus.

"Oh, that's when you use the so called one-time key twice. Then you make it possible for the enemy to decipher that portion of the telegram. The ultimate crime for a cipher clerk." He took a breath, and continued, "Well, they immediately sent me home. I got a Party reprimand, and was sent here to Yoshkar-Ola."

"Isn't that a bit harsh?"

"Maybe. I'd probably have been sent to another Directorate in Moscow, if not for my career."

"What was wrong with it?"

"I had been too good. See, I was competing on a par with the guy who later became the chief of the Directorate. We were both young, both majors back then. Now he's a general in Moscow, and I'm a major in Yoshkar-Ola, in a captain's slot."

"Well, it's tough when you've got such enemies."

"We weren't enemies, we were friends. Our wives were friends. But business is business, see. At least, in the KGB. So, he did me in."

He sighed, and continued, "Well, we came here. My wife, myself," he made a noticeable effort to continue, "and our son Dima. Dima went to a military academy, graduated with honors. Five months later he was killed in Afghanistan." He paused again. "My wife went right downhill after that. A year later she too was dead. Doctors didn't know why. I know, why. From grief. She never could quite grasp that Dima was dead."

Cyrus just shook his head. *And now this.*

"So, now I live alone here." He shrugged his shoulders, "I'm not sure that I live, though."

Cyrus did not know what to say. Vladimir went on, "So, after that my only hope in life was Laura. We were always very close. She's my sister's daughter, such a sweet little girl. And now she..."

Cyrus poured him another drink. Vladimir downed it without even noticing.

After a while Vladimir turned back to reality. He was calm. For anyone who knows anything about human nature this kind of calmness is by far more frightening than any threat. Men in this mode don't threaten. They kill. Without mercy.

"Now, Kirill, we have more or less leveled the field. Was she really helping you, or just.trying to protect you?"

"She was helping. After a while she told me that she was working for the KGB against me. And, she started helping me, saying that it was the right thing to do. That's when we came across some information leading here, she told me about you. She was going to see you and ask for your help."

"This sounds exactly like Laura. The right thing to do. No matter what the cost." He sighed, "Why is it the right thing to do, by the way?"

"Because, if I find the money, it will be officially returned to Russia, and its people will have a chance to make the government spend it for good purposes, for a change. On the other hand, if I don't find the money, it'll most likely be used by former communists for some evil goals. We don't know for what, but that only makes the threat greater."

Vladimir was thinking. "I think you're right. So be it. Let's make a deal. I'll try to help you to find the money, and you'll help me to find who murdered Laura. Those who actually did it are not important. I'll kill them anyway, but I really want the one who made the decision and gave the order."

"So do I."

It sounds almost too easy. Why isn't he verifying anything?

As if he were reading Cyrus' thoughts, Vladimir said, "Aren't you wondering why I seem to believe everything you've said?"

"A bit." Cyrus smiled, "I figured, you have your own ways to verify things. And, you don't have to hurry. I couldn't get too far from here, could I? So, you can have me for lunch any time if I lied or did something wrong."

"True. I like dealing with smart people."

The telephone rang.

Vladimir answered. He was listening without a word for about a minute, turned his face away from Cyrus. Then, he said, "Tanya, please, calm down. I have no words to describe what I feel, you know how much I loved her."

After a few minutes of listening, he said, "Well, you really need some rest. Promise me that you'll take some medicine right now and go to bed. We'll talk tomorrow. Is Ivan with you?"

"All right, then try to get some sleep and listen to him, promise?"

"Goodbye." He hung up and turned to Cyrus, "My sister, Laura's mother. They live in Kursk."

Cyrus did not say a word, just looked at Vladimir.

"The KGB called her to inform that Laura died in a car accident. They apologized that because of some mishap they couldn't find her parents' number in time for the funeral. She was buried today. Well, that's the first confirmation that you're right." He shook his head, "My sister is in total distress. I'm glad she has a good husband, and he's with her."

Cyrus just nodded.

"Well, I suggest we go to sleep, at least you must." He went to another small room off the foyer. "This is my study. The couch is pretty comfortable."

Cyrus was exhausted. He wasn't even interested in seeing what was in the room. *What the hell, if I haven't convinced him, I'm a dead man anyhow.* He was asleep the moment his head hit the pillow.

Despite his exhaustion, Cyrus awoke at six. He lay motionless for a few minutes. Everything was quiet. A truck passed by in the street. A neighbor tried to start his car and, finally, succeeded and drove away. There were no sounds in the house.

Well, it looks like I'm still in business. If they knew of me they'd have arrested me when I was tired, which was obvious last night. That means that I was convincing enough for Vladimir, but it is very dangerous to take it for granted. His soul is in turmoil, you never know how things will turn out.

He stood up and went to the living room. Vladimir was sitting in a chair, his head leaning on the high back. Cyrus slowly walked around. Vladimir's eyes were closed, but Cyrus knew he was not sleeping. Cyrus quietly sat on the sofa beside from the chair.

Without turning or even opening his eyes, Vladimir sighed, "Life is a strange thing, isn't it? You think that you've got nothing to lose anymore, and it proves you wrong right away."

Cyrus nodded, "That's for sure. It proves you wrong no matter what you think of it."

"Surprised that you're still here, not in jail?" Vladimir finally opened his eyes. He obviously did not sleep a minute during the night.

"Not really, but I was certainly glad to find that out."

"Why not?"

"Hard to say. Just a feeling. You would've carried yourself differently last night if that was on your mind."

Vladimir shrugged, "Go by feelings?"

"Do I have an alternative?" Cyrus' smile was soft, but suggestive of his cool awareness of his perilous situation.

"Let me ask you something, Kirill. Are you rich?"

Cyrus laughed, "I'm comfortable." He wasn't offended, knowing that this kind of question was acceptable in Russian culture.

"I mean, do you have to work to live comfortably?"

"No."

"Well, do you need more money to live more comfortably?"

Cyrus was amused by this line of interest. "Not really; however, extra money usually doesn't hurt. Why?"

"I'm just trying to figure out what the hell got you into this story. What's in it for you? Money? You seem to be well off and understand it. Fear? You don't seem to be that type. Adventure? It's just a puzzle for me."

Cyrus felt caught flat-footed. "It's funny you asked. I was thinking about the same thing on my way here and couldn't find the answer. Perhaps I was initially simply intrigued. Bumped into something that was very different from my routine. But then I got involved and found myself unable to make real progress, but also unable to drop it. The answer is that I don't really know. But why do you want to know?"

"Well, you want me to get involved. I was surprised to realize that I do want to get involved, and perhaps I'm looking for a justification. But I'm a very suspicious man; I wanted to know what motivates you and couldn't find the answer."

Cyrus was tempted to ask if Vladimir had found his own justification, but some instinct kept him from it. "Well, welcome to the club. We both feel that it's a crazy thing to try, that it's the right thing to do, and we don't know why."

"I think that you just gave a very good description of the situation. My justification last night was that it's good for Russia. See, since Gorbatov came to power, every Russian, me included, gave a lot of thought to what we'd done, where we are and what's right for

Russia. I haven't heard of anybody finding the answers."

Cyrus nodded.

"Well, let's see if we can pull this crazy thing off." He paused, and added, "By the way, there are two conditions to my involvement. One, I'm not concerned with what happens if we fail, we both know it. But in the unlikely event we succeed, I'll most likely have to leave the country and have to have something to live on. I presume that there is enough money in the whole thing for us that that won't be a problem."

"Absolutely. If I promise you say, ten million, that should do, shouldn't it?"

"Yes. That's enough. Can you get me to America, with citizenship, of course?"

"I'll do my best, and most likely I'll be able to do it. However, I can't guarantee you that. I don't work for the government, you see." Cyrus sounded apologetic and he felt the lame sound of his answer and quickly added, "As a worst case scenario I have friends in several countries, Canada for one, where it would be no problem at all."

Vladimir nodded, "I appreciate your honesty."

"What's your second condition?"

"I need an extra pair of hands to deal with those scoundrels," he hesitated for a moment, "who murdered Laura." His tone became almost apologetic. "I just need some very simple things to be done, so don't worry, it won't be too difficult. It's awfully hard to do everything alone, see."

"I consider it my obligation. You have my word."

Vladimir had no idea what a capable "extra pair of hands" he had just enlisted.

At breakfast Vladimir asked, "I presume that you know exactly what you're talking about and that the money is within my reach. Let's get to specifics."

"Do you know general Katurov?"

Vladimir smirked, "Quite well. Actually, he's the chief of the Directorate I mentioned last night. We were once good friends, as well as our wives. What about him?"

"Did he come here just before the coup in 1991?"

"Yes, that was quite an event. A visit at such a level is a rarity here. It was hushed up, though. Only my deputy and I knew that he was here. What is it all about, and how come you know about it?"

"Some information came my way in Moscow. Do you know who Kruchina was?"

"Yes. He managed the finances and household for the Politburo. Committed suicide during the turmoil."

"It was more like a murder. He knew too much. He was the one who arranged the transfer and placement of the money we're looking for."

"Well, more news every day."

"So, Kruchina made all the arrangements and was taken out. What Laura and I found out was that a week before the coup he arranged a secret meeting between Gorbatov and Katurov at Kruchina's dacha. Apparently, and this was Laura's guess, Gorbatov stopped at Kruchina's on his way to the airport to fly to his Crimea villa. Katurov was already there. It looks like Gorbatov gave Katurov the papers about the hidden money for safekeeping."

"That's interesting and makes sense, come to think of it. But why Yoshkar-Ola? Katurov had a thousand safes and dozens of vaults in Moscow."

"My guess is that he was ordered to put it somewhere that nobody would visit too often. Somewhere that would be hidden from subsequent governments, including the current one."

"Great idea. You're absolutely right. The least frequently used safe in the whole Directorate is the personal safe of the Directorate Chief here, in Yoshkar-Ola." Vladimir was excited. "And I carried the damn thing into the vault with my own hands."

"How did that happen?"

"Well, just as you guessed. At four thirty in the afternoon I got a phone call. Local, from the military airfield ten miles from here. Guess who that was. Katurov. He ordered me to personally pick him up at the air base and to make sure that the only person in the office after five would be my deputy. So, I picked him up and we went straight to the bunker. He had a heavy suitcase with him. Together, we carried it in. When we arrived, he made my deputy leave. Then, he went alone with the suitcase into the inner vault, and I was waiting outside, in the duty room. Apparently he took the papers out and put them in his personal safe, the special one."

"What's special about it?"

"Only the Directorate Chief can open it. Anyway, he came out with the same suitcase, but it was obviously lighter.

"Did you ask him about the suitcase?"

"Yes. He said that it was an urgent change of the emergency ciphers for the Politburo. He also mentioned that his visit was to be hushed up and for my deputy it was just an unannounced inspection which we passed with flying colors. He left the same night and I haven't seen him since."

They were silent for a while, thinking of the chain of events that had created what they faced now.

Cyrus was the one who broke the silence. "At least it looks like we have our target confirmed on your premises. Now we have to find the way to get it." He paused, "And to get out alive."

"That's right. A small thing. But I also want to get those bastards. Why don't we do that first, and then come back here for the papers."

"No way, Vladimir. As soon as you start hitting the KGB people in Moscow, we'll be lucky to make a mad dash to the border. Forget about coming back here."

Vladimir sighed, "You're right, of course. I'm just too emotional. I really want those bastards."

"So do I, don't get me wrong. Well, that's one more incentive for us to succeed here, right?" The cheerfulness of his remark sounded more subdued than was intended. He shifted the gears. "Tell me about the safe."

"As you may know, this complex is an emergency Government bunker in the event of a nuclear war. It also contains the Wartime Government and KGB main Communications Center. An intriguing part of the whole story is that to our best knowledge it was not known to the Americans for all the years of its existence."

"Come on, that can't be true. Our satellites are pretty good at discovering this kind of thing."

"So what? This has been taken care of quite simply. Before construction started, an open coal mine opened a mile and a half away. That was normal. A military unit of no significance, about a regiment's worth, was here even before that. As you may know, we are the world leaders in tunnel construction machinery. So, the whole construction was done underground, and the excavated earth was moved through the tunnel to the coal mine and dumped there without triggering anything in your satellite pictures."

Cyrus was genuinely surprised.

"Well," Vladimir continued, "now it does not matter anymore, but it's a neat little setup. Quite secure, fully ready, and nobody knows about it."

Vladimir paused, clearly enjoying the impression he was making on Cyrus, and then went on, "So, we have our lair in the bunker and, considering the secrecy of ciphers, enjoy practically full autonomy here. In our section we have rooms with mothballed communications equipment, updated once in a while, a peacetime operations center where we are on duty all the time, and vaults with ciphers, also updated from time to time. There is a vault there filled with safes where all the instructions for communications in case of nuclear war are kept. Within that vault there is the personal safe of the Chief of the Cipher Communications Directorate of the KGB, who is the only one permitted to open it. That's our safe."

"Who holds the key to the safe?"

"Nobody. That's the procedure. There are two keys, one for the outer lock, and another for the main door. Both are kept on the shelf in a separate secured and sealed box. The duty officer signs for them, among other things, when he comes on duty."

"This sounds pretty easy, almost a security lapse."
"Not really. First of all, our doctrine, and I must say, it is a realistic one, is that once you've gotten in the inner circle, there is no way to stop you if you have bad intentions. So, we are trusted. On the other hand, there are other methods of dealing in counterintelligence besides just controlling the access, which are more effective under such circumstances."

Cyrus was tempted to poke into those methods, but he knew better. After all, his mission was limited.

Remember, our partnership is not carved in stone, and he is definitely a patriot. He is and will be testing you as a possible spy, so don't push your luck.

"Well, it sounds very easy. You just go in, open the safe, take the box, and we take off."

"Not quite. If I don't reseal the key boxes and the safe, I'll never leave the complex because the next duty officer will be checking it. And I can't leave before that because the outside security knows that our premises are never left unattended. The boxes are sealed with Katurov's seal. I have to replace the imprints somehow. Any ideas?"

Careful. A banker can't know too much about these things. Think of something primitive. "Well, I don't know. We have to think about it. There's got to be something."

There was a long pause, then Cyrus' face brightened, "I've got it. You have a hospital here, don't you?"

"Sure. A small one."

"Doesn't matter. You know that stuff they make a cast from when you break an arm."

"That's good."

My God, no. It wouldn't work. Come on, think better, Vladimir.

"Then I guess it's all solved." *How I can help you without hurting myself?* "And all the details will be imprinted?"

"Looks like it." Then he immediately retracted, "No, wait. No, Kirill, it wouldn't work. The plaster you mentioned is too rough, it wouldn't catch all the fine details of the seal."

Good. "Damn. You're right I guess. We have to better than that."

After thinking briefly, Cyrus came up with another idea. "Vladimir, what about the stuff that dentists use for imprints before they make a crown?"

"That's great. That will definitely work. And you know what? I have a dentist friend. I can easily ask him for some, saying that I need it for fixing something at home. He wouldn't even bother to ask what."

"Now we've solved it."

Vladimir changed, made a quick phone call, and drove off to see his dentist friend. He returned an hour and a half later.

"I'm glad it's Saturday. We have some time to think over the details." Vladimir put a small box with the ingredients on the table and a sheet of paper with the instructions for mixing it on top.

Yeah, the details. Those are what kill you, particularly minor details. It looks almost too easy at this point. I don't like it.

Vladimir acted as if he had read his thoughts. "Kirill, you know, it looks too easy. It makes me suspicious. Does that sound strange?"

"No." Join the club. By he way, are two paranoids better than one?

Suddenly Vladimir's face showed a mischievous grin, "Kirill, would you like a tour of the facility?"

"Have you always had this kind of sense of humor?"

"I'm not joking."

Cyrus felt slightly dizzy. I have a very open mind, but that's a little too much even for me. The whole thing with Vladimir must be reevaluated. Strange, he didn't seem to be insane. Well, isolation in a place like this and vodka can do anybody in.

Vladimir was looking at Cyrus, smiling and clearly enjoying his attempt not to show any confusion. "I know, it's kind of an unexpected invitation."

"You've mastered the art of understatement," mumbled Cyrus.

"Listen to me. First of all, I'm not insane." He chuckled, "Well, for a man in my position to let you stay here was a little crazy, but my insanity doesn't go much beyond that."

He became serious and continued, "But I don't like the easiness of our plan. There may be something beyond what we know. And, two minds are better than one. If something comes out of the blue sky, together we have a better chance of getting through. Sometimes certain things are easier to see with a fresh look. You stop seeing things when you're too close to them for too long."

"Well, Vladimir, I certainly agree with your logic as an experienced operator. The minor snag we have here is that it might not be too easy for me to get in."

"Oh, that's the easy part, don't worry about that." He was not smiling.

"Come on, get serious."

"I am. As I told you, once you're in the inner circle, not much is impossible. Let me give you a little briefing." He took a breath, and continued, "Look, that facility actually is a crypt, and we are the crypt keepers. There isn't much to do. Consequently, there are not too many people employed there. There are several separate units responsible for maintenance in their respective fields. I happen to be chief of one of those units, cipher communications. Considering that ciphers are a very special area, I have the most autonomy of all the unit chiefs. As a matter of fact, even the facility commander does not have the necessary clearance to get into my premises. Nobody except eight officers in my unit ever got inside our lair, bar three cleaning ladies who happen to be wives of our officers."

Cyrus was listening with increasing interest. Vladimir lit another cigarette, and went on, "So, I have the right to order a pass for anybody with no questions asked. I report only to Moscow, to my Department Chief. Technically, the security office at the facility makes and laminates a pass, but I order it, supply the name and a photograph, and only I can put a stamp granting access to my premises."

Maybe I've gone mad too, but it looks more and more attractive. "So, you're saying that you can openly bring me in without anybody even getting suspicious?"

"Exactly. With a properly chosen time and with a very modest level of luck it's not a problem at all. Here is my plan: I take your picture right here. I haven't used my dark room since my wife died, but it should be all right. The store where I can buy chemicals and photo paper is open for another two hours. On Monday I'll make you a pass and let a duty officer go at about four in the afternoon. Just before that I'll bring you in and you'll wait just outside of our door in a small pantry. When he leaves, I'll get you inside. We will have till about nine, when the change of duty officers takes place. Then, we get out."

"Wouldn't it be suspicious that you'd let everyone go at four and then volunteered to do the duty job?"

"Not really. I do it once in a while. One of the guys is on vacation, one is sick, of the remaining six four are on the duty schedule, only one in at any time, so only my deputy and I are on a regular schedule. Routine stuff, you know. As for letting the deputy and the duty officer go, I do it from time to time, when I have to be there anyway, to do some of my bureaucratic chores, like regular reports. They'd just be happy, that's all."

"And what about any record of an extra pass?"

"That's no problem. To balance the numbers, and that's the only thing which counts, I predate my record for a couple of months and show the name of one of the inspectors from Moscow who can come here. I have a guy in mind who has never been here, but he's an old hand in the Inspections, so any other inspector would recognize the name and wouldn't pay any attention. But, we just need a few days, and they may catch something only long after that, most likely never."

There was a pause. Then Cyrus smiled, "As they say, you can't have two deaths, but you can't escape one. I'm crazy enough to do that." *I know, John, I know. But I just can't stand the temptation to tour such a facility. Besides, I have a justification. If I fail, I'd rather do it personally.*

"Vladimir's mind was working full speed. "Now, how are we going to get out? There are a few ways." He went to his study, came back with a map and laid it out on the dining room table.

"I wouldn't recommend flying. You have to show a passport. The best way is here," he pointed at Yoshkar-Ola, skipped south, and turned west, stopping at Moscow.

"Not for me. They may still be looking for me. But even if they've stopped, surely, people who were looking still remember my face. I'd rather go this way." He moved his finger slightly east-north-east, turned north, and then east, ending at St. Petersburg.

"I can't go that route. I'd have to say that I'm going to visit my sister, and that's the other way. Everyone would know the way I left around here. Too small of a town."

They looked at each other. "Then we have to split, Vladimir." Do you trust me that much? No, it can't be true. You have something up your sleeve. Or, you think you do.

"Looks like it. Then we meet in Moscow."

Cyrus nodded.

"Well, I better get going to the store before it closes."

"Yeah, and we've got a day and a half for further planning."

Vladimir quickly dressed and drove off.

Chapter 13

Cyrus had a great meal, and drank a lot of tea. Old intelligence wisdom: during an operation you never know when you will next have a chance to eat, drink, sleep, or go to the bathroom. When you're in need of any of the above with no opportunity operationally, you're weakened. So, you make sure you do all of that every chance you get. He looked at his watch and started slowly dressing. The clothes that Vladimir had bought for him at a flea market had already been carefully fitted and modified yesterday. His training had taught him that clothes are important and should help in an operation, not be an obstacle or distraction.

Vladimir pulled up in his military four-wheel drive, entered the driveway and stopped at the rear house entrance, blocking the view of the door. He entered the house.

"Everything seems to be all right. Here is your pass." He handed Cyrus a laminated card with Cyrus' photo, with pinkish-red watermarks, and three different small stamps.

"That's neat. Certainly looks very interesting. Looks like there's no way to forge it."

"Perhaps. Still a redundancy, though. It's a very small place, peoplewise. In essence, it's still as if I walked in and said 'he's with me.' Any new thoughts on your part?"

"Not really. I think we planned everything as well as we could under the circumstances. There is only one thing I'd say, this is too extravagant." Cyrus glanced at the Russian military officer's field uniform *nakidka* on the back of the kitchen chair. Two layers, one of fabric and one of some sort of very thin rubber made this long cloak, with a removable hood, fully waterproof and warm, very good in the field. "I still think, I'd be better off in a coat."

"You'll have that option when you leave town. Cyrus, please, leave these things to me. I'm local, remember? This cloak is very comfortable in nasty weather like today, and thus, are popular around here. Besides, don't forget that you're a KGB officer, which means that though you're not wearing the uniform, you have one issued to you and stacked away. One more detail, too. This particular one, although the same color, has a layer of wool, not just half-cotton, half-polyester fabric, and comes with a colonel's kit. For you it may mean nothing, but, believe me, sentries notice such things without fail. At first glance at you they'll conclude that you're a KGB colonel on some sort of inspection."

"Well, that's your department." He paused slightly. "Time to go."

"Yes. Let's sit down first."

An old Russian custom. Before a long or a dangerous trip everyone sits down for a short while in silence. They did.

"Now, let's go."

Fifteen minutes later Vladimir turned onto a dead end road with a "No Entry" sign. Three hundred yards later he stopped at the gates with a standard red star in the middle of each half. The gates were painted in standard military green. On both sides of the gates a seven-foot concrete fence, topped with barbed wire, extended as far as could be seen, disappearing in a thick forest and a drizzling mixture of rain and snow. A sentry with an AK-74 at his chest came up from the small checkpoint station building. The building had brick walls on three sides and a glass upper portion. Vladimir half-rolled down his window. From ten feet away, the sentry recognized Vladimir, saluted, turned to his partner in the station, and waved. The gates rolled apart.

To his right Cyrus saw the grounds of a typical small military garrison, surrounded by a large and thick forest. At an intersection a hundred yards ahead, Vladimir did not turn right into the compound. He followed the straight road between the compound on the right and the edge of the forest on the left. Cyrus noticed a line of large trees just off the left shoulder of the road. Their tops covered the road and extended over the right shoulder.

Vladimir noticed Cyrus' interest and said, "That's right. This road is covered by the tree tops and cannot be seen from the air, even in winter. Notice the mixture of trees and the uneven spacing between them. From the air it looks exactly like a natural border for the cleared area of the compound on the right. Even the snow in winter gets cleared to the left, under these trees."

Three quarters of a mile from the first gate they stopped at another, similar one but without stars. Another small station, another sentry. This one did not even move, just saluted and waved to a partner inside. The gates opened, and Cyrus saw the rest of the road, ending about forty yards ahead into an underground entrance. It was a typical heavy bunker entrance, Cyrus had seen one in Colorado. He was surprised to see no parking area or any opening around the entrance at all. The road just dove into the bunker entrance. Half-way down to another gate Vladimir stopped the car. Two remote control TV cameras were pointed at them. Cyrus' face took on the indifferent expression of a mildly bored man. Several seconds later the solid gate started moving. Judging by its thickness, it was more of a wall than a gate.

Vladimir rolled in and stopped again, rolling down his window as the gate slowly closed behind. Another sentry came up and, not paying any attention to Vladimir, looked at Cyrus. After Cyrus flashed his pass, the sentry saluted, walked to the bar ten feet ahead, and opened it. Cyrus was looking at a huge underground parking area, higher than needed to accommodate any truck. *Probably to bring in oversized special equipment when needed.*

"What a place. Isn't it a bit of a luxury to have underground parking here?"

Vladimir chuckled, "If you do something like this, you better do it well. Besides, after the Kremlin, this place looks pretty modest. Don't forget for whom it was built. We have virtually everything here, even a couple dozen tanks mothballed in a garage behind that door," he nodded toward a solid gate in the wall they were passing.

Vladimir parked the car slightly apart from other cars, about seventy feet from a glass entrance with three revolving doors. *Smart. He does not want to bump into somebody parked close, so he'd be forced to introduce me.*

They entered a spacious brightly lit checkpoint. A warrant-officer with a gun on his belt and two sentries at the side walls with AK-74s and a couple of hand grenades each were the only occupants.

"After you, Alexandr Ivanovich," Vladimir invited Cyrus with a wide gesture of respect toward the entrance.

Cyrus walked forward, stepping firmly and authoritatively. He handed in his pass. Barely glancing at it, the warrant-officer saluted, "Please, pass." Cyrus nodded. With the corner of his eye he saw the guy wink while saluting Vladimir, as if saying "Oh, boy, another inspector? My sympathy."

Vladimir caught up with Cyrus and they walked down a twenty-five-foot-wide stair, which after one flight became a slightly downward sloping corridor of the same width. A huge, two-foot thick sliding door was visible in the wall. Twenty feet farther there was a second. After about a hundred feet down the corridor they hit a T-junction and turned right. They walked another fifty feet and entered a foyer with an elevator bank. Cyrus counted twelve doors, six on each side. He was surprised with the distance between the elevator doors which was about twenty feet. *They probably have the shafts separately reinforced, so if it shakes, at least some of them are likely to survive. Do they all serve the same floors, or not?*

Vladimir pushed the button near the elevator with number 4 above the door. Cyrus noticed that the buttons of the even-numbered elevators lit, but not the odd ones. *So, they serve two different areas.* Suddenly, all the other buttons lit and, about fifteen seconds later, the door with number 7 opened and two men came out.

"Vladimir, how many summers, how many winters!" A Russian expression for "haven't seen you for a long time."

Cyrus had turned aside from them and was not looking toward the men. Now he was forced to. Vladimir started moving toward the guy. *Extremely bad, or not? Hard to say. In any event, there's nowhere to go but to talk to them.* At the same moment their elevator door opened.

Saved by the bell. Cyrus stepped into the elevator. Vladimir gestured to the guy, like cutting his own throat, "Hi, Misha. Call you tomorrow. Sorry." He stepped into the elevator behind Cyrus.

Instead of the usual rows of buttons Cyrus saw two telephone dial pads, one on each side of the door. Vladimir quickly dialed a combination and gave Cyrus a look, saying, "Don't talk now." Cyrus slowly nodded. *8-3-7-1-2-9. What the hell is it?* There was no usual display of the floor numbers above the door. The door closed and the elevator started softly, practically without a sound, sliding down.

Cyrus resisted the temptation to glance at his watch and take note of the timing. Instead, he did it mentally, as he had been trained to do. *So smooth, you can't even feel acceleration. God knows what speed it's moving at.* The elevator stopped. *Forty seconds.*

Vladimir got out of the elevator, looked aside, and nodded. Cyrus stepped out. They turned left and walked briskly, Cyrus half a step behind Vladimir. At the first intersection of the corridor they turned right. Cyrus heard a door open somewhere behind, not too far, in one of the adjacent corridors. Luckily, the door with the M on it was on their left. The restroom. They quickly stepped in. Vladimir went inside. Nobody. Cyrus opened a side door off the small foyer of the restroom, stepped inside the closet and closed the door. Cleaner's pantry. Vladimir went outside. Cyrus barely heard his steps in the corridor, dying down to the left.

In a few minutes his eyes adapted to darkness. A small amount of light from a gap between the door and the floor enabled him to see brooms, buckets and other tools of the cleaning trade. He looked at his watch. *Five minutes. Too soon.*

He heard the footsteps he was waiting for. *No, these are coming from the right.* He heard the door open, and somebody walked into the restroom and began attending to his needs. Cyrus was comfortable, almost relaxed, except that it was pretty warm, and he had forgotten to take his cloak off. *Well, it's about the time.* Suddenly, he realized the problem. *Damn it, I might miss my man, Vladimir's duty officer.* The sound of flushing water, as well as of the man washing his hands, was too loud to hear the vital steps in the corridor. *Problems usually come from unexpected small details. But each one of these small details can screw up the whole operation.*

In a few seconds Cyrus went from being calm and almost relaxed to tense and somewhat nervous. He listened desperately for the sound from the corridor, to no avail. *Hey man, go take a shower at home. Stop fiddling around here, damn it. If I miss my man, I don't even know when to get out. And Vladimir can't leave there to come and get me.* Finally, the man finished. The water stopped running almost as suddenly as it started. And, at that very moment, Cyrus heard footsteps in the corridor right near the restroom door. Moving to the right. *Well, if he goes to the right, he probably came from the left.* At that moment the man in the restroom stepped out, the two started chatting, moving along the corridor further to the right. In a few more seconds everything was quiet.

Cyrus looked at his watch. The duty officer had left just in time. He emerged from the closet, opened the restroom door and looked around. Nobody. *I should be all right now.* He walked left into the corridor, and he saw that the big metal door at the end of the corridor was slightly ajar. In a few seconds he was greeted by Vladimir. The heavy metal door closed behind him.

"Well, welcome to our lair, Kirill. Was everything all right out there?"

"Sure, everything was fine, it went just as you said it would." He knows everything around here all too well, but he doesn't understand the impact of minor details. The whole visit in this facility has been very unprofessional. But admit it, you would never miss this chance for the world, be it professional or not. So don't whine.

Cyrus took off his cloak and hung it on a hook next to the door.

Vladimir looked at the clock on the wall. Actually, there were four of them there in a row: local, Moscow, Greenwich and Washington. "Four twenty. We have four hours, it's more than enough. Relax. Coffee?"

"Please."

Vladimir went to a small kitchen just off the room they were in and turned on an electric range with a kettle on it. He pulled a jar of Instant Nescafe Classic, sugar and two cups out of the cabinet.

"You know, it used to be a privilege to have coffee like this. You'd find it in the Center, but certainly not in this hole. Now anybody can have it; it's just expensive as hell."

"Yeah, things have changed a lot in Russia, I imagine. But I've never been in Russia before."

Vladimir sighed, shook his head, and suddenly smiled, "Let me show you around. To put it mildly, it's rare for an outsider to see this crypt, not to mention that you're an American."

"Please. I love seeing exotic places, and this one certainly qualifies."

They went back to the room.

"This is a company room, a central point around here."

It was a small hall with a couple of leather couches and three armchairs, surrounding a large square coffee table, and a small desk with four telephones, a chair and another couch by the wall. Wall-to-wall carpet would have turned the room from cold to neutral were it not for the four clocks on the light-gray painted wall, a constant reminder of the official purpose of the premises. On the left wall there was a six by three feet closed wood cabinet, about four inches deep. The walls were decorated mainly with a calendar and large duty rosters and schedules, and several placards outlining security procedures and demanding vigilance. Cyrus did not see any dust anywhere. Besides entrance door, there were three other closed white wood doors at the corners, and an open doorway into the kitchen.

Cyrus followed Vladimir, who opened one of the doors to reveal a well-lit hundred-foot corridor. "Those doors are to the cipher equipment rooms. All sorts of equipment are housed there. We maintain the equipment so it can be put in use within an hour. The Operations control room, doubling as a duty officer room, and my office are there too. The main telephone lines are duplicated there," he nodded toward the desk in the hall.

"Well, it looks like a pretty big operation."

"It is. We'd take over a lot of functions, so it's even bigger than the current Center in Moscow." He closed the door and walked to another which opened into an identical corridor.

"Here is the communications center, maintenance and repair facilities, parts warehouse, and some sleeping quarters. The first on the left is a restroom."

"Sleeping quarters? I would have thought that you have living quarters somewhere else in this complex."

"We do. This is just in case. Small capacity."

"My God, in case of what? What else can go wrong if you already have a nuclear war on your hands?"

Vladimir laughed, "I don't know. Just the usual KGB redundancy."

He opened the third door and went into another corridor, Cyrus followed.

"And this is the warehouse of mothballed cipher equipment and cipher keys. A good three-year supply." He waved, indicating that it took up a lot of space. Cyrus noticed that all the doors in the corridor were heavy metal. Vladimir walked to the second door on the right and knocked on it. "This is your point of interest." Abruptly, he started walking back. "Our kettle is probably about to blow up. Let's have some coffee."

In the hall, sipping his coffee, Cyrus remarked, "By the way, Vladimir, what floor are we on? I've never seen any elevator system like that."

Vladimir laughed again. Obviously, he was enjoying his role as a guide to a mysterious place. "Oh, you noticed. That's a neat trick, isn't it?" He made a long pause for a stronger impression, and said, "I don't know."

Cyrus smiled understandingly and nodded.

"The funny thing is that I really don't."

"Come on, give me a break. You must have access to everything."

"It's true. But I only have access to everything I need to know. This one I don't. Compartmentalization. The KGB takes it seriously. You just dial a number which is a combination of the floor number and an access code, and the elevator gets you there. Every man goes to his floor, and that's it. Why do you need to know what floor you're on? It's irrelevant."

"Maybe you're right, but for an American that's hard to understand. You must have a whole damn skyscraper here," he wanted to say 'upside down' but that was wrong; he was looking for a word, and then found it, "buried."

"That's for sure."

Suddenly Cyrus realized that all this talk about the place, a virtual crypt, was depressing for him. He realized that there were no windows anywhere, no sounds, and time felt suspended. He changed the subject.

"Vladimir, why do you trust me? Coming here I was scared to death that you wouldn't even listen to me, maybe just put me in jail before asking any questions, and here we are, two days later, sitting in one of the most secret places in the whole country, drinking coffee and about to crack the most sensitive safe in the outfit."

Vladimir chuckled, and smiled coyly. His eyes became two big horizontal wrinkles surrounded by numerous smaller ones. Even the corners of his lips, usually turning down slightly, straightened into another horizontal line with the middle of the lips "That's a good question. Everything is rather simple, actually, except the first moment. I don't know why I even let you talk when you walked in. I felt something, that's all. I don't go by feeling too often, though."

"And then?"

"If you had anything to do with Laura's death, you'd never

come here in the first place. Secondly, I clearly felt that you loved her, just the way you carried yourself, you can't fake that. Then, I know Laura very well, certainly better than her superiors. What you told me was exactly Laura, her inner style; she had an acute sense of justice." He sighed, and continued, "The rest was really easy. On Saturday I came here. It took me ten minutes to find out who you are. See, all the KGB files are duplicated at this facility so that nothing would be lost if we went to war. They update the computer here every Friday. So, from my office I have access to that computer. All Dronov's game with you, vetting included, was at my disposal. So, all it took to find out everything about Mr. Cyrus Grant was a forty-minute detour when I went out. By the way, giving me your mother's maiden name was smart."

Cyrus felt that this was a good time to press a little further. He smiled, "But how do you know that I'm not an American spy? This place is a dream for one."

"One reason is that our intelligence folks are pretty good at vetting. Had you ever even been in training for the CIA, or any other outfit of yours, they'd have known. On the top of that, it's precisely the fact that this place is a dream for any spy that made my check on you certain. You'd offer me money, anything, to get the cipher stuff out of here. But you never showed any interest in ciphers, you couldn't even guarantee me an American citizenship. By the way, if you had tried, you'd be in Moscow in Lefortovo jail by now, I guarantee you that. So, you have nothing to do with the American government. Maybe just have a friend here and there."

Cyrus wanted to give a sigh of relief, but he knew better. Well, we seem to have played it right. So far. Make sure not to show any of your training later. It will tie your hands, but the whole thing won't be blown.

"I see. Did you manage to find anything on Laura's," he stumbled, "murder?"

"No way. This stuff is strictly off the books. Never in the computer." He paused. "But I will. I still have a few buddies in Moscow, and a few strings to pull."

Cyrus looked at the clock. Vladimir noticed that. "Don't worry. It will take just ten minutes. It's five o'clock, so we've got more than three hours."

"Well, I appreciate your confidence, but I'm getting a little nervous. What if something goes wrong?"

Vladimir chuckled, "If anything goes wrong, that's the end of the game. There is no middle ground here, there is no draw in this one."

They were silent for a couple of minutes, then Vladimir said, "All right, I guess you're anxious to see the papers and, frankly, I am too. Let's go."

Vladimir went to the kitchen, plugged in some kind of electric heater, and put a small pot with the standard burgundy sealing wax onto it. "Takes about twenty minutes to liquefy it." Then he returned to the hall, went up to the cabinet on the opposite wall, opened one door, took a key out of one of the numerous pigeon holes, and closed the door. They went back to the heavy metal door of their room in the corridor.

Both ends of a thread, going through a small hole in the skin of the door frame, were affixed to the special indenture in the door frame with a putty seal. Briefly, Vladimir looked at the seal.

"It's my seal. I was the last one there." He took the threads out, breaking the seal, and unlocked the door with the key he had taken out of the cabinet. He opened the heavy door and flipped the switch on the wall next to it. They stepped into a good-sized room. All the space along the walls was occupied by about a dozen massive safes; an opened registry journal sat on a small stand near the door on the right wall. A rough wood table with two well-beaten chairs were the only objects in the middle.

One of the safes, in the farther right corner, was different from the others. It was a little shorter, about five feet high, looked heavier, and was sticking out about eight inches more. Clearly, that was a better grade safe. Some of the safes had outer combination locks, covering the keyhole, others did not. The shorter safe, of course, did. *The safes are backed flush to the wall, there is no way to see if they have electronic security.*

"These safes contain our current stuff and the wartime instructions on implementation of new ciphers for each point we are supposed to be in communication with. But we're concerned with this toy only," he pointed to the shorter safe, "the personal safe of the Directorate Chief."

Cyrus noticed that the seal in the indenture on the face of the safe, half of which was made in the door and the other half on the body, was sealed with a burgundy color sealing wax, not greenish gray putty, like other safes.

"I think, Kirill, we should mix our pie in the kitchen, not here."
"I agree."
They went back to the kitchen. Vladimir put a piece of paper over the counter and put the ingredients on it. *I hope he won't waste too much of the stuff. I wish I could do it for him.*
"Looks like it's going to be pretty messy, Vladimir. How about a vessel of some sort. We have to carry it there, you know."
"Good idea." He took a plastic cup out of the cabinet, toyed with it, then pulled scissors from somewhere, and cut it down to two inches.
"Vladimir, wait. I just realized something. How are we going to apply the mixture to the seal? The seal is vertical, so the paste is going to leak down before it hardens."
"Hey, you're thinking." Vladimir looked happy. "I just thought about it this morning, and I got something out of our tool shop." Triumphantly, he took out a metal cylinder out of his pocket. It was an inch in diameter, it was hollow, virtually a piece of pipe about an inch long. A bottom was soldered to it, making it into a small cup. "Exactly the diameter of the seal indenture."
I'm glad you're smart, and I don't have to go out on a limb with you. "Gee, that's great."
Cyrus looked at the smooth edge of the cylinder. *We really need a rubber seal around this edge. We don't know how fast this paste really hardens.* He took the cylinder, toyed with it a little, put it to the kitchen door, and was looking from the side. *Play it dumb.*
"Good. I'm sure, nothing will leak here."
Vladimir looked from the side, like Cyrus, thought a second, and then said, "You know, Kirill, before it hardens, the paste can be pretty leaky. I'd rather be on the safe side, and I think, I know the answer."
He went back, apparently to the workshop, and returned with a can of rubber glue. He took some of it on a match and put it around the edge of the cylinder. After the glue dried slightly, he added

another layer. He repeated the process several times. That rubberized the edge, as if he had added a rubber washer to it. Cyrus was impressed with this ingenuity. *Good boy.*

"How come you have this glue, Vladimir?"

"Oh, we have a little of everything around here. If we didn't, I'd have thought of something else." Yeah, Russian engineering. You've got to work with whatever you have, but you must succeed. Now is the time for the last detail.

"Vladimir, if this stuff somehow gets on the surface of the safe, we might need some cloth to wipe it off."

Vladimir's face turned concerned. "I don't know if we can wipe it off at all. We have to prevent that somehow."

"Oh, then, maybe we could put some water on its surface beforehand?"

"No, water wouldn't do. Wait. Oil!"

Good. Finally. Vladimir disappeared.

He returned with some oily piece of cloth.

"By the way, is there a chance that this paste will stick to the cylinder when it hardens?" *There is, make no mistake about it.*

"I don't think so, but just in case, let's wipe it with oil too."

"All right." You have to, actually.

Now, I think, we're ready. Hopefully.

Five thirty. They mixed the ingredients of the paste. *Too liquid. Might not work.* They took the plastic cup with the mixture into the vault room with the safes and set everything on the table in the middle. While the mixture was in a liquid state, they poured it into the cylinder to the very top. It stayed liquid.

"Well, we have to wait a bit."

At that moment Cyrus noticed that the mixture, having completely refused to dry for four minutes, suddenly started drying steadily.

"Vladimir! Hurry, it's drying."

Vladimir immediately wiped the safe surface around and below the seal, as well as the seal itself. A very thin film of oil covered the surface.

He was about to take the cylinder, but Cyrus quickly took it and said "Let me do it, you might get a phone call." *He doesn't know how steady the hand must be to get a good impression. And how long you might need to keep it.*

"All right, but be careful."

"Sure."

Cyrus came to the seal and took a comfortable position. Still holding the cylinder vertically, he touched the lower edge of the seal with the edge of the cylinder. At that moment he realized that Vladimir, wiping the cylinder from inside, apparently touched it on the outside as well. Its slippery surface made it very difficult to hold it firmly. *Too late.* With one steady motion, Cyrus turned the cylinder horizontally and simultaneously pressed it to the seal. It didn't slip. He felt some soft resistance of the hardening paste. A few drops on both sides dripped down and stopped a foot lower. *Hold it steady. The seal engraving is too fine to fool with. I'm glad we're not dealing with the putty. This mixture sucks. They should buy some in the States.*

After a couple of minutes Vladimir said, "I guess, that's enough. Must be hardened by now. The dentist said once it started hardening it hardens pretty fast."

"I'd rather be on the safe side and hold it for a while more." God knows how this stuff works. Not too many people know, though, how hard it is to hold it really steady for a minute, much less five.

Three minutes later Cyrus was tired. "I guess, that's it."

He took the cylinder off the seal. The impression was perfect. They waited for a few more minutes for the impression to harden better.

Taking the impression out of the cylinder did not give them any trouble. They shaved some now hardened paste off the perimeter of the cylindrical impression. Now they had a good copy of the Directorate Chief's seal.

Cyrus gave a sigh of relief. Vladimir noticed and shrugged, "Don't worry, everything is going just fine, I told you."

"Sure." Yeah, sure. I'm glad I'm here. Even with my hands tied. But that safe really worries me. I just don't like the look of it.

Somehow, it was five forty. Two and a half hours. We need a break now, just before the final assault. Whatever it brings.

"Vladimir, how about another cup of coffee?"

"Sure." He chuckled, "For a banker with not-too-strong nerves."

He laughed at his joke and, very friendly, said, "Don't worry, Kirill. You're doing great. Very few people would even have the nerve to come here at all."

"Thank you."

They had some coffee. Cyrus was trying to relax. But that safe didn't sit well with him. What's unusual about it? Nothing, really. Just another good safe. What's unusual about its immediate environment? Nothing. Wait, just one thing. A standard sheet of paper, some kind of procedural regulation was framed and affixed to the right upper corner of the door. There are similar looking pages on three other safes too, but those were not framed.

"Vladimir, what's that piece of paper, on the door of our safe?"

"Oh, nothing. The Chief's delusion of grandeur; it's just his letter saying that nobody can open that safe but him. He demanded that it be framed and permanently affixed to the door. Stupid. Like somebody might not know whose safe it is."

"I see. And the documents on the other safes?"

"Just security regulations. We have to post them, but all the walls are covered by safes, so we put them there."

"Well, let's go, Kirill."

Vladimir opened the wall cabinet and took out a five-by-three-by-one-inch metal box. Its sliding cover was sealed with the same seal as the safe. Vladimir brought it to the kitchen., He slid the latching half of the seal seat, breaking the seal. He opened the released cover. Inside Cyrus saw two keys. One, about three inches long, had a thin steel sheath over its blade. The other was a big key, typical of such a safe.

"What's this?" Cyrus indicated the smaller key.

"That's an example of the art of mechanics." With these words he took the sheath off the key. Cyrus saw an incredibly complicated thee-dimensional blade. Some of the grooves were no bigger than two tenths of a millimeter. Inner grooves made the key truly three-dimensional and implied the virtual impossibility of making a duplicate with an impression.

"That's quite something. I've never seen anything even close to it." That was true.

"Let's get going." They went to the safe and Vladimir broke the seal. Then, he inserted the small key into the keyhole of the outer lock. Next, he slid a small plastic strip out of the sheath of the small key. Cyrus saw six numbers printed on the strip. Vladimir dialed the combination on the dial ring of the lock. He paused a second, looked a Cyrus, and decisively turned the key. The key turned softly with no sound. Vladimir lightly pulled the body of the outer lock. Like a small door, it swung open, revealing the keyhole of the main lock.

"See, nothing to it. Many safes here have absolutely the same type of lock. I work with them every day."

Cyrus nodded. But he felt his heart moving up into his throat. As he had been trained to do, he was forcing himself to breathe evenly. *Too easy. Something must be wrong. Come on, Cyrus, don't be stupid. This is better than Fort Knox. Just to get here is a minor miracle. It's logical that the rest should be easy. Besides, Vladimir is an old hand. He knows all their tricks.*

Cyrus automatically moved to the right, beside the safe and behind the soon-to-be-opened door. If there was a blast, this way he had a chance to survive.

Vladimir inserted the big key into the main keyhole. He turned the key. Nothing. Then, he exhaled, and opened the door. His face turned pale.

There it was. Just behind the door, attached to the ceiling inside the safe, there was a horizontal row of white buttons, numbered zero though nine. On the left there was a large red, rapidly blinking light.

"Damn!" Vladimir was paralyzed.

Cyrus' brain started working with lightning speed. *That's it. We should have about twenty seconds.* His voice became firm and calm. "Vladimir, you were friends. Dial in his birthday."

Vladimir, like waking up, quickly dialed six digits. Nothing. The light was blinking. Without a pause, Cyrus gave his next command, "His wife's birthday." Vladimir did. Nothing. Without interruption, Vladimir started dialing something else.

Think. There must be a solution. Calm. Think. What's unusual here? The letter! Cyrus jumped around the opened safe door and looked at the letter in the frame. It has only one number there, the outgoing registration number given by the secretariat.

"Vladimir, dial 3-5-6-0-3-7." Nobody could disobey that voice. Vladimir, most likely, did not even realize what he was doing. Cyrus was prepared to follow with the date of the letter.

The light stopped blinking and went off.

Neither Vladimir, nor Cyrus could say a word during the next couple of minutes. Then Vladimir sat down on the chair in the middle of the room, took out a handkerchief, and wiped cold sweat off his face and neck. Cyrus stepped to the table and sat on it. Subconsciously, both were listening for any sounds of an alarm. And both knew that if there were one, they wouldn't hear it.

Vladimir looked at Cyrus incredulously, "Where did you get that number?"

"Off that framed letter."

"How did you know?"

"I didn't. That was the only number I could come up with, I was just looking at it."

"Well, whatever hit you saved us."

"Yeah."

Suddenly, Vladimir chuckled, "I should have known it. Bastard. You know, years back, they really cracked down on the use of birthdays and so on. Guess what he used for his safe?"

"What?"

"A serial number off a fire extinguisher on the wall next to the safe."

Cyrus laughed wholeheartedly. Vladimir started laughing too. In a few seconds they were almost hysterical. The tension was being relieved.

"Well, let's see what we have got in here." Vladimir's confidence returned.

They stepped to the safe. There was one shelf in the middle. Two file-size boxes were on the bottom of the safe. The boxes were sealed with the same seal of the Directorate chief. Cyrus was more than curious as to their content, but restrained himself. *None of my business.* What attracted their attention was the box on the shelf.

About twenty inches long, a foot wide and five inches thick, this metal box occupied the whole shelf. A bright red seal of some sort was visible at one end.

"That's not from our kindergarten. Never seen anything like that." Vladimir extended his hand to take it out.

Following a sudden impulse, Cyrus quickly and firmly caught his arm. "Stop!"

Vladimir was genuinely surprised. "What's wrong?"

"Forgive me, Vladimir. I don't know. I just don't trust this safe.

Inner voice, if you will."

Vladimir smiled, "I understand. Don't worry. We're in, right? So, the danger is behind us."

Yeah. The biggest danger waits for you when you just decided that it's all over. Have you ever heard of booby-traps?

"Please, don't be mad at me. We still have plenty of time. Let's wait a little. And think."

"All right. No harm to wait a little." He was clearly trying to calm Cyrus down, afraid that he might panic. They sat there, looking at the safe. Cyrus was looking attentively, Vladimir, patiently. Suddenly, Cyrus said, "You know, I'm looking for something unusual here."

"In an empty safe?"

"Yeah, that's a good way to put it. What can be unusual in an empty safe."

"Look, there is nothing there. Three boxes and a dial pad. We have already dealt with the latter. So, what's left are the three boxes."

"And a shelf. Exactly, the shelf." Cyrus was thinking for a few seconds. "I have never seen a Russian safe before, and not too many American ones, so, it's hard for me to see. Is there anything unusual about this shelf?"

Vladimir was surprised. He looked at that shelf, turning his head, looked at it from beneath, with his head almost on the floor. Finally, his tone changed to concerned, "You know, you may be on to something." He shook his head again, and continued, "All the shelves are usually one sheet, usually reinforced with a frame below, but I have never seen one like this, come to think of it."

"I don't get it."

Vladimir gestured at the shelf. "See, it's sheet metal, right?"

"Yes."

"Well, why would you enclose it from below? If you need to reinforce it, put a frame underneath of it, but why would you need to cover the frame from below with another piece of sheet metal?"

"That's it. What if there is a contact below the box, and the contact is covered by the box?"

Vladimir's face turned pale again. "You may have just saved our two skins again."

He went away, and returned five minutes later with a thin sheet of steel and two heavy metal bars. "I think, we can handle this."

He slid the steel sheet under the corner of the box. Cyrus was helping, making sure that the box itself wouldn't move. Vladimir very slowly and carefully slid the sheet under the box deeper and deeper. Then, the sheet met resistance. Somewhere close to the center of the box.

"Here. A contact. Another security string. Bastard."

Trying several times, Vladimir managed to slide the sheet between the contact and the bottom of the box. "Got it."

He inserted the sheet fully under the box, making sure that there was no other contact. There was none.

They took a little break, and started again. Cyrus very carefully slid the box off the inserted sheet, making sure that he did not accidentally lift it. At the same time Vladimir slid the bars onto the sheet, also without lifting them, and followed the box very closely.

In five minutes it was done. The box was out, the steel were on the inserted sheet in place of the box, and nothing happened. Cyrus put the box on the table.

They inspected the box carefully. It was made of steel, the surface painted with dark gray enamel. Obviously, it was not just a metal box. It was machined meticulously. The surface was smooth, the corners slightly rounded with no hint of seams. Two handles on the ends and one on a side were also carefully made. Sturdy, well made and smooth. Like an unusually flat treasure chest, but crafted to the highest mechanical standards.

Vladimir tried to lift it by the end handles. "My God, it's about fifteen kilograms. The metal must be very thick." He knocked on the cover. The sound was dull. "It is."

The thin line of separation between the top and the bottom parts was almost invisible. It ran horizontally around the box, about two inches from the top. No hinges were visible. One end had a seal indenture two inches in diameter and a quarter inch deep. Half of it was in the top of the box, and the other half in the bottom part. A row of six small wheels of a combination lock protruded through the windows in the surface just below the seal. However, the windows were slightly sunk into another smooth indenture in the body, so, the lock wheels would not stick out of the wall plane, preventing possible accidental damage. Cyrus touched one of the wheels. No slack.

Obviously, the lock was made with care and precision. *Well, they put a lot of effort into making this gadget. All the workmanship is meticulous. I bet it holds some surprises.*

Cyrus looked at the seal in the indenture. The sealing wax was bright red. The indenture of the seal was some sort of extremely complex picture. In the middle was a large number 1, in a seventeenth century style, such as is often found at the beginning of the first chapter in the handwritten books of the time. To the right of the 1 was a bas relief portrait of Lenin. On the left side was a picture of the Kremlin, completed in extremely fine detail. Additional fine lines elaborately covered the surface.

Vladimir followed Cyrus' study. "I've heard about this seal but have never even seen its picture. It's the personal seal of the General Secretary. Extremely rarely used, nobody even knows for what occasions."

"Well, now you know one."

"Kirill, I have no idea how we're going to tackle this one. The case is too strong, we can't pry it, we can't break it. I'm not sure it's easy to cut it. It could be some special hardened steel, you know."

I don't even want to try.

"Well, since you're leaving anyway, we don't have to worry about replacing the box. Let's carry it out, and then see."

Vladimir sighed, "You're right. Let's wrap it up."

They were both anxious to close the dreadful safe.

Suddenly, Vladimir said quietly, "Kirill, I don't know how to arm the damn thing back."

"So?"

"That may be very bad. We don't know if they monitor the armed mode. If they do, they'd notice that it's not armed, maybe they already have. It's certainly not as bad as an alarm, but it isn't good at all."

"How much time do we have?"

"No idea. We don't even know where they monitor the signal, in Moscow, or here. But in any case, we should have some time. This is still not an alarm. At worst, it's the absence of 'Armed' signal, which is usually regarded lightly. They'd start with checking the bulbs, then they will call here and ask me to check the seal, and so on. It would take the Chief's trip here to find out what happened. Still, nobody can open his safe." He paused, "And, after all, it's possible that they do not monitor the 'Armed' signal at all. Then, we're home free. The trick is, we don't know. And we'll only find out if we get in real trouble."

We've got one hope here. The blinking red light in the safe went off, not the steady one. That may be an indication the 'armed' mode is not constantly monitored.

"I see. Let's close the damn thing back, and get the hell out of here."

"We can't get out of here until nine. I'm on duty, remember? The guards know that, they keep the log of everybody in here, and they know that this place is never without a duty officer. They'll detain us right away."

"I got the picture. Then we're trapped, hopefully till nine."

"Precisely."

They sarted working quickly. Vladimir closed the safe and locked the main lock. Then he closed and locked the outer lock. The plastic strip was put back into the sheath and the sheath replaced on the small key. Both keys went into the box, the seals were replaced with the sealing wax, using their copy of the Chief's seal. The safe's surface was cleaned of any oil. While Vladimir was busy with something else, Cyrus found a dusty piece of cloth in the pantry, and lightly dusted both the safe and the key box seals. Now the fresh sealing wax didn't shine.

The room was locked and sealed. Everything was cleaned up, put in two small bags, which went into Vladimir's coat pockets.

They were sitting in the hall, tired. The box was on the table.

"Well, Kirill, let's see where we are. We were supposed to come here, get the papers without any problems, and go on with a darn comfortable lead time. Right?"

Cyrus nodded.

"Now, what happened was quite different. We got here all right. Then, we barely managed to escape two traps, and we don't know if we missed the third one or not. Right?"

Cyrus nodded again.

"On the top of everything else, instead of the papers, we have a fifteen-kilos box which we're scared to open, and scared to carry."

Cyrus had to agree. "Yeah, I guess you're right. We don't even know what's in the box. But I'm still scared to open it here."

"Don't worry about the contents, it's our box all right. You tracked it down here independently of me. And I know that if Gorbatov and Kruchina are doing something together it has to be about money. Not nuclear secrets, not intelligence, not any other secrets, just plain, damn money, nothing else." He paused, "Well, maybe power. But that's it."

I hope, you're right.

Vladimir continued, "So, forget about whether we're blown or not. We'll find that out soon enough, and there is nothing we can do about it, anyway. But the question is, what are we going to do with the damn box? If we get out of here, we'll have to make a mad dash to Moscow to deal with those scoundrels. Then, a mad dash abroad. Are we going to carry the damn thing all the time and cross the border with it? Or should we stop somewhere to open it?"

"Well, I'd carry it abroad. It's safer to deal with it there."

"And how are you going to carry it through the border, may I ask? I take it they're still looking for you, and they'll probably look even harder after our Moscow tour, and you're going to travel in style with this fancy box?"

"We'll think of something."

Vladimir shook his head. "On the other hand, somehow, after seeing those two traps, I'm not eager to test my fate by opening the box here. So, in other words, we don't have much of a choice as of now."

Cyrus' training and experience urged him to relax, rest, and fill up before the upcoming uncertainty which might well require all his wits, strength, and stamina.

He stretched his legs on the couch. "Vladimir, I'm starving. Do you have any food around here?"

"Sure. Plenty." He hesitated., "Kirill, how can you eat at a time like this?"

"What's wrong with that? It's half past seven, supper time."

"Must be nice to be able to take it so easy."

"I suggest you do the same. Relax. We may have a pretty rough time ahead, you know. Let's just have a good meal."

Vladimir was shaking his head as he walked to the kitchen to warm some canned meat.

Seven fifty five. The meal was over, and Cyrus was cleaning up the kitchen. "The only thing left to do is to make some sort of harness for the box. I think I can carry it under my coat without attracting too much attention."

"That's crazy. Why don't you carry it in a suitcase? No place to buy it now, but we can drop by my house and take one."

"I'd rather not. The damn thing is too heavy, and a suitcase can break, Besides, if I need to move fast, I'd be better off this way."

Vladimir chuckled, "You sound like you've been smuggling things all your life."

"Not really, just trying to think ahead." *Careful.*

Vladimir disappeared and returned a couple of minutes later with some cord, duct tape, soft foam padding, firm plastic sheets, brown packaging paper and a few tools. Another fifteen minutes and Cyrus had the box, wrapped in brown paper, attached by its end handle to a reasonably comfortable harness around his shoulders, hanging to the side and slightly behind, six inches above his waist down to just above his left knee. It was secured to his left thigh, so it wouldn't bang him as he walked.

Eight twenty. Time. Vladimir opened the entrance door slightly and watched the corridor outside for about five minutes. No one.

Cyrus put his cloak on and walked, limping slightly, to the restroom as fast as he could. He went into the closet and closed the door. He couldn't sit down because of his attached luggage, and standing was not easy. The box was heavy. Finally, he managed to rest the bottom end of the box on a rung of a small ladder leaning against the wall and that took most of the weight off his shoulders.

Fifteen minutes later he heard footsteps going toward the communications section. In five more minutes he heard the footsteps coming back. The door to the restroom opened and closed. Vladimir knocked once and opened the closet door. No words said, just his nod.

They went to the elevator and minutes later they were approaching the checkpoint. This would be Cyrus' first test carrying the box. He barely managed to squeeze a slight smile on his supposedly relaxed face, but all his attention was focused on not limping. He succeeded for the necessary two hundred feet in the sentry's view, and another hundred to the car.

Five more minutes later they had exited the compound uneventfully, and headed east by northeast.

Chapter 14

Vladimir made a couple of turns to get out of town and then took a road leading due north. The headlights illuminated a small sign on the shoulder read "Kotel'nich - 220 km; Yarnsk - 90 km." Vladimir and Cyrus looked at each other. Their sense of relief was obvious, but neither of them was eager to celebrate, their ease tempered by their concern about their inability to rearm the security system of Katurov's safe.

"Well, at least we got out, and I did not see anything irregular at all. The good news also is that there was no phone call saying, 'Hey, we've got a weird signal, what's happening over there?' I had definitely expected that."

"Yes, I understand. Let's hope that it goes on this way, Vladimir."

Vladimir switched to the immediate task. "Your train comes to Kotel'nich at one forty and stays five minutes. It's an express. So, we have time."

The road was not too bad by Russian standards and absolutely horrible by American. Cyrus noticed that Vladimir was doing about sixty miles an hour. Considering the road condition, the sleet on the surface, and the dark, it was definitely too fast. One of the golden rules of intelligence is never drive faster than you have to. "Actually, we have plenty of time. Wouldn't it be better to slow down a bit, so we have a better chance of getting there in one piece -- otherwise, the whole thing doesn't make too much sense, does it?"

Vladimir laughed. "Scared? Don't worry, we drive this way here all the time. Besides, don't be fooled by the time we have. This reserve can evaporate in a heartbeat if we hit some snag down the road. Believe me, there are plenty of opportunities for delays. Anything can happen in this Godforsaken part of the country."

But after a moment's hesitation, he slowed down to fifty miles an hour.

For several minutes they were silent. The car headlights, even on high beam, were not very good. All they could see was a relatively straight road, within a bed of almost non-existing shoulders, surrounded by a never-ending tall, thick forest. There had been no sign of civilization since they left town, and Cyrus knew that it would be like this almost all the way to Kotel'nich.

Finally, Cyrus decided to poke into something that had been bothering him all along. "Vladimir, as a businessman I deal with a lot of different people, and I always know what motivates them to do what they do. Don't get me wrong, I'm very happy with the fact that we are on the same team now, but I'm still not sure what drives you. After all, obviously, you could've accomplished your vengeance without me, without taking this huge risk. And, somehow, I have a hard time believing that it's money."

Vladimir chuckled. "In other words, the 'right thing to do' sounded a little weak?"

"If you will."

"Perhaps it's that proverbial Russian soul, which supposedly is not understood by anybody." Vladimir took a long pause. "Actually, it's rather simple and logical. All my life, along with a lot of people around me, I worked for an idea and ideals. The idea and ideals of communism. How else do you make people work like hell, beyond their capacity, and ask them to sacrifice so much?"

Cyrus did not respond, and Vladimir continued, "Gradually, about fifteen years ago, we started wondering. Started blaming the wrong people at the top for twisting the idea and abandoning the ideals. But it did not add up. Then, all of a sudden, it became clear that the whole thing was wrong. The idea was wrong, the ideals were wrong, the methods were evil. The whole thing was evil. What do you do?"

"Get rid of it."

"Not that simple. People usually need to feel that somebody is at fault, and that somebody has to be punished. Who is at fault, who are you going to fight, and who are you going to punish?"

He took another breath. "The trick is that we all contributed to that, we all are at fault. Some more, some less, but all. From the very beginning. That's the tragedy. And a lot of people realize that now and don't know what to do. See, there are a lot of cute attempts to narrow the blame. But if you're honest with yourself, that doesn't work."

"Well, surely, some people weren't to blame, at least at the very beginning."

Cyrus was carefully hinting at the upper class in pre-Revolutionary Russia, from which his mother's family came. Vladimir promptly understood the hint. He did not get angry.

"That's where you're wrong. Let's start form the beginning and from the top. We had a Czar, who did not want to be a Czar. His obligation was to be a leader of the country, and he was not. He relinquished his power without a fight, and I suspect, with a sense of relief. He just wanted to be a farmer, that's an historical fact."

"Yes, he did."

"We had the upper class, with all its advantages of good upbringing, education, money and power. It was their responsibility to make sure that the country continued to prosper, to guard it against evil and dangers of all sorts. Did they fulfill their obligation? No. What did they do? They were swimming and sinking in their wealth, they were only concerned with how they looked, and quarreled amongst themselves."

While Cyrus was forced to admit that Vladimir had a point there, that notion did not sit well with the way Cyrus had been raised. He was thinking of how many of that upper class died bravely, or were slaughtered, including women and children.

"You are painting with an awfully broad brush, you know. Not all of them, by far, were that way."

"Not all? Surely enough for the result to be as it was," said Vladimir tersely.

Cyrus was getting involved. "So, you want to put all the blame on the upper class, on the aristocracy? No question, that's very convenient."

Vladimir did not notice Cyrus' anger. "Not at all. It's just the beginning. What did the rest of the people do? Even worse. No matter what they said or say, they were tempted by the opportunity to take something that didn't belong to them. To take it by force and to rationalize the robbery somehow. They could whine later that they didn't mean for the whole thing to go so far, but that's nonsense. There is no middle ground between evil and good. And, they got what they deserved later. They were slaughtered."

"Again, not all of them."

"Yes, and again, enough of them for the result to be as it was."

Cyrus didn't know what to say.

"It's funny, but some people are now trying to find a small group to blame for the revolution and for the ideology. One of the latest is particularly cute. Do you know about the Jewish revolution theory?"

"A little. That refers to the fact that over ninety percent of the first Central Committee were Jews?"

"Yes. And that the majority of the original Commissars were Jews too, and that all of them changed their names to Russian ones. They say that it's all Jews' fault. The theory goes, that this small clique of Jews duped the Russian people into all that communist crap, which was merely a Jewish ideological trap for Russia. You know what I say when I hear that?"

"What?"

"We Russians are supposed to be a great and a proud nation. If that theory is true, what greatness and what pride can we find in being duped into destroying our own nation by a bunch of Jews? " He paused. "After that people usually shut up."

"What you just described isn't a pretty picture, I must admit."

"It's just a mildly critical overview with no conclusion."

"If this is not a conclusion, then what is?"

"It's even uglier. Whatever the origins, the result is really horrifying. What happened is that a bunch of criminals hijacked Russia, robbed it and exploited it for seventy-some years, and are now trying to legitimize their plunder without any ideological cover."

"I couldn't disagree with that."

"It's obvious, look at Russia now. There is no distinction between the criminals and the businessmen, or between the businessmen and the politicians, or between the politicians and the criminals. Every sizable business entity contains all of the above. Contrary to popular belief, corruption does not exist here. There is nobody here to corrupt, they already own the damn place, lock stock and barrel. They don't consider that they take bribes, they simply think that they tax you, and, in essence, they are right."

"Well, that's a pretty grim view of the situation."

"It's a sober view, a realistic one. Whether we like it or not."

Vladimir paused again. "So, that's the answer to your question. This understanding drives me. You just showed up at the right time with this hunt of yours."

Yeah, timing is everything.

After a while of driving in silence and meeting only a handful of trucks going back to Yoshkar-Ola, they suddenly saw lights ahead. Orshanka. Just as they entered a clearing in the otherwise dense forest, there was a military police checkpoint.

Vladimir slowed down, preparing to stop. A policeman recognized the military license plate on the car and waved them off. They did not stop.

"There are a few military bases here, two airfields nearby. They man this station around the clock."

"Will they register your license plate?"

"No, they wouldn't bother. They look mainly for soldiers on unauthorized leave to see girls and for trucks with goods stolen from the military. They want their share of taxes too."

Orshanka ended as suddenly as it appeared. Cyrus felt that he had to support Vladimir somehow. He did not like the frightening depth of his disillusionment.

"You know, Vladimir, I want to tell you something, something you probably don't know about the United States. Some people don't realize it, but the real backbone of the American economy is not General Motors, General Electric or General Dynamics."

"What is it then?"

"It's the Ma and Pa corner grocery, bakery, or whatever is there. They are the real engine of the American economy. Natural competition among them allows the best to grow, the worst to go down. People are the most important ingredient of the successful economy, not General Motors. These large companies grow as long as they possess entrepreneurship. They become bureaucracies as soon as they lose it, and die in a while thereafter. It's a natural process. But what feeds the whole process is the people's entrepreneurship." Vladimir was listening carefully. Cyrus took a breath and continued, "So, what happened in Russia, from an economic stand point, was that they killed everybody who knew how to run a corner bakery. They destroyed the very fabric of the economy and were just riding it out on the accumulated wealth. This kind of ride sooner or later comes to an end. Russia was so rich that they had enough to ride on for over three quarters of a century."

"I never thought about it that way, but I think that you're right."

"Well, the logical result will follow, now, while the economy is being freed, even with the major wealth being seized by the current business warlords. Whether they want to or not, they'll give business to Ma and Pa shops. Those crumbs from their table are beginning to feed a grass roots economy. That, in turn, will lead to some of them being successful and growing, growing independently of the criminals at the top. The criminals, in turn, will have their wealth eroded by incompetence and bureaucracy. Eventually this process will lead to a shift in power. That's where the future of Russia rests. If, of course, people here don't destroy each other first in the struggle for the remainder of the plunder."

Vladimir sighed. "That's incredibly interesting. I have to think it all over, and not once. But still, I wish I was as optimistic as you are."

They crossed a long bridge over a lake with the dark water hardly visible in their dim headlights. Vladimir gave a sigh of relief.

"This is a nasty place. In winter you can get stuck here for three-four hours, easy. November is much better."

Cyrus noticed the weather had changed. There was no sign of rain anymore. Light snow was falling and it was not melting on the ground.

They hit a T-junction with a small military police post. Vladimir did not even bother to reduce speed, and the police paid no attention to them whatsoever. They turned right and were moving northwest. Using a flashlight, Cyrus saw on the map that they were following the lake on their right, though he could not see the lake itself. They were on the final stretch to Kotel'nich which was still thirty miles away when Vladimir reduced speed.

"Now I can slow down. Not much uncertainty ahead. I don't want to get you there too early, either."

Cyrus crawled to the rear seat and fixed his gear. He put his colonel's cloak into a military backpack. The backpack was not too full, but certainly did not look empty, which would be suspicious. Besides, Cyrus needed the option of putting the box into it at any time. All fixed and checked, Cyrus crawled back to the front seat.

"So you arrive in Peter very early in the morning on Wednesday. Shouldn't be any problem to catch the morning 'Red Star' to Moscow. So, I'll meet you around seven in the evening as we agreed."

"I wonder if that gives me enough time to hide the box."

"Just put it in a locker at the rail station. Don't be silly, Kirill, don't complicate what is complicated enough. Who cares about those lockers? If you try something too clever, you can get caught right there."

"All right. But, just in case, a fallback meeting at nine next morning, same place."

"I'm flying tomorrow morning. So, I'll have more than twenty four hours to do the groundwork in Moscow."

"I still think that a train is better for you."

"Not after our possible mishap. If they get suspicious, and I've taken off, they'd pull me in. If, on the other hand, I officially asked for time off for family reasons and fly the military flight, they may let me stroll around for a while even if they are suspicious. They'll be looking for anyone I might be working with. This will give me the time I need. Besides, I have to go to Kursk via Moscow anyway, so it's only natural that I fly free instead of paying my own way."

"Well, you know the playground. Where should I stay in Moscow?"

"I'll find something, don't worry."

They were silent again, but this time, with the approaching split, the silence was tense.

"You want to say something, Kirill?"

"Well, strange as it may seem, I've gotten used to you. The separation feels unwelcome."

Vladimir nodded. Obviously, he felt the same.

"One more thing too, Vladimir. I have dealt with a lot of people, but you are, surely, unusual. You trust me on my word for ten million dollars. Particularly now, when chances are better than fifty-fifty that we've got that information."

Vladimir laughed, "First of all, the chances are at least fifty-fifty that we'll get the box out of Russia. Before we had the box, they were small. We don't even realize how small. But on main subject, the fact is that I'm an unusually trusting person. Besides, I'd rather not discuss what I'm sure you have already understood; if I'm disappointed, I know where to find you and I can send some nasty folks, the KGB included, after you. You wouldn't want to trade your enjoyable life for one of constant fear and a rather predictable outcome."

They entered Kotel'nich and Vladimir slowly circled the town for about half an hour. Cyrus crawled to the back seat and put on his harness with the box. Now he could not get back to the front seat.

"Vladimir, can the train be seriously late?"

"In winter, yes. A few hours easy, so much snow everywhere and not enough equipment. This time of the year, no. You've got about thirty minutes. Time to go. I'll wait here to see you off. Just in case."

Cyrus knew that any argument would be useless. Besides, he was uneasy because he looked none too fancy, had no documents and the station police could be a concern. The tickets could also present a problem, and using Vladimir's KGB ID would be a weapon of last resort.

Shaking hands with Vladimir Cyrus felt unexpected warmth.

Cyrus entered an old, shabby, and dirty station. The first relatively large hall contained the obviously perpetual smell of beer, alcohol, dirt, and sweat. Passing the door to the restroom added a sharp smell of urine. *In all of Europe you can find a public restroom by just following the smell, but in Russia it's easier than most places I know of. And, there are more public restrooms, too.*

He went straight to the cashier. He still wasn't quite sure what would be the best ticket. The common car is the least conspicuous, but the police could be a problem. There are plenty of labor camps and prisons along the route. If someone has escaped, I am in trouble without documents. In the 'coupe' I would be more noticeable, but the police would be much friendlier there. First class is out of the question, too noticeable. But right now the main issue is the availability.

With two people in front of him, he waited for ten minutes. He asked for, and bought a ticket for a coupe with no trouble at all. He'd share it with three others.

Ten minutes to the train. Cyrus went to the bar and bought six bottles of mineral water, ten packs of wafers and five large bars of dark chocolate. *Going to the bathroom will be my biggest problem. Hopefully.* He went to the bathroom with all its smell.

People started moving to the platform as soon as the sign showed number three for the express to St. Petersburg. With his motion limited, Cyrus decided to get as close as possible to his car. Limping slightly, he walked with the thin crowd, ranging from several peasants with back sacks to an obviously nouveau riche man with a blonde in a mink coat. The train pulled in only fifteen minutes late. After a slight struggle with the very steep steps, Cyrus was surprised to find his place vacant. He was up on his top bunk quickly, despite his carry-on handicap. His companions were slightly surprised by his taking his coat off up on his bunk. He lay down right away.

One of the passengers, a man of about sixty five, boarded the train with him at Kotel'nich, and the other two were traveling from some earlier point. A young man, obviously a university student, and a woman of about sixty were on their bunks but not sleeping. After the mandatory introductions Cyrus, finally left to himself, took off his harness and carefully tucked the box against the wall, covering it with his body and a blanket.

He participated briefly in a general conversation, then excused himself, saying that he was very tired and not feeling too well, and pretended to dozed.

He was pleased with the set-up. At least, he would have a night, or whatever was left of it, without needing to explain anything. He wouldn't need an excuse for staying in the bunk the whole time. Cyrus could not possibly risk leaving the box unattended, and carrying it around would be difficult. So he'd have to stay put for the rest of the trip. The only exception would be an occasional trip to bathroom.

Cyrus assessed the situation. He could not isolate anything that hinted at his being in danger, or under surveillance. All right, so far, so good. I'm good at least till morning. What are the dangers tomorrow? One -- possible police searches for escaped prisoners; two -- explaining to these folks why I never leave this bunk. He coughed several times, simulating a deep cold and laying his groundwork for tomorrow's "staying in bed."

He was sleeping and he was not -- that suspended state, known to those who regularly face situations where you have to rest and be fresh in the morning, but absolutely cannot afford to fall asleep. His ears monitored the situation well beyond their coupe. When the student on the other top bunk quickly dozed off, Cyrus felt more relaxed. He was monitoring the chat of the older people down below. Both, apparently, had some sleep problem, or they had caught something on the train. Initially irritated, Cyrus soon got used to the chatter about everything on Earth, and it stopped bothering him. He was amused when the conversation turned to him.

The woman said, "You know, that Kirill on the upper bunk, he's really strange."

"Sure, he jumped onto that bunk as if somebody was taking it away from him. On the other hand, who isn't crazy these days."

"He's not well dressed, but did you notice his language? He's obviously educated." She paused, and the man elected not to develop the subject further. Then the woman continued, "Everything is so confusing now. There used to be order. Not anymore. Decent people dressed like bums, bums dressed like decent people. Total confusion. Well, we really need a firm hand, don't we?"

"We definitely do."

They went on developing the theme that despite all the negatives, at least there wasn't such a shameless mess and confusion during Stalin's time.

What material for American sociologists and psychologists! Wasted, and no use to me, and right now I sure, would be happy to swap places with them.

During the night Cyrus did not forget his cough, which made regular appearances followed by his quiet groans. He knew that he was on the right track when he heard the woman's sympathetic voice. "My God, he might get a pneumonia, if he doesn't already have one. I bet he doesn't have a place to stay anymore. Oh, those democrats."

In the morning, as late as he could, which happened to be around nine thirty, Cyrus woke up and declared that it looked like he was sick. He promptly received a dozen uncorrelated pieces of advice on home remedies, blaming of the weather, living conditions, and these days doctors and, of course, offers of help.

No, thank you, everything will be all right, just a slight discomfort. He'd only appreciate if the young man would buy some magazines for him at the next stop. He was not hungry at all, thank you. A short trip to the bathroom took just two minutes, and his traps were not disturbed.

So, Cyrus settled for the day. He was glad to see that Vologda, the half-way point of his trip, went by at two in the afternoon. It was time to plan his next move.

I really can't pull this off without support. Cyrus took a sheet of paper, put it inside the magazine, and started writing. He wrote several sentences, sighed, and added two more. Half a page total. He read it over. *Can't do any shorter than this.*

He took a separate sheet of paper and rewrote his message, substituting all the letters with numbers, and leaving two lines after each written line.

Now, the code. Cyrus took another sheet of paper and started making the key. His personal key was the rain in Spain goes mainly in the plain. He wrote the sentence, digitized it as he had done his message before.

Half the job was done. He wrote down the date, followed by the number of days of his absence from Washington. After that he started doing some arithmetical manipulations between the last number and the digitized 'rain'. The result was almost a page long sequence of digits. He was satisfied so far, and took a breath.

Cyrus rewrote the last sequence under his original digitized message, digit under digit. The rest was simple. He added each digit of the message to the corresponding digit of the key, but he did it in a cryptographic way, where three plus eight equals one but not eleven, and seven plus nine equals six. That was all.

The last operation was to rewrite the result, separating digits in groups of five. Now his job was complete. His message was encoded, and, even in the wrong hands, it would pretty reliably keep the contents private, for John Porter's eyes only.

Cyrus breathed a sigh of relief, made his next trip to the bathroom and promptly disposed of the intermediate results, keeping only the final cryptogram.

The rest of the day was uneventful and Cyrus began to feel the effects of lying still for a long time. By midnight his whole body was aching, but stretching was out of the question. By three in the morning everyone in the coupe was ready for the arrival. By four thirty everyone was in their starting positions.

When the train finally pulled to the platform, the passengers rushing out of the train looked like they were about to miss a train, when in fact they had nowhere to go till the Metro opened at five.

Cyrus got out of the train and went to the main hall of the rail station. Deciding between the Metro and a taxi was not easy. The Metro was more inconspicuous, but walking there with his box could be complicated. Cyrus decided on a taxi.

He gave the address to the driver, and they rolled through the still empty streets of St. Petersburg. Half an hour's ride ended near a large apartment building. Cyrus paid the driver and slowly entered the building. The driver was in no hurry to drive off, apparently hoping for a passenger, but finally decided in favor of better chances at a nearby bus stop and pulled away.

Cyrus stepped out of the building and walked to another high-rise apartment building, three hundred yards away. It was still dark. The windows of the apartments around him began lighting up. People were getting ready to go to work. Making sure that nobody was observing him, he walked slowly around the building. Once around the corner, he rushed as fast as he could to a small side stairway down to the basement. A large lock was hanging outside the door. He pulled the left hinge. As expected, the screws to the door were loose.

Cyrus opened the door, stepped in, and carefully closed it behind, after trying to make sure the hinge did not to stick out too much. He spent five minutes on the landing of the basement while his eyes got used to the almost full darkness. He left his backpack near the door, walked another two flights down and started moving to the far left corner, carefully navigating between the silhouettes of the equipment of the room.

Traditionally this was called a boiler room, though in fact it was not. Like so many others, this building was heated by hot water coming from a nearby power station. The basement was just an entry for those big, two-feet in diameter pipes, one bringing the water in, the other carrying it out. So, as far as heating went, the boiler only contained huge wheeled valves, which were open all the time anyway and did not require any maintenance. Otherwise those basements had no other function except as storage rooms for the building maintenance. Some of them also had bomb shelters, but fewer and fewer new buildings had those.

Cyrus finally managed to get to the corner and find the place where the two pipes entered the basement through a square concrete tunnel, five feet by five. Standard setup. One could squeeze in and walk through but only in dire need. Cyrus was. He took the harness off and carried the box in his right hand, and slowly progressed through the tunnel.

Thirty yards later he stepped into a bigger tunnel, six and a half feet wide, with its ceiling opening to a shaft apparently leading up to a manhole. Cyrus knew that this particular manhole led nowhere. It was closed when someone decided to build a basketball court over it. At last, Cyrus could stand up. He put the box on top of one of the pipes and took a breath.

Then he took a few more steps forward, moving into total darkness. He found the beginning of the bulge on top of the right pipe. Undoing the duct tape was easy. He unfolded the cover plastic and felt a metal mid-size toolbox, he knew it was one of three there. He then carried the toolbox back to where he could stand and opened the cover. Luckily for Cyrus, there was a flashlight taped to the top; he freed it and turned it on.

The rest was easy. The toolbox contained a lot of equipment. Cyrus took out a cellular phone, which was modified with a special module attached. The phone contained a high speed modem and some memory. *I wish I knew whether it's the new model, with an encoder.* Since he had already done his encoding, he would simply use it for transmission in an open mode.

He took out his encoded message, turned the phone on and flipped a small switch on its side. A red light blinked five times and went off. Cyrus started punching the digits of his message into the phone. It required a lot of concentration not to mix up the sequence. In five minutes it was all done, his message was in the phone's memory. He flipped the switch back and put the phone in his pocket.

Now let's see, what else have we got here. He started browsing though the box. He picked two spare batteries for the phone, and a small flashlight. He also took out a leg pouch with hundred dollar bills and a wallet with smaller dollar bills and Russian rubles of different denominations.

Now, weapons. I don't think I need much. Cyrus took a nine millimeter Walther with four extra clips, and a pen. He thought for a second and added a miniature lock picking kit. He added three mini-med kits. *That's it.* He looked at his watch. Six ten. He tucked everything else away, closed the tool box and put it back in place. Then he attached his box at the end of the bulge and camouflaged like the rest of the cache, using material he took from the toolbox. He started making his way out. The Red Arrow departs at nine.

Cyrus took a bus to the Metro and then arrived at the train station. First things first. He spent time in line, bought his ticket, and went out to the station square. He knew that the phone was programmed in such a way that it would use an existing and legitimate number either from St. Petersburg or from Moscow, controlled by a switch. So it would be no problem to get into the international network. It was also programmed to dial John's emergency number, transmit the message through its modem, receive a confirmation, and sign off. In the middle of the square Cyrus turned the phone on and hit the button. He heard the international line's busy signal. After ten minutes of trying it finally worked. The whole transmission took just a few seconds.

Cyrus walked around the rail station, and finally found what he was looking for, a dumpster. He threw his backpack in.

Shopping time. At eight in the morning it could be a bit of a problem. Cyrus walked up to a taxi.

"Do you know of a place I can buy some good clothes? Not far, so I can make a nine o'clock train?"

"This time of the day? Hmm." The driver gave it a little thought. "No problem. Get in, but you've got to buy quick, we'd need to leave the place by twenty to nine." *Nothing is a problem for a real cabby.*

Ten minutes later Cyrus entered one of the new private shops. A young salesman, most likely a relative of the entrepreneurial owner, became available as soon as he realized the potential. He looked at Cyrus' outfit, eyeing it from top to bottom, and quipped, "Made a good deal, huh?"

Nothing is surprising in Russia these days. But Cyrus figured that somehow the owner wasn't stupid when he opened his store that early. There were quite a few people in the store. "Yeah, going on a vacation now. So I've got half an hour."

"No problem, that's plenty of time."

Half an hour later Cyrus dumped all his old clothes in the store, which did not cause any surprise. Russia was the wild West now. The only item he kept, after a slight hesitation, was his colonel's cloak. Tucked away in a suitcase along with the second set of clothing, it was a memento.

The cabby was right on the money, and Cyrus took his seat on the Red Arrow express to Moscow.

Chapter 15

Vladimir was waiting for him. Cyrus noticed a change in his friend; he was calmer, more focused, all business. There was no sign of any emotion.

They briefly greeted each other and went to a parked black Volga, a mid-sized sedan. Cyrus wore gloves so he would not have to worry about his fingerprints. However, that would be more difficult wherever they stay.

"Did you rent it?"

"Yes. I also borrowed an apartment from a friend who is abroad now."

"Is he in the KGB?" Cyrus was concerned that many KGB people might know his face after his less than orderly departure from Moscow.

"No, he's with the GRU."

The traffic was heavy, and it took them forty minutes to get to a large building on the Frunzenskaya Embankment. The eighth-floor two-bedroom apartment was spacious by Russian standards. Ten-foot ceilings reinforced the impression. Cyrus was not eager to unpack. They sat down, and Vladimir started his briefing without any introduction.

"I think we're set. I've found out who the bastards were. Two operatives from the special operations unit." Vladimir took two small photos out of his pocket and threw them on the table, "Personnel photos. The whole thing was cooked up in the FSB, the Federal Security Service, the former Second Chief Directorate of the KGB. The order was given by the deputy chief of the service, general Voronov."

"But why?"

"As you guessed, Laura had found somebody, but I couldn't find out exactly who. Somebody who even she was not supposed to see or to seek. To make matters worse, she arranged a meeting with you."

"Well, you didn't waste any time here."

Vladimir chuckled. "Twenty four hours is a long time. That's not all. It's all set. I managed to find out where these people are, where they live, and how we get to them."

Cyrus was amazed by the plan. He did not want to do something hastily without a real chance of success. "I'm surprised, and I'm ready to listen."

"The two bastards are easy. By the way, they work shifts, and tonight is their shift. Getting them at work is impossible, but at home right after that is not a big deal."

Cyrus did not respond, and Vladimir continued, "Voronov is another story. He's heavily guarded all the time, he rides with guards in an armored Chaika. The only good news is that he doesn't have a tail car with guards. He has one or two guards inside his car."

Cyrus smiled. "Well, that's a relief, but you aren't proposing to hit him with an antitank missile, are you?"

Vladimir smiled too, but with a mischievous smile. "I'm not, though that is not out of the realm of possibilities."

Cyrus just shook his head.

"Look, his residence is in a heavily guarded building. Incidentally, Brezhnev used to live there a long time ago. He works in an even better guarded building. So, both are out. He does not go shopping. That means that the only time we can get him is en route to or from work."

"How?"

"Simple. I bumped into him a few times in my job when I was working here. He has one weakness which used to irritate everyone: he's extremely nosy. Almost to the point of obsession. That's the weakness that we can use."

Cyrus gave him a quizzical look.

"Well, we create some kind of turmoil just where his car always slows down. I can bet you that he'd order his driver to stop to find out what's happening. For that, they need to open a window, and that opening is enough to toss in a grenade. Remember, the car is armored, so there is no danger to the thrower."

Cyrus instinctively liked the idea. *Chancy, a bit original. It might work.* "Vladimir, you're crazy."

Vladimir laughed. "Maybe just a little bit. Any better ideas?"

"No. By the way, what kind of "turmoil" are you going to create?"

"Well, something like blowing up a concrete lamp post and putting it across the Kutuzovsky Avenue, where he lives. See, I'm an old engineer, and they used to teach us everything in those days."

"Vladimir, you really are crazy, and not just 'a little.' But, for lack of a better idea, I'lll go along. It might work for just one reason. It's too crazy."

"Great. I've got the grenades, plastic explosives, and a remote control."

"You really didn't waste any time here."

"Oh, that's easy when you have a lot of friends, particularly those who don't ask questions."

"Well, I had only a modest success. I bought a handgun in Peter."

"Good. I've got a couple of those too."

After a meal they had a planning session.

The shift changed at eight. The Metro ride was about thirty minutes. The bus stop was fifty yards up the street. They parked in front of the bus stop, conveniently facing the Metro station. Virtually everyone went from the bus to the station during rush hour. At eight forty Cyrus began to wonder.

"Well, our guy seems to have gone somewhere else after work."

"No big deal. Even if he does not show up, we know where to find him. Sooner or later, he'll come home, and we'll get him."

"Not after the Voronov thing, I'm afraid."

"Yeah. We'll see."

"By the way, Vladimir, are you sure you can get out of the country with your passport?"

"I think so. At any rate, we don't have enough time to mess with passports now. We'll take care of it in Peter; I've got a few friends there too."

They both saw their man at the same time. They waited until he was right by the car. Cyrus, sitting in the right front set, rolled down the window. "Semenov?"

The man stopped and looked at the car. The black Volga looked official. "Yes?"

Cyrus' voice was commanding. "Get in. Back to the Center."

He opened the door and stepped out.

"Come on, I just finished the night shift. What kind of a joke is this?"

Standing close, Cyrus lowered his voice. "Voronov is waiting. They just missed you when you left and radioed us to catch you. Very urgent. I'll tell you on the way." He opened the back door.

The man groaned and reluctantly climbed into the back seat. *Good. At least I don't have to hit him in public.* Cyrus got in the back seat next to the man. The car accelerated.

In the car the man was clearly irritated and slightly concerned. "So, what's it all about?"

Cyrus pointed the gun at his chest. "Just a small matter to clear up. Nothing to worry about. Now, unbutton your coat and the jacket. Very slowly."

The man's face went ashen. He obeyed.

"OK. Give me your gun. Two fingers only."

With his left hand Cyrus put the gun in his coat pocket. "Good. Now, shut up and enjoy the ride."

The guy knew better than to try to talk. Using mainly small streets, the Volga moved steadily toward the outskirts of Moscow. Vladimir slowed down near a two story red brick building, apparently a small abandoned factory. They drove through an opened gate into the yard, passing the locked main entrance and stopping near a side door.

This certainly did not look like anything the KGB would use. The man became scared. "Who are you? Show me your ID."

"We will." Cyrus got out of the car and gestured for him to get out too. Vladimir opened the door, and all three of them went into a large hall.

Most of the windows were broken, and all the machinery was gone. All there was inside was dirt, filth, and some pieces of metal and brick. Both Cyrus and Vladimir looked intently at the man's face. Cyrus was trying to find a trace of emotion. Outrage or anger, maybe. All he saw was fear.

Cyrus could not stand it any longer. He saw that tiny yellowish Lada on its deadly rainbow arc. He grabbed the man's throat and squeezed. The man's attempt at kicking Cyrus was easily countered and rudely rewarded with a counter kick in the genitals. Cyrus held the sinking body upright with his firm grip on the throat.

Cyrus released his grip, and the body settled on the floor.

"Do you remember a Lada, going from the Moskvoretsky Bridge down to the river?"

Semenov looked at Cyrus and, with visible difficulty, pressing one hand to his throat and the other to his genitals, stood up.

He tried to speak, and after a while, squeezed out of his mouth, "That was orders. You know how it is."

"How many people do you kill in a shift?"

"Come on. It's not like that. It happens very rarely."

"Who gave the order?"

"Voronov. Personally. My partner and I were called in. Nothing on paper," his speech was interrupted by the loud sound of a gun shot. The bullet hit his abdomen and the man was thrown back. He fell on the floor, twisting in pain. Vladimir kept firing, everywhere, except the vital points, obviously trying to inflict as much pain as he could. He emptied the clip and stopped, looking incredulously at the body in convulsions. After a few seconds pause, he changed the clip and fired one shot in the head. The body froze.

Cyrus took Semenov's gun out of his pocket and threw it away. Then he slowly walked to the door without turning. Vladimir followed.

An hour later they drove to an apartment building in Tushino, another suburb on the opposite side of Moscow. They parked the car a building away and approached the target through a connecting yard in order to make a getaway easier should something go wrong.

Cyrus felt a little uneasy. "Vladimir, if he's not alone, we'd better postpone it. I'm not going to take part in any massacre."

"We'll see." Vladimir was in a rage. Cyrus felt that with him it wasn't just Laura. It was also all his frustration, accumulated and brewed over the years. It was his misplaced safety valve.

They walked up the stairs to the second floor. Nobody in the stairway and no sounds anywhere.

Vladimir rang the bell. He had to ring it three times before they heard footsteps inside. *Good. He must be alone, then. Sleeping after the night shift.*

"Who's there?"

Vladimir answered. "Tartov, Michail Petrovich?"

"Yes."

"A telegram for you."

They heard the sound of the chain taken off and then the perfunctory click of a lock. The door opened. Cyrus pushed the door hard, smashing the host. Vladimir quickly followed, and the door closed.

The sleepy man in underwear did not even have time to react. He looked incredulous and then mumbled, "Guys, take anything you want, just don't kill me."

"Do you remember driving a Lada off a bridge recently?"

The man came alive and started begging, "Orders. I didn't want to. Besides, I didn't even touch that car."

"We have our orders too. From the girl you killed." Cyrus did not want to wait for Vladimir's loud gun. Instead he fired two silenced shots in the man's head and watched as the body slid down the wall to the floor.

They drove to the Botanical Garden, parked in its almost empty parking lot and ate the sandwiches Vladimir had prepared the night before. This was to be their last meal before leaving Moscow. Vladimir changed into a work robe and took a tool bag from the trunk of the car. Cyrus got behind the wheel, and they went to lay the trap for their main target.

Vladimir got out of the car on a side street two blocks away from the building on Kutuzovsky Avenue, and Cyrus roamed around for a few minutes. As he was passing the building, heading toward the center of Moscow, Cyrus saw Vladimir. He had opened the metal door in the wiring space at the base of the lamp post and was working inside. Nobody seemed to pay any attention to the electrician. *So far, so good.*

Ten minutes later Cyrus picked up Vladimir on a different side street.

Vladimir was calm. "We're all set. I placed it really well." He smiled. "It's one hell of a prank, even for Moscow, to drop a lamp post across the Kutuzovsky."

Cyrus chuckled. "It is. Until you start throwing hand grenades. At that point the prank turns a bit unfriendly."

They went to the train station and bought a first class coupe for two to St. Petersburg on the evening express. Afterwards they killed some time just riding around the city. At four o'clock Cyrus dropped Vladimir off at the Kievsky train station and headed to the center of Moscow. By four thirty finding a parking space was not a problem, but Cyrus was worried about spending too much time parked near the KGB building.

He wanted to be close enough to see the license plate, but a car in such proximity would undoubtedly attract the attention of security. Vladimir assured him that there was only one Chaika in the building. But what if somebody else was visiting the building in another Chaika and left at that time. Cyrus finally decided on a spot slightly farther off, a block and a half away, where he'd have a narrow but clear view of the cars leaving the building.

Four forty. Cyrus took the cellular phone. He flipped the small switch to "1" so that it operated as a Moscow phone. He flipped another special switch to "Receive" and pushed the "autodial-11." An international line was acquired right away. The dialing went through smoothly, the log-on was successful, and several seconds later the session ended automatically. Cyrus manipulated buttons one more time. John's message scrolled on the display in plain English. Cyrus read it twice, making sure that he did not miss anything. The exfiltration route was being established. Now he felt much better. However, Cyrus was thankful that John had no earthly idea what he was up to now. He disconnected the special module from the main phone and put it in his pocket.

Four fifty. Cyrus switched to the task at hand. Vladimir's plan had one substantial flaw. Since he managed to get only one cell phone, Cyrus was supposed to call him from a pay phone at the time of Voronov's departure. That would trigger the fall of the lamp post about three minutes before Voronov arrived at his apartment building. Time enough to gather a good-sized crowd, but not enough to make a real mess in the street and make it impassable. What Vladimir had not realized was that Cyrus would miss Voronov's car while getting from the pay phone to his car and would under the best of the circumstances trail behind him by five minutes. That would make Vladimir's escape a virtual impossibility. Cyrus would have to use his magic phone to function as a regular one this time, but Cyrus did not mention that to Vladimir.

Five fifteen. Cyrus immediately recognized the Chaika when it slowly rolled out of the gate. Keeping his motor running, Cyrus just shifted gears and drove forward, taking a small short cut. He drove fast, trying to make sure the Chaika didn't catch up with him too soon. Cyrus dialed Vladimir's number.

"Hello."

"He's on his way."

Driving on Noviy Arbat, Cyrus saw the Chaika in his rear view mirror. It was catching up slowly, but steadily. They were next to each other on the Kalininsky bridge. *Perfect. This way I can legitimately be right on his tail to the very place.* He resisted looking at the Chaika's draped windows.

Soon, he saw a commotion straight ahead. The oncoming traffic, generally light at this time of the day, was at a standstill. And in their direction a small traffic jam had formed just beyond Voronov's building. The Chaika took to the right, almost cutting off Cyrus' Volga, and started slowing down. The crowd ahead was growing, and people were standing in the traffic lanes. In a minute it would be a horrific jam. Five thirty.

At this moment Cyrus saw Vladimir. He was slowly walking toward the driveway. The Chaika slowed down more and turned into the driveway. Vladimir was in a perfect position, almost in the Chaika's way, on its left side. He stopped to let it pass. The Chaika almost passed him then suddenly stopped. Cyrus turned his head and saw the rear left window opening. *Indeed, a man is a creature of habit.*

The side street was now just twenty feet in front of Cyrus. He slowed to a crawl, turned right and stopped. He saw Vladimir standing near the Chaika, sixty feet away. On the other side of the side street, Cyrus saw a black Volga with four men inside parked facing the opposite direction. *Hell. Security. It wasn't here before.* Cyrus rolled down his window and held the gun in his left hand, keeping it low.

He saw Vladimir toss something into the opened Chaika window. He did not see the hand grenade itself. In a split-second, another toss. Vladimir turned sharply and started running toward Cyrus. Cyrus expected a dull thump. Instead, he saw Vladimir take off into the air, thrown by a tremendous force. He saw surprise on his face, and in the next instant, a strong shock, accompanied by a double explosion, rattled his car. He also felt a sharp pain in his right shoulder. He more felt than saw pieces of glass from his right window, shattered by the explosion, flying at him.

Vladimir was lying on the walkway. His pose left no doubt. Instantly, Cyrus knew that Vladimir was dead. All this took no more than five seconds, but those were five very long seconds. Cyrus' autopilot kicked in. He accelerated sharply, and with his left hand, he shot at the front tire of the security Volga. He managed four shots, and at least two were in. As he raced down the street, Cyrus saw the surprised faces of the guards as they jumped out of the car. Too late. He turned right onto the embankment. *Go fast. No traffic here.* He turned right again and, doubling back, crossed Kutuzovsky toward the Kiev rail station. Cyrus was surprised to realize that his mad dash had taken only two minutes.

Cyrus glanced in the mirror. Miraculously, his face was not cut. Then he noticed a warm feeling in his right shoulder. It was bleeding. Now Cyrus faced a dilemma. On the one hand, he had to ditch the car, and quickly. By now everybody was looking for it. On the other, he could not afford to sport his bleeding shoulder, he had to fix it, and the sooner, the better. For that he needed a quiet place, a car for instance. Cyrus arrived easily at a compromise when he saw a big parking lot not far from the rail station. He drove in and parked in the far corner, close to a dumpster. It was getting dark.

Cyrus took off his leather jacket and shirt. Now he was happy that at the cache he had not neglected his training and had taken mini-med kits. By touching his shoulder Cyrus realized that the piece of shrapnel had made a deep cut but had not gone inside. He opened his mini-med kit and made a combo shot with an antibiotic, pain killer, and anti-inflammatory drug. He made the cut narrow by raising his right arm, and though he really needed only four, he made six stitches to make sure that the wound wouldn't open with his movement. He finished it off with a dressing.

He opened his bag and put on another shirt, a jacket and a coat. He also emptied the pockets of the bloody shirt and the leather jacket. Time.

Cyrus got out, put his bloody clothing in the dumpster, and took the license plates off the car. Then he re-parked the car in another corner, took his bag out and walked away.

In five minutes he was at the train station. He stopped at the end of the taxi line. The Metro would be as fast, but he was not sure of his appearance and the light was too bright in the Metro. Cyrus looked at his watch. Five fifty eight. He sighed heavily. *It's hard to believe that half an hour ago Vladimir was alive and everything was going smoothly.* From the very first moment he knew exactly what had happened. Voronov's Chaika was not armored. Either it was a substitute, or Vladimir's information was incorrect. He was cursing himself. *Idiot. It never occurred to you to play that scenario. You should have known better, not Vladmir. Too late now. Concentrate on the task at hand.*

Cyrus stopped at the store and bought four bottles of vodka on his way to the St. Petersburg station. The taxi pulled in at the very crowded local train entrance, and Cyrus made his way to the platform. Police and security men were everywhere and looked alert, but Cyrus was sure that they did not know who they were looking for, and his fur hat served well to alter his appearance anyway.

In his coupe Cyrus put all four bottles on the table. When the conductor came in Cyrus played drunk and rudely insisted the conductor drink a large glass. Naturally, he was left alone for the whole trip.

Chapter 16

At the train station Cyrus put his bag into a locker and went to the Main Post office two blocks away. It was crowded. People were waiting on benches near a row of telephone booths for the telephone calls they had ordered, and others waited on the benches not far from the cashiers, waiting for money transfers. Cyrus chose the second group so that he could spend more time waiting without attracting attention.

Not far from the row of cashiers' windows there was another row of widows, which was what Cyrus was interested in. These three windows, designated by their respective alphabetical range, were where people could retrieve their mail. Due to St. Petersburg's number of visitors, it was a popular place. The mail was marked "hold till requested," and to get one's mail, one first had to show one's passport. That was what Cyrus was after: a passport.

Cyrus did not care what letter the last name started with, but he did care a lot about how the holder looked. *Never mind the height and the build, nor the color of the eyes. Just look for a face.* Russian passport photos where black and white. Height, weight, or any other description of the holder was not indicated.

It took about half an hour for a guy with a face resembling Cyrus to show up.

Here is my guy. Definitely not a twin, but enough resemblance to pass. Cyrus watched him move through the waiting line. In fifteen minutes he was at the window, and Cyrus rose, quickly glancing around to assess the situation.

Looks clean. Both plainclothes policemen are concentrating on a Gypsy woman, and a uniformed one is about to walk outside.

Cyrus made a large circle, calculating his speed so as to collide ten to fifteen feet from the door. *So far, so good.* He saw the guy receiving several letters.

Looping near the entrance, Cyrus did not let the man slip out of his sight. The man left the line and, without stopping, put his passport in the side pocket of the coat. *This is really great.* A few steps later, still walking toward the door, the man started looking at the envelopes. Cyrus was only five feet away. He glanced again at the two plainclothes policemen. *Busy. Now.*

Cyrus was just beside of the man. Suddenly, he heard someone, apparently the telephone operator, call his name. He immediately raised his hand to wave, saying "here!" By doing that he knocked all the letters out of the guy's hands.

Cyrus was so embarrassed that the man's rage evaporated before it started. Very apologetic, Cyrus started picking up the letters spread over the floor. The last letter they were picking up together, Cyrus pressed tightly to the man's right side where the passport was in his pocket. The brush contact lasted less than two seconds, and Cyrus started apologizing again. The guy just said "Never mind, don't worry about it." In a minute the incident was over and Cyrus left the post office. Of course, with the man's passport.

Cyrus had plenty of time and, he was in no hurry to get his harness. *Why don't I have a decent meal, for a change?* He did just that. He grabbed a taxi, and went to Nevsky Prospect.

He let the taxi go and walked along, which in itself was rewarding. He realized he was walking down the main street of his mother's family home town. The crowd was colorful and diverse, the shop windows were inviting and the weather was fairly dry, not too common in this city, famous for its cold winds and drizzling rain. After several blocks he saw a restaurant entrance that suggested good food.

The first item on his own menu was his new passport. The picture was close enough. Privalov, Vasiliy Petrovich, born 1961 in Gorky. Married to Tamara Terkova in Samara on October 15, 1987. Daughter Galina, born April 27, 1989. Resides in Pskov, 59 Lenin St., Bldg. 2, Apt. 38. Previous residence Samara, 26 Metallurgov St., Apt. 12. Cyrus memorized the information.

With a day to spare, Cyrus went to the Hermitage and wished he had a week to stay there.

In the evening he found another good restaurant on Nevsky. The maitre'd sized him up and apparently put him in the upper half, but not at the very top. When Cyrus sat down at the table, the maitre'd offered him an escort, having figured that he was alone. Cyrus declined, considering again how much things had changed here.

During dinner Cyrus thought about John's message. The instruction to get a visa to Estonia at the relatively relaxed border was, perhaps, a good solution. On the other hand, if something went wrong there, he'd have to go back to St. Petersburg, and the whole setup would be off for at least a day, and he'd still have to go to the Estonian Consulate here. *Traveling with the box is an additional risk and, really, a pain in the neck. I'm not comfortable with the idea of finding a safe place for it in Kingisepp and leaving it there for a day. And let's hope they have a good reason for me to hang around Tallinn for another day. Well, let's hope that John knows something I don't.*

Cyrus left the restaurant and quickly found a bar. At quarter to one in the morning he was ready to go. He went to the rail station locker, took his bag out, and left. He took a taxi and went to his favorite apartment complex in St. Petersburg. Getting in was no problem. He went back to the cache to replace the telephone and the lock-picking kit. After a little hesitation, he decided to keep the pen. He would dispose of the Walther a little later.

He had chosen the bag carefully; it did not look too empty with the few items inside, but it was expandable to accommodate the box. The bottom was reinforced with a strong plastic plate so the box wouldn't protrude from the bottom, and it was sturdy enough to contain the heavy box without looking extremely stretched. Next, Cyrus took the box with the harness out and closed the cache. He carried the bag and the box into the main boiler room. *One fifty. Now I need a good cabby. Luckily, many of them are connected to the funny business at the nearby border.*

He put the harness with the box in the bag, wrapping it with clothing so that the shape was not too obvious, and left the basement. He carefully closed the false lock and walked to the bus stop. He waited for fifteen minutes without seeing any activity in the vicinity. *Well, somebody's got to come home late. There are a lot of apartments around here. The last thing I need is a police check. Very unlikely, but it can happen.*

Ten minutes later he saw a taxi, but it was occupied. Fortunately, as it passed by, the driver noticed Cyrus. Cyrus saw the taxi turn into a yard at one of the apartment buildings a block away. Two minutes later, the taxi pulled out, and went straight to Cyrus.

The taxi stopped and the driver rolled down the right window without unlocking the door. "Where to?"

"Central rail station." That obviously was a good destination. However, the driver knew that the customer was in a dire situation.

"Hundred thousand." That was triple the normal rate.

"Do I have a choice?"

The cabby grinned, "No."

At that moment they both saw the headlights of a car with a green taxi for hire light a third of a mile ahead.

The driver quickly leaned over and opened the rear door. I have to get his respect now, or he'll keep trying to push me around.

Cyrus put the bag on the back seat. "Eighty."

The driver laughed. "Deal."

Cyrus got into the taxi, and they pulled off.

"Leaving somewhere? There are no trains before five, why are you going so early?"

This guy looks like he knows his way around here pretty well. Let's try him out. "Just in case. Hard to get out of here at four in the morning. Going to Tallinn, see."

The cabby smelled a possible good deal. "Why not a ride to Kingisepp? I'd give you a discount."

"Oh, I don't know. By the way, I haven't been there since the Union broke up. I reckon, you need a visa these days. A friend told me the best way is to get it at the border."

"That's if you know your way around there. So, you haven't got a visa?"

"No."

"Then, buddy, you've got to ride with me. Look, I got a friend there in Kingisepp. He can get you a visa in no time. By yourself, you'd spend half a day and get nothing.

Not true. But it's OK, sell me this ride. "Is it that bad?'

"You bet. What are you gonna do there, anyway?"

"Just go buy some stuff and bring it back here to sell. Business. My partner's there, almost finished, just needs some help."

The driver was getting more excited. "Come on, you're buying so you have money. Incidentally, what are you buying there?"

"Electronics. Computers and stuff."

"Look, my buddy is tied in to everybody. He'll make sure you get all your stuff through with no problems and no duties. As a matter of fact, he goes to Tallinn almost every morning. You can go with him tomorrow."

Now you're talking. "Well, I don't know. But we really need to get the stuff back to Russia. Nobody wants to pay too much to the government. The taxes kill you."

"You bet they do. It's stupid to pay that much. Smart people pay much less to get things through. Everyone wins, see."

"How much?"

"Two hundred thousand."

That was a fair price. But Cyrus new that the cabby was going to get a piece of the deal from his smuggler buddy. "Deal. Let's go straight to Kingisepp."

"Great. By the way, do you need to get money there? I can arrange that."

Feeling out if you can rob me, pal? I don't need any excitement at this time. "No, we have an account in a bank in Finland, so we'd pay with a check in Tallinn."

"I see. Just started your business, huh?"

"Not too long ago, why?"

"You don't seem to know your way around here too well yet. Well, a lot of people are starting these days."

Cyrus didn't want to look too amateurish either. "We just worked through Turkey for three years. Decided to try the waters here."

In half an hour they were buddies, and by the end of the trip they had a few import-export plans for the near future.

Shortly before five in the morning the St. Petersburg cab pulled up to a medium-size house two blocks from the market square. The lights were already on. The cabby introduced Cyrus to his buddy, actually an Army buddy, "served together in Afghanistan," and the smuggler was interested.

He was interested in carrying a truckload of electronics from Tallinn to Russia the next day for a healthy fee, which would be exactly half the regular import duty. But he was particularly interested in a long-term arrangement. Today he was going with his truck and a driver to pick up a load in Tallinn. Of course, Cyrus was welcome to ride with them. Cyrus was interested in a ride. Nothing further was said, but obviously, he'd want to know the level of the smuggler's contact with the authorities. They understood that well; otherwise, why would a businessman be interested in riding in a truck?

Cyrus was satisfied. So far. Now, even if they're going to sell me out to the authorities, they'll wait till I have something of value with me when I return. They wouldn't want to jeopardize their take on my way there. They'll do whatever they can to give me a smooth ride. That's all I care about.

They started rolling at eight. Before eight thirty they were at the border. Nobody even bothered to stop them at the Russian checkpoint. These guys would stop everyone crossing the other way. The truck stopped at the Estonian checkpoint. The smuggler took passports from both the driver and Cyrus and went inside.

Cyrus became tense. His bag with the box inside was in the truck. Cyrus knew that the best hiding place in such situations is in plain sight, but nobody can avoid being nervous when the moment of truth comes. He managed to put an empty box by it so it would not be obvious if someone just glanced inside, but the arrangement wasn't terribly effective.

At any indication of interest in the truck I have to seize the initiative. Hopefully, everyone here is as corrupt as advertised. A couple hundred bucks should suffice and then we'll see. His plan-B was to try to bribe the guard for a future trip back. Then, either he made a deal for the future, and any current inspection would be out of the question, or if he doesn't, their outrage about being asked for a future deal would at least distract the inspectors and they'd forget their intent. The key was to intervene when an inspector started moving towards the truck. Cyrus was ready.

Two minutes later the smuggler emerged, entered the cabin, and returned the passports. Cyrus' was stamped with a visa. The guard waved, and the truck pulled out. The smuggler was delighted to have demonstrated his powers. Cyrus was delighted too.

At eleven they approached Tallinn and stopped at its very active market. They arranged to meet the next day, and the truck pulled away to some mysterious warehouse to pick up some goods to take back to Russia.

Cyrus knew that an American executive had arrived in London yesterday on business. His bored wife did not want to stay in London where she'd been so many times, and decided to take a tour to Helsinki, but then she changed her mind and decided to go on a side trip to an exotic place called Tallinn. The trip was hurriedly arranged by helpful aids from Helsinki. She was going to spend a night in Tallinn and then go back to London. Cyrus glanced at his watch. Eleven ten. The jet should be landing right now. He had about fifty minutes to set himself up.

Cyrus went around the market. In a few minutes he spotted a man selling a few items of Estonian pottery. Cyrus went up to him. The man was uncomfortable. He did not know how to act in this capacity. He was more doing his time than his business. *Corner stand. Good. The next stand is not too close, and the woman is preoccupied by gossip with her neighbor on the other side. She would not hear.*

"Hello. How's business?"

"Hello. Well, slow." The man became more uncomfortable. He was obviously a Russian expatriate living in Estonia.

"You don't seem to have a lot of experience here, do you?"

The man lowered his eyes. "No." He'd rather fall through the surface of the Earth.

"I tell you what. I've got some time to kill here. How much you hope to sell the whole bunch for?"

The man looked at Cyrus with surprise, and hope. He paused, making calculations. "About two million four hundred thousand rubles."

"Let's make a deal. I buy it for two million two hundred and sell it myself. Whatever I can't sell, I'll take back to Russia and sell at a good profit there."

The man's first reaction was disbelief. Then, he got hyper. "Of course. I've already paid for the spot here for the whole day, here is the receipt." His motions became short and rushed, as if he were afraid that Cyrus would change his mind.

Cyrus got behind the table as if he had been selling pottery at a flea market all his life. He turned so the woman next to them would not see and gave him five hundred dollar bills. The man looked at the bills. They were 1993. Pre-1993 hundred dollar bills were commonly counterfeited and thus were not accepted at most places in that part of the world. Then he looked at Cyrus. The man's bearing and expression suggested his bewilderment.

"I prefer to deal on solid terms."

"I can get you more of this stuff tomorrow."

Cyrus did not want to leave the man with too many questions. "Maybe next time. Come here next Friday, we can talk it over. Meanwhile, do me a favor, get me about ten boxes of different sizes. You can't sell pottery without boxes."

The man disappeared and came back five minutes later with a cartfull of boxes. Cyrus was standing at the cart and loudly promoting his product. "Pottery! Come on here, folks! Incredible Estonian hand-made pottery! The best place on the planet to buy Estonian pottery!"

The man unloaded the boxes and looked at Cyrus in awe, as though he had met the master. Master of business, master of sales. Cyrus winked at him, and the man waved and slowly walked away. After only a few steps he began to accelerate, apparently afraid again that Cyrus would take his money back.

Cyrus was taking a short break in his promotional campaign when his neighbor, a hearty woman of about fifty, asked, "Who are you?"

"I'm his partner." Cyrus nodded toward the departed man.

"I saw that man here for three days, but I've never seen you."

"I'm a silent partner."

The woman laughed wholeheartedly and just shook her head as if saying "Clown. But you seem to be a good guy."

Cyrus glanced at his watch. *About time. Where are you, guys?* His style, not unheard of, but still not too common, ceased attracting attention. Everybody turned to their business, and he became just a minor nuisance.

Meanwhile, a black stretch limousine, one of the two in Tallinn, pulled up to the main gate of the market. An aid helped the bored wife of an American businessman out of the car. She started browsing the market accompanied by her two aids and the translator-guide. Five minutes ago she decided that she wanted to see a local market before going to an historic university and having lunch. Her presence did not go unnoticed. The whole market started whispering and nodding. Without even noticing people were almost at attention, like a military parade.

The lady stopped at a couple of places with national souvenirs, bought some, and the aid put them in a large bag he was carrying. Then she heard Cyrus. Without turning, she asked, "What's that loud fellow selling?"

"Pottery, madam." The guide tried to lead her away.

"Oh, pottery? Is local pottery good?"

"Yes, madam. It's very good, and I can show you an excellent place downtown where you can buy the highest quality Estonian pottery."

"Let me see." She started walking briskly away in the middle of the guide's sentence. There was not the slightest doubt in her mind that her entourage would follow, and close enough to hear her every word.

Cyrus, in a hat that covered his forehead and dark glasses, watched the procession.

A good salesman can't miss such a buyer. "Madam, madam, look at the most incredible Estonian pottery! You will not find the same in the whole world!

The lady came close. She looked at the pottery while the guide tried to steer her toward the hotel souvenir shop downtown. Suddenly annoyed, she turned to the guide. "I had the impression that your business is to translate."

The guide quickly realized that it was time for him to shut up.

"What is he saying?"

"He is saying madam, that this is hand-made Estonian pottery."

"I like it. I'll buy it. Ask him how much he wants."

"Which piece, madam?"

"All of them."

"Excuse me, madam, did you say 'all of them'?"

"Of course. I don't have time to sort it out now. I'll do it at home."

The guide turned to Cyrus. "How much for all of it?"

"Six hundred dollars."

The guide was outraged. "What? Four hundred would be too much. Don't push your luck, pal."

"Five hundred. Final." Cyrus did not blink.

"You Russians come here and embarrass us in front of our guests." He turned to the lady. "He is asking five hundred dollars. Do you want my opinion?"

"No. I'll take it." She opened her purse, pulled out the money and gave it to Cyrus. "Pack it, and quickly."

The guide translated.

Cyrus smiled broadly. "Sure. No problem."

He quickly enlisted two boys, and they started hurriedly packing the pottery.

The lady turned to continue her stroll when the limo driver came up and said something to the guide. The guide turned to the lady. He felt a sense of quiet revenge. He was about to spoil this arrogant bitch's tour.

"Madam, they just received a fax at the airport. Your husband has finished his business in London and he urgently needs to go back to New York. He asked that you interrupt your tour and return to London as soon as possible. Your pilot asked us to tell you that the plane will be ready in thirty minutes."

The lady's face saddened. "Too bad. I'd rather stay here for a day. Oh, well, let's go back." She paused. "Let me stroll here while they're packing the pottery." She turned to one of the aids and said, "Jim, help them to pack it, make sure it's loaded in the car, and then find me here."

"Yes, ma'am."

Once packed, the boxes were loaded on a cart, and the boys rolled it to the limo. Somehow, Cyrus' bag from behind the stand was packed in a box and loaded too. The aid followed the cart.

Cyrus took the aid's bag and went off through the market to find the restroom. Three minutes later, the guide walked into the same restroom. Without stopping or slowing down, Cyrus handed him the bag and walked out. He was no longer wearing either the hat or the glasses. His clothes were an exact replica of the guides'. And, surprisingly, he was about the same height and weight as the aid.

Cyrus went straight to the limo and watched for the rest of the entourage. He turned and saw the lady with the other aid and the guide. He waved, and the other aid waved back. The three walked straight to the limo. Cyrus was meddling with a bag in the back of the limo on the right side. The other aid let the lady in and took the left door position. The guide went to the front seat, and the limo rolled to the airport.

A representative from the travel company waited for them at

the airport. The polite girl expressed her sympathy to the upset lady and reassured her that she had taken care of all the formalities. Her gratuity was handsome. Cyrus carried just one box while the others were taking care of the rest. Fifteen minutes later, the Gulfstream-IV was taxiing to the runway. In five more minutes, they were in the air.

The lady smiled, "You know, Cyrus, what was the most difficult thing for me? Seeing the way you looked at the flea market and not laughing. You can't imagine how hilarious you looked."

"Well, Joan, it was not easy to watch you pushing folks around and keep a straight face either."

Joan, John's secretary, hugged Cyrus. "I'm glad, you're back." Her expression changed, and her lips stiffened, "And in one piece. I was worried about you, Cyrus."

"I know." He put his arm around her shoulders and pulled her close.

The next moment he was his old self. "I hope you guys have some scotch around here."

The other aid suggested, "We sure do, but how about some champagne?"

"If you want. I'd rather have Scotch." We still don't know what's in the damn box. The whole ordeal could have easily been for nothing.

Cyrus went to the bar, and when he saw a sealed bottle of Lagavulin, he turned and looked at Joan. *You never forget anything.* She just smiled.

They landed at Gatwick just for refueling. The flight went on to Boston. Another refueling, and the next leg took them to Dulles.

Everyone was tired. Cyrus was surprised to see John at the Dulles Signature Aviation terminal. With very few words said, Cyrus and John took the bag to John's estate. The rest of the team went home.

Chapter 17

Cyrus was finishing his late breakfast in the kitchen when John walked in.

"I thought you'd sleep till the evening. It's only ten thirty. What happened?"

"Oh, just a little insomnia, you know. Getting old."

They both laughed. John was in a good mood. He sat down and poured himself coffee.

"Well, winners don't get judged. Not always, though. I was mad at myself when I let you talk me into letting you go to Moscow."

"There was no other way, John. I knew you wanted this thing badly."

"Not at the expense of losing you. You knew that, didn't you?"

"Well, it's history."

"Yes, but I want to make it clear that it's unacceptable. There is always another way." John sat quietly for a few minutes before finally asking what had long been on his mind. "What happened in Moscow? We saw them looking for you like hell."

"I don't really know. As we'd expected, the General brought me in to search their own bank records. So, I did. I was getting nowhere and then came across one transaction of changing rubles for dollars. I was about to dig into it, and at the same time some rumors of Kruchina's meeting with Gorbatov fell into my lap. And I don't know for sure what upset them. Or anything else, for that matter."

"The interesting twist was that you dealt with their Intelligence. What was going after you was Counterintelligence. We determined that without a doubt."

"That's it, John. Intelligence is trying to find it, along with Yeltsin and Co. Counterintelligence is in collusion with those who hid it, Gorbatov and Co. That's why there's such a mess over there."

"You're probably right. So, you laid low?"

"No, I went to Yoshkar-Ola."

"Where?"

"The Capital of Mariy Autonomous Republic, north of Kazan."

"Good God. You were really looking for adventure."

They moved to the library, and Cyrus told him about his trip. John listened, wondering whether or not it was a fantasy. Knowing Cyrus he was certain that the account was on the conservative side.

John was still shaking his head after forty minutes of brief reporting. He lowered his voice, and said very slowly, "Cyrus, you know the rules. I have to ask you this." He made a pause. "A couple of days ago a Deputy Head of the Counterintelligence was killed in the middle of Moscow in broad daylight. I sincerely hope that you had nothing to do with that."

Cyrus knew that it was a very touchy subject, and he had to be careful with every word. "Well, first of all, I communicated to you that on that day I took a day off for personal reasons."

John grinned. His eyes were saying, "That's precisely what I was afraid of."

Cyrus continued, "I understand that it is a little irregular, but on the other hand, I had to wait a couple of days for the transport anyway."

John was very tense and did not say a word. Cyrus went on, "John, I did not kill Voronov."

John quickly intervened. "That's all I need to know. Your personal matters are of no interest to me whatsoever."

John did not need any translation of the message. Cyrus' mentioning the name delivered the message. He appreciated Cyrus' personal honesty to him while still prudently keeping the record clean. Now, in the unlikely case that John had to answer any questions, he could firmly say that Cyrus reported to him that he did not commit that horrible act. Besides, Cyrus was off the job attending to some urgent personal matters.

John's emotions were thoroughly mixed. On the one hand, he appreciated the incredible drive and courage that Cyrus had demonstrated. On the other, his actions were consistently reckless.

"Cyrus, tell me something. Knowing all I know, what would you do to Cyrus Grant, if you were in my shoes, after this unbelievably successful and incredibly reckless performance?"

Without a trace of a smile, Cyrus snapped, "I'd give him a well deserved vacation."

"Hell you would. You'd nail him to the desk for the rest of his miserable days."

"With all due respect, Sir, I would like to remind you that my task was to play an amateur, and I did it to the best of my abilities."

John could not keep a straight face anymore. He broke into laughter. "Go to hell. I just lost all hope of making you a mature adult."

John changed the subject. "Well, the boys are working on the box in the outbuilding. The preliminary consensus is that it was wise to bring it here." He paused. "God, I just can't get over the vision of you carrying the damn thing through half of Russia when they're after you all over the place. And managing to carry it concealed, too."

At this moment Margaret came in. Noticing her, Cyrus suddenly, with the voice of Morris the cat, pronounced, "A man's got to do what a man's got to do."

They all laughed, and John said, "Margaret, how can we possibly make him grow up?"

"No way. He wants to die young of old age."

John and Cyrus went to the basement, and from there, they went through the tunnel to the outbuilding. In the basement there was a bomb disposal container that John's boys had brought in from somewhere. Inside the container there was a box with a lock-opening robot running through the combinations on the lock.

The robot's arm ended with six parallel "fingers." At the end of each finger was a small rubber wheel which could rotate the wheel of a combination lock. So, the wheels of the "fingers" rotated the wheels of the lock through all the possible combinations until it reached the unlocking combination. In this kind of lock the top did not usually pop open. The way to verify the lock's opening is to try to lift the top. Opening it could trigger an adverse process in the box, like an explosion. To avoid that, this system included a transducer, which was actually an accelerometer that detected a latch release inside the box and gave the robot a stop signal.

The wheels were turning, and the combination numbers were running on the monitor outside the chamber. Cyrus came up to the supervising guy. "How long will it take?"

"Depends on your luck. Could be the first combination. Never seen one, though. As far as the maximum goes, let's see. Six wheels, one million combinations. We couldn't get more than four combinations per second with this lock." A pause. "Comes to about three days max, we are around twenty percent through."

Cyrus turned to John. "Wanna bet?"

"Sure. Got a brilliant idea? They already tried birthdays and stuff."

"Try nineteen-zero-eight-ninety one."

"What's that?"

"The ninety one coup date. August nineteen, nineteen ninety one, Russian format."

John chuckled. "Wait. The box was locked a week before the coup. How could Gorbatov possibly know the date of a coup against himself?"

"There was a theory from the very beginning that he was behind the coup. I kind of lean toward it now too."

John looked at the monitor. The sixth digit was constantly blinking, the fifth was changing every two and a half seconds, the fourth was changing about twice a minute. The first two stayed at 18. "We don't even have to stop the process. Your number will come up soon."

The supervisor stepped in. "Don't worry about that. We'll get it sooner or later. The problem is that we don't know what's gonna happen when we open the thing. We could not get it with the X-ray, the metal is too thick. Is there a good chance there are explosives inside?"

Cyrus answered, "Unlikely. Their goal was to destroy the documents inside in case of an unauthorized opening, not to kill the offender. With the explosion you'd do just the opposite. I'd say they might have an acid in there, or something of that kind."

John said, "Could there be another combination inside, delaying the destruction?"

Cyrus did not agree. "I doubt it. During that delay you could grab the docs, and nothing would be destroyed."

The supervisor shook his head. "The only thing we can work with on the outside is the seal. I don't like it."

"What about it?"

"See, the box seems to be hermetically sealed. If you just break the seal by opening the box, it could trigger something. This seal sticks out as a bright reminder."

John said, "Any suggestions?"

"I'd pick it piece by piece, or try to separate it from the seal, but I wouldn't break it by just opening the top." He paused. "After all, we have nothing to lose here. If it's clean, picking it wouldn't hurt."

John agreed. "Sounds reasonable to me."

At this moment the monitor beeped. They looked at it. The numbers were still. 190891.

"Your guess was right on the money."

Let's first see whether there's any money there.

The supervisor was in charge now. "It's my job to deal with this thing. You better go elsewhere. I'll call you when we're finished. He went out to call his partner to start using the manipulator inside the chamber. John and Cyrus left.

An hour and a half later the supervisor called them. He showed them inside the chamber. The box was sitting in the same spot, but the seal was gone. "We took the seal off. See that wire?"

They saw a thin metal wire, sticking out half an inch where the seal had been.

John nodded. "What do you make of it?"

"Steel. It stuck out when we got the seal off. If you just break the seal by opening the top, you'd pull that wire. Then, something would happen inside."

Cyrus suggested, "As you guessed. Some sort of electric contact?"

"Shouldn't be. Single wire, and steel too. Should be mechanical. Also, we ran a pretty fine current test last night, nothing detected. Besides, in a very long hold you always run the risk of a battery going bad. You're better off going mechanical."

John took a breath. "Well, shall we go on with it?"

"Any time. Here is the game plan. We open the box. If nothing happens, we give you the contents. If the damn thing starts destroying the contents, we save what we can."

John and Cyrus left again. Cyrus was tempted to stay, but that would be inappropriate. A professional himself, he always respected professionalism in others.

Merely five minutes later they were called back again. The box was on the table, not in the bomb chamber. The top was opened. The only item in the box was a tan leather folder, about three inches thick, with a large Soviet Union coat of arms embossed on the face of it.

The supervisor was proud of his work. "That's a devilish setup. You know what that wire would trip?"

"What?"

" The box is a good thick hard steel. Inlaid inside is a layer of magnesium. Guess, what that would do."

"Come on, what?"

"It would ignite. It burns with such a high temperature, that it would burn through this steel, this table, this concrete floor, and wind up in the ground. It burns even without oxygen. The same thing would have happened if we tried to cut it with a torch or even a saw." He then gestured toward the box. "You can take the folder, we've checked it out."

John turned to Cyrus. "Your prey. You carry it."

Cyrus took the folder. Despite his attempts to be very casual about it, he carried it very gingerly with both hands in front of him; he could not force himself to take it in just one hand.

They came to the duty room in the basement of the main house. Cyrus carefully put the folder on the table in the middle. He and John each took a chair and and sat down.

Cyrus chuckled. "Well, let's see if the whole thing was worth it." *All the deaths too.*

He opened the cover of the folder. The folder contained a few loose documents. Cyrus took them out and laid them on the table. He found another clear plastic folder with many documents and some passports. *My God, what is that? Gorbatov's retirement package?*

"Cyrus, let's go step by step. I want to read it from the top. Guess who is going to do all the translating."

Cyrus took the top letter, and briefly looked it through, and turned the page, then another. He was just shaking his head, mesmerized. Then he recalled John was there.

"John, I think, we'd be better off if I just start typing the translation. You just sit next to me and read."

They moved to a computer, Cyrus pulled up the program and started typing.

Top Secret_

Of Special Importance
Copy number 2_

Politburo
Central Committee
Communist Party of the Soviet Union

To my successor, General Secretary of the Communist Party.

If you are reading this letter, I must be dead by now, so conveying this becomes easier on one hand, and more difficult on the other.

We, the Communists, had a great cause and great success from the beginning of the twentieth century. Then, something went wrong. The most tragic thing is that we don't know what or why.

Through great efforts and sacrifices beyond normal human abilities, we achieved our goal. By the mid-century mark we had all the power. Globally, we had positioned ourselves perfectly for expanding our system all over the world; therefore, taking over the whole world would be just a matter of time. Then, something went wrong. We still seemed to have all the power in the country, and nobody was outwardly challenging it, even in the mildest way. But we were losing power. If we could have identified our enemy, we would have destroyed it. Our enemy was elusive. Andropov was the first to recognize the problem, but neither he, nor any of us, could identify our enemy. Now it is up to you, the future generation of communists, to analyze history, identify the enemy, and win the power back.

Fundamentally, everything looks rock-solid. We have always realized that the most powerful incentive for people is not money or anything else. It is power. Careful study of history shows that, given the choice, people consistently give up money for power. We therefore consolidated every kind of power -- military, economic, political, judicial-- into one. The power. And we created a state where the only real currency was power. Everything else, including material well-being and legal protection, was firmly tied to it.

Now, we are coming to a critical junction in our history, and perhaps world history. The simple fact is that we are losing power. We are not losing it to anybody; we are just losing it. This is the most frustrating aspect of the situation. The Politburo is deeply and bitterly divided. Some of us think that the only solution is to crack down, cleanse the country, and enforce order. Others do not see that as a solution, but they do not see any other solution either.

As the General Secretary, my responsibility was to consolidate the Politburo and the Central Committee. Under the circumstances, this was a most difficult and most thankless role. My earlier moves were grossly misunderstood. I see my primary objective as saving the Communist Party and preserving its power for future generations. Not many people realize how dire our situation is and how little time we have before the whole system and the whole country will fall apart. Knowing the real situation, I have to show flexibility worthy of Lenin, combined sometimes with bluffing worthy of Khruschev, to win some time to achieve my objectives. But instead of receiving accolades, I am often blamed for giving away the store. Nothing could be further from truth. In fact, I am saving whatever can be saved. Most people in my position would lose everything.

The competing convictions in the Politburo are at a crisis point. Obviously, a crackdown would be preferable, but I am not sure that it can succeed. I have been under a lot of pressure lately to implement the firmest crackdown. Not being able to contain that pressure any more, I have decided to authorize it but to distance myself from it officially. I have explained to the coup leaders that this way I will retain all the cooperation that I have managed to accumulate around the world and that will enable me to negotiate with the world leaders most effectively. The coup leaders have agreed.

This way we can win either way. The coup group has been instructed to present it as a coup against traitors who, using a pretense of democracy and misrepresenting themselves as a majority, are forcing me to act against my will and convictions. If the coup succeeds, the leaders will come to me and say that they have freed me from those insidious elements. If the coup does not succeed, I will have to sacrifice them for the sake of future communism. I will purge them as traitors, and, with no choice left, I will start the transition.

Now we come to the real purpose of this letter and the arrangement behind it. The transition. Not being able to keep power, we will have to convert it, which is a lot better than simply losing it. To prepare for such an eventuality, which was foreseen by Andropov, in 1985 I ordered some funds to be covertly transferred abroad. Unfortunately, that task proved to be very difficult, particularly due to the substantial amount of money involved and the need for absolute secrecy for the arrangements. Appropriate studies were made, solutions were found, and the transfers have been taking place, starting in 1986. So far we have been able to transfer about 160 billion dollars. As a precaution, the funds were divided into three groups. The materials enclosed in this folder will enable you to take control of one of them, Group 2. By now you, my successor, have either recovered the other two, or know where to find them. I have arranged for a fallback scenario so as not to lose these funds in the event that this succession information is intercepted. If those funds are not reclaimed before the succession, you, as the new leader of the Communist party, will be contacted by two individuals responsible for their safekeeping. They will contact you saying that they have a letter to you from me. To reclaim the funds from them, you have to use the code word Phoenix.

The application of the funds is what makes the whole endeavor worthwhile. We made appropriate studies and came to the conclusion that the best way to save the communist movement is to take over a group of countries. This, as it was with Russia, will make communism legitimate and will enable you to be recognized by the other world leaders. This illuminates one of the axioms of communism: To operate freely and legitimately you must have full control of at least one country. The more, the easier.

We carefully selected the following countries for the takeover: Cuba, Mexico, Columbia and Panama. The appropriate work in those countries started in 1987. Country by country contacts, capabilities and instructions are included in separate documents. I have to emphasize that without these funds neither of the takeover plans can work. In a separate document you will find the suggestions for neutralizing the United States during the time of the takeover. Again, using these funds and the already established infrastructure you will disrupt the United States economy, so the Americans will be preoccupied with their own problems while you take over the aforementioned countries.

Needless to say, if future developments warrant, these funds can also be used to advance goals of the Communist party within Russia. Political and parliamentary confrontations or issues in underground work could require the allocation of these funds.

Good luck in your struggle. I am convinced that together we will overcome all the difficulties, and communism will win.

(Signed)
M.S. Gorbatov

General Secretary

Cyrus stopped typing and looked at John. John said nothing, just winked.

"John," Cyrus began.

John interrupted him. "Let's have lunch. We deserve one."

Cyrus turned the computer off, put the folder in a safe and they went upstairs.

At lunch Cyrus was on edge. The moment he had seen those lines in Gorbatov's letter outlining the goals of the communists, he knew he'd been played, if not directly manipulated by John. He interrupted John's casual small talk.

"John, you knew it all along, didn't you?"

"Knew what, Cyrus?" John was innocence itself.

"John, please. It was just another intelligence operation from the very beginning, and all the stuff about the firm being in trouble was designed just to get me involved, right?"

Cyrus noticed a familiar, fleeting glint somewhere deep in John's eyes. Only someone who knew John as well as Cyrus did could have seen it. "Calm down, Cyrus. It was what I said it was, a way to get the firm out of trouble, no more, no less."

"John," Cyrus lowered his voice, evincing his anger, anger perhaps as much at himself for letting someone deceive him, "You manipulated me. You already knew the real reason for squirreling away that money."

John realized that Cyrus really was offended, and he couldn't simply defuse the situation with a joke. His lighthearted expression of innocence faded away. "Cyrus, I understand your feeling, and it's not justified. One thing I can tell you for sure: I never manipulated you. I have too much respect for the memory of your father, as well as for you."

Cyrus appreciated the sincerity and the depth of John's feelings, but he still couldn't accept the way he'd been drawn into the operation. "But you still knew that all along."

"No, I did not. Listen to me. Yes, I had a strong feeling about the whole thing as soon as I understood the magnitude of their operation. Yes, I had a few hints that something was cooking in those countries, certainly in Mexico and Panama, but those were such intangible hints, intuitions, that I couldn't draw any real conclusions even for myself. So, the answer is no, I did not know."

Cyrus shook his head skeptically. John went on. "Now, what would I do with those intuitions? Go to the President to authorize an investigation? Give me a break! I can only go to the President with a definite and imminent threat to national security. This was neither definite, nor imminent, so I didn't have a prayer," he paused, "with any President."

Cyrus clearly understood the hint. John continued the monologue. "On the other hand, national security is my job. So, I've been facing this dilemma for a couple of years. And, as they say, I didn't have good luck, but bad luck has saved me. What I told you about the situation in the firm is absolutely the truth. All of a sudden, I realized that we could kill two birds with one stone. But it had to be a private endeavor, not an intelligence operation. Then your retirement came very handy. Of course, I took advantage of it, but that's the only thing I'm guilty of." He stopped for a moment. "If I had to confess in church, that would be my confession."

Cyrus did not respond for a long time. Finally, he said, "Yeah, I guess you didn't have much choice." He sighed and, trying to lighten the situation, chuckled, "But you knew I'd agree; you knew how to get me into this mess."

John smiled. "Of course. You're too much of an intelligence operative to refuse a mission as crazy as this."

They summarized what they already knew.

"So, John, what we have here is a nice setup to take over our backyard, to make a major mess in our home, and it's a very well-heeled enterprise. Now you seem to have a good reason to see the President."

"Absolutely. And now it would clearly be a dereliction of duty not to. My major concern now is timing."

"What about it?"

"We don't know how much time we've got. Whoever hid the funds may have the capability to hide them elsewhere. I'd rather move before they have that opportunity."

"Are you saying that you want to move before you report to the President?"

"Precisely. After all, the determination of the timing for the report is up to me. I wasn't tasked on that, was I?"

Cyrus chuckled, "Never trust a politician, huh?"

"Of course. You never know what kind of quiet deal these guys might make with their new chums over there."

"Then let's get cracking." They went to examine the rest of the box.

Cyrus sat at the computer to translate the next document.

It was a short letter written on a plain sheet of paper with no letterhead or security classification.

> For a variety of reasons, including considerations of international laws and our absolute need to operate covertly, all the money in Group 2 was set up in international trusts.
>
> All the money in the Group 2 was laundered and cannot be traced back to its origin. All the keepers of the funds were provided with banking contacts, usually "under a false flag," and the bankers were led to believe in different origins of the money. To avoid any detection by the international banking authorities, the following method was employed.
>
> Step one. We converted our assets inside the country and abroad, such as Western high-grade securities, into hard currency, mainly US, German, Japanese and British.
>
> Step two. We transferred that currency in cash, as well as gold, diamonds, or other assets accumulated abroad from various accounts to a friendly bank, usually an off-shore institution.
>
> Step three. We took a loan in the amount of the assets placed in the bank, using these assets to secure the loan. Specifically, these were loans, representing twenty and eighty percent of the total. Since the loans were well secured, the interest rate was the lowest available. However, the fact that the loans were secured was not reflected in any papers, except in a separate secret document at the bank. Extra income for the bank in the form of slightly higher interest rate

was a reliable way to ensure the bank's cooperation. This arrangement separated our assets from the money in the investment operations. It also avoided the attention of regulatory authorities, since the interest rate was between the typical rates for secured and unsecured loans.

Step four. The twenty percent portion was transferred to another related fund of ours, undergoing a similar procedure. An equivalent of the transferred amount was received reciprocally. This portion was represented to the original banker as our asset money.

Step five. The twenty percent portion, "washed" through the other bank, was invested, using a major investment company, being "leveraged" by the remainder of the loan from the bank. Since the twenty percent portion came from outside the bank, it was treated as our asset that was legitimately transferred from another bank, so the original banker could satisfy all the requirements of the regulatory agencies.

Keeping in mind the dynamics of the current worldwide investment environment, and consequent frequent reinvestments, we estimated that in just a few years these funds would be totally indistinguishable from any other money in the international financial markets. Furthermore, the retained profits would enable us to establish a process of redeeming the collateral and using it for a similar operation in a separate newly created entity.

These steps enabled us to utilize the equivalent of the funds. We could transfer those funds, investing them for profit, as well as placing those investments strategically in such a way that would enable us to control all the economic power we needed to achieve our strategic goals. The loan arrangements also made it possible to operate with virtually no danger of detection. Considering the amounts of money involved, the costs of these arrangements, such as bankers' fees, are negligible.

Cyrus stopped typing. His excitement was obvious. "That's what it was. That's why nobody could find the damn money. How do you like these communists, not even investment amateurs, John, beating us, the investments experts, at our own game?"

"Not bad. I'd never have guessed that. When they get serious these guys, can do some good thinking. They take nothing for granted, accept no set rules and, often, get results."

"You know, we could have looked for that money forever without ever finding it."

"The really frightening thing is that, even now, knowing all we know, we wouldn't be able to find it without knowing the specifics."

"True. Let's take a look at the specifics."

He took the next page and started typing.

> For additional reliability the money in Group 2 was divided into three separate and independent funds: Fund 21, Fund 22 and Fund 23. Three people were chosen to function as keepers. All three were KGB sleepers of unquestionable loyalty in various Western countries. Their identities were well established and maintained for many years. Over those years they did not perform any tasks, except occasional loyalty checks by the KGB, so they definitely have not been compromised in regard to the Western intelligence services. We ordered the KGB to recall them for tasking and to reassign them under the direct orders of the Central Committee. Their personnel files, as well as all related operational files, were removed from the KGB. Comrade Kruchina personally tasked them for this assignment and supervised the production of their support documents. He subsequently removed all traces within the Central Committee. Their identities, contact procedures, procedures for reclaiming the funds, and other related information are contained in the respective envelopes for the funds.

Cyrus stopped typing. "Well, that's kind of short."

"But gets right to the point."

Cyrus opened an envelope with a handwritten 'Fund 21' on it. The content was a bit surprising, and Cyrus fought the temptation to browse.

He took the cover letter from inside the envelope and went back to typing.

The main trustee, registered from the very inception for each of the trusts, is Mr. Peter Rodney Gregory. The first substitute trustee is Mr. John Smith Brendon.

All three funds are currently managed by the following chosen keepers appointed as second substitute trustees. For additional security of the arrangement their backups are another three former "sleepers" who would step in if the current keepers cannot perform their functions.

Fund ...Current keeper......Backup keeper

21......Gunter Braun.........Sancho Rodriges

22......William Blacksmith Rene Germon

23...... Robert Kenworth... Roger Klemmens

Fund 21 is comprised of three trusts:
  BDF International Trust;
  CEG International Trust;
  HKM International Trust.

Fund 22 is comprised of three trusts:
  ACM International Trust;
  GHQ International Trust;
  WIB International Trust:

Fund 23 is comprised of three trusts:
KOG International Trust;
RYP International Trust;
SIM International Trust

You have an option to continue for a while with these keepers or to appoint your own people to the task. These keepers will relinquish their responsibilities at your request. And, of course, they are fully expendable. Their addresses, contact procedures and all other pertinent information are included in separate envelopes.

The authority of the trustees Gregory and Brendon is established through all levels of handling the funds, such as bankers, brokers, investment managers and so on. They supersede the current keepers in all the documents.

For the reclamation of the authority over the Group 2 funds, the photographs of your representatives need to be affixed to the enclosed passports along with the dates of birth. The imprint of the missing part of the seal to stamp on the photo and a typeset for the dates of birth are provided in this package.

Cyrus stopped typing and took two Argentine passports out of the envelope. He looked at John. "Do I understand that correctly, John? All I need to do to get sixty billion bucks is put my face on this passport, go out and show it to some dude?"

John chuckled. "That's right. Only, it's not sixty, it's more like a hundred billion by now. Even at five percent annual, compounded, it would have increased by around sixty-five percent over the ten years."

"All right, all right. I'm just asking, why are they that trusting?"

"They're not. Who in his right mind would play games here, just to get all those nasty, armed, and highly motivated guys after him?"

"Well, you're right. I certainly wouldn't."

They browsed through the contents of the envelope some more, then Cyrus declared, "I don't know how you feel about this stuff, but I need a drink, John."

They locked the folder in the safe and went upstairs to the library.

"Well, it's getting crazier by the minute. What do we do now, John?"

"I don't really know. But I'm inclined to get hold of the money, and then go to the President. Once again, we don't know how much time we have. Or, if we have any time at all. We don't know what means they have to rearrange the whole setup, so that the money would vanish again."

"Yeah, if we move quickly, we could grab the whole bundle."

"Or, we can walk right into a trap. All hell could break loose, and it could become a political impossibility to nail the bastards." John paused for a long time. "It's your call, Cyrus."

"Why mine? You're the boss."

"Because, you're the one who's going to do it. You're the one who speaks the best Russian in our outfit, and you're the one who's equipped to handle an operation like that. With a lot of support, of course."

Cyrus thought for a minute. He was tired, and he was drained emotionally, too. It reminded Cyrus of his hell week back at the SEALS school in San Diego.

"I don't think there's a real choice. So let's do it right. What do you have in mind?"

"First of all, time is of the essence. We have to grab all three trusts in rapid succession, and then go immediately to the President. One is in New York, that's easy. The others are in Bermuda and Barbados; those will take more time."

"We need to keep their guys from communicating for a while after the transfer. They might smell something and demand confirmation that the funds were in place. We don't know if they have an established routine for that."

"True. Let's assume they do. Legally, detaining them would be a bit of a problem, but my hunch is that their ultimate concern is that they could be eliminated. Let's play that card. It should keep them from contacting anybody, and will encourage them to run for their lives instead."

"All right. That should do the trick. I'd start with Barbados, then go to Bermuda, and end with New York."

John called downstairs. Jim appeared.

"Jim, we need to run an operation, fast."

"OK, boss."

"Cyrus is going to deal with some potentially nasty characters in Barbados, Bermuda and New York tomorrow. He needs full backup."

"All in one day?"

"Yes."

"Then we'd better get busy."

"Get two teams, six people each. Going to Barbados and Bermuda. I'll cover New York tomorrow. Two fast planes. In each place reserve a couple of good secluded villas, two mid-size cars, and the largest limo you can find that we can drive ourselves,. The first plane leaves tomorrow night for no later than a Monday zero-seven hundred arrival in Barbados. Cyrus will instruct the team on the plane."

"Arms?"

"Yes."

"Comms?"

"Yes, a scrambled mini-set for each member. Two satellite scrambled phones per team. Questions?"

"Is it strictly covert?"

"Yes. Business travel. Resort purchase negotiations, something of that sort. See what you can come up with."

"Then we might need a couple of females on each team," he chuckled, "they'd make the team look more civilized."

"All right. Anything else?"

"Not at the moment. Villas could be a problem; it's high season there now. I'll call you with the departure time." Jim was on his way out when John stopped him.

"Jim, two more things. Fetch a couple of Cyrus' passport photos, and call Randall to come here in an hour." Jim nodded and left.

Randall was a company lawyer. "Why do you need Randall?"

"So you can legally transfer the ownership, dated tomorrow."

The firm never assumed anybody would live very long. Standard operating procedure.

"Well, let's have a bite, Cyrus, we can discuss the fine detail."

Chapter 18

The Gulfstream IV took off from Manassas Airport at 2:00 in the morning. There were nine people and the crew. Cyrus, Mary, and Joe, and a CPA who specialized in international auditing were the main team. Four men and two women were a special operations support team.

Ten minutes into the flight, Cyrus assembled the whole team.

"All right, guys. Here is the mission. Some people took over a large chunk of swindled money, set up a legitimate operation, and are managing it from Barbados. That's our destination. I have the legal means for taking over the operation. But we suspect they might offer some resistance, perhaps a pretty nasty one. That's where you come in. To make sure that the transition goes smoothly and without major drama."

Jason, the special operations team leader, nodded. The rest sat motionless.

Cyrus unfolded a map of Barbados on the small table in front of his chair, and continued, "The dude's name is Gunter Braun. His office is on Pinfold Street. I've been to Barbados a few times, but I've never operated there. Does anybody know the place well?"

Two hands shot up, and Cyrus waved them closer to the map. "He lives in a villa in Speightstown." He pointed to the map.

"We don't have his full setup, so we'll have to play it by ear. Our tasks are: one, to take over the assets, all of which are accounts; two, to prevent any word about this from getting out for at least 24 hours. We must avoid any major drama as best as we can. Shoot only in self-defense, or in defense of other team members."

Jason stepped in. "Understood. As a practical matter that means we'll have to keep them inside for a while. How many people are we talking about?"

"That's something we don't know. He probably has a staff of three or four. Our sense is that all of them are in the dark, and assume that they're operating a legitimate business."

"Can we rely on that?"

"Hard to be certain. But see, the guy in charge is a KGB sleeper on a very sensitive assignment. I'd be very surprised if he would risk of letting anyone know who he really is."

"Sounds reasonable."

"Well, it doesn't make our task much easier. Regular employee loyalty may be an issue. If someone gets the idea that we're some kind of mob or drug dealers, they might get the police involved. That will spoil the whole show."

"Yeah, it looks like we have to corral them somehow. But most likely in this part of the world they go home for lunch. How about keeping them away from the office before they come in?"

"We don't even know who they are."

Mary jumped in. "Jason, you've just said it. Lunch time. They'll all be gone."

Cyrus caught on immediately. That wasn't the first time his secretary had displayed her wits at a crucial moment. "That's it. Mary, you're great. So, we walk into the guy's office in the morning, keep him busy until lunchtime. When everyone's gone, we take him to his villa, check it out, and then Joe, Mary and I go off, and you guys keep him till morning, and then get out."

"That should work." Jason was happy that his task now looked doable.

"Just in case, another plane will be waiting for you from about fourteen hundred local."

They discussed other details for about half an hour and dozed. Everyone needed rest before the operation.

Just before landing they synchronized the scramblers on their communications gear. Everyone was using the same channel. That could make it congested at times, but it made it easier to coordinate the action. Cyrus was a little concerned with the range limited to three miles, so he decided that if the team split into two groups, they could each use one of the two satellite phones. Cyrus became Alpha, Mary - Bravo, Joe - Charlie, Jason - Delta and so on. Gunter Braun was assigned Tango.

Breakfast was quick, but very nutritious.

The Gulfstream flight was handled quickly and efficiently at the general aviation terminal of Grantley Adams International. The party's regular luggage was whisked away by the service van. It went straight to their rented villa on the beach. The nine people, carrying their attaché cases, laptops, numerous file folders and other attributes of VIP business travel, settled into three cars, the biggest one being a Cadillac. The radio call from the plane crew to the ground operator, requesting that the engines be running to cool the interior of the cars, made the first invaluable impression and set the tone for all the subsequent handling of the party.

Cyrus, Joe and Mary rode with their driver in a black Cadillac Fleetwood. Jason, with another man and one female member, took a white Ford Taurus, and the other couple rode in a light gray Subaru. They left the airport together, and then separated. The Subaru went ahead, the Cadillac was about a mile behind, and the Taurus was trailing another half a mile behind.

The first transmission came five minutes later. "Delta to Alpha. You're clean."

"Roger, Delta."

Mary turned to Cyrus. "Of course we're all clean. Who would tail anybody here?"

"The guys are just following procedure. It's their job."

Mary was navigating. They passed a posh area of old villas, enjoying a good deal of privacy behind tall fences, near the residence of the British Commissioner and the palace of the Prime Minister. Mary looked around. "Looks like there's some old money here."

"Sure. And a lot of it. This is probably the most prestigious part of the island."

They were enjoying the ride through the Park. They also knew that they needed to kill about ten minutes to give the advance group time to survey the premises on Pinfold street. Past that lush park they went right, following the shoreline of the inlet, crossed it via the Constitution Road bridge, and headed downtown.

The next communication came through. "Hotel to Alpha. We're breaking off, going to the villa."

Cyrus answered. "Alpha to Hotel. Go ahead. Report arrival."

They were randomly circling through downtown when Jason's communication came through their ear pieces. "Delta to Alpha. The place is a small two-story office building. The firm has the second floor. The first floor is occupied by a law firm, Krieger and Bland.

The whole street is like that. About a dozen of them around here."

Cyrus nodded to Mary, and she opened the sunroof of the Cadillac. "Alpha to Delta. Any comfortable place for surveillance?"

"Delta to Alpha. Negative. Buildings are well separated by dirt ground, not many cars parked, very few people around. We'd stand out here after ten minutes. Suggest you wait away from the area."

"Alpha to Delta. Roger. We'll wait around the fishing harbor."

Cyrus turned to the driver. "Let's go to the harbor."

Mary dialed Washington. The number answered, and Mary said, "Hello, this is Diana. We're on schedule so far. Please, check local law firm Krieger and Bland. Call back with a derogatory only." She listened through the confirmation, and hung up. Now they had to keep the sunroof of the Cadillac open and the satellite telephone antenna pointed up.

Joe said, "I hope they don't catch anybody's eye down there."

"Don't worry, Jason knows surveillance as well as anybody. With three people and a car they'll cover the area in combinations."

They found a small restaurant near the market on Princess Alice highway open for breakfast. They followed the intelligence precept of always eating when you can. They were sitting on the restaurant terrace and finishing their coffee when the telephone rang. Mary answered, listened for several seconds, and hung up.

She returned to the terrace. "He left the house. Driving downtown. Black Mercedes-600. License plate unknown. The guys are following well behind."

Joe went inside to pay the bill.

Cyrus said, "We have five minutes." He went on the radio, "Alpha to Delta. Tango is on his way. Driving a black Mercedes-600, license plate unknown. Make sure you count heads in the office."

"Delta to Alpha. Roger. One female is entering now. First person in. White, blonde, about five-two, twenty-five. She's unlocking the door. Three people inside the law firm on the first floor already. Any info on it?"

"Alpha to Delta. Negative. Request made. If no response for ten more minutes, we presume no derogatory."

"Delta to Alpha. Second person in. Male, white, brown hair, five-nine, two hundred pounds, about thirty five."

"Alpha to Delta. Roger, two in."

Fifteen minutes later they were approaching the site. As expected, Jason came in, "Delta to everybody. Tango has arrived. Parked behind, entering the building now. Two more people came in the office, one male and one female, both black."

"Hotel ready. We're two minutes away."

"Alpha ready. Hotel, do you have your legend straight?"

"Affirmative, Alpha. We're a couple on a vacation, looking for property. The law firm was recommended as a reputable one."

"How about the referral name?"

"Mr. Max Shredder, whose sister dealt with them. I don't know the sister's name."

"Good enough, Hotel. Make sure you spend a good forty minutes there. Is your clothing fit for vacations?"

"Roger. We changed."

Mary chuckled, but did not transmit anything.

"Alpha to everybody. Weapons ready. Make sure silencers are attached. Delta, you and Echo control the front, Foxtrot watches the back."

"Delta to Alpha. Roger."

The black Cadillac pulled up and parked in the back of the building, next to the Mercedes. The driver opened the back door for Cyrus and Mary. Joe emerged from the front seat. The trio went around the building and the driver got back into the car.

When they entered the front door, on the right they saw a door with a sign "KRIEGER and BLAND, Solicitors." A stairway in front led upstairs. When they were walking up, they heard, "Hotel to Alpha. We're thirty seconds behind you."

Cyrus could not talk now. He answered with two clicks. At the end of the second flight of stairs they saw a glass door with a sign: G. BRAUN MANAGEMENT COMPANY. A smaller sticker in the right low corner of the door informed that the premises were protected by electronic security. Cyrus glanced at Joe, and Joe gave a slight nod. If any drama were to break out, it would be his job to take care of it right away so no sign of trouble got out. Joe opened the door and let Cyrus and Mary in. The reception room was spacious but not large. A standard leather couch with two armchairs and a low table were at their immediate right near a large window at the front of the building. Straight ahead sat a black girl of about twenty, obviously a well-educated local, at the receptionist's desk. Her meticulous dress and her manners were a perfect match.

She smiled politely. "Good morning."

"Good morning. We would like to see Mr. Braun."

On the left there was a window at the side of the building. Behind the receptionist, just to the right of her desk, a door opened into a further room. They could not see if anyone was in that room. To the far right there was another open door. A blond woman was sitting at her desk, facing the reception area. *Should be his secretary.* Their eyes met, and she did not have a choice other than to stand up and walk toward the visitors.

The receptionist's "Do you have an appointment?" sounded a bit late.

The girl is an outsider. The secretary is probably not Braun's confidante. Otherwise, she'd never walk up. Cyrus seized the initiative. He walked decisively toward the secretary, and they met at her door. Joe and Mary stayed behind.

Before the secretary could respond, Cyrus was inside her room. As expected, to the right he saw another door, obviously to the boss' office. In a manner devoid of doubt, he smiled and casually said, "I'm Peter Gregory." With that, he opened the door and cheerfully announced, "Hello, Gunter, old chap!" He went in and closed the door behind him. He moved so quickly that neither the receptionist nor the secretary had any chance to respond. The secretary's face showed outrage.

It was important now to discharge the atmosphere. Mary smiled, "Meet Mr. Peter Gregory. I've worked for him for a good eight years and still can't get used to his manners."

The secretary's expression changed to total puzzlement. Apparently, she knew the name; now it was Mary's time to take charge here. Still smiling, she gracefully walked to the secretary.

"Never mind, dear. He's always like that. Once, he was almost shot by the Sultan's of Brunei bodyguards. Can you imagine that?" She made a small pause, "Hello. I'm Susan, Mr. Gregory's private secretary."

The woman started coming to her senses. "Hello. I'm Penny," she smiled, "Mr. Braun's secretary." She paused and then added, "I saw Mr. Gregory's name on some documents, but lately I began to wonder if he existed at all." She could not have imagined how close she was to the truth.

"Well, he certainly exists for me. For others, I can understand, he might be something like the Flying Dutchman. He lives on an airplane, you know."

Suddenly, Penny realized that she was a hostess. She turned to Joe.

Mary immediately came to help. "Oh, I'm sorry. This is Mr. Sommers, Mr. Gregory's executive assistant. He's a CPA."

Joe extended his hand. "Call me Tim. Pleasure to meet you, Penny."

"Would you like coffee or soda?"

"No, thank you, we just had breakfast." Standard operating procedures absolutely forbade that. Many people failed their missions and paid with their lives for accepting food or drink on the enemy's premises.

"Oh, by the way, this is our receptionist. Annette, could you get us some coffee and soda, just in case?"

"Right away."

Joe was relieved when he saw two men appear in the doorway of the room. Now all the targets were visible. They introduced themselves to the two men, who did not define their responsibilities, just saying "managers." Mary would handle the two women, and Joe's job was the two men. He was ready.

Meanwhile, Cyrus approached the man behind the desk. A balding, happy-faced man of six feet and approximately two hundred and twenty pounds did not make a single motion. His greenish eyes were attentive, but not tense. He was wearing the local variation of business attire, an embroidered and meticulously ironed over-shirt with no tie served as a jacket.

Cool cat. Cyrus approached the desk. He took his passport out of his side pocket, opened it, and put it in front of the man, along with the plastic card.

The man looked at the passport carefully. Now Cyrus could see emotions, but he could not define them. There was a pause.

The man looked at Cyrus. Cyrus met his look, trying to appear calm and firm, but not too firm. He did not want to show any challenge. The man extended his hand and finally broke the silence.

"It's been a long time waiting. Welcome."

He speaks English. Why? Oh, he heard me speaking English to his secretary. Is he testing me? Oh, the password. Cyrus switched to Russian. "Uncle Misha sends his regards. Yes, it's been a long wait for all of us. Hard. I'm not too good at waiting."

The man smiled. He also switched to Russian. "I hope our Aunt's health is still good." He paused. "You can get used to it."

Testing if I know his background?

"Yes, very few people can claim to be as good as you are at waiting. Even before this assignment." Cyrus immediately felt that the message was conveyed and appreciated.

Braun lifted his table lamp, tore off the felt bottom, and took his corresponding card out. His look indicated that it was merely a formality. He compared the two and nodded.

At that moment the comm line came to life. "Echo to everybody. Police car in the vicinity. Two inside, uniformed."

Everyone felt tense. It could be a harmless ride or a response to some hidden alarm call from the office the team had missed.

A minute later they heard, "Foxtrot to everybody. Police car turned the corner. Leaving the area. Steady speed, does not seem to be interested in the environment." They felt like a shell had missed them.

Braun was silent, not willing to ask about the exact purpose of the visit, or the following events. I would prefer for him to start asking questions. I want the psychological advantage. Let's put some more pressure on. By silence.

Cyrus went into some small talk about Barbados and living here versus visiting. Braun followed without showing any signs of impatience. Five minutes later Cyrus heard in his earpiece, "Delta to Hotel. Situation check. Are you OK?" Two clicks followed.

Jason's nerves were strained. "Delta to Alpha. Is everything OK?"

Cyrus clicked twice.

Realizing that Cyrus was in charge here and that he was not about to bring up his agenda first, Braun cheerfully asked, "Well, what's our plan for the day?"

Cyrus was non-committal. "I'd like to see your setup here. Then, we'll see."

Braun could not hold off any longer. "I presume you're taking over."

"Officially, yes. In reality, I don't know. My orders are to conduct a full and careful inspection here, establish my authority over the trust and report back." They will tell me whether to stay here, or to supervise from a distance with you doing essentially the same job you did before."

"I see." Braun paused. "So, I either report to you, or get reassigned."

By the sheer tone of his voice Cyrus knew that Braun fully understood the meaning of "reassignment," quick elimination. What he did not know was whether Cyrus had the authority to decide his fate. Usually, in a clear-cut case, Cyrus could settle it right on the spot. Otherwise, the Center was to be the judge.

"Precisely."

"Well, let's get on with it."

Cyrus did not need another invitation. "Who has access to the trust around here?"

"Only I do. My secretary is just a secretary. She types letters, she knows with whom I'm dealing, she takes my messages. That's about all. She doesn't know any particulars, the amounts involved, although she has an idea that I'm dealing in big money."

"All right. How about the others?"

"The receptionist knows nothing. The two guys are managing other funds. See, I couldn't afford to manage just the trust. I had to have other business too, otherwise the whole thing would be too suspicious."

Cyrus chuckled, "So, you expanded the business, right?"

"Yes. You have to understand, by dealing with the kind of money I do, I naturally attracted other business. I didn't need to ask for it." He could not predict Cyrus' reaction and was almost apologizing. "When business comes your way, and you decline it, you raise a lot of eyebrows."

Cyrus smiled. "I understand."

Braun quietly took a breath, feeling relieved. "So, the black guy manages some local stuff, and the other one handles all the international business. Both know what they're doing, so I really don't need to supervise them much."

"All right. What do they know about the trust?"

"Nothing. Just the fact that I personally manage a large trust."

Cyrus shook his head. "So, you single-handedly manage a huge chunk of money?"

"Yes, and no. I don't really manage any investments per se. I just hire large companies to do that. They do their jobs, I watch the results. The worst two performers in a given year lose their business with the trust. I redistribute one of those two funds among the three best performers, and find a new one for the other. Simple. I just have to sum up all the results." He paused. "Well, I also have to deal with the banks on the original loans, too."

"That's a lot for a guy and a secretary, you know."

"Look, I haven't had a vacation in ten years, OK?" Braun was irritated by the questioning of something that had been his pride. "I've told you that nobody else knows about the trust. I'm responsible for that. If you don't trust me, you're welcome to check it out."

Cyrus decided to ease up for the moment. "Whether I trust you or not, I have to verify everything. It's my job, and you know it. OK?"

"Sorry." Braun realized that his irritation was out of order. Under the circumstances.

"Do you have any hard copies of the portfolio performance?"

"No. As ordered."

"How many electronic copies do you have?"

"Two. One here, in my computer, updated daily. The backup is in a bank vault, updated weekly, along with all the paperwork, original and the subsequent. All the originals are there."

Damn. We absolutely forgot. One more target, one more place to get to. I hope not the original bank?"

"Of course not. Bank of Nova Scotia, a short ride from here."

"So far, so good. And now I'd like to see the portfolio summary."

Braun took a piece of paper, wrote a long number on it, and gave it to Cyrus. "This is the access code to my computer." He started punching the numbers in the computer.

Critical moment. If we goofed somewhere, and he's got an idea what is going on, all the records will be destroyed right now. What can I do? Nothing. He was watching Braun, making sure that the numbers he was punching in were the same numbers written on the piece of paper. They were.

"At the same time his earpiece broke silence. "Hotel to Alpha. We're out. Do you want us to stay here?" Cyrus clicked once. Negative.

Braun got the information up on his computer screen. "I think you better sit down in my chair, so you can browse through. *No way. How do I know what you've equipped your chair with?*

"Not to worry," Cyrus turned the monitor so the screen faced him. "just pass me the board." Braun did.

At this moment the door opened. Mary walked in with a sheet of paper in her hand. "I'm very sorry, gentlemen, this is an urgent message for Mr. Gregory." She handed the paper to Cyrus.

"Oh, Gunter, this is Mary, my private secretary." Mary and Gunter shook hands, and Cyrus looked at the paper.

"Your mike button is stuck." Operational misfortune. When one of the sets has its mike button stuck, this set broadcasts whatever is said in front of this mike continuously, and nobody else can use the frequency. In the circumstances, the worst possible set to go out was Cyrus'. Murphy's law.

Cyrus quickly wrote, "OK. H, I - buy IBM Pentium hard disk, stand by. Find mike button replacement. Next - Bank of Nova Scotia, deposit box." He gave the note back to Mary and, turning away from Braun for a second, through the fabric of his sleeve, he pulled the thin wire out. Now his mike was disconnected and the frequency was free again. But he could only listen.

The frequency came alive. "Delta to Alpha. Jam released."

Then, Mary's voice came in. "Bravo to Hotel. Leave the area. Go find an IBM Pentium hard disk, after that stand by in the area. Bravo to Delta. Our next move to Bank of Nova Scotia, deposit box."

She must be in the bathroom.

"Roger. Any sense of timing?"

"Bravo to Delta. Negative. Alpha is in a private conversation, we are in a reception area."

"Delta to Bravo. Roger." Jason chuckled. "Private conversation." Jason was amused that Cyrus' "private" conversation had been broadcasted to all of them. They smiled. "Bravo to Delta. Alpha needs mike button with the wire replacement. Suggest Echo's set."

"Agreed. Ready in two minutes. Suggest a brush contact at the front door."

"Bravo to Alpha. I need a reason to get out. Will be in the reception area in fifteen seconds."

Cyrus looked at his watch. 10:05. *They probably go to lunch at 11:30.* "Gunter, what about going to the bank at lunch hour? Then we can go through the papers in the afternoon."

"As you wish. That bank is opened during lunch."

"Good. Then please call Mary in here."

Braun pushed his intercom button and made the request. Mary immediately materialized at the door. "Yes, Mr. Gregory?"

"Mary, please tell the driver that we're going out for lunch around noon."

"Yes, Mr. Gregory." She disappeared as quickly as she showed up.

"Bravo to Delta. Brush contact with Echo at the front door, thirty seconds."

"Delta to Bravo. Roger. Thirty seconds."

A minute later Cyrus heard Mary's voice over the frequency. "Bravo to everybody. We're leaving for the bank around noon."

Cyrus was browsing through the list of investment managers working for the BDF Trust. *My God! This is the Who's Who in the investment industry.* He knew some of the people involved, and he certainly knew all the companies involved.

"Gunter, this is a good setup. Top notch companies."

"As ordered."

"Let me see this year's income statement."

"Sure," Braun punched a few keys. "Here."

What Cyrus saw impressed him. *That's capitalism in its purest form. Given the amounts of money involved, these guys have every reason to be very motivated. This outperforms most of the funds I know of.*

"This is really good. I'd like to see the balance sheet for the whole fund now."

"At your service." Braun punched a few more keys.

Cyrus's eye slid quickly down the document. He wanted to see the bottom line. When he saw it, he was not sure that his face was as motionless as he wanted it to be. In the row "net worth" he saw a number 37,564. Combined with an unobtrusive note at the top of the document "$millions" it meant that the trust was worth thirty seven and a half billion dollars.

You may look a little excited. Not good. Cool down. Cyrus looked at Braun and smiled, "I wish all our funds were performing that well." Mr. Gregory had just made his first slip.

Braun brightened. For him it was an invaluable piece of information. One, it confirmed that he was not the only one doing this job, and two, it confirmed that he was doing a better job than others, and is probably going to be in the Center's good graces .

"Gunter, why don't you let your folks go for lunch. I'm sorry about the formality, but we have to check out their computers. I'm sure you understand."

Braun sighed. "I do." He called Penny in.

"Penny all of you can go for lunch. We'll go a little later."

"Thank you, Mr. Braun. Do you want me to make a reservation for you?"

Braun looked at Cyrus. "Peter, what do you prefer?"

"I don't know. Seafood, maybe. But we don't know the time yet." He paused for a second. "Why don't you leave a couple of restaurant names and the phone numbers with Susan. She'll handle it for us later."

"Delta to Bravo. Two males and two females are leaving the office."

"Bravo to Delta. It's OK. Lunch. Bravo to India. Bring two computers in the office."

The driver had been sitting all this time, and he was happy to stretch out. "Echo to Bravo. Two computers in."

"So, Gunter, you've got four trusts total, right?"

"That's right. Initially, I had three. The order was to keep no more than ten billion in one trust."

"And, you split each trust into ten accounts."

"Of course. Again, to keep them under a billion."

"So, you personally get the results for each account, sum them up in each trust, and then do the same for the entire fund?"

"Yes. Nobody sees more than one account."

"How often do you sum up all the trusts for the fund?"

"Once a month."

"A lot of work."

"Well, with a computer it's easy. I paid a lot for the software, but it's worth it."

"How do you handle computer security?"

"No big deal. Every account has the daily results for me in my E-mail slot in their computer. Once a day I connect the modem to the line, this computer automatically calls up all my E-mail slots, sweeps the data and processes it, updating my files. Then I disconnect the modem."

The earpiece came alive again. "Bravo to everybody. We're finishing sweeping the data from two secondary computers now. Bravo to Alpha. The computers do not seem to contain any relevant information. If you want us do destroy all the data in them anyway, call me in and ask for a glass of water."

Cyrus glanced at his watch. 11:50. *Two more areas to go.* Gunter, I noticed a lot of trading on margin here. Any comments?"

"Frankly, I thought you knew that. Some tax considerations are involved. And, we're paying the initial debt off."

Careful here. Don't push it. "Don't count on me knowing too much. You know how the Center likes to inform you. The less you know in advance, the better. Then, when it's time to go, the rush starts, and a lot of stuff gets overlooked."

"Yeah, I know." Braun sighed. "I guess this happens to every one of us."

"Hotel to Bravo. Hard disk is here. We're two minutes away. Request instructions."

"Bravo to Hotel. We're on schedule so far. Give the disk to India. Remain in the general area."

"Hotel to Bravo. Roger."

"Bravo to India. Bring the disc to the office."

"India to Bravo. Roger."

"All right, Gunter. I think, we're moving along pretty well. By the way, where's the list of collateral in the vault deposits?"

"In the original bank. I have a copy here." He nodded at the wall.

Do you have two safes here?"

"No, just one." He paused. "Want to see it, of course?"

Cyrus just nodded. "And while you're at it, let me have the

combination."

Braun once again took a piece of paper and wrote down the number, and handed it to Cyrus. Then, he walked to the wall, opened a panel, and dialed the combination.

"Bravo to Alpha. We've finished."

Cyrus casually looked through some papers in the safe. "All right, close it back. Now, I would like you to talk to Tim Sommers, my accountant. I imagine, he'd like to ask some questions on your records in the computer. Meanwhile, I'll drop by the men's room, and off we go to the bank."

While Braun was closing his safe, Cyrus leaned over the desk, and punched the intercom button. "Tim, can you talk to Mr. Braun now?"

Joe walked in, and Cyrus left. In the reception room Mary whisked him into a corridor and then into the restroom.

Cyrus chuckled. "You're getting aggressive, I like it."

She just laughed, "Oh, shut up. Just get your shirt off."

Cyrus obeyed. Mary quickly switched the mike buttons, and connected the new one. "Try it."

While Mary was putting his shirt back on, Cyrus pushed the new button. "Alpha to Delta. Radio check."

"Loud and clear. Glad to have you back on line, Alpha."

"Sure. Alpha to everybody. Leaving to the bank in five minutes. Tango rides with me. Delta, Echo cover us in the bank. Go to the lobby. Hotel and India cover Charlie, pick him up when he's done. Proceed to watch the residence."

"Delta to Alpha. Roger, bank lobby."

"Hotel to Alpha. Roger. Staying with Charlie, then to the residence."

"Alpha to Charlie. When I ask you to go, insist on staying in."

Two clicks came in response.

Cyrus gave Mary two pieces of paper. "Codes for the computer and the safe. Slip them to Joe. Then he went back to Braun's office.

"All right, gentlemen. I think it's a perfect time for lunch now. After a short stop at the bank."

"Well, Mr. Gregory, I have no idea what we're dealing with here. I'd be more comfortable if I could stay here and work."

Cyrus turned to Braun. "Any objections, Gunter? By the way,

Tim manages more than this, so there's no worry on that side."

Braun was not sure. "Well, I did not realize that you were in a hurry."

Cyrus took him aside. "The sooner I turn in a report, the better it is for both of us." Then, he added, "At least, a preliminary report. I'd rather work around the clock. There are a lot of nervous people around, you know."

"I guess you're right. If it's all right with you, sure."

Cyrus waved to Joe. "We'll bring you a sandwich."

They walked outside. Mary was meddling with her bag, and stayed behind just long enough to give Joe the numbers.

Mary was riding in the front seat of the Cadillac, Cyrus and Braun took the back seats.

When they were getting out of the car in front of the bank, Cyrus asked, "By the way, is my name on the access list to the vault?"

Braun chuckled. "Still trying to catch me? Of course it is."

The management knows him here. We're going to carry out a lot of stuff. Dangerous. We'd better bump into a manager.

When they entered the bank, Cyrus slowed down, looking at the large hall, ceilings, walls, everything. Sure enough, they attracted attention. The security man in the corner became attentive. A man in a business suit saw them and obviously recognized Braun. He walked straight up.

"Hello, Mr. Braun. Glad to see you again, sir."

Cyrus noticed that Braun glanced at him and slightly nodded. ·

"Hello, hello. Mr. Gregory, this is the bank's vice-president, Mr. Fisk. Mr. Fisk, this is my boss, Mr. Gregory."

That was the guy's lucky day. He gasped. "Oh, what an honor. Why don't you gentlemen step into my office. We can have a quiet chat. Our president will be here shortly, and I'm sure he'd be happy to meet you, Mr. Gregory."

"Thank you, but we'll have to do it some other time. I'm a little behind schedule and we have an awful lot of papers to go through. Knowing Gunter as I do, I can bet you right now that we'll have to carry a hundred pounds of papers from the bank to work with."

The vice-president laughed. "Yes, I know what you mean. We can carry them for you."

"Oh, don't worry, I have a driver here."

They left for the vault.

The attendant seemed to know Braun. "Good afternoon, Mr. Braun. Would you please sign here." They entered the first chamber, and the massive grill door closed behind them. While entering, Cyrus glanced back. He saw Mary at one of the customer stands, looking for something in her bag. He heard, "Bravo to everybody. Nothing unusual. They're entering the vault." He knew that he would not hear anything else until he was back outside the vault. The vault itself was an electromagnetic shield, and the radio waves could not penetrate it.

The attendant opened the huge steel vault door, and they followed him into the vault itself. In addition to the numerous safe deposit boxes on the two side walls, the vault also contained several large, high grade safes along the front wall. The attendant remained at the entrance door and turned around. Braun went straight to the third safe from the left. He dialed the combination, and opened the door. On the bottom there were two full size leather file cases, formerly used by pilots and now favored by lawyers. Another similar file case sat on the shelf along with a black attaché.

As expected. Everything neatly stored, and ready to go any minute.

Braun turned to Cyrus. "Are you sure you want all of it now? We can take it case by case."

"I'd rather take it all now." He smiled. "Don't worry. If we lose one of these, as far as both of us are concerned, it's the same as losing the whole thing."

Braun quietly said, "I know."

He took both cases from the bottom and put them on the floor beside the safe. Then he followed with the third one and the attaché. When he closed the safe, Cyrus took the attaché and one of the file cases. Braun took the other two, and they proceeded to the exit.

"Thank you, gentlemen, good day," was a welcome sign of relief for Cyrus. As he was exiting the chamber, he heard, "Delta to Alpha. All quiet. Delta to India. Go to exit. Do not take the bags, keep your hands free." With the corner of his eye Cyrus saw Mary closing in from behind, covering his back.

As they proceeded through the hall, Cyrus spotted the bank vice president and nodded to him. Fortunately, it was too late to arrange help. At the car, they put the cases in the trunk. Everybody felt relieved.

Cyrus let Braun in and sat next to him. To Braun's total surprise, the other back door opened, and Jason took the other side seat. Mary took the front seat, and the Cadillac rolled off.

Without a word, Braun looked at Cyrus. He just shook his head.

Cyrus said, "Don't worry, Gunter. Standard procedure. Until the inspection is complete, and you're fully cleared, just pray that nothing happens to us."

A smirk was Braun's only response.

When they approached the office, without being asked Braun said, "My car key is in the left side pocket. Jason put his hand in and took the keys out. At the office, the car stopped for a second and Mary jumped out. Jason's car with Foxtrot behind the wheel passed them and took the lead. The Mercedes with Echo behind the wheel and Mary next to her followed.

Cyrus pushed his mike button, and as softly as he could, asked, "Gunter, who's at your home now?"

"Nobody. The maid has left and my girlfriend will be back in the evening." Everybody on the team heard that. Cyrus let the button off.

"Hotel to everybody. We're at the residence. No sign of people inside. Should we call the door?"

"Bravo to Hotel. Affirmative. We're ten minutes away."

A minute later the voice came on again. "Hotel to Bravo. No response from inside."

"Bravo to Hotel. Roger. Alpha, Delta, India and Tango are in the Cadillac. They go inside. The rest will cover them outside."

"Hotel to Bravo. We're ready."

"Bravo to Charlie. Was everything all right?"

"Charlie to Bravo. That's affirmative. The safe's clean, and the hard disks switched on the computer. I have all the essentials on three floppies."

Cyrus turned to Braun. "Gunter, listen to me carefully. Everything is in your hands now. You know the procedures as well as I do. I'm sure that you've done a great job and you have a good future. That is, if you don't do anything foolish, or try to hide something. We need to check everything you have at home. And remember, time is of the essence."

Braun did not respond. Cyrus grinned. "I don't know the reason, but every one of us seems to think that all unpleasant things are reserved for others, and we are genuinely surprised if they happen to us."

"Come to think of it, you're right." Braun sighed. "All right. No games. We need five minutes inside for me to hand over everything."

That was precisely what happened in the house. They emptied both his safes, a regular and a covert one, in five minutes. He wrote a note to his girlfriend that he'd be away, entertaining guests for two or three days, and he asked her to pass on the message to his office.

The line came alive again. "Hotel to Alpha. Phone call from home. Team shortage at the next stop. They suggest that you take two more people in the plane. Your discretion."

Cyrus gave two clicks.

Ten minutes later the Cadillac carried Braun, flanked by two men, to the team's villa. The Mercedes and the Subaru followed. Cyrus, Mary, Joe, Hotel and India were heading to the airport in the Cadillac.

There were no speeches on the tarmac. The Gulfstream took off at 14:25 with the flight plan filed to St. Kitts. Soon the flight plan was amended in the air to go to Bermuda.

Cyrus dialed John's number over the satellite telephone.

"John, we are almost on schedule. We've got everything. No drama. Clean as a whistle."

"Great. We have a bit of a problem in Bermuda, though. First, the scale is to big for an outfit like ours. That's why I asked you to take two more people with you. I managed to get only four there."

"That's no big deal. What else?"

"Do you know Bermuda well?"

"Not really. Been there once on vacation."

"Have fun. Pretty uncomfortable operational environment. First, no visitors are allowed to rent or drive cars there. Mopeds or bicycles only. I had to pull quite a few strings on short notice to get two cars with two people permitted to drive them. Two, their customs are pretty nasty, and we can have a major slip-up there. So, make sure that you take only camouflaged weapons. Everything else has to be concealed in the plane."

"Will do. We won't have too much fire power, though."

"I know. The team there has some more for you."

"John, we might have another problem. Timing. Most of the papers in Barbados were in a bank's vault. That could well be the case there too. So, we may need to slip to tomorrow."

"I see. How long will the Barbados thing hold water?"

"Two days. I told Jason to let the guy loose then, with a good piece of advice."

"OK. Then it's your call. You know the risk increases every day. Do you want to call the rest of it off?"

"No. Let's follow through. We'll start tonight. We'll go to the bank tomorrow morning. Then we can do New York tomorrow afternoon."

"All right. I'll keep New York at ready till tomorrow, and then we decide."

"Agreed."

"Cyrus, what about the notifications to the fund managers?"

"I don't know. I'd probably hold it till tomorrow. Joe is ready to get all the pertinent particulars to you through a modem after we hang up."

"Looking forward to it. I guess you're right. It's not too much of a risk. Let's hold till tomorrow."

"OK, have fun."

"You too."

Joe went to work. The rest of the team fell asleep immediately after their meal.

Chapter 19

While going through customs, Cyrus appreciated John's warning. If not hostile, the customs officers were unfriendly and unpleasant. Paul, the leader of the Bermuda support team, met the team at the airport.   Three of them barely fit in a tiny Toyota, and Hotel and India had to take a taxi.

"What a place." Cyrus was concerned, "I'm glad we didn't have to ride bicycles from the airport."

Paul smiled. "You could have. They are crazy around here. You need to attend a local college for four years to know all the restrictions around here. Only the residents can drive cars, only one car per household, and only the local driver's license is recognized."

"How did you manage?"

"Well, two of us just got hired this morning by an international company, established residences, and got local driver's licenses."

Cyrus chuckled. "That's an achievement in itself. What other good news should we know?"

"Well, the good news is that, since you're clearly not locals, you don't have to wear the Bermuda shorts. The bad news is that some of us will have to go by moped. The good news is that our guy is still in his office. The bad news is that he's a hell of a target to follow. The good news is that our villa is right on our way to his office. The bad news is that we have to stop there, so he might leave his office."

"All right. Still, let's make the stop, but quick. What about the office itself?"

"Two-story building, second floor. One other company on the second floor. A real estate office on the first floor. Two entrances. The rear one does not seem to be regularly used. Eight people in the office today, functions unknown. There were no visitors. His investment management company is registered with BIBA.

"What's that?"

"A local business association. Supposedly all the members are reputable companies."

At the villa they spent ten minutes getting weapons and synchronizing the comm sets to Paul's, which had been previously synchronized with the rest of the Bermuda team. Their radio call signs were retained from their Barbados operation. Paul was Delta and William Blacksmith was Tango. They quickly conducted a radio check.

Cyrus, Mary and Joe with his equipment rode with Paul, and Hotel and India took the mopeds.

The Bermuda line came to life. "Delta to Echo. Report situation."

"Echo to Delta. Three people left the office, no other changes. Workday ends in fifteen minutes, so Tango may leave any minute now. Request instructions."

Paul looked at Cyrus. "Your game now."

Cyrus was not certain what to do.

"Alpha to Echo. What's happening in the real estate office?"

"They're pretty much finished. Last two people are about to leave now."

"OK. Count heads. If Tango leaves, follow at a safe distance."

"Roger, Alpha."

By the time they arrived in the vicinity of the building, three more people left. Cyrus was still undecided. *I just don't have a feel for the place and the situation. Jumping in at the very end of the day can be dangerous.*

They stopped about sixty yards up the street.

"Well?" Joe was nervous.

"Let's wait a little."

At that moment they saw two women coming out of the entrance.

"Echo to Alpha. All out. Tango's there alone." That was the first break for them in Bermuda.

I still wish I had more time to groove in. "Weapons ready. We're moving in. Hotel and India, thirty seconds after we're in, take positions at the staircase. If nothing happens in three minutes, go outside. Echo remains in the car at all times." Cyrus turned to Joe. "Joe, you wait here."

Cyrus and Mary walked briskly to the entrance. Mary went

ahead at the stairway, Cyrus followed. The glass door on the second floor was locked. Mary, hugging a large envelope, knocked at the door. Cyrus was aside, near the wall, not visible from the reception room of the office.

There was no response. Mary knocked a little louder. A dark-haired man of five nine in Bermuda shorts and a shirt without a jacket walked to the door.

Mary smiled. "Hello, I'm Susan Roth from Arthur Anderson. Terribly sorry that I'm late. Could I possibly leave a package for Mr. Blacksmith?"

"Certainly. Mr. Blacksmith is authorized to take a package for Mr. Blacksmith." The man smiled at a pretty young lady. He unlocked the door. Mary made a couple of steps inside, blabbing apologies. "Oh, Mr. Blacksmith, I did not mean to bother you."

"Not at all."

At this moment Cyrus quickly and decisively stepped inside, one hand in his pocket. The man understood his mistake, old as the world itself. Too late. His face paled, but he had enough nerve not to make a single motion.

In Russian Cyrus said, "Mr. Blacksmith, I'm Peter Gregory. Uncle Misha asked me to pass his regards. I hope we are alone here."

Now the man's face went completely colorless. "I see." He paused, thinking quickly. "Oh, yes, we are alone. However, I expect my associate to come back any moment."

Cyrus looked at him. *I don't like it. Obviously he's lying. Why? Watch out.*

The man did not feel comfortable. He did not meet Cyrus' silence.

"Well, he may just go home, but he intended to return here."

Cyrus did not respond.

"Well, not to worry. I'll send him away. Won't you come in?" He gestured toward the corridor, apparently leading toward his office.

Cyrus nodded to Mary, and she moved forward. "After you." Blacksmith followed Mary, and Cyrus closed the file.

In the office Blacksmith looked at Cyrus and chose not to try to go behind his desk. Cyrus handed him the passport. The man looked at it very carefully, nodded, and returned it.

Without a word, Cyrus gave him the plastic card. *I'm glad the computer is running.*

Blacksmith said, "I have to verify it."

"Of course." *I really don't like his demeanor. Be ready for anything.*

Blacksmith went to a file cabinet and pulled the handle without unlocking the knob, rolling the whole cabinet forward. He opened the panel behind it, revealing a safe. When he kneeled to dial the combination, Cyrus came over and pushed his pen against the back of Blacksmith's head.

"Make sure you don't make a wrong motion."

With deliberate slowness, the man opened his safe. Then he took a small envelope from underneath the file of papers.

"Don't close the safe."

Blacksmith obeyed and sat down in the visitors' chair next to his desk. Cyrus followed. He looked at Mary and gestured toward the door with his eyes. She went out of the room.

"Bravo to Charlie. Come in."

"Charlie to Bravo, roger."

Mary returned to the room when Blacksmith finished his verification.

"Everything is in order. Now we can talk." When he said that, Cyrus could feel the man's spirit deflate.

Why? This does not feel right.

"Well, Mr. Gregory, what are we going to do now? Are you taking over?"

"We both will have our orders in a few days. Meanwhile, I am going to make a thorough inspection."

"That's what I thought."

"What bank are the main documents in?"

"Butterfield."

"Do you have the whole safe there, as instructed?"

"Of course."

"The combination."

The man sighed, and wrote it on a piece of paper. He stopped, sighed again, and wrote three more combinations.

"This safe, your home safe, and the computer?"

Blacksmit nodded.

"You are becoming more cooperative. Thank you." *I'm glad I* started that way. He probably thinks that we'll torture him right here and now.

Blacksmith saw Joe coming in and looked like he wanted to shrink in his chair. Suddenly, he stood up and smiled a sad smile like an old man with no hope of being understood by the rest of the world.

"Please, forgive me. I'm still a host here. Would you like any drinks, coffee or refreshments? I'm afraid that's all I have here."

"No, thank you, we're fine."

"I see." He nodded understandingly. Then he recalled something else. "Oh, I have some jelly beans here too. Want some?"

He reached to his desk, took a jar, opened it with a look of a good host, and offered it to Mary.

Mary shook her head. "Thank you very much."

The man smiled. "As you wish, but they're good, I personally, love them." With this he put his hand in the jar, fished a little, and took out a green one. He carefully closed the jar and put it back.

At that moment Cyrus realized what he had not liked. From ten feet away, he jumped to tackle the man. It was too late.

Blacksmith quickly put the jelly bean in his mouth and clenched his jaws. At that moment Cyrus caught his hands and knocked Blacksmith down on his back. Cyrus raised his head and looked at the man who now wore a look of sad victory. In seconds his body jerked in a series of short convulsions, his eyes turned glassy, and white soapy foam bubbled on his lips.

"Damn. I should have known." He looked at Blacksmith. "Gone." Mary tried his pulse and shook her head.

"Joe, get on with the computers. Mary clean up the safe." He pushed the mike button. "Alpha to everybody. We have a mishap here. Tango's dead. In case of any police interest we will abort and get the hell out of here. Meanwhile, we'll push as far as we can."

"Delta to Alpha. Do you need help there?"

"Negative. It may arouse suspicion if anyone comes to the office that late. When do they clean the offices?"

"Early in the morning."

"Alpha to Delta. Park one of the cars somewhere nearby for the night and come back. We'll have to drive Tango's car out of here, but we have only two legitimate drivers. I don't want to take chances here."

"Roger, Alpha."

In half an hour all the computers were checked out, all the information from Blacksmith's computer copied, and the hard disk erased. *I'd rather have the disk removed, but there's no way here. Everything has to be quiet till we're out of the bank tomorrow.*

"Joe, open the back entrance. There's probably a security system."

Joe left. Cyrus verified the code for the safe, as he had done for the computer before the information was erased. Both were correct. *What's the chance that he gave me the wrong code for the safe in the bank? Let's judge that by the code to his safe at home.*

"Charlie to Alpha. The door is open."

"Roger, Charlie, stand by."

With Mary's help, Cyrus put Blacksmith's jacket on the corpse. Cyrus took the car keys from Blacksmith's pocket and gave them to Mary.

"Alpha to everybody. Charlie, come here. Delta, take the keys at the back door and bring Tango's car there. Report when ready."

Mary went downstairs and came back. She and Joe took all the materials and moved them to the back door on the first floor. Cyrus checked that the office was clean and nothing was left there.

"Delta to Alpha. Ready to go."

Cyrus and Joe carried the corpse to the back door. They locked the office.

"Alpha to everybody. Let's go. Delta, bring the car."

In a few seconds the car stopped at the door. In twenty more seconds Blacksmith's car with Cyrus, Mary, the corpse, and Paul behind the wheel slowly rolled out of the alley. Joe got into another car. The four other members of the team were enjoying moped rides.

"Alpha to Charlie. Go ahead and deal with the security system at Tango's villa. We'll take a scenic route. How much time do you need?"

"Charlie to Alpha. I have no idea what the system is. Twenty minutes, maybe."

"Try to be a little quicker. We have a boring guy with us."

"Will do my best, Alpha."

Paul slowed down and took the scenic Harbour Road. By the time they approached Tamarind Vale, the radio came alive.

"Charlie to Alpha. You can come in." That was a welcome call.

At Blacksmith's villa they found the safe and opened it without any problem. After cleaning it up they put the body in the bedroom. They spent more than an hour looking for the safe and making sure there wasn't another one in the house. They left Blacksmith's car in the garage.

"Paul, what time does the maid come in?"

"Today it was nine thirty. Comes on a moped. Should be the same every day."

"If that's the case, we should be in the clear by that time. But I'd rather be on the safe side. Joe, you jam the lock here so she won't get in for a while. Make sure she feels like the lock broke, but when they come in, and the investigation starts, it will be locked from inside. Can you do that?"

"With this lock I can only do both. The lock broke, and it's locked from inside. Coincidence."

"No way. Too sloppy. Then we'll have to do it differently. We need to steal the key from the lady. Do we know where she lives now?"

Mary said, "Yes, the address and the phone number are in the kitchen."

"Paul, you put two people on it."

"OK."

"Let's get out of here."

When Joe started complaining about the small car, Cyrus noted, "Joe, it's still a hell of a lot better than riding with a stiff."

Back in Hamilton, they took their other car and went to their villa.

Ten minutes later Cyrus was on the phone with John.

"John, we're doing kind of OK here."

"What happened?"

"Our guy bailed out. My fault, John. I should have known better."

"Damn. But why?"

"Who knows. I guess there are a couple of possibilities. One, he thought that he'd be disposed of anyway, after some rigorous questioning, which is not unheard of in his kindergarten. Two, he might have been squirreling away some of the decimal dust off his accounts, and knew the price he'd pay."

"Well. Cyrus, I'd like to call the rest of it off. You don't even know if he put you on the access list or not."

"John, he gave us four access codes. Three of them have been verified as good. There's a good chance that the fourth one is OK too. And, he had to put me on all lists. It was done in the very beginning and it was strictly a standard operating procedure. Ten years ago he wouldn't dare."

"I can buy that. But what if the code is false?"

"If I'm on the list, it's OK. They won't know yet that he's gone. So, I'll have time to vanish. If I'm not on the list, I'll make a scene to insist on getting to the bottom of the mistake, and leave with dignity."

"Don't you have the feeling that you're pushing your luck lately?"

"John, leave it to me, OK? I'll be careful."

"Hell you will. But, somehow, I can't stop you."

"Thanks, John."

"All right, how about the official transfer notifications?"

"Wait till noon. I hope we can give you the second batch, and you can shoot it off while we're on our way to New York."

"All right. You've got till noon tomorrow."

At a quarter to nine next morning, a limousine by local standards, and a Mercedes sedan by the rest of the world's, pulled up to the Arthur Andersen building. By request, uncommon outside an airport, the car carried two foot-wide placards. One was on the windshield, and the other one on the rear window. The driver was surprised to see Cyrus, Mary and Paul exit the main entrance the moment he pulled up. They got in and went for a short drive to the Butterfield bank.

At nine sharp the bank door opened, and the manager was obviously in front of the lobby. The car, with its placards could not be unnoticed. The manager came to the door.

Cyrus walked confidently in with Mary and Paul following two steps behind.

"Good morning, Sir. Arthur Andersen is one of our best clients. Good business people start their day early."

"Good morning. Absolutely. Especially, if you have to do three audits in a week."

"How can I help you?"

"I need to get to the vault."

"This way, Sir." The manager lead the way to the entrance.

Cyrus shwed his passport to the attendant. "I'm Peter Gregory. To the Blacksmith Management safe."

"The attendant was surprised. He looked at the register. "Oh, yes, Mr. Gregory. Your name is even above Mr. Blacksmith. But I would expect Mr. Blacksmith to accompany you." He looked at the manager.

Cyrus chuckled, and handed him the passport. "I don't want Mr. Blacksmith to accompany me. However, you're welcome to call him." He saw the manager nod to the attendant. *Well, human psychology again. Now I just told them enough that they know a little secret: Mr. Blacksmith is in some kind of trouble. And that made them very proud to be in on it.*

"No need, Mr. Gregory. Your name is number one on the list. Please, sign here."

Cyrus signed the register.

"This way, Sir."

At the safe Cyrus felt something resembling jitters. Well, it's either yes, or no. At least there shouldn't be any tricks here. Not like Yoshkar-Ola.

He dialed the combination. The safe opened. No tricks. Cyrus took a breath. *This is the last time I'm pushing my luck.*

There were two large file cases on the bottom, one file case and an attaché on the shelf. Cyrus stifled the laughter welling up in his chest. *That's what big organizations are. Discipline and uniformity.* He brought two file cases to the door.

"Would you be so kind as to get my assistant over there." He nodded toward Paul and went back for the other two pieces.

Two minutes later he carried a case and the attaché, and Paul and Mary followed with the other two cases. The limo driver was let go at the Arthur Andersen entrance and ordered to come to the Bermuda Commercial Bank building three hours later. The trio walked toward the building when the limo left. They stopped on the sidewalk, and within fifteen seconds a small Toyota pulled up. Getting in took a matter of seconds.

At the same time, Blacksmith's maid was riding her moped to his villa. Suddenly, a young lady, obviously a tourist, lost control of her moped, and veered sharply toward the maid. The maid desperately tried to avoid collision. For the maid, well in her fifties, and not too light, it was too much to cope with. She fell on the shoulder of the road. Her pride suffered much more than her body, and the moped received a slight scratch.

The young lady and a young man following her came to help. They made sure that the lady did not have anything serious, like broken bones, and then they helped her with her clothes and her bag. The young lady felt very guilty, so she offered five hundred American dollars as a conciliatory gesture. Though still visibly upset, deep inside the maid would have been happy to repeat the exercise. Less than ten minutes after the incident began, she was on her way to her employer's house. Without the key, of course.

An hour later the Gulfstream took off from the Bermuda International Airport with the flight plan filed for Puerto-Rico. The flight plan was amended to go to New York.

Cyrus called John.

"John, we're on our way to the Big Apple."

"Great. I was worried about you in that dreadful, snobbish place. Glad, you're out."

"See you soon, John."

Nobody wanted to sleep on that plane.

An hour into the flight, Cyrus was looking out the window when Joe came to his seat.

"Cyrus, I was playing with the computer for a while. I think I know why the guy freaked out."

"Why?"

"He diverted a lot of money to a few strange companies. I bet he owned them all."

"He also had two spare passports in his home safe."

"Yeah. It looks like he started about five years ago."

"How much did he steal?"

"Hard to say right now. I'd say close to a billion."

"Those guys would hang him by the balls for that, and he knew it. Poor bastard."

Just past noon the Gulfstream landed at Kennedy International Airport. Two stretch limousines were waiting. Cyrus, Mary and Joe got into one and took off for Manhattan. The other limo followed.

Inside the limo, John greeted the group. "Welcome back. That was something to remember, wasn't it?"

"Yeah, you don't come across something like that too often." Like everyone else, Joe was happy to be on American soil.

"I don't think you guys really comprehend the whole thing right now. It's all right, you'll have time to reflect later. Meanwhile, we have a job at hand. Mr. Robert Kenworth."

Cyrus switched gears. "What's the setup here?"

"As expected. Big player, low profile. Known in investment circles as a manager of a few international trusts. Rumor has it, for quite a few shy Arab customers. Owns a small, tightly managed outfit, RMK Management. Lives in an uptown condo, has a large house on Long Island. Changes girlfriends about once a year, broke up with the last one just two weeks ago. Now flirting with an owner of a small public relations firm. Has not left for a vacation during last ten years. That's about all."

"So, how do we tackle this one?"

"Just head on. I don't see any problems. There are the comms set to synchronize, fresh batteries, and the weapons in that box." He nodded toward a box on the floor.

They started fiddling with the hardware, and John continued, "He's at lunch now. Hopefully, we'll be there before he's back. Then, we'll intercept him just before his office. When we're finished I'll give him to the FBI."

"Why, John? Those guys can blow anything of a sensitive nature in a heartbeat. They're good at criminal work, but not where any finesse is needed. They're just not equipped."

"Well, we're in the United States, Cyrus. There are certain rules, and I'd better adhere to them. He's a foreign agent, operating on American soil, remember? Besides, I want to get a brownie point with them."

"How about us?" Cyrus didn't want to blow anyone's cover.

"They'd move in when we're out. I haven't warned them yet."

Cyrus shook his head. "I'd wait on that, but you're the boss." After a pause, he asked, "How about the transfer orders for the funds?"

"Being faxed as we speak. The main trustee, Mr. Gregory is taking sole authority over all the accounts. He authorized Jones &

Bleach to handle the investments for him."

They had to wait for forty minutes before they heard over the radio line, "Lima to everybody. Tango is leaving the restaurant."

When they received a message that Tango was a block away, walking toward the building, the trio got out of the car and went inside. Joe and Mary remained in the lobby while Cyrus took an elevator to the eighth floor. Two guys of the support team were already there. At Cyrus' request, they moved out of sight.

Luckily, Tango emerged from the elevator alone. Cyrus, apparently waiting for the elevator down, stepped up. "Excuse me. Mr. Kenworth?"

The tall, well fit man of about forty stopped.

"Yes." His demeanor was a question mark.

"I hope you remember me. I'm Peter Gregory."

The man shifted gears effortlessly. "Oh, yes, of course. Buenos Aires, isn't it?" He extended his hand.

Cyrus shook his hand. "Yes." He lowered his voice and switched to Russian. "Uncle Misha sends his regards."

Softly, the man answered in Russian, "I hope Aunt's health is still good." He raised his voice to a normal level and continued in English. "Well, let's go to my office, we have a lot to chat about."

They went through the reception area, and moved on. Passing his secretary, he said, "Jacqueline, hold all my calls." He turned to Cyrus, "Coffee?"

"No, thanks."

They went inside. Cyrus handed him his passport and the plastic card. To his surprise, the man took his corresponding card from the front drawer of the desk. Seeing Cyrus' surprise, he chuckled, "The most secure places are the most accessible ones."

Cyrus just smiled. Kenworth made the comparison and, satisfied, sighed. "Well, it's been a while. So, where do we start?"

Cyrus pushed his mike button. Now everything he said would go to the comm line. He looked at his watch. "About two minutes from now my assistants, a man and a woman, will come to see you. Please make sure they are let in without a big fuss." He released the mike button.

"No problem." He pushed the buzzer. His secretary appeared at the door. "Jacqueline, there are going to be a man and a woman to see me very soon. Please usher them in here." The secretary nodded and left.

By now Cyrus had enough experience to handle the situation confidently.

"Robert, you know the rules." Kenworth nodded, and Cyrus went on. "Well, my orders are to make a full inspection, and report. I'm taking over, but I have a lot of other things to do. If everything is all right, you will, probably, stay on. Obviously, I cannot guarantee that, but that's my hunch."

Kenworth looked very confident. "As expected. Any peculiarities?"

"No. Just everything is to be verified."

At that moment Joe and Mary showed up. After the introduction Cyrus suggested, "The sooner my report is made, the better. Why don't we leave these two here and go to the bank?"

"Suits me." He pushed the buzzer again. "Jacqueline, Susan and Tim are going to work in my office. Make sure they are not disturbed. They can do whatever they want. Mr. Gregory and I are going away for a while."

Cyrus watched the secretary's face. She was well trained and showed no surprise at an obviously unusual request. Her eyes, though, showed a little flicker at the name Gregory.

Cyrus and Kenworth went to the lift. "I have a car at the door."

"You seem to be very well equipped and very confident. I'd like to work with you."

My God, I seem to have acquired one more profession. The Politburo inspector.

An hour and a half later Cyrus and Kenworth came back, having visited the bank and Kenworth's apartment. Cyrus remained in the limo, and Kenworth went to his office. Five minutes later Joe and Mary appeared in front of the office building.

An hour later, in the Gulfstream on its way to Washington, Joe transmitted all the particulars of the Kenworth files. The remaining transfer orders would be faxed within an hour.

With the four of them in the plane, John took Cyrus to the back of the cabin for a private talk.

"Cyrus, I don't need to tell you that you've done a super job, well beyond what anybody could order or even ask for. Now we're entering a critical stage."

"Are you going to the President?"

"Yes. You'll drop me off at National and go on to the base."

"You seem to be concerned. Why?"

"Well, you absolutely never know what kind of trick a politician can play. My hunch is that everything could be swept under the rug."

"You mean that they'd just give it all quietly to Yeltsin?"

"Precisely."

"I can't believe it, John."

"Just wait. But I'm not about to let that happen."

"Neither am I, that's for sure."

"That's precisely the point. I need ammunition. Up until now this has been only a commercial enterprise. Do you remember how I got you into this?"

Cyrus chuckled. "Sure."

"Well, it was the truth, and it still is. The President did not suggest this operation, and he did not authorize it. Further, if I went to him for authorization, I'd be fired on the spot."

Cyrus interrupted, "And replaced by some relative from his home state."

John laughed. "Perhaps. But you went into this venture to earn money commercially, right?"

"Absolutely."

"So, you've found it, and you control the information about it."

"John, come to the point. What do you need?"

John smiled. "I may know you well, but you know me well enough too. The only way to prevent the whole thing from being hushed up is to report that the whole affair will be in the media very soon, somehow. I don't need to specify more."

Now Cyrus understood. "Well, but of course. I heard a rumor that some interviews have already been set up to publish if not the whole thing, at least a major portion of it." He paused, his face growing grim. "John, with what I've been through in this thing, it's a little more than politics for me. I got people, good people, working and dying for me and making it happen with my word that I'd make sure the money went to the Russian government publicly. So there would be a better chance that this money would be used for the benefit of the Russian people, not spent on some games and looted by the crooks."

"I understand."

"I'm afraid you don't. No matter who says and does what, if I see any sign of an attempt to hush it up, I'll make sure that it's advertised on every fucking bulletin board from coast to coast, as well as in Russia and Europe. You have my word on it."

John looked at Cyrus with the concern of a father. "Cyrus, I do understand. You need rest now, a lot of rest. I got what I wanted, which was just a small portion of what you've just said. Now let me play the game. I'm still not too bad at it, you know."

Cyrus was too exhausted to feel sorry for his emotional display. He said nothing.

John tried to lighten things up. "Oh, as a manager, I have to make sure that I know all my costs for the transaction. Besides our colorful British friend, who has been taken care of, who else is to be paid, and how?"

Cyrus was silent for a while. "Vladimir, who made it happen, died. I promised him ten million in case of success. He has a sister in Russia. We should find her and give her his share."

"No problem."

"New York was your play. So, that's up to you. All the other guys were very good. When I took chances, nobody gave me that look you're afraid of when operating. They have to be paid well."

"Of course. They'll get their one full year take for this operation."

"With a take like this, you should do better, John."

"Come on. These guys are the best of the best, and they don't come cheap, believe me."

"Two years, John."

John sighed. "I'm glad you're not the manager. OK, two. Anything else?"

"By the way, how about Nicholas?"

"That's a thing in itself. We paid one million pounds, as you promised. That includes his promise not to do it again. We paid him one more to keep quiet about it."

"I'm glad that's taken care of."

"The thing is that the NSA went crazy over it. They think that by the time people wake up, they'll extract a good chunk of goodies from everybody. I wanted to protect you at all costs. So, we made a deal with them that they'd start using it tomorrow."

"I hope you didn't tell them where it came from?"

"Of course, not." John made a pause. "Now, the main thing. What about your compensation?"

Cyrus laughed. "That was a commercial enterprise, remember? So, my service ain't cheap either."

To his surprise, John said, "Absolutely. The way we deal with an independent contractor, but with a slight discount. How about thirty percent of whatever the firm gets? And the firm picks up all the tabs."

Cyrus looked at John. *I'll never figure you out.* "Are you serious?"

"Certainly." John was smiling.

"Sounds like a good deal to me."

"Done."

"What's our total fee going to be?"

"I think, I can swing one percent."

"I thought one could do better than that."

"Not with this amount."

Cyrus smiled. "All right, let's not be greedy."

"Yeah. I'm afraid I'll have a hell of a time figuring out how to motivate you to work, though. I might take less just for that reason."

Cyrus laughed.

"By the way, Cyrus. I told everyone involved to stay low for a while. We don't know what these guys are up to, but they're nasty. They may need some time to come to grips with reality and to cool down. Mary and Joe will go to Wyoming. You do not leave the base under any circumstances. Too much is riding on your head right now."

"John, they don't even know that I'm involved."

"Hopefully. They're not stupid, Cyrus. And they have their way of figuring things out."

"OK, you're right. I'll test your hospitality."

"By all means."

Chapter 20

Cyrus slept most of the next day while John monitored the confirmations of the trusts' authorized transfers. Considering the size of the accounts involved, the investment managers gave the faxes their undivided attention. When John returned from Washington, Cyrus was asleep for the night.

At four in the morning Cyrus awoke, and at five he and John boarded the Gulfstream at the small Manassas Regional Airport. The airplane took off and set the course for Eielson Air Force Base in Alaska.

"Read this. You may find it entertaining." John took a folder from his file case attaché and handed it to Cyrus.

Cyrus opened the folder. Inside was a summary of investments for the entire Group 2, as well as the full list of investments. However, it did not give any information either on the management of the investments, nor on the separation of the trusts and the accounts.

Cyrus glanced at the bottom line. "One hundred and seven billion dollars. Well, overall, they didn't do too shabbily. As well as anybody over the whole period."

"Of course. You know who was doing the job for them. The best of the best in the investment community, without ever knowing it."

Cyrus browsed through the list of investments. "A model portfolio. They have everything here, except real estate. I wonder, why."

"They need it for operational use, which means that they have to stay more or less liquid. Real estate may take a long time to sell. They have to be ready to roll on short notice."

"Yeah, makes sense." Cyrus returned the folder. "How was your meeting with the President?"

"As well as expected. He was outraged at the setup at first, but not as much as one of the previous Presidents would be, those who dealt with Gorbatov and were fooled by him." John sighed. "Then he realized the magnitude of the situation. He understands that the issue is big enough that it required an urgent personal meeting. On the other hand, he's mad that we're taking time from his busy schedule, particularly considering that he was here just a short while ago, and the elections aren't too far away."

So, you didn't get a lot of praise, did you?"

"Give me a break, Cyrus. He was most upset that we didn't manage to handle it quietly, gave me a lecture about the subtleties of diplomacy, in the great tradition of his paradigmatic Secretary of State. At the end he scolded me for sloppy tradecraft and expressed his sincere hope that it would not happen again."

"What was he so upset about?"

"As I told you before. That we did not arrange it in a way that it would be hushed up between him and Yeltsin."

"It's kind of hard for me to comprehend. So, he is more mad at us than he is at the communists and the Russians, right?"

"Of course. He thinks that we're the ones who presented him with a headache, not the communists, not the Russians. And one of his ways of showing his displeasure is not to take us on Air Force One for the meeting."

"As a matter of fact, I'm happy to travel separately. By the way, who is accompanying him?"

"Tony Blake, the National Security advisor. I hope that he won't take the Secretary of State."

"Can he double-cross us somehow?"

"I don't think so. Under the circumstances, he doesn't have a choice. He cannot discount the possibility of publicity of a media frenzy. So, he cannot afford to screw it up with the upcoming elections."

"Tell me something, John. Does he understand that this money was being strategically placed and represented a direct threat to this country's national security, to this whole region? Does he understand that if it is hushed up, never mind the Russian people, our own interests are in jeopardy? If the Russian government takes the funds over quietly, they'll just leave them in place and will have a perfect weapon against us. A weapon which they can use at any time."

"I'm not sure if he understands that clearly, or not. But I'm sure that he doesn't want to understand that." John made a pause. "Look, Cyrus, let's change the subject."

"All right." Cyrus leaned back. In five minutes he was sleeping, and he didn't wake up until the engine's sound changed. The plane was making its approach at Eielson AFB, Alaska.

Air Force personnel delivered military parkas on board, and Cyrus and John were ushered into the officers club. They had to kill a couple of hours with the deputy commander of the base and three men of the Secret Service advance team.

The President walked into the room with Tony Blake and the base commander two steps behind.

"Mr. President, let me present Cyrus Grant. He is the one who actually pulled the operation off."

The President shook Cyrus' hand and slapped him on the shoulder Luckily, it was the left one. "So, you're the guy." He suddenly laughed. "Didn't they ever teach you to operate quietly?"

"Yes, Mr. President. But I retired a while ago. Lost the touch, I guess. Besides, it came up unexpectedly, in a purely commercial way."

"Don't worry. You pulled it off, and it wasn't easy, I'm sure."

No, it wasn't. Mr. President. Cyrus did not say a word.

At that moment an aid came into the room. "Mr. President, Yeltsin's plane is landing in five minutes." On such occasions pilots and air traffic controllers usually coordinated the planes' speeds, so neither party would have to wait for too long.

"All right. Let's see how my friend Boris feels after his heart trouble. I'll meet him at the tarmac." He turned, and the whole procession followed in the same order they came in.

Twenty minutes later the procession, double in size, flooded in. The Presidents took their seats across from each other in the middle of the long table. Somebody pushed Cyrus slightly toward the last chair on the left flank of the American side. John was seated next to him. Cyrus raised his eyes and saw a ghost. General Yuri Dronov was sitting across the table from him.

"Boris, I already extended my apologies that I called for this urgent meeting with me. I know you have to get back quickly, but so do I. Let's get to business."

Yeltsin nodded.

"The first question which I would like to raise is money."

Yeltsin quipped, "When you start talking about money, I get worried, Bill." Everybody laughed.

"Boris, as I hinted to you over the phone, it concerns the money missing from Russia a few years back."

Yeltsin nodded again.

"So, I have good news and bad news for you. The good news is that we've found the money, one hundred and seven billion dollars. And, we are prepared to return it to you immediately."

Cyrus noticed that neither Yeltsin, nor anyone else on the Russian side showed any surprise. He saw only poker faces across the table.

Yeltsin slowly said, "We appreciate your help in this matter."

"So, we can start converting the investments and transferring the money immediately. Last time we met you mentioned that Russia is running a little short of cash. I'm sure that this will help to improve the situation."

"Yes, it is a substantial amount. But I'm not convinced that it will entirely solve all our problems.

That's what it is. He doesn't want to lose the foreign aid money.

"I understand." The president lowered his head. "The bad news is that we discovered something very disturbing." The President opened a folder in front of him, and handed Yeltsin a piece of paper. "This is a copy of the letter we came across. Signed by General Secretary Gorbatov."

Everybody was silent while Yeltsin read the letter. He shook his head, and passed the letter to Primakov, sitting next to him.

"We would like to see the original."

That intimation was a hopeless bluff, and the President felt it was inappropriate. "Mr. President, are you questioning the authenticity? We can provide all sorts of proof, I was just trying to avoid any possible embarrassment." He looked Yeltsin straight in the eye.

Yeltsin immediately understood his mistake. "No. I'll have to look into it, and we'll find those involved." He hesitated. "Now I see why you asked for this meeting."

There was a long silence at the table. Finally, Yeltsin said, "Bill, I do not see any reason why we can't settle this matter quietly between us and avoid a lot of controversy. As you are well aware, there are some people in both our countries that would love to damage our friendship and to find irreconcilable differences between us."

"I'm certainly all for that, but…"

Yeltsin interrupted him. "For instance, we can keep the investments in place, and borrow money instead, using them as collateral. I think that's a good idea."

"I'd love to do that, Boris. Unfortunately, the funds were discovered accidentally, and not by the government but by an American investment firm." He opened his folder and looked up the name, Jones & Bleach. Let me introduce," he glanced into the folder again, "Mr. Porter and Mr. Grant. They are top notch international investment bankers."

John and Cyrus half-raised themselves from their chairs. Yeltsin looked at them and nodded.

"But what is the problem?"

The President looked at Cyrus. "Mr. Grant?"

Cyrus looked Yeltsin straight in the eye. "Mr. President, I'm just a banker, and I know nothing about diplomacy, but our firm is used to acting discreetly. And we are always sensitive to publicity. In this case, however, it is not possible to contain the matter. Quite a few people were involved in this transaction, and I am sure that very soon the story will get to the media."

"I see." Then, suddenly, Yeltsin smiled. "This is the first time in my life I have met somebody who found a hundred billion dollars."

"It's the first time for me too, Sir." Everybody cracked up with laughter.

Yeltsin, apparently, took the opportunity to discharge the atmosphere. "Well, since it was a commercial transaction, how much would you charge us for finding the money?"

Cyrus looked at John. John said, "This was not our usual modus operandi, so I did some research on the matter. I think one percent would be in order."

"One percent." Yeltsin paused, "But that's one billion dollars. That's a lot of money."

John is on the spot. I think I can help. Cyrus stepped in, "Mr. President, a usual insurance recovery fee is ten percent."

Yeltsin laughed, and said, "I wish I had salesmen like that.

You've got a deal. One percent." He stopped, and then continued, "With one condition, though. Your company is a reputable investment banking firm, so you shouldn't be interested in publicity over such affairs, right?"

John lowered his head.

"Then why don't we take the credit? We'll announce that our SVR discovered the stolen money." He looked at the President. "I'm sure Bill wouldn't mind."

Bastard.

John looked at the President, who looked back sternly, and nodded. "Of course, Mr. President."

"Very well. Then it's all settled. You'll give all the particulars to Mr. Primakov."

Cyrus felt a slight fury. He understood that the President was not going to say no. *To hell with it, I'm not a politician.* "I'm sorry, Mr. President, but we didn't find any particulars, we just found the money." He deliberately looked at Yeltsin, but with the corner of his eye he saw that the President was outraged with his tactlessness.

Yeltsin was irritated. He was outplayed. He knew that he had no other choice than to laugh, which he promptly did.

"Well, this issue is resolved."

John gave the President a long look. He clearly was not thrilled with that, but he knew his final obligation on the matter. He stepped in, "Oh, Boris, one more detail. Since Jones & Bleach is already involved, I'm sure that your government would be interested in hiring them to manage the transfer."

"Well, I think that's logical." Then he smirked, "I hope they won't ask for another billion."

"Everybody laughed, and John said, "Just a regular commercial rate."

The President finished the issue. "Well, why don't we tackle a couple of other things we planned for today?"

That was the cue for Cyrus and John to leave.

Just outside, Cyrus saw General Dronov coming out of the conference room as well.

"Cyrus, can I have a word with you?"

Cyrus did not move.

"Please."

The General took Cyrus by the elbow, leading him to the next room. Cyrus abruptly freed his arm.

"Cyrus."

Cyrus interrupted him. With a very quiet, slow and calm voice he said, "General, I hope I'll never see you again. I'm a very peaceful man, but if I see you again, I'll break your neck. There will be no other warning."

To Cyrus surprise, Dronov chuckled, "I believe you. That won't be the first neck you've broken, would it? Or do you prefer blowing somebody to pieces?"

Cyrus was stunned. *How does he know?* He did not say a word.

"Are you surprised? You may want to know something I can tell you. If you listen to me, your next ten minutes will be well spent."

Cyrus went to the club bar, and the General followed. They took their drinks to a small table in the corner.

"First of all, I'm sorry about Laura." Cyrus clinched his jaws. "I really am. Let it be known to you, I tried to save her. And you. I was just a little slow, unfortunately. Let me tell you a story."

Cyrus took a sip from his glass.

"There are two parts of the KGB. Intelligence and counterintelligence, call it external and internal. They were always very different, even during Stalin's time. They worked more or less together until Gorbatov split them. Then all the old rivalries came to the surface. The internal part was far more rigid, more repressive, more conservative. The external was more open to new ideas. Are you with me so far?"

"Yes."

"Well, guess which part the communists relied upon to retain the power, and to try to regain it when they lost? Of course, internal." He made a pause. "And which part did the new government employ to find the stolen money? The external."

He sighed. "Yes, it is true, I was working on a special assignment and tried to recruit you to do the job for us. Yes, it is true, I tried to manipulate you. But I never tried to harm you. Or Laura. The intelligence people were working against us."

"What are you saying, General, the KGB against the KGB?"

"Precisely. They were protecting the communists' little secret. We only realized the full extent when it was too late."

"But if what you are saying is true, they knew the secret in the first place."

"That's where you're wrong. You have to know the KGB to appreciate that. They did not know. They were protecting the general area. And, as soon as you get into that protected general area, you're doomed. If that was me, I'd be dead too."

Now Cyrus was presented with a series of question marks. What does he know? Does he know of my trip to Yoshkar-Ola?

The general came to his help. "I don't know how you managed to hide in Moscow for that long. Obviously, you're not about to tell me." He made a sufficient pause.

Cyrus said nothing and kept watching the general.

"Of course, not. That's OK. The internal service turned Moscow and the suburbs upside down. We did twice that trying to find you before they did. You'd just vanished." He sighed. "I always said, 'don't underestimate an amateur. Particularly one with a brain.'"

Cyrus smiled. Do they know about the disappearance of the box?

"Well, the hunch came to me when I heard about Voronov being blown to pieces in broad daylight. Speaking of breaking necks. I made the connection and figured that there were only two people interested in the same set of stiffs. You and Laura's uncle. And the set was Voronov and two little bastards. I immediately set off to find the two. Guess, what I found."

"What?"

"Cyrus, so you play poker? You must be pretty good."

"Go on."

"Cyrus, you made one mistake. Easily forgivable for an amateur. You should have dumped the bloody shirt farther away. I took it to the lab and we compared it to the sample off your laundry in the hotel. We always keep things for a while, just in case. And guess, what? A perfect match. Bingo! The getaway car driver and a banker at the Savoy are the same guy."

"Must be a mistake."

"Obviously. Don't worry. Only I know about it. Nobody even knows that I had that shirt in the first place. And an old friend made the comparison, off the record."

Cyrus shook his head. "I'm not sure where you are going with this, General."

"Be patient. So, I figured you and Vladimir Portnov were connected. Considering his job, he was likely to be the one who brought you the information on a silver platter. He probably had had it since Gorbatov entrusted him to keep it. But I was not sure how you managed to get in touch with him and lure him to Moscow. Tell me, Cyrus, did Laura bring him in?"

Why is he so interested in a closed case, especially where everyone he's concerned about is dead?

Cyrus did not answer again.

"All right. You, probably think that I'm upset about Voronov. Wrong. The bastard should've been dealt with a long time ago. I don't know of a single person who didn't hate him. Even his own dog hated him. So, on a freelance basis I might have conceivably helped you."

Careful. He's still pressing with what Laura did. Why?

"General. Suppose, for the sake of argument, there is a fraction of truth in what you've just told me. Why would you tell me all that?"

"Good question. I don't know."

"General, I had the opportunity to see you in action on a few occasions. Do you expect me to believe that you do anything without knowing exactly why? Let aside that you allegedly covered something up for me?"

Dronov laughed. "What if, however unlikely it may sound, I also have a sense of right and wrong?" His eyes became serious and tired.

Cyrus shook his head.

"Well, believe it or not, I came to like you. I also happen to know of a few conversations between you and Laura. And I came to the conclusion that you're right about what should be done with the money. And I watched you maneuvering today to achieve that. Do you really think that I did not realize that you knowingly infuriated your own President? Do you think I don't realize that if not for you, the whole thing would be hushed up? To do what you did takes a strong sense of right and wrong, and a lot of courage. So, I salute you."

"Thank you."

Dronov extended his hand. Cyrus shook it.

Suddenly, he realized that there was a note in his palm.

The general said, "If you want to meet me after reading this, you'll know how to find me."

He abruptly turned and walked away.

Cyrus put the note in his pocket. He walked through the facility and found a small empty reading room. He sat in a chair and opened the note.

"Dear Cyrus,

There is certain news I must convey to you. News that is of great importance to you. I deliberately avoided discussing these issues in person, not being sure of your immediate reaction. I want you to take your time, think everything over in a calm manner, and make your decision.

First, I have great news that Laura is alive. It may sound like a miracle, but it's an indisputable fact. Let me explain what happened.

Naturally, we were intercepting all your telephone calls, live. Luckily, an officer on duty at the time could speak English. He quickly alerted our Service of the situation. At the time, Laura was suspected of dereliction of duty, trying to make a private deal with you. So, she was arrested immediately after the phone call to you.

Our next task was to save you from pending action by our sister Service. At any cost we needed to find you before they did. In an attempt to avoid scaring you off, we quickly put another female officer in Laura's car and she drove off to meet you. Other cars were converging at the meeting place. Unfortunately, we did not realize at the time that our sister Service was planning an acutely active measure against Laura as well. So, to our great regret, the female officer was killed in the line of duty. In other words, what you observed was Laura's car, but another woman inside it. We missed you at the Rossiya hotel by less than five minutes.

Now I have to convey the bad news. Laura is still under arrest, and her future is not bright at all. The pending charges of dereliction of duty have been expanded to treason. I'm sure I don't need to explain the likely sentence under this charge.

Finally, the good news. Laura's fate is entirely in your hands now. Our Service was so impressed with your performance in the issue that we both worked on, that I was asked to offer you a deal. If you agree to participate in a continuation of the search, and find another part of the subject of the search, Laura will be released to you personally and allowed to emigrate. Needless to say, we guarantee your personal safety and our full cooperation.

Very truly yours,

Yuri

P.S. My speculation about your possible past actions is exactly that, my personal speculation. I assure you that no one else is crazy enough to imagine anything like it. And it shall never be brought to daylight again.

P.P.S. You can find me in the same hotel where we had our first breakfast meeting. I will arrive there a week from today and will stay there for three days.

Cyrus realized that he had stopped breathing while reading the letter. Now his breathing was heavy. He walked briskly through the facility. Dronov was nowhere in sight. He went outside. Dronov had vanished.

Cyrus walked up to one of Yeltsin's guards.

"Have you seen General Dronov?"

"The General went to the plane."

Cyrus rushed to Yeltsin's plane. Two Russians were guarding the stairs.

"I need to talk to General Dronov. It's urgent."

The answer was very clear. "The General is resting. He asked not to be disturbed."

Cyrus looked up at the plane's windows. Only one window was lit. He saw Dronov's smiling face. Dronov saluted him and lowered the curtain.

THE END

ACKNOWLEDGMENTS

I would like to thank Sara Hallman for editing the original manuscript.

I was fortunate to have the talent and experience of my editor and agent, Roger Jellinek, contributing to this book.

I am grateful to Olga Sheymov who applied her talent to designing this book's cover.

ABOUT THE AUTHOR

Victor Sheymov is a computer security expert, author, scientist, inventor, and holder of multiple patents for methods and systems in cyber security. He was responsible for coordination of all security aspects of Russian cipher communications with its outposts abroad when he was exfiltrated with his wife and daughter by the CIA in 1980. He worked for the National Security Agency for a number of years and is a recipient of several prestigious awards in intelligence and security.

Victor Sheymov is also the author of *TOWER OF SECRETS: A Real Life Spy Thriller*. This memoir describes how Sheymov, ace troubleshooter for the KGB super-secret Eighth Chief Directorate, operating out of the infamous Lubyanka Moscow Center, was head of security for cipher communications worldwide, and thus had a rare knowledge of the entire KGB system. A star player, headed for the top, his contacts ranged from party elite to the dissident community and the Moscow underworld.

Victor Sheymov is also the author of *CYBERSPACE and SECURITY: A Fundamentally New Approach*. We have now been staring at the cyber security problem for a quarter of a century without any effective action. Our entire infrastructure, finance, communications, fuel and transportation, and Internet systems are extremely vulnerable, and we do not know how narrow is the window of time we have to protect ourselves. This book establishes that our legacy computer security systems are failing for a simple reason: we tried to adopt security methods developed in our physical space for protecting cyberspace objects. These two spaces are so different that methods effective in one do not necessarily work in the other. Our physical space security methods are generally static. In order to adapt to the highly dynamic environment of cyberspace, we need to base our security on dynamics and secure virtualization.

This book's multidisciplinary concept approaches cybersecurity from a fundamentally different direction.

CYBERSPACE and SECURITY consists of three parts: I, Security; II, Cyberspace; III, Cyber Security. The book reviews the history of what we have been doing to establish access security; analyzes the nature of cyberspace and its fundamental difference from our physical world; analyzes the applicability of our legacy security measures to cyberspace; determines what has been fundamentally wrong with our legacy approach to cyber security; and presents a fundamentally new approach to security that is effective in cyberspace.

9 780985 893071